BREAKING THE FLAME

SHADOW'S FIRE BOOK 3

CHRISTOPHER PATTERSON

Breaking the Flame

Rabbit Hole Publishing

Tucson, Arizona, 85710 USA

The only thing necessary for the triumph of evil is for good men to do nothing

— Edmund Burke

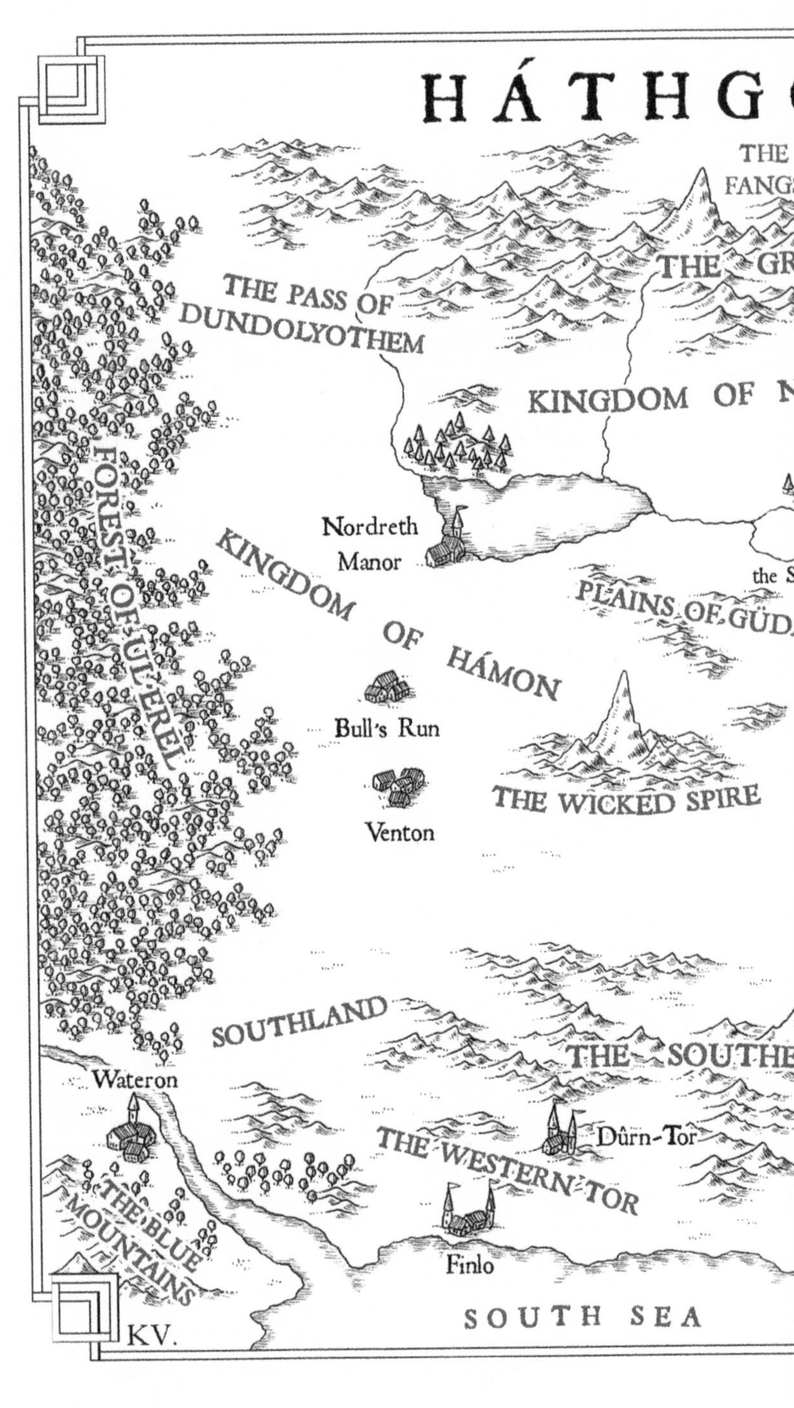
HÁTHG
THE FANGS
THE PASS OF DUNDOLYOTHEM
THE GR
KINGDOM OF N
FOREST OF UL'ERÉL
Nordreth Manor
KINGDOM OF HÁMON
PLAINS OF GÜD
Bull's Run
Venton
THE WICKED SPIRE
SOUTHLAND
THE SOUTHE
Wateron
Dûrn-Tor
THE WESTERN TOR
THE BLUE MOUNTAINS
Finlo
SOUTH SEA
KV.

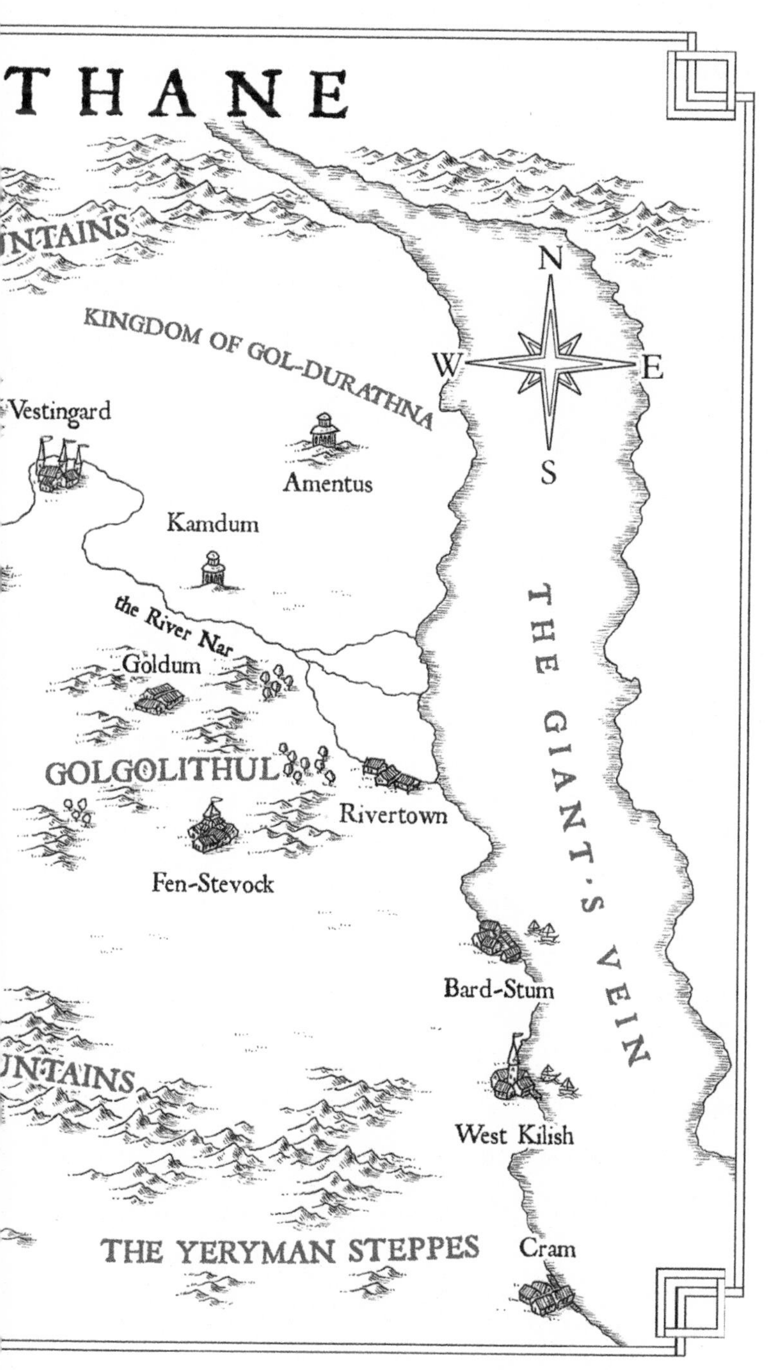
THANE
NTAINS
KINGDOM OF GOL-DURATHNA
N
W
E
S
Vestingard
Amentus
Kamdum
the River Nar
Goldum
GOLGOLITHUL
Rivertown
Fen-Stevock
THE GIANT'S VEIN
Bard-Stum
NTAINS
West Kilish
THE YERYMAN STEPPES
Cram

1

They came closer. Erik could feel them. He shivered as the air grew cold. He could smell them.

"Get to the center of the hallway!" Balzarak yelled, his voice echoing off the walls and ceiling of the ancient hallway they expected —hoped—would finally lead them to Orvencrest.

"You look after Befel," Wrothgard added with a tug on Erik's sleeve.

A purple glow filled a small part of the hallway as Bryon unsheathed his sword. It didn't shed much light, just enough to see a thin, ghostly arm reaching out from the darkness and towards Erik. He jumped back as his cousin brought his sword down. A high-pitched scream filled the hallway as the arm and hand fell to the ground. But when Erik looked to where the appendage should have been, it was gone.

More light, bluish-white, filled the hallway, and Erik looked over his shoulder to see Balzarak, a sapphire studded circlet around his head. The gemstone glowed brightly and, as more light filled the space, the voices seemed to grow more and more distant. But they were still there. They lurked in the dark spaces beyond the light, in the shadows.

As Bryon and Balzarak looked one direction, they—whoever they were, the undead, ghosts—crept closer. Erik felt something brush his leg. He looked to Bofim, a line of blood on his cheek where something scratched him. Wrothgard rubbed his chest where a blunt object struck him.

"What the bloody shadow is this?" Switch yelled.

He sounded scared. He never sounded scared.

Erik saw another hand reaching towards him. Erik struck the arm away with one hand and pulled out his sword with the other before he jabbed into the darkness, which quickly consumed the edges of the light. As Erik attacked, almost blindly at whatever might be there, he heard more screaming. It didn't sound like screams of pain, but anger and evil. When he withdrew his blade, it was covered in a black ichor. Then he remembered something.

Erik sheathed his sword and removed his haversack. Opening it, he found the bag he assumed the moon fairies had given him.

"When darkness consumes and all hope seems lost," Erik said.

He opened the bag and the brightest white light Erik had ever seen shone upward from the moon fairy dust. As the screaming and screeching voices became more distant, he grabbed a fistful of the dust and threw it up into the air. Like a thousand stars, each speckle of dust began to glimmer brilliantly, and it was as if it was daytime in the ancient hallway.

Within moments, *they* were gone. Erik didn't hear them, couldn't feel them, couldn't smell them. The chill in the air disappeared, and a comfortable warmth replaced it. The stale air became fresh, and everyone breathed easily.

Beldar still lay on the floor, unconscious, the shards of a battle axe scattered about him, the result of the dwarf trying to chop at the wall in front of them. His breathing was still shallow, although he seemed a little better. Befel lay next to him, also unconscious, the strange voice that controlled him before he collapsed in a cataleptic heap still rang through Erik's mind.

"What was that?" Wrothgard asked.

"I don't know," Balzarak replied.

"Was it *them*?" Erik asked.

Balzarak stared at him for a moment. A part of Erik suspected the darkness and shadow that had attacked them were the undead from his dreams, but there was something else there, something stronger, something more evil.

"I don't know," Balzarak replied after a long moment of silence.

Erik couldn't help realizing the other dwarves stared at him, some in surprise, some in irritation, and Turk with a small smirk on his face.

"Who is *them*?" Switch asked.

"No one," Balzarak snapped.

"No one?" Switch asked, exasperated.

"No one you need to be concerned with right now," Balzarak said.

"Well, if *they* are going to continue to try and kill us from the shadows," Switch said, "and it seems like this place is full of shadows, assuming we can even get past this damned wall, I think we should all be concerned."

"They won't come back," Balzarak said. "At least for a while."

"Oh great," Switch muttered, his voice full of sarcasm as usual.

"What do we do Lord Balzarak?" Wrothgard asked.

"Between the light of Bryon's sword, my circlet, and the moon fairy dust," Balzarak replied, "we have nothing to worry about. We need to wait for Befel and Beldar to recover, as well as everyone else for that matter."

"And then what?" Bryon asked.

"Then, we figure out how to get through this wall," Balzarak replied.

"It's not a wall," Balzarak translated, as Gôdruk inspected their obstacle. "It's a door."

Befel and Beldar had just regained consciousness, Beldar with a splitting headache and Befel with absolutely no recollection of what had happened.

"Then bloody open it," Switch said.

"We are trying," Balzarak replied evenly, but his lack of patience with Switch's endless complaining was clear.

Gôdruk traced a hand over the words written in blood, reciting what he knew to himself. Thormok and Threhof joined him, but they couldn't figure out what exactly it said.

"You understood your brother?" Turk asked while everyone else tried to figure out the door.

"Yes," Erik replied. "It sounded as if he was speaking Westernese to me."

"That is interesting," Turk said, rubbing his chin.

"What language was he speaking?" Erik asked. "It almost sounded like Dwarvish at first."

"It wasn't Dwarvish," Turk replied. "Related to it, perhaps. It is an ancient language—an evil one."

"You know it?" Erik asked. "You understand it?"

"Enough to know that it should not be spoken," Turk replied, "especially here."

"Could it be like the door at Aga Min?" Wrothgard asked. "Perhaps there is a lever or a button somewhere."

Gôdruk shook his head.

"What's the matter, Erik?" Turk said, seeing the concerned look on his face. "Your brother will be alright."

"It's not that. I mean, I am concerned about Befel," Erik replied, "but ..."

"What?" Turk asked.

"After he collapsed," Erik explained, "there was another voice. It sounded powerful, dark and evil. It said something that didn't make sense."

"What?" Turk asked, and Erik realized that Balzarak and some of the others were now listening.

"It said, *your chains are not made of iron, but of flame. You cannot break the flame.* I can't think of what that means, or whose voice it was."

Gôdruk spoke to Balzarak with hushed words.

"We must figure this door out," Lord Balzarak said, "or else, I fear, shadow will befall us."

"Can't you just say we'll die," Switch complained.

"That's just it," Balzarak replied. "We won't die. It is a fate worse than death."

"You speak in riddles," Wrothgard said.

"Aye," Balzarak replied, "and perhaps I will give you the answer to the riddle soon, but for now, we must get past this door."

"What black magic is this?" Wrothgard asked to no one in particular.

"The blackest," Threhof replied, and Balzarak nodded in agreement. "But this door ... no, this is no black magic. This is dwarvish magic."

"And why would dwarves put a door here," Switch asked, "to keep other dwarves out?"

"Maybe they put it here when they abandoned Orvencrest," Threhof said with a shrug. "Maybe they knew treasure hunters would come looking to pilfer what was rightfully theirs."

Switch rolled his eyes.

"Perhaps," Balzarak said. "However, I fear this door was not put here to keep people out, but rather, to keep someone—or something—in."

"Truly comforting," Bryon muttered.

"So, is there some code word you need to say?" Wrothgard asked. "Some ancient secret word, perhaps?"

Balzarak shrugged. Erik couldn't help thinking the general looked defeated. The dwarf put both of his hands on the wall, breathed heavy, and with a sigh of resignation, rested his forehead against the stone. Suddenly, the sapphire in the middle of his circlet began to glow brighter than it already had been, and the ground shook ever so slightly.

"Oh, by the gods," Switch said. "Can we just get this over with? If I'm going to die, just get it over with."

But rather than darkness and the undead returning, torches in high sconces appeared all along the walls of the room. Looking back, Erik could see that the stairway from which they came had reappeared.

"Dwarvish magic," Threhof said with a smile.

"It must have been your circlet," Turk said.

Before Balzarak could reply, the door shook with a low voice. It was Dwarvish, or some form of it, but certainly not what Erik had heard before. Balzarak listened intently. It was such a different dialect and Erik, only recently proficient in the language, didn't understand.

Balzarak said something in return, and in an instant, a giant, dwarvish face appeared in the door disguised as a wall. It bulged out from the stone as if it were pliable cloth, stretching this way and that, looking about.

It spoke again, and Balzarak replied. This went on for many moments until Balzarak finally bowed. The face also bowed and then returned to a normal looking wall. Then, in the flutter of a fly's wing, the wall was gone, revealing more hallway, as tall as the one in which they stood, built of the same large stone that, despite many years of seclusion, looked almost polished.

It was wide, deep enough that Erik couldn't see the end, and perfectly straight, another testimony to the architecture of dwarves. Suddenly, the hallway lit with a myriad of torches, and Balzarak stood still, staring at the open hallway. He looked distant, lost in thought. Thormok and Gôdruk began speaking, almost arguing, until Balzarak hushed them.

"General, what just happened?" Threhof asked.

"What language was that?" Erik asked.

"Old Dwarvish," Balzarak replied. "It was a guardian, a type of lock dwarves used to use often. They rarely use them anymore."

"And, so, your circlet was the answer to the riddle?" Erik asked.

"Somewhat," Balzarak said, still staring forward. "The guardian opened the door because I am a descendent of Stone Axe."

"So, what are we bloody waiting for?" Switch asked, stepping forward.

"Stop!" Balzarak yelled, turning hard to face Switch.

The thief was so taken aback by the change in the general's demeanor, he stopped cold, staring.

"General?" Threhof asked.

"The guardian wasn't put here to keep people out, as I suspected," Balzarak explained, "but to keep people in."

"I don't understand," Dwain said. His admission was met with nods and agreeing grunts.

"This place is cursed," Balzarak said, shaking his head and dropping his eyes to the ground.

Gôdruk and Thormok began arguing again and, as Balzarak turned to the awaiting tunnel, others started chattering as well.

"General," Erik said, stepping up next to Balzarak.

"Once we pass this point," Balzarak said, eyes trained on the hallway, "we will not be able to return. This doorway will close behind us."

"So, this guardian means to keep us in," Erik asked, "trap us in the city?"

"Not us," Balzarak replied. "*Them.*"

"Who?" Erik asked. He felt the hair on his arms stand up and a chill crawl up his spine like some phantom spider.

Balzarak turned slowly to look at Erik.

"Evil, Erik. The Shadow's minions. We shouldn't talk about it here," he said. "Let us move on."

2

"They are there," Andragos said.

He sat at his table in the living quarters of one of his homes. Being such a powerful man in Golgolithul, the rulers of the east had awarded him many such homes, some in the middle of cities, others in the countryside, a place he might retreat to in order to rest. This was his favorite home, close to their northern borders with Gol-Durathna. The land was often green here, and his little cottage, even though it was surrounded by a stone wall and guarded by his Soldiers of the Eye, felt quaint and simple. It reminded him of his childhood, so many years ago.

"Who, my lord?" Terradyn asked. The large man poured tea into a small cup for the Messenger of the East.

"Erik Eleodum," Andragos replied with a smile. "He and the men he travels with have found the lost city."

"Who is Erik?" Terradyn asked.

"The boy from Finlo," Andragos said, looking up at his man. "And he is no longer a simple porter. I knew it would be him. I knew it when I first saw him in that tavern, so out of place."

"He is by himself?" Terradyn asked.

"No," Andragos replied. "He is with others. Dwarves."

"Dwarves?"

"Yes." Andragos laughed. "What a remarkable, resourceful young man."

Andragos took a sip of his tea, and his face scrunched into a look of irritation as he shook his head, grunting angrily.

"Is the tea bad, my lord?" Terradyn asked.

"No," Andragos replied. "I cannot see them anymore."

"Shall I darken the room and light some incense, my lord?" Terradyn asked.

Sometimes, when Andragos' magic seemed to wane, certain things helped him concentrate. He was still more powerful than any other mage in Golgolithul, but compared to a hundred years ago, two hundred years ... Andragos shuddered at the thought of how strong he used to be. But this wasn't the same. However, he felt better, more dangerous than he had in a while.

"No," Andragos replied. "It is something about that place ... about Orvencrest. There is a powerful magic presence there, something I haven't felt in years that reminds me of ..."

Andragos' eyes widened with a distant memory. He stood quickly, knocking his cup of tea to the ground. The small, porcelain teacup shattered when it hit the stone floor, and Andragos looked to the door. It swung open, and a strong wind, as if it brought night, rushed in and darkened the room, extinguishing all candlelight and the fire that burned brightly in the Messenger's fireplace.

"My lord!" Terradyn yelled.

Andragos couldn't see his manservant. Blackness consumed him. Then he heard another set of footsteps.

"Terradyn! My lord!" Raktas yelled. He must have seen the darkness from outside.

The darkness swirled around like a tornado. Andragos could hear things breaking in his quarters, wood snapping, and glass shattering. Within the darkness, he could hear chattering and laughter. And then he heard a voice—a deep voice—speaking an ancient language, one he hadn't heard in hundreds of years.

Andragos began to chant, using words from a language almost as ancient as the language he heard in the darkness. His voice grew louder and louder and, as he almost shouted his cant—over and over again—the deep, ancient voice laughed louder, the amusement shaking the walls.

And then the darkness was gone.

"My lord!" Raktas said, running to Andragos.

Terradyn was on the other side of the room, wide-eyed and afraid. It wasn't often Andragos saw one of his manservants afraid.

"I'm fine," Andragos said. "Ready a carriage. I must travel to Fen-Stévock and meet with Syzbalo."

Andragos seldom used the Lord of the East's name around his men, even Terradyn and Raktas, but his visions were so dire, he didn't really care at the moment.

"*She* is in Orvencrest."

Traveling down the new hallway, they had found a fountain, water fresh and cool, and when Erik woke from a deep sleep, the sound of water was comforting. It reminded him fondly of home. Collectively, the party decided this would be a good place to stop and rest. Erik was glad for it. Beldar and Befel looked worn, even more so than everyone else, and it gave Turk time to tend to them. Switch, after scouting around, rushed back, cursing about the door being closed.

When Balzarak told him he knew that would happen, the thief stomped off rather than arguing with the general; Erik wondered if he'd ever see Switch again. A short while later, he found the slight man snoring softly as he leaned against a wall, and Erik wondered how such a despicable fellow could look so peaceful.

Befel and Bryon still slept. In fact, the only other person awake was General Balzarak. He stood in front of one of the walls, just staring. As Erik collected himself and walked to the dwarf, he saw markings carved into the stone, along with pictures of creatures he had never even heard of.

"A dragon with one head seems formidable enough, let alone one with three heads," Erik said, pointing to one picture.

He knew Balzarak wasn't aware of his presence, but if he had startled the dwarf, he didn't show it.

"Creatures of the ancient days, Erik," Balzarak replied.

"Scary," Erik said.

"Terrifying," Balzarak added. "And terrible."

"Why would An, the Creator, allow such creatures to exist?" Erik asked, looking at one carving of a fire-breathing creature that looked like the combination of some giant lizard and a spider.

"Sin corrupts even the purest things," Balzarak replied, "and evil blackens even the brightest hearts."

"What do these runes say?" Erik asked.

"That is very astute," Balzarak said, "recognizing that these are ancient runes."

"We saw some as we entered the territory of Thorakest," Erik said.

"I only know what they say because of my intensive schooling. Most dwarves wouldn't be able to read them. Maybe Gôdruk will be able to. I doubt anyone else here could."

"And what do they say?" Erik asked.

"They are names, mostly," Balzarak replied, "and chronicles, a history of our people. These are lost clans—Blood Axe, Stone Hammer, Red Steel, Golden Blade, Bone Breaker."

"Myths." Threhof's voice startled Erik. He was stealthy for a dwarf and had even snuck up on the general, evident in the dwarf's eyes when he turned around to see the former guardsman standing there.

"Perhaps," Balzarak replied. "Even a year ago I might have agreed with you. But now ... today, I don't know. I think not so much myths, but lost truths."

"General?" Threhof said.

"Today's events," Balzarak explained, "yesterday's, this week's, by An, the events of these past several months, have led me to believe that what our people have heralded as ghost stories are actually not. There are dwarves who believed that even the lost city of Orvencrest was a tall tale," Balzarak said.

"I once thought a world outside my farm a myth," Erik said. "A painful realization perhaps."

"Very painful," Balzarak agreed.

"This is not the only truth once thought a myth, though," Erik said, "revealed by these runes, is it? What happened to the lost clans? What happened to the city of Orvencrest?"

"I think every type of people in this world have a dark past," Balzarak replied, "even we dwarves. The legend of Orvencrest, lost to many, is one that some of us who were born to lead learn, so that this doesn't happen again."

"General," Threhof said, almost hissing.

"Calm yourself, Threhof," Balzarak said. "Speaking of a ghost doesn't magically make it appear."

"I don't understand," Erik said.

"Orvencrest wasn't lost, as most think," Balzarak replied. "It was attacked, taken from the dwarves, and those lucky enough to escape have kept what happened a secret."

"Why?" Erik asked. "And who? Who could attack a dwarvish city?"

Threhof said something to Balzarak in Dwarvish, and Erik couldn't quite catch what he said. The general put a hand up, silencing the elder dwarf.

"Dwarves, Erik," Balzarak replied.

"Dwarves?" Erik repeated.

"Aye," the general replied. "Dwarves. Dwarves that had been twisted by the Shadow. Dwarves that had been turned against their own people by the promise of treasure and power. It is such a dark part of our history that most dwarves won't even speak of it. It has become a bedtime story we tell our children if they are misbehaving. *Be good or the dwomanni will come take you away.*"

"Is that what you call them," Erik asked, "the traitors?"

"Yes, the dwomanni," Balzarak replied. "Xenophobic. Power hungry. They are remotely related to dwarves now, but once, they were our brothers and sisters. Most think it's just that—a bedtime story. But some of us knew better ... or, at least had an idea."

"The dwomanni rebelled," Erik said, "and as the dwarves abandoned the city, they put up guardians to keep them in."

"Not just them," Balzarak replied.

"I don't understand," Erik said.

"According to these runes," Balzarak replied, "Orvencrest was the holding place of a powerful weapon—a weapon that would make the wielder god-like."

"A god-like weapon?" Threhof asked. "That seems far-fetched. Dwarves are powerful, but that would mean something magical ... more than magical."

"Aye," Balzarak said. "I wish you could read the runes for yourself. Certainly, something ... or someone, powerful and magical."

"The dwomanni stole this weapon?" Erik asked.

"It is doubtful," the general replied. "This is new to me. I had never heard of this weapon in my studies, whatever it might be. But, believe me, if the dwomanni had uncovered this weapon, and knew how to use it, they would have done so already. It is foolish to think they would simply stay here in Orvencrest and die away. They dug deep into the earth. Many of them, according to the few writings I have on them, have spread throughout the deepest parts of the world, hiding in darkness. Given something that has god-like powers ... they would have used it against us by now."

"Another myth," Threhof said.

"Haven't we already proven that these supposed myths are no longer myths?" Balzarak asked.

"This weapon is still hidden within the city," Erik said, as much to himself as to Balzarak.

"Aye," Balzarak said.

"But the runes don't say what exactly it is?" Erik asked.

"No," Balzarak replied. "It's vague. The language is old. I don't quite understand it. It could be some siege weapon imbued with powers. It could—could have been—some ancient animal. It could be a spell. I don't know."

"I wonder if the treasure that the Lord of the East wants us to find is related somehow," Erik said.

"I thought you said it was a writ of lineage," Threhof said, "some record of his family history."

"That's what the Messenger of the East told us when he met us in Finlo," Erik recalled. "That is what he told those people who accepted his offer of service and took a map to Orvencrest."

"I wouldn't put it past the Lord of the East to lie about what he seeks here in Orvencrest," Balzarak said.

"How could a scroll be related to a weapon?" Threhof asked.

Balzarak shrugged, thinking for a moment.

"Directions to where it is hidden," he said. "Instructions on how to make it. A spell to reveal it, maybe."

"If it's related to some mighty weapon," Erik asked, "then why send mercenaries? Why not the Soldiers of the Eye?"

"Waste less resources, perhaps," Balzarak said. "Keep his hands clean. As Threhof said, up until now, this was just a myth."

"So deceitful," Threhof grumbled.

"Does that surprise you?" Balzarak asked.

"If this *thing* that the Lord of the East wants us to find is truly related to something so powerful," Erik said, "and we find it, should we deliver it?"

"Absolutely not," Threhof replied, raising his voice a bit.

"I don't know," Balzarak said. "Who would you rather have this weapon, the dwomanni or Golgolithul?"

"Neither," Threhof argued. "We take it to King Skella."

"Perhaps," Balzarak said. Erik couldn't help recognizing that look of uncertainty on the dwarf's face. "If we take this scroll to a dwarvish city—and it is directions on how to find or create this thing that the Lord of the East wants—are we foolish enough to think the Lord of the East wouldn't wage war against us?"

"Let him wage war," Threhof replied, puffing out his chest. "Let his soldiers crash and die against the might of the dwarvish army."

"War is never so simple," Balzarak said, his voice sad and somber. "And we don't know if the Lord of the East even knows how to use this weapon. He may read this scroll he desires and think it nothing but gibberish."

"He has the black mage," Threhof argued.

"That he does," Balzarak said. "And he is a powerful wizard himself."

"If the dwomanni haven't found it yet, after all these years, why would you be worried about them finding it?" Erik asked.

"They know we are here," Balzarak replied. "They will follow us. If we find it, they will undoubtedly try to take it."

"Do they look like any other dwarves?" Erik asked.

"No," Balzarak replied. "They have gray skin and white hair and are short, spindly creatures, shells of their dwarvish past. They hate the sun and the surface and worship dark gods. The truly zealous dwomanni blind themselves in reverence to their gods. They are becoming bold as of late; only recently have we seen evidence of their reemergence."

"The young dwarf in Strongbur," Erik muttered, remembering the accusation of Fréden Fréwin. The mayor had accused men of twisting a young dwarf's heart, causing him to spy on his own people, but as Balzarak spoke, Erik knew it was these mutant descendants of the dwarves that had coerced him. It made sense. It was a perfect plan. Cause friction within the dwarvish people as they fight, whether or not men are the enemy, all the while sowing the seeds of dissention with those dwarves power hungry enough to listen.

"Yes," Balzarak replied.

"So, is the mayor in league with the dwomanni?" Erik asked, wondering if Fréwin had gone beyond simply listening to the young dwarf.

"No," the general replied. "And I don't think he would ever be. He is xenophobic, just like they are. They are no longer dwarves. He would look at them just as he looks at you. But there are many like him, prideful and suspicious."

"What do we do, then?" Erik asked.

"Be careful," Balzarak said. "This place is more dangerous than I originally thought. It is the realm of the Shadow, which means more than just dwomanni. They will be serving a master. They may inhabit this place, but they are not its masters."

"We are the masters of this place," Threhof said. "It is our right, by blood. It is your right, Lord Balzarak."

"No longer," Balzarak said.

3

Fréden Fréwin sat in his throne-like chair knuckling his chin in frustration. A young servant walked up the steps to the dais on which Fréden sat. He held a silver platter in his hands, a single, silver cup resting in the middle. The servant knelt and bowed when he reached the mayor.

"Get out!" Fréden yelled, slapping the cup off the platter. Wine spilled from the cup, some of it splashing the young servant in the face. The young dwarf gave a short yelp, bowed, and turned and ran down the stairs.

Fréden Fréwin stared at the splotches of purple wine, slowly running into the cracks of the stone that made up his dais.

He knew it would leave a stain. He felt his face grow hot and red.

He looked up, wanting to call his servant back, but he was already gone.

"Clumsy fool," Fréden muttered.

He looked back at the wine. The purple stains on the stone, the dirt on the floor, it all made him grip his armchair with white knuckles.

"Is someone going to clean this mess!" he yelled. He stood. "Someone clean this, now!"

The hall was silent. Few of the citizens of Thorakest meandered through the mayor's chambers, but those few who visited quickly left. Another dwarf, one dressed in a livery of gold and red with a burette of blue velvet and leather shoes that curled at the toes, walked up Fréden's dais. Fréden Fréwin sat, and the other dwarf bent down to speak with him. He whispered and Fréden knew he meant what he said only for his ears. He hated it when Nalbin did that.

"My lord, people are watching," Nalbin said.

"I don't care who watches!" Fréden screamed, his voice echoing through the hall of his keep. He looked to Nalbin. Any other dwarf would've cowered at that look, but not Nalbin. He never cowered to Fréden. That infuriated him even more. "Whose hall do they congregate in? Whose favor do they seek?"

He stood up, glaring at the few aristocrats and merchants, the local business owners and artisans that still stood in his hall. They all stared at him, frightened, perplexed, offended.

"Get out!" he yelled. No one moved. They just stared. He looked down at his feet. The silver cup rested just at the foot of his chair. He picked it up and threw it at the closest dwarf he could, a fat merchant dressed in wide, brown robes, barely missing his head. The merchant turned and made for the hall's door, not bothering to wait for his servants or the two guards that protected his goods. The other dwarves in the hall followed suit.

"Get out!" Fréden yelled again. He slumped back into his chair as soon as his hall was clear, sighing heavily and resting his chin on his chest. The only dwarf left in the hall was Nalbin.

"My lord," said Nalbin. Fréden gave him a sidelong glance and huffed.

"Skella welcomed these men into Thorakest," Fréden spat at the mention of men, "as if they were long lost cousins."

"He did imprison them, for a time," Nalbin suggested.

"Imprison?" Fréden questioned with pure disdain. "They had access to the greatest city in all Háthgolthane ... in all the world. How is that a prison?"

"They were not free to come and go as they pleased," Nalbin said with a quick shrug of his shoulders.

"And should they be?" Fréden said. "They are men. They encroach on our territory more every day."

"All men, my lord?" Nalbin asked.

"Does it matter?" Fréden hissed, leaning forward and clenching a fist. "The one who encroaches on our lands the most is the very one who sent these men into our midst."

Nalbin just shrugged his shoulders again.

"The Lord of the East, you imbecile," the mayor said. "And we are to believe they have been sent on some mission to find the lost city of Orvencrest."

"Is that so unbelievable?" Nalbin asked.

"Orvencrest is a myth," the mayor replied, slamming a fist on the armrest of his chair and staring out into his empty keep. "It is a rouse, to get men journeying into our lands, an attempt to plant spies in our midst."

Fréden Fréwin clenched his teeth as he groaned.

"And all the while that fool of a king allows more and more men into our lands, under the guise of truce and peace and trade," the mayor whispered, giving Nalbin a sidelong glance, not sure if his advisor heard him. He trusted Nalbin ... mostly. But in reality, he didn't trust anyone. Then, he added, "He is singlehandedly going to destroy our people."

"Doesn't that seem a little far-fetched, my lord?" Nalbin asked. "The Lord of the East sending mercenaries on a fool's mission just to plant spies in our lands?"

Fréden just glared at Nalbin, anger and malice in his eyes. Nalbin backed up a step.

"What if the lost city isn't a myth?" Nalbin finally asked after a long silence.

"What if ..." Fréden replied. King Skella had done so many things, made so many policies, so many mistakes, on what ifs. But Fréden had entertained the thought, as fanciful as it might be.

"If Orvencrest was real," Fréden said, "then the riches there would be enough to change the course of dwarvish history."

"I don't understand," Nalbin said.

"Of course, you don't, you dimwit," Fréden accused. "We could sway dwarves loyal to our people to our side. We could raise an army to fight back against the hordes of men intruding on our lands."

"An army, my lord?" Nalbin asked. "What of King Skella? What of the dukes?"

"Traitors," the mayor seethed. "We do as we would any traitor ... we depose them."

"Are you serious?" Nalbin said, lowering his voice to an almost inaudible whisper. "This is insanity."

Fréden's hand slowly moved inside his robes. His fingers tickled the small knife held by his belt.

"Are you with me or not, Nalbin?" he asked calmly. Nalbin was useful, but not enough to spare his life if he wasn't going to support him.

Nalbin's back straightened as he stood firm, a resilient look on his face.

"Must you even ask, my lord," Nalbin replied. "Of course, I am with you."

Fréden suddenly began to think of the mounds of treasure, the ancient weapons, the histories in the lost city of Orvencrest, as fanciful a thought as it might be.

"We need someone to follow Skull Crusher and General Balzarak," Fréden said.

"I think I know of just the person, my lord," Nalbin said, retrieving a letter from his pocket and giving it to the mayor.

Fréden read the letter and then looked at his servant, his face red hot with anger.

"You are just now giving this to me?"

"I was waiting for the right time," Nalbin said, backing away again. "He reached out to us. He knows Skull Crusher has betrayed his people."

"Yes, I read the letter," Fréden replied. "Can we trust Belvengar Long Spear, once having been such a close friend with Skull Crusher?"

"Yes, I believe so, my lord," Nalbin replied. "His family has long been critical of King Skella, and his father before him."

"We must use Long Spear, then," Fréden said. "He is an adept assassin. It is why he left. Send a letter to him. Tell him we wish to enlist his help. Even if there is no lost city—which I doubt there is—if anyone could kill General Balzarak, it would be Long Spear. The death of the Lord of Fornhig while in our lands would do much to drive a wedge between King Skella and King Tharren. It might even sway the north to our cause."

It was a long shot. Fréden knew that. Thrak Baldüukr had long been allies with Gol-Durathna. But if he could convince King Tharren that men had a hand in the death of his nephew, he might at least support their efforts in the south of eradicating those surface-dwelling dogs from their lands. King Tharren might even support a new king in Drüum Balmdüukr—King Fréden Fréwin. The mayor liked the sound of that.

"It is time to make our move, Nalbin," Fréden said. "It is time the Fréwin name took its rightful place in dwarvish history."

4

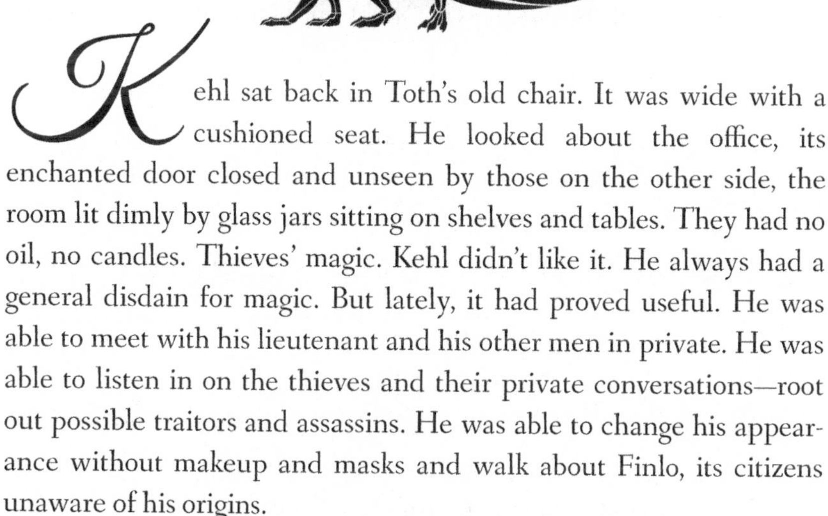

Kehl sat back in Toth's old chair. It was wide with a cushioned seat. He looked about the office, its enchanted door closed and unseen by those on the other side, the room lit dimly by glass jars sitting on shelves and tables. They had no oil, no candles. Thieves' magic. Kehl didn't like it. He always had a general disdain for magic. But lately, it had proved useful. He was able to meet with his lieutenant and his other men in private. He was able to listen in on the thieves and their private conversations—root out possible traitors and assassins. He was able to change his appearance without makeup and masks and walk about Finlo, its citizens unaware of his origins.

"Have we purged the disloyal ones?" Kehl asked.

"Yes, Im'Ka'Da," A'Uthma replied, bowing low.

"Are we certain the ones that remain are loyal?" Kehl asked.

"As loyal as these dung eating dogs can be, Im'Ka'Da," A'Uthma replied.

"That does not make me feel very secure," Kehl replied. "I am to lead these thugs. I cannot do this if I fear a knife in my back every moment."

A'Uthma bowed again. "Im'Ka'Da, I dispatched the ones that were outwardly disloyal quickly, disemboweling them while they still breathed, burning their entrails as an offering to Ner'Galgal. I ripped their still beating hearts from their chests and offered them to Nan'Sin. I did all this while the others watched."

"And?" Kehl asked.

"Those who were not loyal, but did not choose to say so outwardly, left in the night," A'Uthma replied. "A dozen men, perhaps. Albin and Flemming tracked down at least half of them and killed them."

"And those that remain?"

"They have pledged loyalty," A'Uthma replied, "to the death. They have been branded with the mark of The Slayer on their left breast, the mark of the Mistress of Night on their right hand, and the mark of Master of the Morning Sun on their left cheek."

Indeed, a symbol of loyalty. To brand the symbol of just one of their gods on the body would certainly be a sign of loyalty, but all three? The death's skull, the moon, and the sun. These thieves were truly loyal to Kehl. After being branded, he did not doubt that. And if they weren't, A'Uthma, Flemming, and Albin would take care of them.

"How many in total?" Kehl asked.

"Two score men," A'Uthma replied, "and a dozen women."

"Whores," Kehl hissed. He didn't despise whores, but to have them in his employ would prove distracting to his men. "Sell them."

"They are not whores, Im'Ka'Da," A'Uthma replied, bowing

again. "They are adept thieves and assassins and spies. Of this, I have been assured."

"We will see," Kehl said.

"Has this violence reached the ears of the Council of Five?" Kehl asked.

"Not that I know of, Im'Ka'Da," A'Uthma replied. "Should we be so worried about the Council of Five?"

Kehl shot A'Uthma a hard look. His fellow Samanian bowed his head and stepped backwards.

"They are brutal," Kehl replied, "the Council. They care nothing for allegiances, loyalties, good or bad, righteous or iniquitous. They care nothing for the plight of the poor or the corruption of the rich. They only care for the law—and care only for those who follow the law. In this city, we must be careful. If the Council knows there is an unlawful element in their city like us, they will be quick to extinguish it, and with terrible force. Why do you think Toth took such care to keep his lair secret?"

"I understand, Im'Ka'Da," A'Uthma said. "What is your plan?"

"I wish to leave this place, eventually," Kehl said.

"You wish to go home?" A'Uthma replied.

Kehl nodded.

"With our connections in Crom and Tyr, and with new connections in Finlo, we can be rich men—aristocrats with power and influence—in Saman."

"I beg a thousand pardons, Im'Ka'Da," A'Uthma said, "but your tone does not sound like you are convinced this is a wise thing to do."

"It is wise," Kehl replied. "It is the wisest thing to do."

"But ..."

"But I have unfinished business," Kehl replied. "I have my brothers' deaths to avenge."

"You wish to go to Waterton," A'Uthma said.

"Yes," Kehl replied. "I will burn that dung heap of a town down; I will enslave its people, and I will sell them in Saman when we return."

"How many will you take with you, Im'Ka'Da?" A'Uthma asked.

"I do not wish to take many of these thieves," Kehl admitted.

"You do not trust them, Im'Ka'Da?" A'Uthma questioned.

Kehl shook his head. "If you trust them, I trust them."

"Then why would you not take them to raze Waterton?"

"I fear that will be a hard fight, destroying the town of Waterton," Kehl said, "and these new members to our guild are valuable and skilled."

"Guild?" A'Uthma asked.

It was true. Kehl had never referred to their band of slavers as a guild before.

"Yes, A'Uthma," Kehl said with a smile. "A slavers' guild. I think that has a nice ring to it. Don't you?"

A'Uthma smiled.

"Yes, Im'Ka'Da. If you wish to not take members of your guild, then who?"

"I will take a dozen," Kehl said, "and Albin. For the rest ... I wish you to spread word. Spread word that there is a need for swords—anyone who is a skilled fighter and has a taste for gold and women. Despite the Council of Five, there should be enough dispensable alley rats in this city that would be willing to follow me to Waterton for the glimmer of a gold coin and the pretense of membership into the newly formed slavers' guild of Finlo."

"Am I to not go with you?" A'Uthma asked.

"No." Kehl shook his head. "I need you and Flemming to stay here. Ready our departure for Saman. Purchase a ship. Make preparations. As for me, I will travel to Waterton under the guise of someone else."

Kehl thumbed through a book that rested on his—Toth's—desk. It was a book of disguises, both simple and intricate, one he had found amongst the vast books that sat on Toth's bookshelves. He could simply change his eyes or mouth, or his whole face, or his body, his sex, his voice, the complexion of his skin. He could even change his race—a dwarf or goblin. Towards the back of the book, he found spells that even suggested he could change into animals—a cat or wolf.

"As you wish, Im'Ka'Da," A'Uthma said, bowing.

Kehl's lieutenant turned to leave when the Samanian slaver stopped him.

"The women in our guild," Kehl said. A'Uthma looked to Kehl over his shoulder. "Are any of them from Saman? The pale skin of these Háthgolthanians makes me sick. I wouldn't mind lying with a woman from my homeland."

A'Uthma turned to face Kehl, a wry smile on his face.

"I do not believe we have any women from Saman, Im'Ka'Da," A'Uthma replied. "However, one of the women is from Nai Na'Kinasa. Her shoulders are strong, her hips wide, and her skin dark and beautiful."

"What is her name, A'Uthma?" Kehl asked.

"N'Jeri," A'Uthma replied.

"And would N'Jeri be willing to please me?" Kehl asked.

"Im'Ka'Da, her willingness is inconsequential," A'Uthma replied. "You are master of this slavers' guild. You take as you wish. However, yes, N'Jeri has the heart of our continent. She is tired of living among these dogs. I do believe she would be more than willing to lie with the Im'Ka'Da."

"Then send her in."

Kehl spoke a silent word, and the door to his office appeared and opened. As soon as A'Uthma left, the door disappeared again. He sat for a while, waiting for N'Jeri, thinking about his plans.

I don't really care if I take any slaves from Waterton if all I do is kill that fat, disgusting dog. But I must give A'Uthma a reason to go. I will return to Saman, and I will be rich.

He sat and thought, thumbing through the same book of guises before opening a book of simple tricks—lighting torches with a snap of his fingers, causing a fog with the blink of his eye, commanding a shadow to fall over him with a simple word. Then, he saw them. He saw the heat of two people on the other side of his door. They wouldn't be able to see the door. Magic hid it from the naked eye. But he could see the heat a body emanated through the wall. Kehl spoke a few words, and the door formed.

A'Uthma opened the door but did not enter. He simply ushered in a tall, dark woman before bowing and closing the door. Kehl spoke again, and the door disappeared.

Kehl tried saying something while this woman stood before him, but her beauty made him mute. He felt his pulse quicken, his face grow hot, his manhood become excited.

"You are N'Jeri?" Kehl asked.

She bowed low. "Yes, Im'Ka'Da."

"You are beautiful," Kehl said. He stood.

"I am glad my appearance pleases you, Im'Ka'Da."

She was tall, almost as tall as Kehl. Her skin was dark, her hair black and braided, falling to the middle of her back. The muscles in her arms undulated as she moved slightly. Her jaw was strong and firm. She reminded Kehl of home. Kehl could see the brands on her hand and cheek blistering, but they did not take away from her beauty.

"You wish to lay with me?" Kehl asked. He felt boyish. He didn't know why, but he did.

"I wish to do whatever pleases the Im'Ka'Da," N'Jeri replied. She reached up and undid the clasp that held up her dress. It fell away, revealing her breasts, large and round, and the blistering brand on the left side of her chest. There was another brand on her stomach, an old one, raised and gray against her dark skin.

"What is that a brand of?" Kehl asked.

"The Kinasan god of war," N'Jeri replied, "Oguan."

"I have heard of Oguan," Kehl replied, "although I have never worshipped her."

N'Jeri bowed low.

"It has been a long while since I have lain with a woman from my continent," Kehl said walking to the front of his desk.

"Then I will remind the Im'Ka'Da of what it feels like to be with a real woman," N'Jeri said, stepping close to Kehl, so close he could smell the oil on her skin. She grabbed him, gripped his crotch hard. "I will make you forget the filthy wenches from this place, who open their whore legs to any tiny prick with a copper penny that walks their way."

Kehl grabbed her and pushed her onto his table.

"You will be mine," Kehl said, excitement in his voice. "You will stand next to me as I rise in fame and fortune."

"I am yours, Im'Ka'Da," N'Jeri said before she kissed him, and Kehl was putty in her hands.

5

Erik looked over his shoulder as they left the hall and the well and fountain. He could still here the distant trickle of water, but as he stepped into the adjoining tunnel, leading to somewhere within the city of Orvencrest, the torches that lined the large hallway extinguished, the distant sounds of water stopped, and in the darkness, Erik heard voices.

"Do you here that?" Erik asked Demik, who walked next to him.

"Hear what?" Demik replied.

"Those voices," Erik said.

They both stopped and stared into the darkness. Erik could see the dwarf straining to hear what he had heard.

"No," Demik said, shaking his head. Then, he shivered. "But the warmth of this hallway seems to have disappeared with the light."

"That is *them,*" Erik said. "They are here, in the darkness."

"Who?" Demik asked.

"Demik. Erik," Balzarak called from the front of the company, "we must go."

At the edge of their own torchlight, and the light of Bryon's sword, Erik could see the tunnel was short and opened into another wide hall. On both sides of the hall were platforms, both with broken stairways.

"Guard posts," Turk said.

A long spear rested against the wall on one platform. Under that same platform, they found a pile of clothing—armor—and under the armor, old bones, brittle and ancient.

"Why don't these torches magically light?" Erik asked, pointing to the sconces on the wall holding ancient sticks covered in pitch.

"I don't know," Balzarak replied. "Perhaps the magic of the guardian only extends so far. Whatever the reason, be careful. Be ready."

Beyond Balzarak's circlet, Erik could see a wide darkness, blacker than the shadow around it, gaping like an open maw.

"A doorway," Erik said.

"Aye," Demik agreed.

The large double doors that once stood strong and tall at the end of this hall—a smaller version of Thorakest's Gröde Hadenhall—hung open, rotten and dilapidated. The darkness from beyond the doors spilled into the hall as if it were sunlight, only its shadowy, evil twin. At this end of the hall, stood two more guard stations. The remains of one dwarf, now skeletal, hung over the edge of one platform while the remains of two other dwarves rested underneath the other platform.

Trauma was evident on these remains, a clear tale of battle from within and treachery, with cracked skulls, broken weapons, and shattered bones.

"They were taken by surprise," Dwain said.

"How do you know?" Wrothgard asked.

"We only see the remains of four or five guards," Dwain replied. "If an alarm had gone off before they were attacked, this hall would have been filled with the remains of hundreds of warriors."

"Maybe time has washed the evidence away," Wrothgard suggested.

"No," Balzarak said. "Something surprised them."

"*They* surprised them," Erik added, and Balzarak replied with a quick nod. Erik couldn't help seeing the disapproving stare Threhof gave the general.

As they passed through the great, dark opening, Erik heard them again, shadowy voices from the darkness, the memory of the dead.

"We are here," they hissed in one, sickening chorus. "Come to us."

Erik turned as the others passed through the doorway. The light around him faded, and only Demik stayed, with his torch. Erik could almost see them, at the edge of the darkness.

I'll see you enough in my dreams.

He looked at Demik with a sidelong glance. He knew the dwarf didn't hear them, but he knew something was there nonetheless. Still, it didn't stop the questioning look on his face.

"Coward!" they hissed.

"Maybe," Erik replied. "Or maybe I'm just smart. Maybe I will fight you on my terms."

Their laughter seemed to rattle the walls.

"You are in our realm now," they hissed. "You will fight on our terms. This is the realm of the dead."

"Let's go Demik," Erik said, and they turned to follow their companions.

The broken doorway opened into a huge cavern, the ceilings beyond sight so Erik could only discern the outlines of buildings and walls. Balzarak and the other dwarves stood just inside the door.

"Is he bloody crying?" Switch asked.

"I think so," Bryon replied.

"This is it," Balzarak muttered, more to himself. "This is the lost city."

"I doesn't look like much," Switch said.

"If the fires were only burning," Dwain added, "you would see its grandeur."

"Where are its mirrors?" Erik asked. "Are they broken?"

"No mirrors," Bofim said. "Time before mirrors."

"Ah I see," Erik said. "So, they just used torches to light the city."

"Giant fire pits," Bofim replied.

"You know, you can speak to me in Dwarvish," Erik said.

"If I speak Dwarvish," Bofim said, "I no get better at Westernese."

"What if I speak to you in Dwarvish, and you speak to me in Westernese?" Erik asked.

"Deal," Bofim replied.

The shadows of buildings rose around them, most distant memories of what they once were. Wood had rotted away. Stone had crumbled.

"No farms," Befel said.

"No," Turk replied. "Their farms would have been on the surface somewhere."

Erik felt something under his boot. He bent down and picked up a child's doll, a thing made of cloth that had somehow avoided the ravages of time, with string hair and buttons for eyes—although one of the blue buttons was missing. It reminded him of the gypsies, which seemed so long ago. He remembered a little girl carrying a doll similar to this one. She had reminded him of his sisters. He felt a lump in his throat. Families had lived here. This wasn't just a city of hardened dwarvish warriors. When the dwomanni attacked, women and children fell victim to their shadow.

"What's that?" Befel asked.

"Nothing," Erik replied. "Just an old doll."

"Still intact?" Befel asked.

Erik nodded, lifting the doll up, close to his face. He could almost smell the child that had held this doll. It smelled like his sisters, like their hair. Their hair always smelled sweet, like his mother's roses.

"Seems odd," Befel said.

"There are no dwarvish remains," Wrothgard said. "No bones, clothing, armor. There isn't any evidence of an attack."

"Keep moving," Turk said as he passed Erik, Wrothgard, and Befel. "It isn't safe to stop."

Erik tucked the doll into his belt. As he followed his dwarvish friend, he felt *them* watching. He knew they were there, beyond the shadows. He could smell their stink and tried thinking of the smells of his mother's garden. They came to an open place.

"The main marketplace of Orvencrest," Threhof said.

It was a large space. At its center, as with almost any marketplace, was a fountain. Whatever massive statue that once rose as the centerpiece of the fountain was gone, crumbled away into dust, but the remnants of a sitting space that surrounded the fountain still remained.

"It still has water in it," Bryon said, peering into the fountain.

"Bryon," Dwain said, "be careful."

Beldar and Bim stepped next to Bryon as he reached to dip a finger in the water. But as he touched it, they saw that it wasn't water. It was sticky and black and bubbled when he disturbed its surface. Both Beldar and Bim grabbed Bryon's arms and pulled him back, almost dragging him away from the fountain. In their light, Erik could see steam rising from the fountain, and he heard a rumbling like boiling water. Bryon flicked the sticky stuff from his finger onto the floor, and where it hit, it hissed and smoked.

Everyone readied their weapons, but after a few moments, the smoke dissipated, and the rumbling stopped.

"Don't touch anything," Balzarak hissed. "Everything here is tainted."

Erik looked at the doll hanging limply in his belt. Everything?

The marketplace was vast, broken remains of carts and shops scattered all over. The sound of boot steps on a cobbled street echoed through the cavern in which the city rested.

"I don't like this place," Switch said. Erik saw the thief shiver. "Treasure or not, this place is cursed."

"Cursed indeed," Wrothgard agreed.

"Yes," Balzarak said, "very much cursed."

Once they passed through the tomb of what once was a marketplace, they could see the distant walls of the castle of Orvencrest. This part of the city seemed even more decrepit, with very few buildings left standing. As Switch rested a hand against a beam of wood that leaned against the stone foundation of another building, the old wood crumbled away, turning to dust instantly. The smell of fire and smoke hit Erik's nose, and he bid Demik bring his torch closer. The dust was black. The floor was black. The stone of the other building's foundation was black.

"Fire," Erik said.

The walls of the next building still stood, albeit crooked and pockmarked. Wrothgard and Turk stepped through what was once the front door.

"I think we finally found dwarvish remains," Wrothgard called out.

Erik saw what looked like a gray statue of a dwarvish child. Next to it, were a dwarvish man and woman, also stone-like.

"What is that?" Befel asked.

"Are they encased in ancient ash?" Erik asked. "I've never seen anything like that."

"The fire would have had to have been so hot to do this," Turk said. "I have never known a fire to get this hot."

"Never," Demik agreed.

"I've seen this once," Dwain said.

"Truly?" Wrothgard asked.

"Truly," Dwain replied. "Melted rock flows like rivers, deep within the earth. It is like yellow blood. It is so hot, it can melt even Dwarf's Iron in an instant. Sometimes, the heat builds up, and it erupts through the surface of the earth."

"A volcano," Wrothgard said.

"Yes, a volcano," Dwain replied. "An eruption happened, once, near a village of men, near the Yerymann Steppes. I was a member of the dwarvish force that went to help those who had survived. The temperature of the air was so hot when the volcano erupted, when ash fell and the air cooled, it *froze* the people it covered. Those images still haunt my dreams to this day."

"So, this hot blood of the earth erupted here?" Switch asked.

"I thought Orvencrest was attacked," Erik said.

"It was," Balzarak said, "and no, hot magma did not erupt and destroy Orvencrest. There would be nothing left."

"Then what could have made the air so bloody hot to do this?" Switch asked.

Balzarak looked to Gôdruk and Thormok. They whispered, and the look on Gôdruk's face was enough for anyone to realize it wasn't a pleasant conversation.

"Bloody magic, that's what it was," Switch said.

"The bloodiest," Balzarak said, "and the blackest."

They found more bodies encased in ash and more buildings blackened and charred. This whole area of the city looked to have been ravaged by fire, anything flammable was gone. There were even blocks of stone that looked to have been melted.

Beldar said something to Threhof.

"A fire in a mountain cavern, with nowhere to go, would be devastating," Threhof said, nodding his head. "As it rages, it sucks away all the oxygen. These dwarves probably suffocated before this ash ever touched them."

"Then why does the evidence of fire stop at the marketplace?" Erik asked.

Balzarak looked back at the young man, worry in his eyes.

"Maybe there was no more air," Threhof said with a shrug. "Fire can't burn without air."

Threhof didn't believe what he was saying. Erik knew that. He could tell by the tone of his voice. And the look that Balzarak gave him said he didn't believe him either.

6

Cliens and Ranus had seen a group of men and dwarves they recognized from Finlo, from the Messenger's meeting. But there were other dwarves with them. Cliens couldn't figure why men and dwarves were traveling together. But shortly after they saw them exit an entrance into the mountain, dwarvish patrols began to increase. They hid for several days, wanting to follow the mercenaries but concerned about being seen by the keen eyes of some scout. That meant they lost track of the mercenaries, the group of men from Finlo, and they were not happy.

It was their solemn duty, their task direct from the General Lord Marshall, commander of all military forces of Gol-Durathna, to follow these mercenaries, these minions of the Lord of the East. They were to follow them and find out what it was the Lord of the East wanted, what thing he could possibly desire, hidden deep within the ruins of an ancient dwarvish city. And what were they to do when they found this thing ... or found the men who found this treasure. That command was somewhat ambiguous. Take the thing and let them go? Capture them? Kill them? The thought gave Cliens a shiver.

Risking coming more out into the open, they found a large bridge that crossed a massive ravine that split the Southern Mountains into two ranges. Camping there, the next morning Ranus spotted a gigantic bear.

"Cave bear," he had told Cliens.

It limped, missing several claws on one of its paws, as it paced back and forth on the other side of the bridge, perhaps wondering if it could cross. Cliens shuddered at the thought of what thing could have caused such an injury to this prehistoric beast. The bear disappeared into the mountain forest when a dwarvish patrol showed up, the soldiers congregating at the bridge.

Ranus tapped Cliens on his shoulder and jerked his head sideways, signaling that they should go. Cliens nodded in agreement, but stopped moving when he heard talking, not in Dwarvish, but in Shengu.

A company of men marched along the edge of the ravine, apparently unaware of the dwarves as the dwarves were just as unaware of them.

"Golgolithulians?" Cliens whispered.

Ranus shook his head and pointed to the man in the lead and his iron breastplate.

"Patûk," Cliens hissed.

Ranus nodded his head.

"Damn it," Cliens cursed. "Now we're stuck between them."

Ranus suggested they go around, but that would take them away from the ravine by another day or more. The mercenaries they had been following were the closest to finding the fabled lost city of Orvencrest. If anyone could show them a way to recover that which the Lord of the East sought so desperately, it would be these mercenaries, with the seeming help of dwarves from Thorakest.

"We wait," Cliens said.

"They'll be long gone," Ranus replied.

"What? The master tracker cannot follow their trail?" Cliens chided.

"Even my nose for tracking has its limitations," Ranus replied.

Just then, the men and dwarves saw one another. Ranus and Cliens pushed away from the ledge overlooking the ravine and began to descend down the slope. The sounds of metal clanging—and dying—rang out only moments later, soldiers shouting in both Dwarvish and Shengu.

"Son of a whore," Cliens cursed.

They hiked east and then started climbing the steep mountain slope again, so they might see the ravine and find another way across, away from the land bridge and fighting. Cliens followed his nimble friend as quickly as he could, but Ranus always seemed more adept at this sort of thing. Ranus stopped, just before the crest of the hill.

"What is it?" Cliens said through labored breaths. He hadn't realized how tired he truly was until they stopped.

"More easterners," Ranus replied. He went down onto his stomach and pulled himself forward, slowly.

Cliens followed suit and, crawling up next to his friend, saw half a dozen men, all armored like the others—leather breastplates and wooden shields. Cliens huffed.

"If we keep running to the east," Cliens whispered, "we move farther and farther away from the mercenaries."

Ranus nodded. He looked to Cliens. Cliens nodded back.

The stealth of Ranus always amazed Cliens. He stood shorter than most men, but he was well muscled, and all that muscle seemed to slow most down. Ranus jumped behind one of the easterners—the man unaware—with his two-pronged spear in one hand and a long, curved dagger in the other. He jabbed both blades of the spear hard into the base of the soldier's head. The soldier lurched forward, collapsing in a heap. As the soldier next to the dead man turned, Ranus brought the blade of his dagger up under the man's chin. Blood exploded from his mouth, and he gurgled a muffled scream. Another soldier ran at Ranus, but Cliens leapt at him, sword in hand. The steel blade easily passed through the man's leather breastplate.

The other three soldiers, now aware that they were under attack, lined up, shield to shield, with spears extended. Ranus jumped, his feet easily head level with the eastern soldiers. As one of the soldiers tried to stab upwards at Cliens' friend, Cliens came in hard with his sword. He felt his blade break ribs as it slid through the soft meat of a man's diaphragm. The soldier lurched to the side, crashing into the man next to him.

As they tumbled backwards, Ranus came down onto the other soldier, foot kicking out and catching his enemy in the nose. The easterner dropped his guard, eyes watering as blood ran freely from his nose. That gave Ranus all the opportunity he needed, and he jabbed upwards with his two-pronged spear, catching the soldier in the throat.

"What are you doing here?" Cliens asked the surviving soldier in Shengu, the language of Golgolithul.

The soldier rolled over to face Cliens, and as he did, jabbed up with a sword. Cliens easily swatted the weapon away and slashed at the man's wrist. The soldier groaned and clutched his arm to his chest. Cliens' steel had almost removed the man's hand.

"What are eastern traitors doing here?" Cliens asked, again in Shengu.

"Traitors?" the soldier seethed. "It is that imposter that is the traitor."

Cliens looked at Ranus with a smile.

"Who do you serve then?" Cliens asked.

"The east," the soldier replied, his face paling. "I serve Golgolithul and its people."

"You know what I mean," Cliens said. He put the point of his sword to the man's chest. His steel easily slid through the leather breastplate and into flesh. The soldier groaned again, this time louder.

Cliens saw Ranus step forward. He had a concerned look on his face—a disapproving look. Ranus hated his questioning tactics. Cliens certainly did not wish to torture enemies. He would rather give them a quick death, contrary to the officers and inquisitors of Golgolithul. But when there was a need to extract information, Cliens found a way.

Cliens returned the hard look Ranus gave him.

"What do you want me to do?" Cliens asked in his native tongue. "Do you want me to wrap him in a blanket and give him treats?"

Ranus shook his head. "No. But no need to cause him extra pain. Give him a quick death, and be done with it."

"Patûk Al'Banan or Pavin Al'Bashar?" Cliens asked.

Cliens suspected General Al'Banan, with the regimented way these soldiers moved and the breastplates bearing the symbol of the Aztûkians, the former ruling family of Golgolithul. When the soldier didn't reply, Cliens pressed his sword into the man's shoulder harder.

"Curse you," the soldier seethed. "May Ga'an Yû curse you, in this life and the next."

"Don't believe in him," Cliens said, smiling, "so I don't really care about your curse. Now, who do you serve?"

"General Patûk Al'Banan," the soldier finally said. He seemed tired. He was losing blood.

"And why are you here?" Cliens asked.

"Just kill me already," the soldier said.

"Soon enough," Cliens replied. "Why are you here?"

The soldier waited a moment, closing his eyes.

"The imposter wants something from the dwarves—a lost city or something like that. It's something of importance to him. I don't know what it is. Of course, rather than look for it himself, he commissioned mercenaries to find it for him. We have been ordered to stop them."

"I see," Cliens said. "And the dwarves are making that difficult."

The soldier nodded slowly.

"Aye. Stupid tunnel diggers. We have had three or four skirmishes with dwarvish patrols just in the last few days."

"You are to stop these mercenaries, or find the city for yourselves?" Cliens asked.

"I don't know." The soldier leaned his head back. His breathing slowed. "I'm just a soldier. It's all too complicated for me. Give me ale and women, and I'll be happy."

Before he closed them, the soldier's eyes took on a vacant look and then, as if he was watching his life slip away, a wide smile appeared on his face. Cliens drew his sword from the man's chest and placed the tip of his blade at the base of the soldier's throat. Most men flinched when that happened, knowing what was coming. This man could have cared less. Blood pooled around him, flowing freely from his wrist. His skin had paled almost white. He probably didn't even feel the steel at his throat.

Cliens pushed hard, the blade passing through skin, throat, and spine easily. The soldier didn't move. He didn't even flinch.

"The dwarves are coming," Ranus said, pointing to the west.

Cliens turned. He couldn't see anything, but he heard the growl of a bear, heard distant shouting in Dwarvish. He looked back to his friend, who jerked his head sideways, motioning down the hill to the ravine.

"The land bridge is just back that way," Ranus said.

"Let's go then," Cliens replied.

They raced down the hill, the yelling dwarves behind them.

As Ranus stepped out onto the bridge, Cliens looked back, once again. At least half a dozen dwarves, all clad in mail and plate armor, glared down at them. They shouted and pointed, and again, Cliens heard the great growl of a bear. The beast came into view—a giant of a brown bear covered in plate barding—and took a swipe at the earth before stomping up and down.

"Come on," Ranus said as he nimbly crossed over the bridge.

"Sure," Cliens muttered to himself, "says the one who could walk across this ravine on nothing but a piece of thin string."

Cliens stepped out onto the land bridge, trying his best not to look over the edge and stare at the darkness that consumed the space below him. He expected the shouting dwarves to get closer, expected to eventually have to run across the bridge, but that never happened. Halfway across, he heard more shouting, this time in Shengu. Cliens stopped and turned, watching as the other force of eastern men clashed with a dozen southern dwarves.

"Are you coming?" Ranus yelled.

"Yes," Cliens replied, looking back at his friend who already stood on the other side of the ravine. "Yes, yes. I'm coming."

"Quickly, perhaps?" Ranus chided. Cliens could sense the amusement in his friend's voice. "Or are you planning on waiting until the dwarves kill those men?"

"No, damn it," Cliens replied. "I'm coming. Calm yourself. I'm not as nimble as you are."

When Cliens finally reached the other side, he asked, "Can you track them?"

Ranus gave Cliens a disapproving, frustrated look.

"Just a question," Cliens said defensively.

"I can track them," Ranus replied.

"Then let's get to it."

7

"Fires happen in large cities," Switch said, quite confidently. "In fact, they happen all the time. And they're the kiss of death. Fires and epidemics."

"I realize that," Erik replied. He had gotten tired of listening to the thief try to convince him that nothing out of the ordinary had happened here, in Orvencrest, even though he could hear the uncertainty in the man's voice. He was trying to convince himself more than anyone else.

As they moved closer to the castle, its ancient towers—those that still stood, at least—rose taller and taller in the distance, gigantic, shadowy monsters of mystery in the relatively dim light of torch, magic sword, and magic circlet that was almost washed out by the vastness of Orvencrest's cavern.

Now, the dwelling places and shops of Turk and Balzarak's ancestors disappeared, little more than ages old dust where stone and timber once stood. Here and there they found a few foundations or lumps of hardened iron or steel or some other metal, melted in the great fire. But mostly, they found empty space, buildings destroyed a thousand years ago and gone from memory.

"If this was just a typical fire," Erik said, "then why does it end at the marketplace? Why does the damage just stop?"

"Like the old tunnel digger said," Switch said, pointing a thumb to Threhof, "it used up all the air in the cavern. It bloody killed itself, basically."

"Did anyone look at the gate?" Wrothgard asked.

Erik didn't quite understand what the soldier meant, and by the silence, he suspected neither did anyone else.

"The gate leading into the cavern," Wrothgard repeated. "Did anyone look at it?"

"It was broken," Turk said, "barely hanging from its giant hinges. Why?"

"I remember it being black," Wrothgard said.

"Everything here is black," Switch said with an irritated huff.

"No," Wrothgard said. "Black ... as in burnt. I guess I didn't think of it when we first entered Orvencrest—I had no reason to. Perhaps it was just blackened by time and decay. But, as I remember looking at it—only briefly as we passed through the entrance—it looked brittle, as if it had been touched by fire."

"What does it matter?" Threhof said. He sounded irritated as well.

Bim and Beldar started arguing in Dwarvish, Nafer quickly jumping in on their heated conversation as well.

"So, fire obliterated this part of the city," Bryon said, "and burned the main gate, but barely touched the marketplace and the first part of the city?"

"Was it just the dwo—" Erik began to ask, but Balzarak turned on him hard, putting an open hand into the middle of the young man's chest.

Erik knew dwarves were strong, but the force with which the general had struck him knocked the air out of his lungs. He hadn't expected it. Neither had anyone else. Both Bryon and Befel moved next to Erik, swords ready. Nafer and Demik looked confused. Gôdruk and Thormok moved next to Balzarak. Turk tried to step between the two groups, only to be held back by Bofim. Erik could see that malicious smile growing on Switch's face.

Balzarak stepped back quickly and gave Erik a quick bow.

"I am sorry, Erik," he said. "I didn't mean to strike you."

"It's alright," Erik replied, rubbing his chest where the dwarf had struck him.

"This is not the place to mention their name," Balzarak said and Erik nodded, understanding.

Threhof gave the general a hard look and the one Balzarak returned showed his worry ... and fear.

The walls of the castle rose so high, the torch and magic light could not reveal the merlons at the top, but Erik could see that black char covered the stone. The wall had crumbled in some spots, and every length they inspected was pockmarked and showed signs of age and deterioration. Erik presumed, like in Thorakest, a great wooden gate once stood at the castle's main entrance, but it was gone, and the giant portcullis hung halfway closed, warped and partially melted.

The darkness that lay beyond the opening, and the broken portcullis, made it look like a rotten mouth with crooked, nasty teeth, open and snarling. The courtyard presented little in terms of standing buildings. Crushed rubble lay where buildings once stood. The walls on this side were pockmarked as well and leaned in haphazard directions. If there was wind in this cavern, one strong gust could have toppled the whole castle.

"There is the keep," Dwain said, pointing to a tall, square building stained black.

As they all entered the courtyard, Erik heard *them*—the undead, the ghosts that haunted his dreams—congregating outside the walls. He heard them goading him, cursing him, crying out for his blood. But something told him they could not enter the castle. He didn't know why, but he was certain, they would stay on the other side.

"Not even ghosts would haunt this bloody tomb," said Switch.

"Somehow that is true," Erik muttered to himself. "What magic protects this place?"

Erik felt cold walking through the entrance of the keep. When he breathed, he remembered the coldest winter mornings, back on the farmstead, when he could see his breath and his lungs burned because of the chill.

The first part of the keep was a large room with a high ceiling and two staircases on either side, directly across from one another. When their lantern and torchlight flooded the room, a golden hue filled the hall.

"Is that melted gold?" Switch knelt and ran his fingers over a mound of yellow metal that held no distinguishable shape.

Erik scanned the walls and surmised that, before the fire, gold and silver ornamentations hung from the wall, or sat on small, stone daises. Now, even the iron sconces once held torches, but they were all gone. All that was left were countless mounds of melted metal, a distorted remnant of the opulence that was once the keep of Orvencrest.

"Could it really have been so hot in here that all the metal melted together?" Wrothgard asked, even though what they saw answered his question.

"Is that so hard to believe?" Threhof asked. "We saw melted Dwarf's Iron, for An's sake."

"But, dwarf, this room is untouched by fire," Wrothgard said. "Do you not understand? The heat in this room, even though it was untouched by fire, was so hot it melted gold and silver. General, what happened here?"

Switch had begun working a pile of melted gold loose with one of his daggers. He looked like he was in a trance, his eyes focused, his mouth twisted into a weird smile. Erik thought the thief might salivate.

"Don't concern yourself with that pile of melted gold," Balzarak said. "It is said that the treasury of Orvencrest has so much gold it will make that look like a pittance. We need to keep moving. Find the throne room ... find the treasure room ... and find a way out of here."

The room must have been magnificent, and as they moved through the keep, Erik noticed how many piles of melted gold and silver there were. There were places where tapestries must once have hung, now gone with time. Just the construction of the room spoke of its grandeur. Even the two stairways leading to the next levels of the building, though now thoroughly distorted, suggested artfully carved and molded handrails, with inlays of gems and precious metal in each step. Everything spoke of opulence, and again, Erik couldn't help noticing how the thief eyed the gems—emeralds, diamonds, and rubies—set within the steps.

As they moved behind a wall that extended from the ceiling of the first floor to the floor, at the back of the keep stood two large doors, intricate scenes of battles and ceremonies carved into their wood. As well as being untouched by the heat or fire, they also showed, after so many years, no signs of warping.

"That is the throne room," Dwain said in hushed tones.

"Draw your weapons," Balzarak commanded.

As they got closer, their light picked out two bodies lying in front of the double doors, nothing but skeleton. Their armor had melted, although they looked as if they had been untouched by fire, and bone and steel were now one.

Beldar stepped over the remains of the two guards. He looked back at Balzarak.

"Offne," Balzarak said with a quick nod.

Erik tightened his grip on Ilken's Blade. As the doors opened, he could hear his dream crawlers, from the other side of the castle walls.

They cried out and screamed and cursed. A chill crawled up Erik's spine, and goose pimples rose along his arms.

"This is the bloody throne room?" Switch asked, walking in after Beldar.

"Aye," Balzarak replied, following the thief.

"It's tiny," Switch added.

"The doors would normally be left open," Balzarak explained, "so that it felt as if it was a part of the main keep. But for security, these doors could be closed and barred."

"Little good it did them," Bryon said, pointing his sword at the remains of two more guards.

Old torches rested in rusted sconces along the wall. Demik lit them, and they illuminated the room. There were two thrones up against the wall opposite the door, the remnants of a small table with no chairs—although half a dozen might have sat comfortably around it—and a marble pedestal that was big enough for a vase and pitcher. The skeletal remains of an animal rested next to the table. Erik recognized the skull.

"What was that?" Switch asked.

"A bear," Erik replied.

"Cave bear," Turk added.

The remains of two more guards lay in front of the two thrones and another skeletal body still sat on the larger of the two thrones, thick bones covered by robes that had survived the decay of time. Erik imagined the dwarf whose bones these belonged to as a stout soldier, wide shoulders and thick chest. This was once a powerful dwarf, a decorated warrior. A crown resting on its skull had slipped down as the flesh disappeared, the golden headdress stopping just above the nasal cavity, blocking out the eye sockets.

"The king," Erik said.

"Fire Beard," Balzarak gasped.

And then Erik could see him. He saw the dwarf, standing on a distant hill. It was the hill from his dreams, and he knew that he had seen the dwarf in his dreams. Why had King Fire Beard been in his dreams? Under his robes he wore plate mail that gleamed with a reddish hue. His crown was studded with rubies, and he still looked majestic, resting his hand on the handle of his battle axe.

Erik looked over his shoulder and saw Balzarak, along with the rest of the dwarves, kneeling.

At first, it appeared as if the smaller throne simply contained a pile of clothing, but as Erik moved the cloth aside, he saw more bones that seemingly had collapsed and a skull, much smaller than the king's, had rolled back and it nestled in the corner of the throne. A child.

Back on the hill, Erik saw him, a young dwarvish boy, standing next to Fire Beard. He looked scared, and the king lovingly looked down at the lad—his son—as the boy clung to his leg. He looked like the king, with his red hair. The king rubbed his back and said soothing words to his son, even as the boy whimpered and began to cry.

"It will be alright," the king said.

"I'm scared, Papa," the boy replied.

"I know, my son," the king said. "So am I. But no matter what happens, we will be alright."

"Do you promise?" the boy asked, looking up at his father.

"Yes, my son," the king replied. "Have faith. Have hope."

Erik could see both sorrow and hope in the king's eyes. He knew they were going to die, but that wasn't the hope he spoke of. He knew they would die, but then they would be together again, in the halls of heaven. Such strength in the face of death. He heard prayers. It was the king's voice. His son joined him. So did the guards in the room. They all stood on that hill, resilient, praying, and looking evil in its face.

"Do not touch it!" Balzarak yelled.

Erik stepped away from the remains, his leg brushing the child's clothing and, as it did so, a small doll fell to the floor from underneath the clothing. Erik bent down and picked it up. It looked like a little warrior, all wood but painted gray as if it wore armor. One hand held a spear, a thin stick really, and the other held a shield.

"His son," Erik said. "The prince."

"Why is the king just sitting here?" Turk asked. "And why is his son with him, waiting for death?"

"Does a warrior not welcome death?" Threhof asked.

"Certainly," Turk replied, "but surely, their guards would have escorted them away if escape was possible. And the king, especially with his son here, would not have just sat in his throne and waited for someone, or something, to kill the both of them."

"They knew they would die," Erik said, facing his friend. "At least, King Fire Beard did. That is why he sat here and prayed with his guards and his son, comforted them in their last moments as any good king would."

"You sound awfully sure of that," Switch said.

Erik just shrugged. But it wasn't just that the king knew he was going to die. There was more to it than that. His hip tingled. His dagger agreed with him. The king certainly would've welcomed death. But his son? The king was protecting something. And the thing that he protected, the thing that he kept secret and safe, was so important, he was willing to not only sacrifice himself, but also his son and his most trusted guards.

"We must all say a prayer for the lost king," Balzarak said, "and his son."

"This is truly hallowed ground," Threhof added.

"Aye," Dwain agreed.

The dwarves all bowed their heads and muttered quiet prayers. Erik couldn't help feeling tension in the room, especially as Wrothgard looked about, and Switch ran his hands over the walls.

"Where is the treasure room?" Switch asked.

"There are no doors in this room," Wrothgard said.

"Perhaps in another part of the castle?" Erik asked, but the dwarves still remained inattentive as they prayed.

"Is the door hidden somewhere?" Wrothgard asked.

"Turk? Demik?" Bryon asked.

No one answered him.

"Damn it!" Switch yelled. "All this bloody praying and reverence. It's a bloody skeleton. We're here for the bloody treasure and for some *thing* the Lord of the East wants. That's it. Not for some gods be damned day of remembrance. All this way, people dead, so we can sit here and cry over a damned dead dwarf!"

Switch moved towards the throne, and all in unison, the sound of steel echoed through the room as the dwarves, including Turk, Demik, and Nafer, readied their weapons.

"No touch," Bofim said.

"Or what?" Switch asked defiantly.

"You die," Beldar replied.

Switch threw up his hands dejectedly.

"The entrance to the treasure room should be behind the king's throne," Balzarak said resolutely, moving slowly past Switch and next to the dead king.

"How do you know that?" Threhof asked.

Balzarak didn't answer but stepped between the two thrones and crouched so he could place his hands on the side of the king's throne. He began to push. Erik heard the sound of something sliding on stone and saw the king's final resting place move sideways.

"Help him," Wrothgard said.

Switch needed no more prompting. He joined the general in pushing the throne. So did Beldar and Bim. Slowly, as the chair moved away across the floor, a dark passageway was revealed. As soon as there was enough space for someone to pass through, they stopped.

"This is the way to the treasure room?" Switch asked, putting his hands on his hips and trying to catch his breath.

"This is the way to the treasure room," Balzarak replied, reluctantly.

Bim and Beldar muttered something to one another, excited.

"I almost can't believe it," Turk said, running a hand over his face.

"Beldar," Balzarak said.

The dwarf needed no more prompting. He took a torch and stepped into the dark tunnel.

"Switch," Wrothgard said. "Maybe you should go with him."

The thief needed no more prompting either, he grabbed a torch and followed.

"Was there no queen?" Erik asked as they waited for Beldar and Switch to return.

"I don't know," Balzarak replied. "Bim, Bofim, Gôdruk."

All three bowed and left the throne room.

"They will explore the rest of the keep," Balzarak explained.

The three dwarves returned before Beldar and the thief and Gôdruk spoke with Balzarak.

"They found the queen," Balzarak explained, sorrowfully. "Her quarters. Everything was melted and burned. Her remains, the remains of two daughters, the rest of the king's guard. They all deserved better."

"They were all protecting something," Erik said under his breath.

"What was that?" Balzarak asked.

"Most people who find themselves on the other end of evil intentions deserve better," Erik said, thinking of the people from Aga Kona and his friends, the gypsies.

It had been a while since Switch and Beldar had left when Erik caught the glimmer of light coming from the tunnel behind King Fire Beard's throne. He heard heavy footsteps and shouting, distant and inaudible. Within moments, the light grew, and he saw Switch, holding a lantern that gave off ten times as much light as any torch.

Both Beldar and Switch entered the throne room, bending over and trying to catch their breath. When the thief finally stood, he couldn't stop smiling.

"Did you find it?" Wrothgard asked.

Neither one of them said anything.

"Beldar," Balzarak said. "Speak."

"Well?" Turk asked.

"By the bloody gods!" Switch finally cried.

"An be good!" was Beldar's cry.

"We found it," Switch said.

"Bloody shadow," Bryon said, "I think Switch is crying."

Switch reached into his pants and pulled out two handfuls of gold coins and gems and necklaces. There was more in his hands than Erik's father would make in ten lifetimes. A dozen coins twice the size of Hámonian pounds spilled over his fingers. A diamond, almost transparent and the size of a cow's eyeball, slinked against the ground.

"The treasure of Orvencrest," Switch said. "We found it. It's like nothing I have ever seen. By the gods, we found it."

8

"Never ..." Erik muttered.

"I would have never thought I would see such a thing," Wrothgard said.

"I knew it would be here," Turk said.

"An is good," Balzarak said.

"How much do you think that is?" Bryon asked, and Erik shook his head. No one could ever even estimate the worth of all that lay before them.

"So much precious metals, gems, and coins that they just started piling it up in the middle of the room," Befel said.

"Here are your rivers of gold, Bryon," Erik said. "The treasures that the east has to offer. Now you just need a harem."

"Very funny, cousin," Bryon said, but for once he did not respond angrily to the sarcasm.

Erik walked down a long ramp that led into the room. About fifty paces on all sides, it was rather simple although it had a ceiling higher than five homes stacked on top of one another. As he walked around the five giant piles of treasure that sat at the center of the room, he felt his heart quicken.

Beldar, Bim, and Bofim had lit all the torches in the room, but there still wasn't much light. Dwain found a small trough that ran along the length of the treasure room walls on every side, and when he put his torch to it, the oil in the troughs lit, finally revealing the true grandeur of Orvencrest's treasure room.

The light reflected an eerie golden-red hew along the walls, and piles they had built cast even stranger shadows. The corners of the room, the places farthest away from the light, still looked dark and ominous. Erik wondered if they—the dead—could hide in those small, black spaces. The odd light and even odder shadows gave the room a somewhat discomforting feel, despite the massive wealth that rested there.

And it wasn't just gold and jewels that sat in the room. Rich carpets and tapestries had been stored on one side of the room, some giant creations of craftsmanship, made from material native to faraway lands. Another part of the treasure room held furniture—tables and chairs and armoires and mirrors—that were suited for only the greatest of kings, with their intricate carvings and expert manufacturing. And yet another part of the room had rows and rows of shelves filled with books and scrolls.

Perhaps that is where the Lord of the East's treasure is kept, in some chest on a shelf, Erik thought, but then realized that that would be too easy, this deadly thing simply sitting on a shelf.

The real treasure—according to some of the dwarves—sat opposite the books and shelves ... an armory. Racks of weapons and armor, anything from basic swords and spears to the most exotic looking implements, sat there, grander than anything any soldier could imagine, certainly grander than the armory of Thorakest. This was something Erik never thought he would ever see, and despite the shiver the eerie light and odd shadows gave him, he allowed himself a tiny smile as he surveyed the room.

Switch lay in one of the piles of treasure, wiggling his arms and legs in the gold and laughing. He wore a dozen bracelets on each arm, as many jeweled necklaces around his neck, and several circlets studded with gems on his head.

"This is his heaven," Befel said, smiling and shaking his head at the same time.

"I bet, if we checked, he'd have a bracelet hanging around his manhood," Bryon said.

"A bracelet may be a little generous," Erik said with a laugh. It felt good to laugh.

"A ring then," Bryon replied, also laughing.

"A small ring," Erik added as the other two wandered off.

"Come, my friend," Balzarak said, as the other dwarves also started to walk about the vast room, "Fill your haversack with the bounty of the dwarves. We cannot deny you your reward."

"Where did all this treasure come from?" Erik asked.

"Dwarves have always been a frugal people," Balzarak replied.

"That doesn't really explain a treasure room filled with more gold and jewels than I think exist in all of Háthgolthane," Erik said.

"No, I suppose not," Balzarak said. "We dwarves typically give a portion of our wealth each year to the king. It is an offering, and the expectation is that it would be used for the good of the city and the people in a time of need."

"So, this is all from offerings?" Erik asked.

"Some," Balzarak replied, "but then, this would be the place where we would store the spoils of war, those things like important documents and histories, treasured pieces of art that aren't being displayed at the time. Orvencrest was the capital of the Southern

Dwarves for hundreds of years before it fell. This is wealth that had been amassed over centuries."

"Does Thorakest, or the cities in the north, have a room like this?" Erik asked.

"They have a treasure room, for sure," Balzarak replied, "although I have never seen Thorakest's, I am certain it's nothing like this."

"Seems dangerous," Erik said, "to have so much treasure in one place."

"Rest assured, Erik," Balzarak replied, "that this is perhaps the most secure room in the whole city, its entrances kept secret."

"And yet we got in fairly easily," Erik said. He didn't know why, but this place didn't seem so secure. It seemed more like a beacon to would be conquerors. "How did you know how to get in?"

Balzarak just shrugged and smiled at Erik.

"Please, explore the magnificence of dwarvish treasure," the general finally said, joining his dwarvish companions. "Everyone can take their fill, and it will barely make an impact.

As Erik headed to join Turk, the dwarf standing hands on hips in front of the shelves of books and scrolls, he stopped and turned to look at the tunnel that led to the throne room. They were there, waiting, but something stopped them from following him into the throne room of the treasure room. He didn't know what it was that stopped them, but he knew they wouldn't follow. They would be waiting for them when they left.

"This is the *real* treasure," Turk said as he and Erik walked by each shelf.

Erik had no idea what it was he was looking at, or for, but the look on Turk's face told Erik that the dwarf was serious when he said this was the real treasure. In that moment, Turk could have cared less for all the gold in the world.

"You contradict those who said the armory took that title," he said, and Turk flashed him a look.

"Some of these books are worth more than all the gold in this room, Erik," Turk said.

"A book worth more than bloody gold?" Switch exclaimed, walking by Turk and Erik and shaking his head. "Poppycock."

"He wouldn't understand, Erik," Turk said. The dwarf ran his fingers along the spines of the books. "These are our histories. Some of them lost. Languages. Arithmetic. Science. Commentaries on our faith. Commentaries on other people's religions. It's priceless, Erik."

"I understand," Erik said, "but why are they here. I asked Balzarak, and it didn't seem to make sense to me. He said the dwarvish people give offerings to the king, just in case of famine or tragedy in the future. But this place seems like more than anything any kingdom ... two or three kingdoms, would ever need. Why is there so much value in this one room?"

"It is a large room," Turk said, laughing.

"Still," Erik said, not sharing in his friend's mirth.

"What is it that concerns you, Erik?" Turk asked. "I mean, look at the wealth of knowledge here. This one is on medicine and healing."

Turk put several of the books in his haversack.

"It just seems so unnecessary," Erik said, more to himself than to Turk. "There is so much here—gold, jewels, furniture, art, books and scrolls, weapons. Why is it hidden away and not used to ... to better the lives of your people?"

"Erik, why are you worrying about what my ancestors did right now?" Turk asked. "We found something that has been lost to my people for millennia. Take a moment and enjoy it."

But Erik was having a hard time doing that. The treasure room was more of a mystery to him than a magnificence, and he couldn't help thinking that its opulence had consumed the senses of even his good, dwarvish friend Turk. He wondered if hoarding such wealth was the reason the city of Orvencrest fell. Perhaps, this was a lesson the ancient dwarves had learned, and no one had found the city for that very reason. His father always warned him about the dangers of greed and wealth and the righteousness of humility. He shook his head.

"Do you think the Lord of the East's treasure is hidden on one of these shelves?" Erik asked.

"What was that?" Turk asked, nose plunged deep into a book, wide smile on his face.

"The scroll, the heirloom the Lord of the East wanted us to find," Erik said. "Do you think it could be on one of these shelves?"

"Oh," Turk said with a sudden look of realization, and then shrugged. "I don't know. I guess, at the moment, I don't care. Let us not think of the Lord of the East for a moment."

Erik nodded with a smile, but he couldn't stop thinking about their mission. Men had given their lives for this mission. Drake, Samus, Vander Bim, Mortin ... more.

As Turk continued to peruse the books, Erik made his way to the other side of the room, joining Wrothgard as the man looked through the myriad of weapons hanging from racks, sitting in stands, or simply leaning against the wall. The soldier seductively rubbed his fingers along a mail shirt.

"Do you think it will fit you?" Erik asked.

"It looks like there are weapons and armor here to fit all sizes of people," Wrothgard said, pointing to a giant of an axe just lying on the floor.

"Spoils of war," Erik muttered.

"Can you imagine the size of the man who would yield that?" Wrothgard asked.

"You will not find weaponry or armor better crafted," Balzarak said, walking up behind the two men.

"Why are there armor and weapons that were clearly made for men ... people larger than men?" Erik asked. "Were they collected on some battlefield?"

"Some, perhaps," Balzarak replied. "But some were crafted for men, gifts, offerings of friendship, and signs of peace to be given at treaty signings. To be given a suit of armor, a sword crafted by an ancient dwarvish blacksmith, would be an honor greater than almost anything else."

"It is still strong, after all these years?" Wrothgard asked.

"It looks that way," Balzarak said with a smile.

"I would think even good steel would have been ravaged by the hands of time," Erik pondered.

"I have found that sometimes it is best to simply accept things, rather than continually asking questions," Balzarak said. "Please, take what you wish. Mail shirts, swords, helms. You won't find the likes ever again."

Erik nodded with an insincere smile, and Wrothgard began to examine things more closely. Erik shook his head and wandered among the armor.

If this place is cursed, then what about this armor? What about this treasure?

He mulled over a coin he had picked up. It was gold, and the slight bend in the money said it was pure. One side of the coin had an etching of a wall with a single, arched opening. The other side had a symbol carved on it, something he didn't recognize. He let the coin fall from his hand.

Erik grabbed a mail hauberk. It looked sturdy and heavy, but when he put it on, it felt as light as a cloth shirt. He donned steel plates that covered his shoulders and arms and legs, and again, despite looking cumbersome, they were light and allowed for almost maximal movement. He even found a mail coif that fit his head and a helm that would protect his nose and cheeks and jaws.

For a moment, looking down at himself, seeing the glimmering steel—what he assumed to be Dwarf's Iron—of his new armor made him smile. Erik remembered playing knights and warriors as a child, envisioning himself as an armored warrior riding into battle, slaying the evil enemy, and rescuing the damsel in distress. For a moment, he was that warrior.

The shouting and cheering broke him from his trance. It was Switch again, throwing coins and gems into the air, letting them fall back down upon him as if they were a gentle, cooling rain. Bryon sifted through the mounds of treasure as well along with several of the other dwarves. Others marveled over the weapons and armor with Balzarak. Even Befel inspected a diamond the size of a fist, hemming and hawing over it with wide eyes. Erik felt overwhelmed. How could all this treasure—just the treasure alone—make someone happy?

Switch was never happy. Threhof was never happy. Bryon was never happy. And the simple gleam of gold and gems, the glimmer of Dwarf's Iron, even the smell of ancient books, made them happier than they had ever been in their lives.

Erik walked away, towards the chairs and tables. He found a large, cushioned chair and sat. He wanted to be alone. They were here for a purpose, to find some lost family heirloom for the Lord of the East. The sooner they did that, and the sooner they left, the better. This place was a prison, a tomb, guarded by ghosts.

All this wealth, and all this treasure. For what? What good did it do Fire Beard and his son and his wife and daughters? His guards? His people? For all this treasure, they're trapped down here, forever. Always running from those dream crawlers.

A shiver ran along his spine, and he knew they were there, just on the other side of the castle walls. They could read his thoughts, and he could feel them squirm as they so desperately tried to cross into this realm, whatever that was. It was like his dreams, the dead crowding around the base of that small hill, but never able to step on it. Erik wondered what force kept the dead—and the dwomanni —at bay.

Looking at his feet, he saw several gold coins scattered about the ground. That shouldn't have seemed so odd in a vast treasure room, but these coins were marked with a large X or cross, deep grooves dug into the metal. He bent down and picked one up. The profile of some patriarch was on one side. The other side should have been the image of a laurel, but the deep lines marred the picture. There were seven coins in all, all with the same markings, and he gathered them and put them in his belt pouch. As he put them in, he touched the smooth service of a rock. He retrieved two stone-sized rubies that sat a dull red, reflecting no light. And yet, in the dim corner of the treasure room in which Erik sat on a wooden chest, they seemed to glow.

Marcus, your gifts are as curious as you. I wish I could have gotten to know you better.

He still had no clue what these stones were and wondered if they had some mystery locked away like Marcus' flute and dagger. Then, an image flashed into his head, one that looked like a giant red sun. The words he heard told him he would understand what they were soon enough. Erik looked at his dagger, feeling the surge of energy at his hip. Remembering the first situation in which Erik learned about his dagger—a fight with slavers—made him a little uncomfortable with that revelation. He pushed his mind back to more immediate matters.

How will we ever find the Lord of the East's treasure?

He looked at the simple vastness of the room. He looked at all the treasure. It would take a hundred lifetimes to sift through ever single piece of treasure, to find this thing the Lord of Golgolithul wanted.

His hip tingled.

It is hidden.

"How do you know?" Erik asked.

It is something that the dwarves wanted to hide away. They knew of its power.

"It's a family heirloom," Erik said, "a script of lineage, according to The Messenger."

Laughter. The dagger was laughing.

And you believe him?

"I guess not," Erik said.

The dwarves would have hidden it away, separate from everything else. They knew he would seek it.

"How?" Erik asked. "The dwarves lived here a thousand years ago. Was Golgolithul even a country then?"

City-states, ruled by the families that now serve as Golgolithul's aristocracy.

"What are those?" Erik asked. "And if Golgolithul didn't exist, how would the dwarves know someone from there would be looking for this thing? This is all too complicated."

Yes, his dagger replied.

"Is this some deep magic?" Erik asked. "Some ancient, mysterious magic, like the moon fairies?"

But then, it wasn't the voice of his dagger, consuming and almost controlling his thoughts. It was a vision. A great dark space with stars and streaks of vivid colors and suns. The cosmos. Erik didn't even know what that meant. He looked to the ceiling. It was the place beyond the sky, past the sun and moon; if someone could travel there, that is what this would look like. Other worlds. Other suns. And then he understood. There were things that transcended time. Somehow the dwarves knew they possessed something that a man would eventually seek.

A prophesy, Erik thought.

In a way.

They—Fire Beard—knew the Lord of the East would seek this treasure, so they hid it away, somewhere in the vaults of Orvencrest. Erik's stomach twisted with another revelation. Fire Beard knew the dwomanni would come. He knew his city would fall and be forgotten and that his wife and children would die.

Fate, but no, not fate.

Erik felt he understood, then, that Fire Beard could have avoided it. He could have saved his family. But then this treasure, this thing that the Lord of the East now sought, would have fallen into the wrong hands. It would have been used for evil, in service to the Shadow. So, he sacrificed himself, his family, his city, and his people so that it would remain hidden.

"The Lord of the East is somehow better?" Erik asked.

No, but you are.

"But I ... we are to hand it over to the Lord of the East. How is that better?"

When the time comes, you will know what to do.

That was all his dagger said. Erik shook his head. This was too big for him. It was too big for his brother and cousin and Switch, and even Wrothgard. He would give this *heirloom,* if they ever found it in the vastness of Orvencrest's treasure, to Balzarak. This was something a general and a lord could understand. But then what? Watch his back for the rest of his life? Just wait until some assassin from Golgolithul murdered him and his family in their beds, assuming he still had a family and assuming he could even find what this thing was.

"What are you doing, Erik?" Turk asked.

Erik snapped out of his internal conversation with his dagger and saw his dwarvish friend standing there and staring.

"Just sitting," Erik replied, "and thinking."

"About what, if I can ask?" Turk said.

"Aren't we supposed to find something for the Lord of the East?" Erik asked. "Wasn't that the original intent of this whole journey?"

"Yes," Turk replied.

"And yet, here we are, reveling in the spoils of a lost treasure room," Erik said.

"What would you have them do, Erik?" Turk asked, slightly exasperated. "We wondered if this city even existed. Not only have we found a city that has been lost from my people and from the world for a thousand years, we have found a treasure that is beyond anyone's dreams."

"I suppose so," Erik replied with a quick shrug.

"On top of that, we have all made sacrifices to find this place," Turk said. "Shouldn't we take time to celebrate that which we thought was impossible?"

Erik thought for a moment and then nodded.

"Where do you think this treasure of the Lord of the East's is?" Erik asked.

"I don't know," Turk replied. "I suppose it could be anywhere in here."

"I don't think it is in the treasure room," Erik said.

"Really?" Turk said. "And what makes you say a treasure wouldn't be in a treasure room?"

"Just a hunch," Erik said, thinking of his dagger. Turk eyed him suspiciously.

"Where, then?" Turk asked.

"Somewhere in the keep," Erik replied. "Somewhere secure. Hidden."

"Lead on, then," Turk said with a nod.

Erik and Turk left their companions to their revelry, walking back through the dark tunnel that led to the throne room. Erik could feel their presence, the undead. He could smell them and hear them, but, again, something kept them at bay.

"And now?" Turk asked when they entered the throne room.

Erik looked around the room. It seemed too obvious, too simple, and too close to the treasure room. Surely the king wouldn't hide something so valuable in the throne room?

"The queen's quarters," Erik suggested, to which Turk nodded.

They walked up the staircase, heavy with soot and dust, although it showed no signs of fire damage. It wound up and up until they reached a heavy door that sat open. At the end of a long hallway, another heavy door stood open, and when Erik and Turk entered the room, the air seemed thick and heavy.

Erik could smell the death in this room. He could hear crying and sniffling and a woman's voice trying to console her daughters. He heard prayers and then he heard the sound of deafening thunder and felt the room shake with a great earthquake. He felt his hair grow searingly hot and thought his skin might melt. He looked to Turk. The dwarf felt, heard, and smelled none of it.

A large bed sat at the other end of the room, curtains around it drawn and exposing the bodies of three people. They were the skeletal remains of an adult and two children—the queen and her daughters. The remains of others lay about the room—guards most certainly. Erik saw no signs of trauma, no broken bones.

Erik found pieces of wood—the legs of chairs or tables—that could serve as torches and lit them, stuffing them in the iron sconces hanging from the walls. The room was large, and Erik could tell at one point it was a fancy place. Pieces of tapestries and pictures still hung from rusted hooks on the wall. Several chests of drawers and armoires sat along the walls, a deep, cherry wood, albeit warped and unsteady now. A rug consumed almost the whole of the floor, once brilliant colors, now faded and stained by dust and soot and full of tatters and tears.

Erik looked out the room's single window, looked out into the darkness of the city. It should have been pitch black, but he saw a faint glow hanging over the city, one not bright enough to fully illuminate anything but enough to break through some of the darkness. It was a sickly deep red, like dried blood.

"Them," Erik muttered, peering in between what he supposed to be the effigies of buildings. He thought he saw movement out there, in the city.

"Where do we start?" Turk asked.

"You're the dwarf," Erik replied with a smile.

"The chest of drawers, the armoire, the chest at the end of the bed," Turk offered.

Erik nodded with a shrug of his shoulders.

They searched through everything and found nothing but old, dilapidated clothing. Erik even looked under the bed, and behind it, in the corners. He even, to the protest of Turk at first, looked under the blankets of the bed. They gently moved the bodies of the queen and her daughters and cut open the mattress of the bed even.

When they had determined that it wasn't in the queen's quarters, they began to search the other rooms, a dozen of them, at least, over four stories. They had all but ransacked the rooms, anywhere from quarters with ancient corpses to storage areas. They even started feeling the walls, checking for loose stones and bricks in the walls.

"It's not here, Erik," Turk said. "Perhaps it is in the treasure room. Or maybe it is hidden somewhere in the city."

"I'm not going back into the city," Erik replied. "Something evil is out there. The dwo—"

"Hush, Erik," Turk said. "Do not speak their name in this place."

"Will speaking their name suddenly bring them down on us?" Erik asked, but a part of him actually wondered if that was what kept them at bay, that no one dared speak their name in this place.

They walked back to the throne room, looking about, feeling the walls as they had in the rest of the keep.

"They're so consumed by their treasure, they probably don't even know we've been gone," Erik said, nodding to the tunnel that led to the treasure room.

"Why did he just sit here?" questioned Erik, looking again at the king's skeleton. "When he knew death was coming."

"Maybe he was protecting something," Turk said, "to the end. He was protecting the entrance to the treasure room perhaps."

But then, Erik had a thought. He wasn't protecting the treasure room. He was protecting something else, and that required him to remain on his throne. Erik gently felt underneath the king, the arms of the throne, the sides. Nothing. He was moving around the side, wanting to look behind it, when the toe of his boot knocked against the foot of the throne. It looked like gold, but it wasn't even solid. He tapped it again, and a hollow sound reverberated around the small room.

"Did you hear that?" Erik asked.

Turk nodded, wide-eyed.

Erik bent down. He felt about the foot of the throne. It was simple wood, painted to look gold. It wasn't warped, and the paint hadn't chipped—charms or magic for sure. The piece of wood wouldn't budge. He removed from his belt the hand axe he had taken from the weaponry in Thorakest and aimed. It struck the wood hard, and he heard a crack. Another strike, and then another, and then another, and the wood splintered and broke. He could reach inside.

Erik cleared the broken wood away to reveal a small compartment in the bottom of the throne. A small chest sat in the compartment. A small lock sealed the chest, but three hefty strikes from the axe, and the lock fell away. A case, one that might be meant for a scroll, rolled and sealed, sat inside it. It was solid at one end and corked at the other.

"Is that it?" Turk asked.

"I don't know," Erik replied. "If it is, we can't open it according to the Lord of the East."

"Look," Turk said, pointing to an etching on the outside of the white case.

"Is that a rune?" Erik asked.

"I don't know," Turk replied. "I have never seen one like it."

Then, Erik recognized the symbol. He had seen it, once, on the map. Maybe one of the many mysteries of the map that even the dwarves couldn't figure out. This must have been it. It was the symbol that would tell the finder this was the treasure.

How did the Lord of the East know this symbol would be on the case?

Magic. Curses. Sorcery.

Erik grabbed the case.

"We'll look at the map," he said, holding the scroll case and letting the small chest fall to the floor.

As Erik held the scroll case, the floor underneath him rumbled, the walls shook, and the torches in the room flickered and dimmed.

9

"Please tell me you felt that," Erik said. "Tell me you saw that."

"Yes, I did," Turk replied, eyes wide, mouth slightly set open.

The torches in the room sputtered and seemed to brighten and dim as some whim fancied them.

"We should get back to the treasure room, get the others and get out of here," Turk said.

"Agreed," Erik added.

As they entered the tunnel that led to the treasure room, Erik heard laughter behind them.

"Did you hear that?" Erik asked.

"Hear what?" Turk said.

Erik turned and stared into the throne room from the darkness of the tunnel. A pallid red seemed to consume the room. They were there.

"Nothing," Erik said with a shake of his head.

Befel and Bryon met Turk and Erik at the bottom of the tunnel's ramp.

"Where were you?" Befel asked.

"Searching for the real reason we are here," Erik said curtly.

"What?" Bryon asked.

"The Lord of the East's treasure," Erik said.

"Why wouldn't you search for it in the treasure room?" Bryon asked.

"It wouldn't be hidden in a treasure room," Erik replied.

"Of course, it wouldn't," Bryon said, rolling his eyes. "It's treasure."

"No, you fool," Erik seethed. He had had enough of Bryon's sarcasm. "It's too important to be hidden with simple treasure. It would be concealed somewhere else, like a secret compartment of a throne, on which a dead king sat, staring death in the face."

"Truly?" Bryon asked with a hint of disbelief in his voice. "And how do you know?"

"I just do," Erik replied.

"We found it," Turk added.

"Really?" Befel asked.

"Aye," Turk replied. "At least we think we found it."

"How can you be sure?" Befel asked.

"There is a symbol—a rune—on the scroll case," Erik said, retrieving the thing from his belt and showing it to his brother and cousin. "I think I saw the same rune on the map. I wonder if that is a sign, an indicator that this is it."

"I do not recognize the rune," Turk added, "and I think we all thought it might just be some cartographer's embellishment, but now ..."

Turk smiled and shrugged.

"Wrothgard," Erik said. The soldier and dwarves were all congregated near the armory of the treasure room, marveling in their newly acquired weapons and armor.

"Erik, my friend," the soldier said with a wide smile, "where have you been?"

"Can I see the map?" Erik asked.

"I beg your pardon," Wrothgard said with a cocked eyebrow.

"The map, Wrothgard," Erik said, "can I see it?"

"Well, certainly," Wrothgard replied, retrieving it from his haversack and handing it to Erik.

Erik unrolled the parchment and found the symbol on the map that looked like the symbol carved into the case of the scroll. It was a series of triangular lines, and if he looked closely and studied it, Erik might have thought it was some ancient symbol for a claw or teeth. He pointed to the symbol, drawn in the lower corner of the map, away from the directions.

"What does this mean, Balzarak?" Erik asked.

Balzarak peered close to the symbol. He shook his head, ever so slightly.

"It means nothing, Erik," Balzarak said. "It is a simple embellishment."

Erik pulled the scroll case from his belt and presented it to the general.

"It matches the symbol carved on this scroll case," Erik said. "Could it mean this is what the Lord of the East wants us to find for him?"

Balzarak's eyebrows rose, and his eyes widened.

"Where did you find this?" he asked.

"It was in the throne room," Erik explained, "hidden in the bottom of the throne, in a small compartment."

"How did you know to look there?" Threhof asked, chiming in and looking over the general's shoulder at both the scroll case and the map.

"We searched the whole keep," Turk said. "We considered that this thing might be important, and so, it would not be kept with the rest of the treasure. Finding it was fortuitous."

"This could very well be a marking that signifies it is what the Lord of the East desires," Balzarak said.

"What is in there?" Threhof asked. "Why would dwarves, a thousand years ago, care to hide this thing away, right underneath where the King sits?"

"We haven't looked inside," Erik said. "We were commanded not to."

"You were commanded not to look," Threhof said, grabbing at the scroll case, "but we were not."

He tried to pull the case away, but Erik pushed the dwarf and stopped him from grabbing the treasure. As Threhof stumbled back, he drew his sword, and Erik complied, doing the same.

"It belongs to the dwarves," Threhof said.

"No," Erik replied. "The deal was we get to keep this and return it to the Lord of the East. I thought you owed me a blood debt. This is how you honor such a debt?"

"This is how I honor my people," Threhof replied. "General."

Balzarak shook his head.

"No, the King's wishes were that these men would be allowed to return whatever it is the Lord of the East is seeking back to him ... if we found it."

"It's the Lord of the East," Threhof said. "It's Golgolithul."

"It does not matter," Balzarak replied. "These are King Skella's wishes."

Erik looked to Wrothgard.

"Do you want it?" Erik asked.

"No," the soldier replied. "You keep it ... keep it safe."

Erik didn't want to keep the scroll safe. He didn't want to have anything to do with it, especially as the dwarves—and Switch—eyed him coldly like starving animals ready to make an unadvised attack simply for an empty belly.

"It is time to finish gathering what you want, what you can carry," Balzarak said to everyone. "We need to leave this place. We can revel in our find, and our treasure, when we return to Thorakest."

As everyone dispersed, gathering what final treasure they wanted or could physically carry, Switch walked up behind Erik.

"I know you're there," Erik said.

"Of course, you do," Switch said. Erik could feel the smile in his voice.

"Then why are you trying to sneak up on me?" Erik asked.

"I wasn't sneaking at nothing," Switch replied. "If I wanted to sneak, I would've done so."

Erik turned to see the thief, thumbs tucked into his belt.

"I don't believe you," Erik said.

"Believe what you want," Switch said, then gave his chin a quick tilt. "Let's have a look. What do you say?"

"I say no," Erik replied.

"Come on. Aren't you at least a little curious?"

"No," Erik lied, He was but not enough to want to deal with the Lord of the East when he had to give him the scroll."

"How do we even know we'll make it to Fen-Stévock?" Switch asked.

"We've made it this far," Erik said.

"How will he know?" Switch asked. He inched closer.

"He will," Erik replied. He didn't doubt The Messenger when he had told them, in Finlo, that the Lord of the East would know if they had looked at his treasure.

"I don't think so," Switch said. "I think it's all troll scat, just to scare us into not looking at what he has here ... at what the trolls have here. Come on, let me look at it."

Switch stepped forward again and extended a hand.

"No."

"Don't you want to know what Vander Bim and Drake gave their lives for?" Switch asked.

"Not really. You don't care about them anyway."

"That hurts," Switch said, and then shrugged his shoulders. "But it's true. Let's find out what has caused all this trouble. What do you say?"

"No."

"All right," Switch said with a smile which soon faded, "then I'm done asking. Now I'm telling. Give me the damn scroll."

"No," Erik repeated.

"They're too far away too help you," Switch seethed, a knife appearing in his hand, his eyes squinting.

"Good," Erik said. He gripped his sword with both hands.

"I'll have you gutted by the time any of them get here," Switch hissed.

"You can try," Erik replied. He felt a smile growing on his face.

"You little welp," Switch spat. "You think all that training you've been doing with Wrothgard will help you? It won't do you a bloody lick of good."

Erik smiled. "Come and see."

Switch hesitated a moment, then straightened his back and huffed.

"It's not worth the trouble."

Switch sheathed his knife, kicked a silver cup at Erik like a petulant child, and walked away.

Erik cursed silently as the thief left.

Watch him. He'll try to take it again.

"I know," Erik replied to his dagger.

As he turned to walk away from Switch—far away from Switch—he thought the light in the throne room looked a little dimmer, and he felt the floor underneath him move. He looked to his dagger, then to the scroll case, stuck snuggly in his belt.

10

Bryon never thought he would pass up a coin the size of a Hámonian pound, but diamonds and emeralds the size of his fist were worth hundreds of Hámonian pounds. He would be rich. When they reached Fen-Stévock and delivered the Lord of the East's treasure, he would buy a villa. He would have everything he ever wanted—servants, women, the richest food.

Bryon was running out of space in his haversack and becoming selective about what he took, picking mostly coins that looked unique and large gems. As he sifted through a small mound of treasure, the glint of a huge diamond caught his eye, sparkling in the firelight of the treasure room. He had to have it. Bending down to pick up the gem, he heard something growl, and it startled him, causing him to lose his footing and fall backwards.

"Damn it," Bryon cursed.

When he pushed himself up, he gasped and scooted backwards.

"What, by the shadow, are you?" Bryon muttered as some ugly, mongrel dog-like creature stared back at him.

It gave another growling whimper.

It was larger than any dog he had ever seen, perhaps the size of a wolf, but maybe even bigger. Bryon went to one knee, right hand on the handle of his sword. He dared to lean closer. The creature backed up a bit, a low grumble coming from its mouth. It had red eyes void of pupils, and its head looked too big for its body. Its eyes followed Bryon, as he scooted away from the treasure and onto more solid ground. As the creature's eyes followed, its head tilted.

It was green with no hair. Its skin looked wet almost. And when it tilted its head, it looked like it was going to fall over. Bryon cracked a smile. He dared to stand. The creature moved as well, and he could see it had short, squatty legs and a long, almost scaly tail. Now it looked something like a mountain lizard, although, they didn't have ears.

The creature seemed less apprehensive now and yelped, showing a row of fangs, long and sharp. As silly as it looked, Bryon suddenly didn't want to be on the receiving end of its teeth. Or its claws, for that matter, which were long and black.

The creature moved closer, and Bryon, keeping his right hand on the handle of his sword, extended his left. He crouched. The thing moved even closer. It sniffed at the ground, watching Bryon all the while. Bryon extended his hand farther. The creature moved closer, sniffing.

"I am no enemy," Bryon said. "I won't hurt you."

The creature sniffed at Bryon's hand. Its breath wasn't warm, but hot, almost uncomfortably so.

"Where do you come from?" Bryon asked. "How did you get in here?"

It licked Bryon's hand with a long, red tongue, leaving sticky saliva all over Bryon's skin. His hand itched, almost burned, where the tongue had touched.

Bryon stood. The creature nuzzled his leg.

"See, we're fine," Bryon said. "Now, you go about your business, and I'll go about mine."

Bryon turned, but the creature kept nosing his leg.

"Go on," Bryon said, pushing the thing away with his leg. It yelped again and pushed its nose hard against Bryon's leg.

Bryon almost fell forward. A large dog could be strong, but it would have taken more than a simple nudge with its nose to push Bryon over. This creature was strong. It clawed at his boots. Bryon's hand tingled and felt numb where the creature had licked, and being around this mongrel made him feel uncomfortable. The thing's yelps turned to growling, and the second time Bryon swatted at it, it tried to bite him.

Bryon pulled his hand back in time. His hand went back to his sword. The animal nudged his leg again, licking at his pants. He tried to kick it away, but the creature was too heavy. The licks turned to nips. Bryon stepped back, avoided the small bites, until the creature fully opened its mouth—wider than Bryon thought possible—and tried to take a bite out of his leg.

Bryon drew his sword, its purple magic hissing as it hit the air. He raised his sword up, gripping the handle with both hands, and waited. The creature hissed like some giant, demonic cat. As it hissed, steam spilled from its nostrils.

"What are you?"

The creature bit at the air and growled, hissing more and more. It reared up on its hind legs, and jumping forward, it bit at Bryon. He swiped his sword at it, but it kept moving towards him, crouching like a predator with its prey in sight.

Bryon stepped forward, ready to swing, when the creature leapt at him with blinding speed, almost flying through the air. Its claws easily passed through Bryon's dwarvish shirt of steel scales, easily passed through the leather jerkin underneath it, and dug into his flesh.

Bryon cried out as he fell back. He wasn't able to use his sword as the creature pressed down on his chest, so he unsheathed a dagger from his belt and plunged it into its ribs. It howled, and it was just enough time and space for Bryon to escape from underneath it. He stood, sheathing his dagger and once again holding his sword with both hands. He felt woozy and swore the room began to tilt.

The beast hissed and growled. The steam that left its nostrils and mouth filled the space between it and Bryon, and as it touched Bryon's face, it stung his eyes. As he breathed it in, it caused his lungs to burn. He could feel the growing splotch of blood on his chest.

Bryon wanted to faint. He wanted to hunch over and catch his breath, or splash water on his face, but this creature was about to attack. That much Bryon could tell through blurry vision and labored breaths.

The creature readied itself again, but before it could attack, Bryon swung hard. The animal dodged the attack, swiped with its claws, and then leapt forward. Bryon ducked out of the way, and as the creature slid along the ground, slipping on coins and gems, Bryon rushed the thing. He felt himself stumble forward clumsily, but as he did, he cut deep grooves along either of the beast's sides, his magical sword searing its flesh as it cut it. It lunged forward again, trying to bite him. Bryon stood, unsteadily, and as the creature attacked, Bryon brought his sword down hard on the creature's neck.

The beast faltered but was still alive. Bryon brought his sword down on the neck again and again until its head finally fell loose from its body, its blackish-green blood spewing over gold coins.

As Bryon looked down at the dead creature, his chest burned with even more intensity. His consciousness waned, and his vision blurred until he fell backwards, seeing only black. He could hear distant voices.

"What happened?"

Bryon tried to focus on the blurry figure speaking and finally could make out the face of Balzarak. The dwarf knelt next to Bryon. He felt tugging at his armor and realized it was Turk removing his mail and inspecting the wound on his chest. He saw his cousin, Erik, as well.

"It burns," Bryon wheezed. It hurt to speak. It hurt to breathe.

"What did this?" Erik asked.

Bryon shook his head.

"I don't know. Some dog, lizard, cat-like thing."

"Dog, lizard, cat-like thing?" Balzarak repeated.

"Well, then see for ... see for your ... for yourself," Bryon said, having to take breaths in between each couple of words. He pointed to where the dead creature lay.

"This is not good," Bryon heard Balzarak say.

"What's not ... not good?" he asked, closing his eyes hard as Turk pressed on his wound.

Then he heard another dwarvish voice say, "Drak Vurm."

The room dulled, the luster of the treasure fading. Bryon sweated. He knew some of it was due to his wound, but it had also gotten decidedly hotter in the treasure room. He heard frantic yelling, mostly in Dwarvish.

"What's going on?" Bryon asked, his voice slow and slurry.

"Be still," Turk commanded as he worked on Bryon's wound.

Bryon lifted his hand, the one the creature had licked. It was red as if he had burned it. He saw blisters appearing.

"My hand," he said.

Turk pushed Bryon's arm down.

"Yes, I know," the dwarf said. "Your face is blistered as well. But this wound is much more pressing."

"Doesn't Drak Vurm mean dragon?" Bryon heard Erik ask.

"Aye," Balzarak replied.

"How?" Erik had asked.

"I don't know," Balzarak replied. "This is the realm of the Shadow. Dragons are minions of the Shadow."

"Focus on me," Turk said, and Bryon looked at the dwarf's face. "I am sure your vision is a little blurry, but the dimness of the room is not your vision."

"Why does my wound hurt so much?" Bryon asked.

"A dragon's wound is poisonous," Turk replied.

"Dragon," Bryon muttered. "That was a dragon?"

"Aye," Turk said. He pressed hard on Bryon's chest, and Bryon felt not only burning pain, but something oozed across his skin.

"I thought a dragon would be bigger," Bryon said with a smile on his face, "from what I had seen on all the tapestries in Thorakest."

"That was a mere baby," Turk said.

"Of course, it was," Bryon said. He lifted his head just enough to see all of his companions running about. Then, he felt Turk's rough hand on his forehead, and the dwarf pushed his head back down.

"We must do this later," Balzarak said. Bryon saw the general's face as the dwarf stood over him, looking down at Turk and him.

"He has a fever," Turk said. Bryon closed his eyes and pretended not to hear. "His wound is already infected. Without the best of care, he will not survive."

"We have to leave," Balzarak said, "or none of us will survive."

"Very well," Turk replied.

Bryon opened his eyes. "Will we go back through the keep?"

Balzarak shook his head. "No. She is out there."

"Who?" Bryon asked.

"The mother," Turk replied.

11

She opened her eyes, one at a time. Her joints and muscles were stiff, and she stretched, shaking the unconsciousness from her body. She felt the cavern around her vibrate with her movement. It was dark in this place. There was no way of telling how long she had slept. Eons perhaps. Her minions were there, but they would not show themselves. Why? They were tasked with caring for her ... caring for her children. She could smell their fear. Something was wrong. Clearly. She was awake. Why was she awake? Cursed dwarves. Cursed dwarvish magic.

That smell stung her nose; it had been so long since that happened. Her slaves carried that smell, but it was faint, waning.

This was strong, and she hated it. Their taste was even worse—hairy, tough little things—and she spat. She remembered a world without them, a world primitive and simple, a world before they plundered the deep depths of the earth and stole what the earth had to offer, stole what the Shadow had put there for her and hers. But why would they be there? How would they be there?

She crouched down and slithered through the opening, her back sliding across the ceiling. She had settled in this place because it was hidden. Only her children and her slaves knew where it was. She stretched her long neck and looked out over the city, the skeletal remains of the once shining dwarvish citadel—so dead and, yet, so alive. If she could, she would have smiled.

She felt some of the old buildings, burnt and brittle, crumble under her feet as she walked through the ruined city, gone with the quick inhalation of her breath. That smell was here, but faint. She moved her head from side to side, and she caught it. They were here. They had come back. She winced at their smell, he body shuddered, and the walls shook.

With her keen eyesight, she looked into the darkest of places, the most hidden corners. Nothing. Then, she looked to where she had killed the one the Shadow called the king, him and his offspring and mate. That's where they went.

She walked closer. Yes. Their smell was the strongest here. She growled, and the walls shook again. Clearly, they had found it, the cause of her slumber, her cursed hibernation. They would pay, those imbecilic creatures, those insignificant beings. So ignorant, so weak, and, yet, they thought they were so strong. She had showed them true strength before, and she would show them again.

Anger got the better of her, and she spat, roared, and screamed. The walls shook. She was awake because they had found the spell. Then, she wasn't angry anymore as a new feeling came upon her, one she had never felt before. Fear. Where were her offspring? Even in her cursed slumber, she knew they would have fed on her teats, slept in her hidden place. So her waking would have surely summoned them. She let out a loud call for them. They still did not come.

She roared loudly and called for them again, and the male appeared. He slinked towards her, shaking with fear. She nudged him and smelled him, and she tried to comfort him with licking; he wet the ground. His tail, short and stubby, curled as far as it could under his body. She grunted, and he understood. He slinked back to her sleeping chambers. She grew more impatient, more indignant. Where was her other offspring, the female who would continue her line, would grow their number? She howled again, calling to her in her most ancient of languages, and the walls and the ground shook as she moved closer to where she had killed the king.

12

Andragos stood in front of the Lord of the East's dais, waiting. Two men, covered from head to toe in black robes, stood on either side of the Lord of the East's chair. A giant curtain hung just behind the chair and extended the whole length of the hall, and Andragos knew the Lord of the East was behind it. The Messenger clenched his teeth. He didn't like being made to wait. Kings had died for making him wait this long.

Naked men and women lounged on rugs at the foot of the stairs that led to the dais. They giggled and caressed one another and kissed. Two tigers lay in front of Andragos, white with black stripes. They watched him lazily. They wore diamond-studded collars.

All this extravagance. Andragos' lip curled. The Great Hall of Fen-Stévock used to look very differently, even under Morken, the Lord of the East's father. Now, it looked like some fancy whorehouse.

"You do not like being made to wait," the Lord of the East said as he passed through the curtain and sat in his seat. The robed men standing next to him didn't move.

The Lord of the East wore thin, black pants that billowed just above his calf length boots, flowing gently over the arm of his chair as he draped a leg over it. His robe, open and showing a well-built chest, spilled over the sides of the chair as well. The Lord of the East's hairless skin had a pallid color to it, although not a stark pale, and it glistened with sweat, as if he had been exercising. Or doing something else.

"Should I be made to wait?" Andragos replied. "My news is important."

"You will wait as long as I wish you to wait," the Lord of the East said, haughtily. "My father gave you too much power, Andragos."

The Lord of the East pushed some of his long, black hair off his face. Most of it had been pulled into a tail, held back by a leather thong, but some had escaped during whatever his exertions might have been. He looked down at Andragos over his nose, his jawline flexing as he smiled. His face, even and handsome, belied his age, and Andragos knew the magic that kept the Lord of the East so young was strong, even though this ruler was but a baby compared to The Messenger's own age.

Be careful, my lord, for magic always has its price. This I know personally.

"As you say," was all Andragos said.

"What is so important anyway?" the Lord of the East asked. "I am busy."

"With them?" Andragos asked,

Exercising indeed.

The Lord of the East sat up straight. He squinted hard at the Messenger. The muscles in his chest flexed, and as he rolled his head, his neck popped. He was powerful. Andragos knew that, but not as powerful as he thought he was.

"It is none of your concern," the Lord of the East said.

"If it concerns my nation," Andragos said, "then it is my concern."

"This is not your nation," the Lord of the East hissed, "and you forget yourself."

Andragos bowed quickly. The naked people lounging at the bottom of the stairs stopped. They didn't even move. The tigers seemed attentive now, staring at the Messenger.

"They have found her, Your Majesty," Andragos said. "They have awoken her."

The Lord of the East looked surprised, only for a moment. Then he sat back in his chair and hung a leg over one of its arms again.

"Yes," the Lord of the East replied, "I know."

He was lying. Andragos knew it. He was powerful. His witches were powerful. His *mentor,* Andragos' thoughts hung on that word with disgust, was powerful. But they weren't as powerful as he was. Those bitches poisoned the Lord of the East's mind and that cheap hedge wizard was a simpleton compared to him.

"It was some of the ... the mercenaries I engaged at Finlo," Andragos said before he added, "they are with some dwarves from Thorakest."

"Why should I care?" the Lord of the East asked. "Dwarves are of no concern to me."

"They will know she is there," Andragos said. "They will know *they* are there. We don't need them as an enemy right now."

"Keep following them," the Lord of the East said. "Inform me of changes."

"Are you not worried that the dwarves might try and take it?" Andragos asked.

"Take what?" the Lord of the East asked, suddenly paying no attention to Andragos and watching two men and a woman lounging with one another on a chaise.

"Your prize," Andragos said sternly. "The scroll you sent these *mercenaries* there to look for."

"Why would the dwarves care to look at it?" the Lord of the East asked lazily.

"They are not necessarily our allies," Andragos replied.

"So?" the Lord of the East said.

"Your Majesty," Andragos said, stepping forward.

He looked to the trio of people that the Lord of the East once again fixed his attention to. They giggled and moaned as they began fondling one another. The Messenger felt his face grow hot. He narrowed his eyes and snapped his fingers. The three people turned into small frogs, bouncing around the chaise and croaking.

The Lord of the East glared at Andragos, no longer a nonchalant look on his face. He squinted and pursed his lips.

"The dwarves do not trust you," Andragos said. "They will want to look at this scroll you want from one of *their* cities. When they find out what it is, they will want to keep it."

The Lord of the East stood, shoulders pulled back, and a resolute look on his face.

"It is no longer their city," the Lord of the East said, "and if they do try to take it, it will be to their destruction. Their time in this world is nigh ... whatever happens."

The Lord of the East snapped his fingers, and the frogs turned back into the three people. They looked confused and scared, but the Lord of Fen-Stévock then waved a hand in front of him, and they calmed and went back to caressing and fondling one another.

"Keep following them," the Lord of the East repeated. "Let me know of any changes."

"Your Majesty," Andragos said with a quick bow.

13

"Why is it getting so hot in here?" Erik asked.

"She is near," Turk replied.

"The dragon?" Erik asked.

Turk nodded.

"Fire is her element," Turk said. "Her very presence changes the climate."

Gôdruk yelled something to Balzarak, who in turn replied, and then yelled something else to Threhof.

"They found scales," Turk said, "back by the weaponry. This is not good."

"Scales?"

"Aye," Turk replied. He pointed to the headless body of the baby dragon. "Dragon's scales. If there was any doubt before that this was a dragon, now there is not. We must leave now."

"But we can't go through the keep," Erik said. He looked to the dark tunnelway back into the throne room. He could still hear the dead screaming, though they did not seem to be any closer.

"No, we cannot," Turk replied. "Even if we wanted to, that thing's mother will be there, waiting for us."

"Then how?" Erik asked.

"There will be an exit," Balzarak said.

"Where?" Erik asked.

"There always is," Balzarak continued. "In case of cave ins, or siege, or anything else that might trap the royal family in their keep, dwarvish architects would always have built a rear exit."

"Where is it?" Erik asked.

"I don't know," Balzarak replied. "I would suspect that it is in here somewhere. Where, I do not know. But we must find it."

Erik shook his head. Dwarvish tricks were beginning to annoy him.

"Gôdruk," Balzarak said, "you and Thormok search the far wall. We are looking for a doorway."

Balzarak's cousins complied as the others—except Bryon who looked to be slipping in and out of consciousness—quickly joined them. Even Turk left his charge.

They ran their hands along the walls of the treasure room, the dwarves sticking their noses almost against the stone, looking for some hidden doorway. Threhof even took to searching the floor in front of the wall, and Dwain looked through chests large enough to conceal an opening and stairs. All the while, the temperature in the treasure room grew hotter, the walls continued to shake, and Erik thought he heard distant thunder, as if the monsoons had somehow snuck into the deepest parts of the Southern Mountains.

"Is there a trigger, General?" Turk asked. "Maybe something that would reveal the door?"

"Perhaps," Balzarak replied, "just keep looking."

Erik vigorously wiped sweat from his brow. The air in the treasure room had almost become suffocating.

"Where would it be?" Turk asked over his shoulder, his stubby fingers moving over the wall as if they were playing a musical instrument.

"I don't know," Balzarak replied, now looking himself, "but I would guess, if it isn't in here, it would be in the throne room."

The general seemed uncertain of his answer, and as Erik looked to the tunnel that led to the throne room, he could now hear the dead up there, congregating, laughing. Part of the barrier had broken, the thing that had held them back. Perhaps it was the dragon. The finding of the scroll. Anything. But the dead were coming closer, but he had to check.

"I will look in the throne room," Erik said. "Turk, keep an eye on Bryon. General, you and everyone else, keep looking in here."

The general nodded, seemingly accepting that Erik might start giving out orders.

"Thinking about it, as much as we may find a door, I believe we will also need a key," Balzarak said.

"Truly?" Erik asked.

Balzarak simply nodded.

"And I suppose you don't know where that is," Erik said.

"I would guess ..."

"The throne room," Erik finished.

Balzarak nodded again.

Erik walked towards the tunnel, and as he did, he heard Balzarak say in Dwarvish, "We are doomed."

He could feel them, hear them, smell them. They were there, in the throne room.

The ground underneath Erik's feet shook. He saw a ripple in the stone, heard it cracking off in the distance, heard some of it breaking loose from the ceiling and falling.

"Hurry, Erik," Balzarak called. "As she nears, it will get hotter in here. We will all die before ever meeting her."

"So, what we saw, walking through Orvencrest?" Erik asked over his shoulder as he made his way up the ramp.

"The dragon," Balzarak replied. "Melted stone, existence completely obliterated ... and now the attack on Bryon ... it's the only explanation."

He could sense their excitement heighten, knew they were there, waiting for him. He unsheathed Ilken's Blade and readied his shield.

This isn't a treasure room, or a city. It's a giant tomb.

The earth rolled again and then something that sounded again like a crack of thunder ripped through the treasure room. Erik found himself down on his knees, clutching his ears. In that thunderclap, he heard a voice, an ancient voice speaking an ancient language that sounded ugly and hateful. The dragon.

Another deafening roar and the walls shook in its wake. As he reached the end of the passageway, Erik heard Switch screaming, dwarves yelling, men praying. He felt the floor roll under his body and had to work hard to get back to his feet. He steadied himself and stared resolutely at the tunnel's entrance in front of him. A deep, blood-like hue crept from the firelight in the treasure room and now it continued to dull and dim.

Erik felt it as he passed into their realm. The moment he stepped further toward the reddish darkness that was now the throne room, a thick, inkiness overwhelmed him, and he knew he now dwelt in a place that crossed between dreams and the waking world. This world down here, this world within the mountain, was pure evil and, if the Creator ever allowed it, Erik had never felt so afraid in his life.

His strongest desire became one to leave this place and never return, but then, with a further twisting of his stomach, he knew he would have to come back. When he left, he would have unfinished business in this place. He sought to shake off all such thoughts and told himself to get moving.

He didn't need a torch in this place. There was enough of the reddish light that he could see. He felt hands grasping at him as he walked up towards the throne room. He felt fingers brush against his arms. He swiped with Ilken's Blade, and as his sword passed through rotting flesh, he heard their screams.

Sweat poured from Erik's brow as the heat rose and the air grew thick.

Erik stopped. Fox, rotting and decayed and black with death, stood in front of the opening to the throne room.

"You," Erik said through gritted teeth.

Fox nodded his head slowly, seemingly leering at Erik from black, eyeless sockets. A bit of flesh, purple and rotted, hung from a cheekbone and his red hair stood on end in haphazard splotches, crusted and barely clinging to decaying scalp. Erik felt the others behind him. He felt them clawing at his legs and arms. He stepped forward.

"How are you here?" Erik asked. "Is this some place that crosses the land of the living and the land of the dead?"

"You thought you could rid yourself of me," Fox said, his smile revealing broken teeth. Insects crawled from his mouth, and as a centipede tried to escape the rotting maw, Fox extended a blackened tongue and licked the bug back into his mouth. Erik could hear the crunching of exoskeleton. The smell that came from the dead man's mouth was so sickening he felt his stomach churn and bile rise up in his throat. When Fox wiped the back of a rotted hand across his mouth, a bit of his lip tore away, revealing dead teeth and gums regardless of whether or not he closed his mouth. "But now you have stepped into my realm, the realm of the Shadow, the place where she is master."

"She?" Erik asked. "The dragon?"

"She is powerful," Fox hissed, "and your death, the deaths of your brother and cousin, will bring her great pleasure. I will live once again and be more powerful than any who might call themselves leader."

"You're a fool," Erik replied. "You were a fool in life. You're a fool in death. You're a slave, a pawn. And you don't scare me. Now move."

"Your thoughts betray you," Fox said. "We know you are scared. Terrified even."

"That's no mystery," Erik replied. "Any man would be scared. Now move."

Erik felt them creep up behind him. He turned hard, swinging Ilken's Blade. The sword caught bone and rotting flesh. Screams filled the tunnel. The stink of pierced, bloating skin filled the space. But Erik cut through them easily ... too easily. It was a rouse, a distraction.

Erik turned, and Fox was almost on him. The undead man had no weapon, only bony fingers. One of them, one of those black, boney appendages, grazed Erik's cheek. The wound burned. Erik brought his knee up hard into Fox's stomach as the creature lunged forward. The attack sent the dead slaver backwards. Erik attacked with his blade. The Dwarf's Iron caught Fox's ribs, and as it opened his flesh, worms spilled out. Fox screamed. Erik kicked out, catching a knee, breaking it. As Fox lunged again, he blocked with his shield, pushing the undead back again. He slashed, opening the creature up, maggots crawling from the wound.

"You're not that powerful," Erik said, and then slashed, slashed again, and punched his blade through Fox's chest.

Fox erupted into thousands of insects—maggots and roaches and beetles—spilling to the ground and scurrying away. Erik heard the undead behind him. He turned, cutting one down after another, backing towards the throne room. They kept coming, throwing themselves at him, but they were no match for Ilken's Blade.

When Erik stepped into the light of the throne room, they stopped ... waited in the darkness of the tunnel.

"I'll see you tonight, in my dreams," Erik muttered with an insincere smile.

Erik inspected the room. As they had before, when they were looking for the treasure of the Lord of the East, he touched everything, pushed every stone, pulled every melted trinket, and moved every dilapidated piece of furniture. He looked to the throne. There was no lever or button. He felt all around it, even inside the small compartment that had held the Lord of the East's scroll. Nothing.

I'll find the key first. Then, maybe the way to open the door will reveal itself to me.

He inspected the remains of the king, still where they had left him. He didn't find anything that could pass as a key. He frantically looked through the pockets of the king's robes, practically scattering the dwarvish bones. The room grew hotter, and as the temperature rose, Erik's breath quickened. His hands trembled, and his mouth went dry. He was sure he had only been in the room for a little while, but with the screams of the undead coming from the tunnel, the rumbling thunder of the dragon, and the thought of his dying cousin, it felt as if he had been in the room for hours. He tried to concentrate on slowing his breathing, closing his eyes for a moment.

He looked down at the scattered bones of the king. Balzarak would have killed him if he saw this, and Erik's stomach knotted. The dwarvish king deserved better. Then his gaze drifted to the prince. Could it be so simple?

"Fool," Erik whispered to himself as he lifted the robe that covered the dwarvish child's remains and saw a long, thin, cylindrical pendant hanging from his neck, one end studded with what looked like a diamond. The key.

He broke the chain on which the key hung so he didn't have to disturb the prince's remains like he did the king's. What did it matter? The dragon would probably disturb everything when she came.

Erik felt lightheaded as he stood and inspected the key. He could barely see past the sweat streaming down his face, and another roar in the distance shook the room. He stared at the tunnel. Rotting hands reached out towards him from the reddish darkness. They laughed and screamed as he inched closer.

"Keep laughing," Erik yelled. "I'll send each and every one of you back to the Shadow."

We're already in the Shadow.

It would be a hard fight, making his way back to the treasure room. He already felt weak. And each roar, each roll of the earth, threatened to throw him to the ground. This may have been a fight he could not win. But then he remembered the moon fairies and their dust. He retrieved the bag from his haversack, took out a handful of the dust, opened his hand, and blew it towards the tunnel.

As if some errant wind had found its way into the ancient city of Orvencrest, the dust blew towards the darkness, each speck lighting up and floating haphazardly. In the flutter of a fly's wings, it lit the tunnel up, and the undead fled in one ear-piercing chorus. Erik thanked the moon fairies, wherever they were, for their gift. As he stood in front of the tunnel, he looked at the throne. Something had to open the exit in the treasure room.

But then, he saw it—a single sconce with a torch set snuggly in it just inside the tunnel. He could see it clearly, enlightened by the fairy dust. It was so dark in there, he hadn't seen it before. The torch looked as if it had never been set afire. It made sense. Erik pulled on the torch, and it and the sconce moved as one. He heard a click, and then the throne began to move behind him. He smiled.

"Dwarvish trickery."

As the throne moved behind him, returning to its original position, and closed off the tunnel to the throne room, he heard yelling from the treasure room. He could make out that a doorway had appeared.

Erik raced down the tunnel, bracing himself with one hand against the wall. As he entered the treasure room, he heard another rumble, this one louder and, like the one before, he thought he heard a voice buried somewhere within the sound. It was angry and evil.

"I think I found the key!" Erik yelled.

"Everyone, to the door," Balzarak commanded.

As Erik burst into the treasure room, he could see the silhouette of a door must have revealed itself as the throne slid back into place. Turk and Befel lifted Bryon, still practically unconscious, and carried him as the rest ran to the door.

"How do we bloody open it?" Switch asked.

"A key," Wrothgard, "Erik said he found a key."

Erik produced the pendant and looked for something that matched its shape until he found a small hole in one top corner. The pendant was a perfect fit, the diamond at one end lighting up as Erik slid it into the keyhole. It stopped, and Erik heard a clicking sound and turned the pendant. The door rumbled, moved inward, and began to slide open.

Erik retrieved the key as darkness glared back at them.

"Freedom," Switch said.

"Perhaps," Erik replied.

14

They stepped into the darkness of the tunnel. The light from torches and lanterns, and even Bryon's magic sword—which Wrothgard held—and Balzarak's circlet, seemed to do little to illuminate the passageway. The blackness around them drank up the light, extinguishing it just as it left the flame. Another deafening sound shook the wall, the floor, the ceiling. Erik heard the voice again.

"Hatred," Erik whispered.

"What?" Turk asked.

"The roaring, the rumbling, the sound," Erik said, "it is filled with hatred."

"That is what a dragon is," Balzarak said. "A dragon is hatred. It is living death. It is famine and pestilence. A dragon is the stuff of anyone's worst nightmares. A dragon is the minion of the Shadow."

"I hear a voice in the dragon's roar," Erik said softly.

"A voice?" Turk asked.

Erik nodded. "Aye, a voice. It's a language I don't understand, but I hear a voice, and it speaks with pure malice. It reminds me of the language Befel was speaking in the hallway when we first entered Orvencrest."

Erik turned and looked over his shoulder. The treasure room seemed almost a pinpoint of light, but then it glowed brightly, lighting up like a red sun and casting that same dark, reddish light that Erik remembered from the tunnel that led to the throne room. As the treasure room cast its sickly light into the tunnelway, a deafening roar echoed past the men and dwarves, this one louder than ever. It shook the ground, the walls, the ceiling, the whole earth. The dragon now was truly angry.

She crawled through the hole high in the cavern ceiling. She had dug it out centuries past, an easier way for her to get to the treasure room. Her slaves could not come here, could not enter the treasure room. An ancient spell. But she could—once. The treasure held no value to her but recognized its power to corrupt and create evil. She fed on evil. Once, she was able to bask in the magnificence of dwarvish gold. But then that put her to sleep. Never again.

She dropped through the ceiling, dispelling the illusion of the room being covered she had put there years before, and walked through the treasure room ... and saw her offspring's tail. And she smelled that stink, so fresh. The smell of dwarves. Why did her daughter not answer?

She crawled over the mound of gold and saw it. The body lying limp at the foot of the hill, the head, severed. She rushed to it, her wings spread and rattling with such hatred. She nudged the dead body. She whimpered and cried as it lay there, motionless. Now her rage had never been greater. They would pay. All those stinking creatures that walked on two legs. She would wage such a war on them, and all would know her presence, tremble at her sound, her sight. And her mate, he would know too. She would make sure of it. So far away, she would signal him, and he would join her. They had killed his offspring too.

She screamed and spit fire and flapped her thunderous wings. Her tail snapped like lightning against the wall, and it cracked. Gold and iron melted under her breath. Her wings hurled coins and gems into a glimmering tornado. She saw the door and with all her strength ripped the opening away into a gaping hole. Oh, how they would pay.

"What happened?" Switch asked.

Erik couldn't see the thief, but knew he was right next to him.

"I don't know," Wrothgard replied.

Even Bryon's sword and Balzarak's circlet gave off no light.

"I can't even see my hand in front of my face," Befel said. Erik could hear the panic in his brother's voice.

"Bryon's sword isn't even hot anymore," Wrothgard said. "It's as if the magic is just ... gone."

"Can that happen?" Wrothgard asked.

"This is an even deeper magic," Balzarak said. "An ancient, evil magic. She is one with the Shadow."

"Blood and guts and magic," Switch hissed.

Erik heard it. Chuckling. Giggling. A child's laughter off in the distance. A whistle. The shuffling of feet. Something scratching the wall.

"We see you ..." The voices of the dead echoed through the dark tunnel.

"What, by the Creator?" Befel muttered.

"An be merciful," Balzarak said.

"We see you." It was a chorus of voices, ones Erik recognized. "We can taste your fear."

"A deep, evil magic," Balzarak repeated. "Be ready."

"You can hear them?" Erik asked.

"Aye," Balzarak said.

"This is truly evil magic then," Erik said.

"What?" Wrothgard asked.

"Those are the dead from my dreams," Erik said. "Those are the voices of my nightmares."

The dead laughed.

"Of course, they can hear us," the dead said. "This is our realm."

"No more dreaming for you, Erik." Fox's voice cut through the blackness, resounding over the other voices.

"We'll see," Erik replied.

"Your fear tastes exquisite," the voices said. "Don't worry. It won't be much longer."

"Piss off!" Switch screamed.

"Darkness," the voices said. "Darkness. Forever."

Erik smelled them. He felt them, their hot breath. Their stink filled the tunnel. He heard them get close, heard their shuffling feet, heard their cackles. He heard the scraping metal against flint.

"Bloody light," Switch said. His voice shook. He breathed heavily. "Damn you. Bloody light."

Erik heard Balzarak's voice. It sounded methodical. He was talking to himself, praying.

"They're close," Erik said.

He swung out. Ilken's Blade caught rotten bone and putrid flesh. The smell proved that much. Others attacked, swinging recklessly in the darkness.

This was an ancient magic, but more ancient than fairies? More ancient than the first creations. It had worked twice before, why not again? Eventually, it would all be gone, but he could not worry about that now. If the others could hear them, then things had changed. And certainly, for the worse.

Erik opened his haversack and retrieved the bag. He took a handful of the dust and threw it. The tunnel lit up with a pale light, and he could see their faces, rotting and distorted. They screamed and growled, and for a moment, everyone could see what they were attacking, but then the light was gone.

He heard them. They were on them again. Something brushed Turk's face. Something cut Demik's cheek. Something grabbed Dwain's ankle. They would kill them.

"More, Erik!" Balzarak yelled. "This is much more powerful than before."

Erik threw another handful, and another, and another. Soon, flecks of dust floated all about. When they touched one of the undead, the creature burst into flames and screamed as it was incinerated. Even if the fairy dust didn't touch the dead, it injured them. They grabbed at their eyeless sockets and tore away already rotted flesh. As blackened skeletal hands reached out, they dissolved into black dust when the light hit them.

They cut some down. Others burned away when the fairy dust touched them. Others disappeared into the walls of the tunnel. And the dust hung there in the air, casting its eerie moonlight onto the tunnel. Half the bag was now gone, but they were alive.

The tunnel, narrow and constricting at first, widened and gave such a sudden and steep incline that Balzarak and Wrothgard, leading the party, almost fell when they first came to it. They continued to march upwards, the thundering and roaring still raging behind them, shaking the tunnel.

"The walls are going to collapse on us!" Switch cried through one deafening roar.

"These are dwarvish walls," Demik replied. "They'll never cave in."

Just as Demik spoke, the wall shook and cracked. The sound was almost as deafening as the dragon's screams. The fissure in the wall grew upwards like some crawling weed, and as it reached the ceiling, the wall opened and ancient rock spilled onto the walkway, as if the wall was a belly that had been opened to spill its intestines. There was so much debris that everyone had to find their footing. Erik found himself slipping and bracing himself with a hand on the other wall. He heard more cracking, felt more shaking, knew that more rubble spilled from the supposedly unbreakable dwarvish walls.

The ever-growing heat said the dragon was right behind them, but the fairy dust seemed to cool the air a little around them. However, the tunnel leveled off, and the heat returned, apparently too powerful for the fairies' magic to stave off.

The tunnel curved suddenly to the left and, as they turned the corner, Wrothgard gave a sharp cry, and Erik found himself stepping right into the back of Dwain.

"Just bloody great!" Switch cried. "Now what? Is Erik going to pull some wings out of his ass so we can fly across?"

The tunnel had opened onto a wide ledge. Erik stepped up and saw that the ledge abruptly dropped off. He looked down. There was no floor. Only darkness. Erik looked upwards. There was no ceiling. Only darkness. He looked forward. He could see an opening—another tunnel—on the other side of the chasm.

Even though the fairy light still illuminated the air around them, something else lit up the wide gap. It looked like red water, only thick, like porridge. It spilled from a crack in the mountain wall across from them, just below the tunnel opening. It poured like honey in thick clumps and gave off a reddish, fiery light that combatted the pale whiteness of the fairy dust.

"Magma," Balzarak replied. "The earth's lifeblood."

As Balzarak spoke, another roar rumbled through the tunnel and shook the ledge on which they stood. Erik heard what sounded like a whip cracking from somewhere up above, far beyond the light and, only moments later, a large rock—a piece of the mountain—fell past them and down into the darkness below.

"So, here we are," Wrothgard said, shoulders slumped, "stuck again. I don't suppose, despite what Switch said, you have something else in that haversack of yours, Erik, that might save us."

Erik shook his head, but then saw something, something odd, out in the expanse of the chasm. He hadn't seen it before. Maybe, it hadn't been there until the great piece of mountain had broken loose and fallen past them.

Another distant scream shook the world.

"Is that ..." Erik said, speaking to no one.

"Is that what?" Switch asked.

"Look. Don't you see it," Erik said, pointing. "More dwarvish trickery."

"What are you talking about?" Dwain asked.

"It's dust, sitting out there, sitting on nothing," Erik said, huge smile on his face. "At least, that's what the ancient dwarves wanted us to think."

The mountain shook again. Another piece of mountain broke free.

"Bloody wonderful," Switch said, "but as you stand here laughing about tunnel digger tricks, we're going to die."

Erik dug into his haversack again, again removing the bag of fairy dust. Dipping his hand into the sack, he removed a small handful. He stepped forward and threw the dust into the space before, into the air, to seemingly descend into the ravine below.

"A lot of good a lit-up gully will do us," Switch said.

"Just wait," Erik said.

The dust floated through the air, dropping slowly as the mountain rumbled and shook around them. When the dust should have continued floating into the darkness below, it came to rest, midair.

"What, by the gods ..." Wrothgard said.

"Floating fairy dust." Switch shrugged. "So, how is this going to save us?"

"I see it," Turk said.

"Aye, so do I," Demik agreed.

"It's a bridge," Erik said, "made to look like the side of the ravine. Step out. You won't fall."

"You step out," Switch said.

Erik shrugged and did as he was asked. He looked down, and it looked as if he might fall into the darkness as he let his foot down, but he stepped onto stone and stood in what must've looked like midair.

"Clever tunnel diggers," Switch said, smiling. He almost sounded as if he believed it.

"Clever indeed," Turk grumbled.

Erik ran across the land bridge. He could hear his companion's footsteps as they followed. The tunnel at the other end of the bridge was short and, even though the fairy dust stilled followed him, it glowed with the sickly red glow of the melted rock that flowed through the mountain.

The short tunnel opened again into a large chasm. This one had a clear bridge running from one end to the other and a river of the fiery, melted rock flowing under it, lighting up the whole of the chasm so Erik could see in either direction as far as his eyes would let him.

The river gurgled and moaned as it flowed under the bridge. Large bubbles emerged and then popped, spewing the stuff into the air like some geyser. The other end of the bridge wasn't as much of a tunnel as it was a wide shoreline that rose up from the river and extended back into darkness.

"I will go first," Balzarak said. "Turk, you follow with Bryon."

The general stepped out onto the bridge, Turk—half dragging Bryon—after him, and it seemed solid. Then, the mountain shook again.

"She sounds closer than ever," Erik said. He clasped his hands together, trying to stop them from shaking.

Rock and rubble from the mountain fell into the river, and it hissed and sizzled as they melted away into the red magma. The flow undulated, and some of it spilled over the bridge like a flood rushing over a dam. The bridge steamed where the magma had been.

Behind them, Erik heard more rumbling and roaring. He heard

stone cracking and rock falling. As he looked backed through the tunnel and into the cavern behind them, it lit up as if the sun had somehow been stuffed inside the mountain and a blast of hot air struck his face. He saw his fairy dust fall away, float to the ground and blink out, like the heat had sapped away its strength. Sweat once again poured from his brow. He could feel it pooling under his arms and in between his legs and at the small of his back.

He heard them again. He heard their laughter and their screams. He smelled them, their rot and death. And then he froze. His hands seeming to be tied to his sides, his muscles rigid, like stone, his eyes were locked when he saw her.

You have to move.

The thought passed through Erik's mind as if it was his own, but he knew his dagger was speaking to him. He wanted to answer, even if he answered in his own mind, but even that seemed frozen. Her very presence paralyzed him, and he heard the dagger again.

You must fight the fear, or all is lost.

Erik finally blinked his eyes. He felt tears spill down his cheeks as he closed his eyelids tightly. His eyes stared at the swirling reds and purples and pinks of the backs of his eyelids, the images of the mountain, the fire ... her, all tattooed there when all he searched for was darkness, blankness ... nothing.

Creator, help me.

He moved his hands, opened and closed them several times. Then his arms moved. He felt his knees buckle, and he almost fell but caught his balance. Then he opened his eyes.

"We must go," he said, looking to his companions as they slowly crossed the land bridge, avoiding more of the fiery river's undulations and floods over the top of the walkway.

"What do you bloody think we're doing," Switch replied.

"No," Erik said. "Faster."

He could hear them. He could hear her. Just behind them. Coming. Fast.

His companions seemed to crawl across the bridge.

"Move!" he yelled. "She is right behind us! She's in the cavern! I saw her! Move!"

The dwarves needed no more encouragement. Their snail crawl turned into an outright sprint, and the men needed nothing else other than the fear of their dwarvish companions to spur them on as well.

Balzarak and Turk and Wrothgard, carrying Bryon, were the first to reach the other side. Then Switch and Bofim. Erik found himself in the back, Bim and Befel in front of him. As he reached halfway across the bridge, her deafening roar ripped through the cavern, followed by the sound of rock breaking, cracking, crumbling. Erik turned to see the wall behind him—the wall all around the tunnel opening and as far up as he could see—crack and bend.

Then he saw her again. Her head poked through the tunnel opening, taking some of the mountain with it. The scales on her face were golden-green, her head long and slender, lizard-like. The nostrils at the end of her long snout steamed, and her eyes—red with black, cat-like pupils—squinted when she saw them. Erik could sense intelligence in those eyes as they scanned the cavern. The dragon's head—attached to a long neck—poked farther into the cavern, breaking off large chunks of rock. Large spines—fan-like ridges—ran down the dragon's neck and, as her body pushed through the tunnel, Erik could see they ran down her back as well. She was so powerful, she simply pushed herself through rock, breaking the mountain at will.

As the dragon emerged from the mountain wall, standing partway onto the bridge in order to fit her whole, massive body into the cavern, the tunnel behind her crumbled and caved in. Erik stopped and stared. The sight of her, her very presence, caused him to stand in awe, unable to move. Her body was long, and those same golden-green scales covered her all the way to the tip of her tail, which she slapped against the mountain wall, cracking it and sending debris everywhere.

She surveyed the cavern, glaring the whole time at the party—at Erik. Wings protruded from the dragon's back, just behind her shoulder joints and just above her forelegs. She spread them, and as they stretched, they rattled. She lifted her head and dug her claws into the stone of the land bridge. Looking upwards, she sucked in a deep breath of air.

All sound left the cavern. It was as if Erik had gone deaf. The movement of the burning river below. The falling of rock from above. The cries of the dwarves behind him. Nothing. And then ...

The dragon opened her mouth and a pillar of fire erupted. She blew her fire high into the cavern and with that came a roar so loud it pushed Erik to the ground. He clutched his ears, pressed as hard as he could, and still he couldn't drown out the deafening sound. He felt something wet coming from his ears and, when he looked at his hand, saw blood. When the sound stopped, all Erik could hear was ringing, constant ringing, and his vision went blurry. He heard something behind him, someone yelling, but couldn't make out the sound, the words. He turned to see Turk at the other end of the bridge, waving at him, yelling. It looked like he was telling Erik to run.

His voice finally reached Erik's ears, and the pain, the fear in the dwarf's voice, brought him back to his feet. He had never heard such raw terror in Turk's voice, never seen such horror in his eyes.

Erik looked back at the dragon. She took a step further out onto the bridge. She stared at him with a high-arched, craned neck, and again, Erik sensed intelligence in those eyes, something far beyond a simple animal acting on instinct, something beyond the intelligence of any man. He ran.

Another roar erupted from her mouth, and a pillar of fire burned the stone where Erik had been standing. He pushed Bim and Bofim and yelled to his brother.

"Run Befel!" Erik cried. "Don't look back. Just run!"

As they ran, the bridge shook, and Bim fell. Erik ran past him, but Befel stopped.

"What are you doing?" Erik yelled, still running.

"We have to help him," Befel replied.

Erik stopped and watched as two spears glanced off the dragon's armored neck. He looked over his shoulder to see Gôdruk and Threhof throw two more. Nothing. The dragon looked at them before focusing on Erik, her piercing eyes suggesting she mocked their pathetic attempts to attack her.

Befel helped Bim to his feet, and they both returned to running. The dragon took another step and then turned. For one moment, Erik thought she was going to retreat, but then her tail flicked at the roof of the cavern. She could fight them in more than one way; she wanted to take her time before her fire did its last terrible act.

From high up in the darkness, a shower of rocks, large and small, came crashing down, and Bim caught the worst it. One huge boulder hit his lower back, and he went down before smaller rocks half buried him. Even though Erik couldn't hear his screams above the dragon's roaring, he saw them. Bim squirmed on the ground, clawing at the huge stone of the bridge and pounding his fists. Befel regained his feet and bent down to help Bim up, but the stone was too heavy. Befel grabbed a hand and tried dragging the dwarf, but he could not be moved.

"Befel! Leave him!" Wrothgard yelled.

"Hurry!" Turk cried.

"Run!" Bofim yelled.

The silence came again as the dragon sucked in all the air in the cavern in one, heaving breath. It was as if she sucked out life too.

"Run, brother!" Erik yelled.

Flame consumed the spot where Befel and Bim once were. Erik couldn't breathe. He grabbed at his chest as he fell to his knees. He couldn't blink. Even the beating of his heart stopped. When he found the power to breathe once again, his breaths came in short, sporadic spurts.

Pathetic.

It wasn't his thought. It wasn't his dagger. It was the voice of a woman, one of dignity and nobility, almost soft. Erik looked up to see the dragon standing over him, looking down at him. Her eyes now definitely mocked him. As her mouth moved, it could almost have been a sneer.

Pathetic. Pathetic little insects.

Erik just stared.

You are doomed. All of you. Doomed. You. The dwarves. Your people. But you—I won't kill you yet. Oh no. First, you will suffer. Then, you will join them.

Erik heard the laughter of the dead, the voices from his dreams snarling and screaming. How could she know?

"Come on, Erik!" Wrothgard's voice yelled. "You'll do no good dying today!"

We're dead anyway, no matter how fast we run, we're dead.

Yes, yes you are.

As her voice rang in his head, Erik felt the familiar pinch at his hip, but his dagger was telling him something. It was something about another gift Marcus had given him—two stone-sized rubies that refused to glimmer in the light. He dug into his belt pouch and retrieved one of the red stones. His dagger told him what to do.

He held out his hand, the ruby-like stone sitting in his palm. The dragon looked down at him. He heard her cackle, the softness gone, and she threw her head up and spouted forth flame. The cavern shook, and more debris fell, causing the river of magma to spill over the bridge. But Erik didn't move.

He saw a white light begin to glow, appearing from deep inside the dull stone. The light grew brighter and brighter until it consumed the whole stone. It looked like it should be hot, but it wasn't. It just glowed and gave off a reddish-white light that seemed to combat the red, eerie glow the dragon brought with her.

Erik heard that sucking sound again, felt the air and the sound go out of the cavern. He knew she was preparing to attack, preparing to kill again, douse them with fire.

As his dagger had instructed him, Erik threw the stone, but not at the dragon. Instead, he simply tossed it into the river of fire, and when it touched the magma, it glowed even brighter, filling the cavern with a light that challenged even the midday sun. It didn't sink but simply grew brighter and brighter until it forced Erik to close his eyes.

Erik heard an explosion, felt a heat even more intense than what the dragon brought with her against his face. He opened his eyes to see a wall of fire before him. It was as if the river below rose up and surrounded the dragon. He heard a deafening roar and screaming. He heard the undead screaming. He heard the dwarves and men behind him screaming. He just watched.

The wall of fire fell back into the river as a splash in a pool of water. As the ripples subsided, Erik looked up, and the dragon was gone.

"Where's the dragon?" he heard Switch ask.

"Is it dead?" Demik added.

"It must be," Wrothgard said. "Erik killed the dragon."

"Erik?" Demik questioned.

"Impossible," Balzarak replied. "A dragon doesn't die so simply."

"You've seen one die then?" Switch chided.

"It's not there anymore," Turk said.

"He must have. Erik killed the dragon," Wrothgard said, his voice with the awe of a child receiving it's most desired gift.

Erik could hear joy in Wrothgard's voice, but he felt none of it. He felt the hair on the back of his neck rise and goose pimples rise up along his arms. He felt his face grow hot and a knot in his stomach.

"Befel," he muttered. "Where are you?"

He couldn't hold back his tears. He tried, but he couldn't. He couldn't stop them from pouring down his face. He couldn't help the gulping, gasping sobs as they involuntarily racked his body.

"Please," he whispered through weeping cries.

He buried his face in his hands.

Erik felt a hand squeeze his shoulder.

"Erik." Wrothgard's voice returned to its normal tone. "Erik. I'm sorry. I'm so sorry. I wish we could do something, but we have to go."

Erik's tears stopped. He bit his lip. Anger raged over him. He shrugged Wrothgard's hand off his shoulder and stared at the soldier. The look caused Wrothgard to take a step back, and Erik simply walked past him.

Turk stood in front of Erik who balled up his fists.

"There is no greater love than to lay your life down for another," Turk said. "Befel did that. He died—willingly died—trying to save Bim. There is no greater honor than to know a warrior, man or dwarf, who sacrificed so much. Bim and Befel will go down in dwarvish history as heroes, warriors willing to die for their friends, willing to fight a dragon. They will surely be at peace this day, resting in the halls of An."

Turk smiled at Erik, even looked to offer a comforting hug, but Erik put up his hands and backed away. He didn't scowl. He didn't yell. He didn't cry. He just stared past Turk, at another mountain tunnel and the pinpoint of light at its end—the pinpoint of light that signaled an escape from this underworld.

"I don't want a dwarvish hero," Erik said. "I want my brother back."

Erik walked past them all and into the tunnel. It was dark, save for that pinpoint of light. He couldn't really see, but he didn't care. He knew they might be there, the undead. He didn't care about them either. Part of him hoped they would be there. Maybe they would end this pain.

15

"Did you hear that?" said Patûk as he put down his cup of hot, spiced wine.

Usually, it helped chase the chill of the mountain morning away, but this morning, the general had drunk more than one cup. He rarely drank two, but this morning, he had drunk four already and was working on his fifth. He even chastised Li for questioning him when he asked for the last cup. Was it just the wine?

"Are there clouds gathering?" General Al'Banan asked.

"I don't believe so, sir," Andu replied.

"Well, go check, man," Patûk hissed.

He heard it again. It sounded like thunder, but not quite. Patûk

Al'Banan hadn't seen clouds in several days. It hadn't rained in a week.

"Wine," Patûk hissed. He slapped the cup of spiced wine away. "No more wine in the morning, Li."

"Yes, my lord," Li said, bending to pick up the cup but ignoring the red spatter on his clothes. Making a fuss over that would have caused even more ire in his master.

Patûk looked over his shoulder. He hated the way his seneschal seemed to sneak around, seemingly always looking for the shadows.

"Is there something else you would prefer in the morning, my lord?" Li asked.

"What else is there?" Patûk snapped.

"Tea, my lord." Li seemed unfazed by Patûk's mood. That made the general even angrier. Most men bowed and cowered when he raged.

"A woman's drink."

"Yes, my lord. Certainly," Li said. "What about coffee?"

"What is that?" Patûk asked.

"It is a drink normally served hot," Li replied, "from Wüsten Sahil. It is made from a bean. They grow it on the Feran Islands and Isuta as well."

Patûk Al'Banan grunted.

"It is dark and bitter, my lord," Li said. "A rich and bold taste. A man's drink, my lord."

"I'll try it," Patûk said.

"Yes, my lord," Li replied. "I have some now, and when we reach civilization, I can get more ... if you like it."

Andu reentered the tent.

"Clouds?" Patûk asked.

"No, sir," Andu replied with a bow.

Patûk heard it again.

"Do you hear that, seneschal?" the general asked. "Or is it the wine?"

"Yes, my lord," Li replied, "I hear it."

"What, by the gods, is that?" Patûk asked. He stood. The wine had affected him more than he had originally thought. He felt dizzy and grabbed the arm of his chair to steady himself.

"Not thunder, my lord," Li replied.

"Then what, damn it?" Patûk hissed. He walked past Andu, pushing him aside, and stepped outside his tent.

His men were standing and looking around. Patûk looked to the sky. He heard it again. The sound rolled over him. He felt his heart stop as the sound wave hit him. He felt rigid and stiff as if he couldn't move. Just after he heard the thunder, a gust of wind blew through the camp, but it wasn't cold and crisp like a normal, mountain morning wind. It was hot and putrid. The smell made Patûk want to retch. He never retched.

"No, not thunder," Patûk said to himself.

He heard it again, this time louder. He froze again. He tried moving but couldn't. His men froze as well. No one moved. The sound paralyzed them. And then the hot wind came again.

"Not thunder at all," Patûk muttered. "That sounds like a roar."

"A bear, sir." Andu's voice weak and subdued, caught Patûk by surprise, and he spun on the sergeant, the back of his hand slamming hard into the man's face.

"That's no bear, you fool," Patûk Al'Banan hissed.

"I'm sorry, sir." Andu slowly pushed himself to his knees.

"Are you crying?" Patûk asked. His hand went to the handle of his sword, but then he released his grip. "Damn wine."

He stepped out into his camp. He had trained his men well. Thirteen thousand men, all trained to his strict standards. And despite his training, much of his camp had fallen into disarray. The thundering sound, the fear that paralyzed even General Al'Banan, the waves of heat, sent his soldiers running about, confused. His mountain trolls met each thundering boom with a roar of their own and then pissed themselves. Even his officers seemed perturbed. Patûk looked down at Andu again. He scoffed.

"A bear. You fool. The only thing I have ever heard make a sound anywhere close to that," Patûk said, not really to his sergeant, but to himself, "was a dragon lizard from Boruck-Moore. But nothing like this."

Patûk saw Lieutenant Bu with his corps of spies. They seemed a bit calmer than the rest of the camp.

"Lieutenant!" Patûk yelled.

Bu came to his general. He knelt before Patûk. General Al'Banan could see the lieutenant look at Sergeant Andu. He heard the lieutenant's disgusted sneer.

"Focus on me, Lieutenant," Patûk commanded.

"Yes, my lord," Bu replied, bowing lower.

"Where are my captains?" Patûk Al'Banan asked. "Why are my men in such disarray?"

"I do not know, my lord," Bu replied.

"Why are your men so steady while everyone else is running about like idiots?" Patûk asked.

"You have trained them well," Bu replied.

"No." Patûk Al'Banan shook his head. "You trained them well. You are now a captain. You are now Captain Commander. You are a captain of captains. Organize my camp. Organize my troops. Organize my officers. I need to address them."

"Yes, my lord," Bu replied.

"After I speak to my men," Patûk said, "I want you to send your spies out to our other camps to deliver my message. Is that understood, Captain?"

"Yes, my lord," Bu replied.

Bu stood to do as he was commanded, but then turned.

"My lord, what is that?" he asked.

"What is what, Captain?" Patûk asked.

"The noise, my lord," Bu added.

"I don't know," Patûk replied, "but I intend on finding out."

"My lord?" Bu said.

"Yes, Captain?"

"Are we still following the mercenaries serving the imposter?" Bu asked.

Patûk smiled. At first, he felt a flash of anger rush through his body, but Bu was an officer. He wasn't just an officer. He was an officer of officers. He deserved to know what they were doing. He deserved to know their course of action.

"Do not worry," Patûk replied. "I have a plan. I have someone who is tasked with retrieving something for me that will turn the tables in our favor, Captain."

"My lord?" Bu asked.

"It is a powerful weapon, Captain," Patûk said, "but we will still need help to execute our plan. We need Pavan Abashar. If he is willing to come under my command, we will join our forces in our fight against the Stévockians."

"And if he isn't willing to come under your command, my lord?" Bu asked.

"We will force him," Patûk said. "We will give his men the opportunity to join us. Those that don't, will pay with their lives. Now, gather the men and break camp."

Patûk spoke to the men. It wasn't all of them, of course. Over half his forces were spread throughout the Southern Mountains and beyond. But it wasn't even to the whole force that he directly commanded. He spoke mostly to the officers and sergeants and corporals. The rest of the soldiers busied themselves with breaking camp, packing and readying for a journey unknown.

Bu stood to the back of the gathering, listening absentmindedly to the general speak. It wasn't that he didn't care about what the general had to say. He simply knew what it would be.

Through a sidelong glance, Captain Bu could see Li step up beside him. He thought he saw a smile on the seneschal's face.

"What are you smiling about?" Bu asked.

"Does my smile upset you, Captain?" Li asked.

"No," Bu replied.

"I told you, Captain," Li said.

"What did you tell me?" Bu asked.

"I told you, you would continue to rise in favor," Li replied. "The general will continue to recognize your worth."

"Yes," Bu replied. He hated to agree with a snake like Li, even if it was in his favor. "You told me, didn't you? You are so wise."

Li gave him a condescending look, making Bu want to slap him.

16

Erik simply kept walking, his eyes trained on the pinpoint of light. No matter how long he walked, it always seemed so far away. It never got bigger, but he didn't care. His aim was to focus on nothing, and the distant light offered the perfect solution.

Several times Wrothgard or Turk called to him. He even heard someone try to catch up to him, once. He just walked faster. Ignored the calls. He didn't care.

With only the pinpoint of light, and the lanterns and torches some distance behind him, Erik's path was dark. He found himself stumbling several times, catching some stubborn rock stuck in the ground, or not seeing some undulation in the pathway. He righted himself and kept on. He didn't care.

Erik heard his companions—he shook his head and scoffed at the word—behind him arguing.

"We should stop and rest."

"Bryon doesn't look good."

"What if our lights go out again?" someone asked.

"What if those things come back?" another said.

"We're going to bloody die down here, dragon or no dragon."

Erik didn't care.

Finally, the light grew brighter, larger. Erik felt the air around him cool. It felt fresher as he breathed in, and then he realized he could smell rain. He touched the tunnel wall and found it wet. He felt little crawlers and vines clinging to the mountain wall as if planting them had been interrupted, an unfinished project. He was getting closer to the surface, to freedom. He sped up, walked faster, and then stopped and closed his eyes. He didn't care. The darkness of the world beneath or the light, bright colors of the world at large, neither offered benefit because nothing ever would.

He saw his brother. He saw the look Befel gave him right before he died. It was a look of fear, but it was a look of acceptance as well. It was the same look Befel gave his mother or father, whenever they gave him some new chore, some new responsibility. Erik always thought it was silly, how Befel could be afraid. Afraid he was in charge of shoeing the horses. Afraid he was in charge of plowing the cornfields. Afraid he was in charge of irrigating the apple trees. But he wanted to be the best. He wanted to make his mother and father proud. That's who Befel was. Make everyone proud—even his little brother.

Erik felt the tears again. He tried to hold them back, but couldn't. That look ... the look of resignation ... that was the look he gave Erik just before he died.

"I'm proud of you, brother," Erik whispered through tears. "I am so proud of you. If I could have only been the man you were."

Perhaps that was why Befel had started questioning himself, questioning their quest, their decision to leave. He had thought he was doing what was best, and when he realized he had made a mistake ...

"And all I could do was chastise you for it," Erik muttered. "And now father's eldest is gone."

Erik thought of having a boy—three or four or five boys. He thought of the joy they might bring him. But he thought of that first boy—the oldest. He would be the first one. It would be he who Erik taught to fish and hunt first. He would be the first to learn to plant and sow. He would be Erik's future. That was Befel Eleodum to Rikard Eleodum, and he was gone.

"It should have been me," Erik said. "I ran past them. All I cared about was myself. I should have been the one who died back there."

He felt a pinch at his hip.

You're not being fair to yourself.

Erik ignored his dagger.

The light grew increasingly brighter until Erik could see that it was an opening. Rocks were piled up in front of it, so there was only a face-sized hole, but nonetheless, Erik could see the outside world, all cloudy and rainy with the day's light waning.

Roots poked through the ceiling of the tunnel as Erik got closer, and he pushed them aside. Some were tough, and some he had to cut away. But he reached the opening to feel the cool wind of a rainy, mountain day on his face. He started pushing rocks away, and the opening widened. One large boulder splashed against the wet ground, sending flecks of mud up onto Erik's face, but he continued to clear the opening.

"Erik," Turk called, "wait for us. We will help."

He ignored the dwarf.

Pushing enough rock away, he poked his head through and saw that the day was truly almost over, and he knew they would have to camp soon, so he left a wall of rocks, knee high, in front of the opening.

"We will probably camp in here," Erik said to himself, "and this will keep out the water."

Erik stepped over the wall of rock and out into the mountain rain. It was cold, but it was a welcome contrast to the heat of the underworld, of Orvencrest, of ... her. The rain plinked off his mail shirt in a metallic chorus that Erik didn't like. He took it off. Now, the rain just thudded against the soft leather of his jerkin. That was better.

Erik heard the others behind him.

"Well done, Erik," Turk said.

Erik heard someone moving the rocks.

"Don't touch those," he snapped.

"And why not?" Switch spat back.

"Because we're going to camp in there," Erik retorted, "and unless you want to sleep in puddles, those rocks will keep most of the water out."

"Camp here?" Wrothgard asked. "Why do you think we are going to camp here?"

"It is almost dusk," Erik said. "Do you see any other place we can camp? Someplace dry and relatively warm?"

"No," Wrothgard replied, "no, I suppose I don't."

Erik didn't like the look Wrothgard gave him. It was one of disappointment. Part of Erik felt bad, but then he just shrugged.

Darkness came quickly. Dwain tried to build a fire, but the dampness made it impossible. They kept a torch burning, for light, but other than that, the night, cloud-covered as it was, passed by in cold, wet darkness.

Bryon sat against the wall, Turk tending to his wound. He groaned often. His face looked red, redder even in the firelight. He would shake, then seemingly fall asleep, and then come to again with a start and a short cry. It reminded Erik of his brother, just after he had hurt his shoulder.

"Will he be all right?" Erik asked.

"I'm surprised you care," Turk replied without taking his eyes off Bryon's wound.

"I don't," Erik said. He bit his lip and clenched his fists, but it was a lie. "No. I do. He's my cousin. I care."

"Is that the only reason you care?" Turk asked.

Erik didn't answer for a while. He just sat and watched shadows dance along the tunnel wall, listened to the rain pound against wet dirt and grass outside their little sanctuary. He shivered as a quick gust of air doused him with rainy, nighttime air.

"No." Erik shook his head as if Turk could see it.

This time, Turk took a while to respond.

"Honestly, I don't know," Turk finally said. "This is like no wound I have ever seen before. It has taken all of my knowledge of medicine and the body, all of my ..." Turk paused a moment, "skills, to stem his fever and keep the pain at bay. This is no ordinary wound, with no ordinary poison."

"But he will all right?" Erik asked again.

"I don't know," Turk replied, "I think I can treat him well enough until we get to Thorakest. Once we get there, it may take some time, but I believe he will heal."

"I've never asked about your ability to heal wounds," Erik said.

"What about it?" Turk still seemed short with Erik, agitated and curt. Erik couldn't blame him but offered no apology.

"Is that something all dwarvish warriors learn how to do?" Erik asked. "Work with medicine? Heal wounds and tend to injuries?"

"Some, yes," Turk said. "Not all."

"And why are you exceptionally good at it?" Erik asked. "Did your father teach you?"

"No," Turk replied. "I happened to learn on my own."

"How—"

"You know," Turk said, cutting off Erik and staring at him. Erik couldn't quite see Turk's eyes in the dimness of the lantern light, but he imagined those hard, gray eyes glaring at him. "You are not the only one who has lost loved ones. You are not the only one who has lost a friend on this journey. I am sorry for your loss, Erik. I know not how it feels to lose a brother, but I have lost friends that were like brothers to me. I know it hurts. And no one would ever fault you for grieving. But you act as if no one here knows what loss is, as if no one here has ever had to deal with the death of a treasured friend. Mortin and Bim were—are—beloved warriors by the dwarves here, with us now, and by those at home, including their families. They had wives and children. And, I fear, we may lose even more before our journey is done."

"It just hurts," Erik said. He could feel tears coming to his eyes. He looked away even though Turk would not see him.

"I am sure it does," Turk said, "and I wish there was some sort of medicine in this world that could heal that hurt, but there is not. An knows, many try to heal this kind of hurt with ale and wine, or tomigus root, or kokaina, or any other thing that might numb their mind, but for this, there is no cure."

Erik stayed silent, staring into the darkness.

"You are a good man," Turk said. His voice softened. "You're a righteous man, and I consider you a good friend. But the way you acted ... it isn't right. We all care about you, and we all cared about Befel."

By the faint light of a torch, sputtering in the mist of the rainy, mountain air, Erik couldn't quite see Turk, but he thought he saw tears in the dwarf's eyes.

In the darkness, Erik remembered words his grandfather had said to him when he was just a little boy. He was scared, during a thunderstorm. It was dark then, too. And Erik cried.

"Don't be afraid," his grandfather had said.

"Why?" Erik asked, still sobbing.

"Because, the Creator is always with you," his grandfather had replied, "even in the deepest, darkest places."

"The deepest, darkest places?" Erik had asked.

"Yes," his grandfather had replied.

"Even in the deepest, darkest places," Erik muttered, and he wished he would believe his words.

The dreamless night passed by quickly, and Erik woke to a rainy, mountain morning. The dim gray of clouds cast eerie shadows throughout the tunnel. Turk and Bryon were the only two awake as Erik stirred and stretched. He looked across to the other side of the tunnel as his eyes found focus.

"Don't tense up," Turk told Bryon as he pressed around the wound on the man's chest. Bryon's bare chest revealed an angry, reddened wound that seeped with not blood, but a greenish-yellow puss. "It will only make your wound hurt more and harder for me to bandage it."

Turk spread some of his cooling ointment over the wound, pressed a clean cloth against it, and then bowed his head and seemed to pray. Bryon leaned his head back and closed his eyes.

"Is he all right?" Erik asked, but Turk didn't answer.

Erik gathered his things as the others woke and stepped through the tunnel's opening and out into the wet, mountain air. It took only moments for the rain to soak his hair and only a few more moments for Erik to feel the wetness through his mail shirt and leather undershirt.

Erik walked off, not caring to wait for his companions. The trees were less thick in this area of the mountain than Erik thought they would be. There was no recognizable path, and he suspected it had been many years since dwarf or man had been here. He passed by several clumps of blackberry bushes and through a grove of white-barked ash. Rabbits and squirrels and other small animals scurried away as he walked by.

Finally, he came to a ledge. Stepping to its edge, he could see, far below, a stream. It could not have been a large stream. The chasm at which Erik stood was barely twenty paces wide. But at some point, he knew it must open into a much larger river. This was, after all, how all raging rivers began.

I wonder if you eventually flow into the Giant's Vein.

It was too far to hear, almost too far to see, but he could imagine the sounds of gurgling water spilling over rocks, of rain plunking into the rushing stream. He imagined it flow and widen and grow into a larger river. He imagined what a river the size of the Giant's Vein might look like. The Blue River was big, big enough to require a bridge. But what he had heard about The Giant's Vein ...

I wonder if it's like the ocean. I can't imagine anything that big.

He remembered the deep blue of the South Sea, staring at it from so far away atop a hill overlooking Finlo. He had never seen anything like it.

I thought mountains were big. I do believe the South Sea could swallow all the mountains in Háthgolthane. I would like to see the South Sea again, perhaps when I am not so worried about getting on a boat sailing east.

Erik would see it again. He was sure of that ... almost sure. Befel ... Befel would never see anything again. Erik didn't think his brother was aware that he had seen the look on Befel's face when they first saw the South Sea. But that look, it was one of pure awe, of amazement, as if he had only dreamed of something so big, so magnificent, only to find out it was real.

That look reminded Erik of the first time one of Befel's crops—big, fat, red tomatoes—grew buds and then bloomed and then gave a fruit. He was there. Befel had that same look then. Awe. Amazement. Something he had touched actually grew and produced food. He was also with Befel when they both first saw a mare give birth to her foal. Awe and amazement.

So simple. Tomatoes. Horses. The sea, and yet, so amazing.

Erik wiped his cheeks. The rain was steady, but he knew that some of the wetness there were his tears. He looked down at the tiny stream again.

They'll torment you, Befel. The dead. They'll chase you, stop you from getting on the caravan, make you one of them. You don't know how to fight them.

He looked down at the stream again.

I know how to fight them. I could jump. I could find you, stand by you, chase them away.

Erik stepped closer to the chasm's edge.

"Even in the deepest, darkest places," he whispered as he stared down into the ravine. Then, he asked the question, "Even there, in the realm of the dead."

As he wondered what it would feel like, hitting the floor so many paces below, he heard water sizzle against fire.

"How are you feeling, cousin?" Erik asked.

"How did you know it was me?" Bryon asked in reply.

"Your sword," Erik answered. "I heard it sizzle in the rain. I'm glad to see its magic isn't gone forever."

"Magic gone?" Bryon asked. "What do you mean?"

"Nothing," Erik replied. "It was something that happened in the tunnels of Orvencrest when you had passed out from your wound."

"What are you doing out here?" Bryon asked. Erik could hear the weariness in Bryon's voice. It was usually so commanding, even if the forceful nature of his voice was pretense.

"Minding my own business," Erik replied.

"The dwarves were wondering where you were."

"Oh," Erik said, "and not you."

"No ... I mean, yes, I was wondering too," Bryon said.

"How are you feeling?" Erik asked again, not turning to face Bryon.

"Better, I guess," Bryon replied. "Not very good, really. My whole body hurts ... burns."

"So, is that all?" Erik asked. "You know where I am. Is that all you wanted?"

"You're too close to the cliff's edge," Bryon said. "You're going to fall."

"You are suddenly worried about me," Erik said with a smirk. "That's interesting."

"What are you doing?" Bryon asked. Erik could hear him step closer. Erik inched forward.

"Why do you care?" Erik asked.

"You're my cousin," Bryon said, "my blood. Now, what are you doing? Why are you so close to the edge?"

Bryon's voice was still shaking and weak, but Erik could hear the intensity in it, a mix of fear and anxiety.

"I'm not going to jump," Erik replied, "if that's what you're worried about."

"No, of course not," Bryon said. Erik knew he lied. He could tell by the tone of his voice.

"Good. Well, you can go now," Erik said.

"What?" Bryon asked. Erik could hear the irritation in his voice.

"Go away," Erik said slowly. "I am fine. You are feeling better. Now you can go back to the dwarves as they sing funeral dirges for the dead."

"Why don't you come back with me?"

Erik shook his head. "I think I'll stand here for a while."

"Why?"

"Because I want to watch the mountain. Because I wish to listen to the sounds of the wind through the treetops. Because I wish for the rain to completely soak my breeches. Because I wish to kill myself. What do you care why I want to stand here alone?"

"Those words hurt," Bryon said. "We are kin. We are all we have left now."

At that, Erik wheeled on Bryon. He could feel his face redden, his ears grow hot. For only a moment, the paleness of Bryon's face, the sunken look in his cheeks, took him aback, but then he regained his composure.

"Those words hurt?" Erik questioned, seethed, hissed. "What hurtful words have you spoken recently, Bryon?"

Bryon stepped back. He looked surprised and then resigned.

"Many, I suppose," Bryon replied.

"It seems to me that you took your leave of our kinship long ago," Erik accused.

"So, do you wish to make up for all the hurtful things I have said by saying them back to me?" Bryon asked. His pale face turned a pinkish hue, and Erik saw tears collecting at the corners of his cousin's eyes. "Befel was like a brother to me, too."

Erik turned back around. "For a time, I suppose."

Erik waited for a few moments, watching the rain, staring at the stream below.

"I can smell fresh tilled earth." Erik closed his eyes. He saw fields of golden stalks fluttering in the wind. "I can smell wheat, the rain on the farm. Befel loved that smell."

"I used to love that smell too," Bryon said, "until I realized it meant more work, more hours under the hot sun."

"And this isn't work?" Erik asked.

"It's different."

Erik shook his head. "How?"

"I see the riches of my work. I feel the weight of gold and silver in my haversack. All I saw on the farm, even when my father was sober and talked to me about owning it one day, was more work. Never riches."

"I think you misunderstand the true meaning of riches." Erik wiped a tear away from his cheek. He might have just thought it was the rain, but he could tell it was a tear, the way it felt, the way it smelled.

"Are you trying to sound like your father?" Bryon asked. Erik could hear the derision in his voice.

"What good are riches to Befel now?" Erik asked. "What good is all this gold and silver? What good will your gold and silver be if that wound on your chest kills you?"

"At least I won't be on a farm with a drunken father," Bryon said. "And Befel didn't want to end up working on a farm either."

Erik clenched his fist.

"You think that was the last thing on his mind," Erik said through clenched teeth, "when fire consumed him? Do you think the last thing he thought, the last thing he was thankful for was the fact that at least he wasn't working on a farm?"

There was a long silence. Erik loosened his hands and leaned his head back, letting the rain hit his face. It quickened and hardened, and he could hear the small stream below start to rush as water flowed from higher upstream.

"What do I tell my mother?" Erik asked, looking down again and catching his cousin's eye.

"What do you mean?" Bryon asked.

"When I see her," Erik said. "When I return home without my brother, what do I tell her?"

"I don't know," Bryon said.

"I'm afraid I'll forget his face." Erik dropped his chin to his chest. "I'm afraid I won't remember."

"What?" Bryon asked.

"Befel's face," Erik replied. "I'm afraid I'll forget it, along with Tia's and Beth's. And my mother's and father's. Simone's."

"How could you forget your brother's face?" Bryon asked.

"I don't know," Erik said. "His face is just a memory now—just a fading memory."

"You'll see him again, won't you," Bryon said, "in your afterlife?"

Erik turned on Bryon.

"How dare you?" Erik spat.

"What?"

"You mock me and my faith. You make fun of my belief in the Creator. And then you try and use it to console me?"

"I'm just trying to help," Bryon said, stepping back.

"Well don't."

Erik turned around again to look down from the ledge, trying to ignore Bryon. He felt his cousin, knew he stood there for a long while, watching him. When he eventually walked away, Erik fell to his knees and wept.

17

Del Alzon rode quietly, looking back over his shoulder ever so often. He wasn't as heavy as he was when they had left Waterton, and he found himself riding longer, horse tiring more slowly. Of course, he was a far cry from what he was when he fought for Golgolithul, but as he looked down at his belly, it disgusted him less than before. Just the day before, he had poked a new hole in his wide girdle. He thought the simple Yager would never stop laughing when he stood up in the middle of that inn in Dûrn-Tor and his belt slipped off his waist and collected on the floor and around his ankles. The thought made him smile.

"Del, what are you looking for?" Danitus asked, riding up next to the former soldier.

"I don't know," Del Alzon replied. "I hoped ... I hoped ..."

"You hoped to what?" Danitus asked. Del Alzon could hear the irritation in the man's voice.

"I guess I had hoped we might run into them," Del confessed. "I hoped we might see them, that they would come back."

"Del, this is crazy," Danitus said.

"I know," Del Alzon agreed. "It's just ... I don't know what it is."

"You saved those children," Danitus said. "And the others. People we didn't even know. If you're trying to make up for something you've done in your past, surely you have."

"You don't know what I've done in the past," Del Alzon said.

"You must have been some terrible bastard to be that conflicted, my friend," Danitus offered, a small smile on his face.

Del Alzon laughed.

"Aye, a terrible bastard I was." Del Alzon closed his eyes and breathed in the cool air of the Abresi Straits.

"Smells like home," Del muttered.

"I don't quite know what home smells like," Danitus said with a smile.

"I suppose I know what you mean," Del Alzon replied. "I've lived in so many places too."

"Aye," Danitus agreed.

"I've lived in Waterton the longest, though," Del Alzon added, "so I suppose, Waterton is home."

"Isn't that a sad thing to say?" Danitus asked.

"What's that?" Del asked.

"Waterton is home," Danitus repeated.

Del Alzon shrugged with a smile.

"I don't know. There are worse places to live."

"Like where?" Danitus asked.

"The bloody east," Yager said, riding just behind the two men. "Fer sure, the bloody east."

"And how would you know?" Danitus asked.

"All in the past, mate," Yager replied, "but I've been. I've lived there—sort of—and I can't think of a worse place than the east. Golgolithul and Gol-Durathna."

"Aren't you originally from Golgolithul, Del?" Danitus asked with a smile.

Del Alzon nodded his head.

"And you're from Gol-Durathna, aren't you Danitus?" Del Alzon asked.

Danitus nodded.

"Don't care," Yager said. "Big cities. Lots of people caring nothing fer no one. Cruel, brutal governments created by greedy bastards. No thank you."

"Then, where is home for you?" Danitus asked.

"Waterton, fer sure," Yager replied. "But, that's not really home. Home is where my wife is, where my boy is. Home is in the woods, in the world, where the laws of nature rule."

"And nature isn't cruel?" Del Alzon asked.

"Oh, sure she is," Yager replied. "A cruel, harsh, brutal bitch at times. But she's always fair, nature is. No greedy politician bending the rules fer this or that."

Del Alzon thought about that for a moment.

"I guess you're right. Although, I rather enjoy the comforts of a town."

"We should be getting close," Danitus said. "I think I see the bridge's flag up there."

"I'll be happy to be back in my bed," Del Alzon said. "I hope Quintus was able to get those poor children—those poor people—back to Waterton safely."

"Do you hear that?" Yager said. He nudged his horse, his animal trotting ahead of Del Alzon and Danitus, and leaned forward in his saddle.

"I don't hear anything, woodsman," Danitus replied.

"Hush," Yager hissed. "I can't hear over yer jabbering."

"You asked us a question," Danitus snapped back, "and I'm simply—"

"I said shut yer mouth," Yager retorted.

Just as Danitus was about to say something again, just as he was about to curse Yager for his wood-brained ignorance, Del Alzon heard something as well. The merchant put a hand on Danitus' shoulder.

"I hear it," he said.

"Aye," Yager agreed.

"Screaming," Del Alzon said.

"Aye," Yager agreed again.

"Let's go," Del Alzon called, jabbing his heels into the ribs of his horse.

They galloped, and the flag that flew above the Blue River Bridge came into view. Black smoke billowed over the town, and Del Alzon heard the cracking of timber, heard more screaming, more yelling. He heard iron strike iron. He heard someone's curdling cry as iron cleaved flesh. He saw a body, lying a dozen paces in front of the bridge. It was a lumberyard worker, a middle-aged man, his chest opened by a gashing wound. Then, Del saw two more, men he didn't recognize. They looked dirty, like vagabonds or ...

"Brigands!" Danitus yelled.

"Forest thieves!" Maktus added.

Del Alzon saw half a dozen more bodies, lying in front of and on the bridge. He looked up to see the flag—a simple white flag with a blue river painted in the middle—fluttering in a light breeze, its edges tattered.

"The militia," Danitus said as he pulled up next to Del Alzon.

"Four of them, yes," Del replied.

A shrill scream cut through the air and caught Del's attention. He heard fire. He heard more screaming. The clang of metal. The grunting of dying. Then he heard a horn ... a Samanian horn.

"Those damn slavers," Del said before kicking his horse and

galloping across the bridge. "They're back for revenge. I know it. That Samanian prick."

Del Alzon drew his war sword. Dust and black smoke blocked his way, blinded him from anything that might await him on the other side, but he rode forward anyway. The smoke and dust whipped around him, swirled about his horse as it galloped on and revealed a town in flames, in complete chaos as men fought and as women and children ran for their lives.

Del Alzon passed by *The Wicked Beard*. A chair, its legs smoldering, flew through the single window that sat in the front of the tavern. A scream followed that chair as the door was flung open, Bill tumbling backwards onto the inn's front porch and down its three steps. Del saw that the man's bald head was bloodied, and he lay there, unmoving, barely breathing. Another man, long sword in one hand and Bill's daughter in the other, followed Bill out the door.

Del Alzon pulled on his horse's reins, bringing the animal next to the porch, and, as he rode by, brought his blade down upon the thief's head. Bone cracked, blood spouted up, and the man went to his knees, releasing the girl, who promptly ran to her father and cradled his head in her arms.

"*Get him inside!*" Del commanded, "and stay in there. Do not come out until I come back and get you."

Danitus rode past Del Alzon, Maktus and Gregory close behind. He looked to Del over his shoulder.

"*Get the women and children inside!*" Del yelled.

Del Alzon heard the blow of that all too familiar horn, but before he could see from where the sound came, two more men rushed to him. Del Alzon dug his heels into the horse's ribs, but before he charged his assailants, an arrow struck each one of his attackers in their chest. Del Alzon looked to see Yager's wife—a tall, slender, but well-muscled woman who always wore a hooded cloak —nodding to him with a wink. She turned, Yager now at her side, and loosed three more arrows with blazing speed. All three arrows found a home—a man's neck, a chest, and a belly. And then Yager loosed his arrows. One after another, Yager and his wife fired arrows at the enemy. Four, five, six, ten, a dozen attackers fell, dead, even as Waterton's militia retreated to the market square, led by Danitus.

Del Alzon heard the horn again.

"That cursed horn," Del hissed, more to himself. He looked about, ignoring the fighting for a moment. Then, he saw him. In the shadows of *The Red Lady*. It was a man holding a horn that Del Alzon recognized, but he didn't recognize the man. He was stout with blond hair and a bushy blond beard. He blew the horn again, and then he shouted. His voice was that of a westerner, harsh and simple. He was disguised somehow, but there was only one person that could be.

"Kehl." Del Alzon gritted his teeth and ground so hard his jaws hurt. "*Kehl!*"

The man didn't respond, perhaps didn't hear him. He looked nothing like Kehl, but there was something about him, the way he moved, the way he watched the brigands attack the people of Waterton, the way he hid in the shadows, said he was. Regardless, he was the leader of this attack. He blew his horn again, directing the fray of slavers as they attacked and killed the citizens of Waterton.

"They're here for more slaves," Del Alzon said to himself. "Replenish lost reserves."

But then he saw one of the brigands cut down a man, someone he could have easily captured, dragged away to sell in some sea port. Del shook his head.

"No. They are here for revenge," he muttered and then wheeled his horse around. "*To the square!*" Del Alzon yelled, and Yager and his wife followed him.

Del Alzon grimaced as they rode to the square, the dead bodies littering the road were mostly citizens of Waterton trying to flee the grips of the slavers. When they reached the square, Del Alzon saw the dwarvish blacksmith that called Waterton home swing a mallet hard, crushing one man's face. Four or five militia members, all clad in black leather and carrying a mishmash of weapons, staved off several more brigands.

"How many are there?" Del Alzon asked.

"Enough," Yager's wife said, and she again loosed arrows with the precision of an expert marksman.

"I didn't know your wife was so handy with a bow," Del Alzon said.

"Aye," Yager replied, "where do you think I learned?"

She leapt onto the fountain—part of it broken—that centered the square with a nimbleness that Del Alzon had never seen. Underneath her, as she rained arrows down on at least a dozen of Kehl's men, the dwarvish blacksmith continued to swing his hammer, crushing knees, shoulders, and skulls. Yager stood next to the dwarf, firing arrows as well. All the while Danitus and Maktus and Gregory cut more men down.

"*Get into your homes!*" Del Alzon yelled to the chaos of women and children and men who could not—or would not—fight. "Get to your shops! Stay there!"

Del Alzon dismounted. He gripped his sword with both hands. The thieves, the slavers came, and he cut them down. Arrows continued to rain. A dwarf's hammer crushed bone. And the onslaught began to retreat.

"You fat pig!" the stout, blond-haired, bushy bearded man shouted.

Del Alzon turned to face him.

"I will feed you to swine," the attacker said as he lunged at Del, swinging a curved sword with blinding speed.

The steel caught Del on the hand, and then the arm, and then the chest. That was definitely Kehl. He moved like a Samanian, even if his voice and body lied. Some trickery. Some magic.

"The next one will be across your fat, disgusting belly," the blond man hissed.

Del Alzon didn't say anything. He didn't reply. He didn't have the energy to. If this man was Kehl, somehow disguised, he wasn't worth a response.

He's right, you know, Del Alzon thought. *He's going to kill you. You're one, sorry excuse for a soldier. At least you'll go out having done something worthy. At least you'll die a man and not some slobbering, fat fruit merchant.*

The man came hard, and Del knew this would be the death blow to end his sad life. Just, maybe, he could kill this Samanian dog at the same time. Maybe he could at least take Kehl with him.

But then an arrow struck the attacker in the shoulder. He cried loudly, clutching at the arrow and breaking the shaft, just before it entered his flesh. At the same time, the tip of Del's sword grazed his cheek, and in the blink of an eye, the ruse wore away, and Kehl stood in front of Del Alzon, blood pouring down his cheek.

"You bitch!" Kehl hissed, glaring at Yager's wife. Then he turned his eyes to Del. "You fat bastard."

Del turned to see Yager's wife standing next to him, shoulder to shoulder. The hood of her cloak had fallen back. He had never seen her without her hood. Now he knew why. Her ears. She always covered her ears. They were long and slender, pointed at the top.

"She-elf scum!" Kehl hissed as he backed away and then turned to run. "Figures that you fatherless whores would let a she-elf fight your battles."

Kehl ran, and those of his men that still lived—and there were only a few of them—followed.

"Should we go after them?" Yager's wife asked.

Del Alzon didn't answer her. He just stared. Her eyes met his. They were blue—crystal blue, the color that sky might have been on the first day it ever existed.

"Del Alzon," she said. She put a hand to Del's face.

Her touch. It was so soft. Goose pimples ran along his skin as she touched him.

"Del Alzon, should we give chase?"

Del Alzon heard her. He heard her words, but they sounded a distant echo, some far off sound that barely touched his ears.

"Del." Yager's voice cut through the distant echo, and Del Alzon realized the woodsman was shaking his shoulder.

"What?" Del Alzon asked.

"Do we give chase?" Yager's wife asked.

"Chase to who?" Del Alzon asked.

"The brigands," Yager replied. "The slavers who are fleeing. Should we follow them?"

Del Alzon shook his head.

"No. Let them go."

"Let them go?" one woman said as she walked through the charred remains of her home's front door and into the market square. "After what they did, and you want to just let them go?"

Del Alzon could see tears welling up in her eyes. He could see her face turn a bright red. He saw her hands clenched at her sides and her arms shake.

"We need to take care of ours," Del Alzon replied, softening his voice. "We need to tend to our wounded. We need to bury our dead and comfort their families. We need to assess the damage done to our town and figure out what it will take to rebuild."

"We need revenge!" the woman screamed. Del Alzon put his hands up, moved to rest a hand on her shoulder, but she backed away. "Don't touch me! You speak of *our* town. You speak of *our* dead and *our* injured. Since when did you care about Waterton and its people?"

A young man ran from the woman's home. He ran to his mother, put his arms around her and, even though she struggled, began dragging her back to the home.

"I apologize," the young man said. "My mother—she is distraught. My father died just last year. My younger brother, well, he was one of those that left in the gypsy caravan, captured by the slavers, and, even though he returned—by your good graces—he isn't the same."

"Don't be sorry," Del Alzon said. "Please, don't be sorry. And, mother, as for when was this town ever my own ... today, Waterton is my town. Today, Waterton is my home. Today, Waterton's citizens are my brothers and sisters."

The woman stopped struggling with her son and, instead, buried her face into his chest and wept.

Del Alzon noticed a crowd gathering around him, around the fountain. The blacksmith dwarf stood there, with him, as did Yager and his wife ... the elf.

"It's an elf," Del heard one person murmur.

"We are cursed," said another.

"It can't be," one woman said. "They are a myth."

"That is why we have been attacked," said yet another.

"See for yourself," someone replied. "Bringing with her dark magic."

"What do we do?" asked yet another person.

And then Del Alzon heard all the answers he knew he would hear, all the answers he dreaded he would hear.

"Imprison her."

"Banish her."

"Kill her!"

"You would ask the person who saved your lives to leave?" Del Alzon said to the gathering crowd. "You would try—quite unsuccessfully, I think—to kill the reason more of you are not dead, more of your homes are not burnt to the ground?"

"But she is an elf?" one person called.

"And you are an idiot," Del Alzon replied.

Some laughed. Some growled. Then, Del Alzon heard more commotion ripple through the crowd.

"Make way for Simon!" called a hard voice. "Make way for the mayor!"

The gathered people parted as a short, pudgy man walked into the square, preceded by four militia members and followed by another four volunteer soldiers. The militia entered the square and surrounded Del Alzon, Yager, the woodman's wife, and the dwarf.

"Mayor," Del Alzon said flatly and gave the dignitary a short bow.

"The fat fruit merchant from the east," the mayor said in a nasally voice, "although, perhaps, not quite as fat."

"And what gives you cause to grace us with your presence?" Del Alzon asked.

"You left without my permission," Simon the Mayor said.

"I didn't know I needed your permission," Del replied.

"With able-bodied men," the mayor added.

"I didn't know they needed your permission," Del said.

"Who would have helped in the fight against these brigands," the mayor said. "You are under arrest, Del Alzon."

The militiamen following the mayor stepped towards Del Alzon.

"And where were you during the fight, Mayor?" Del Alzon asked. "Where were your men, those who guard your mayoral house so diligently?"

"It is not your place to ask where I was," Mayor Simon said.

"Were you barricaded in your manor?" Del Alzon asked. "Were you away and safe with your guards, hiding under a table while your people were dying?"

"And what of it?" Simon asked. "What happens to Waterton if I die?"

"We get a new mayor," someone from the crowd of people shouted.

"I think we need a new mayor," another cried.

Del Alzon began to smile. The mayor's militiamen stopped advancing on him.

"Del Alzon should be mayor," someone else yelled.

Del's smile faded. He shook his head.

"No," he mumbled, but as the crowd began to agree, as the crowd began to shout his name, he raised his voice. "*No!*"

"Why not?" Yager's wife asked.

"Because, I don't want to be mayor," Del Alzon replied.

"Good," Simon replied, "because you're not going to be. You

won't ever be, especially after I have you tried for civil unrest and cast you out with naught but the clothes on your back. Men, take this fat pig to the jail. And then, burn this woodsman and his she-elf's home down and throw them out of our town."

But the militiamen that accompanied the mayor didn't move.

Del Alzon looked at Yager.

"I don't want to be mayor of Waterton," he said.

"I think that is what make you most qualified," Yager replied.

"Aye," Danitus agreed. "How many shoddy leaders have you followed? Leaders who lead purely because of money or birthright?"

"Too many," Del Alzon replied.

"Then let us have a leader we want," Maktus said. "Someone we wish to follow. Someone who has earned our trust."

"Too many men have died under my command," Del Alzon said. "I don't expect you to ..."

"Then you've learned from your bloody mistakes," Gregory said.

"Stop fighting the inevitable, Del," Yager said. "Fer sure, you're gonna be our new mayor."

Del nodded. He laughed quietly to himself, eyes closed and head shaking. Who would have thought?

"Take Simon to the jail," Del said.

The eight militiamen that had accompanied Simon looked to one another, only for a moment. One of them, a larger man Del Alzon knew as Cody, nodded, and the others surrounded Simon. Two of them grabbed his arms and, even though he struggled, they easily began to drag him away.

"You can't do this!" Simon yelled. "Damn it! You can't do this to me!"

"Kill him!" the people of Waterton began to shout. "Burn him!"

Del Alzon looked at Simon's face. It had turned bleach white. He looked as if he was going to vomit.

"No," Del Alzon said. "He will get a fair trial, but we will learn what he has done to rob this town for his own good."

Del Alzon turned to the men that had traveled with him.

"Gregory," Del Alzon said, "will you go with the militiamen? Go with Cody and make sure Simon is placed in jail without incident please."

Gregory looked at him for a moment and then smiled and bowed. "Surely."

Del Alzon looked around at the crowd. The people of Waterton. *His* people. He tried not to, but he smiled widely.

"We need to assess the damage, Danitus," Del Alzon said.

"Are you asking me to lead those efforts?" Danitus asked.

Del Alzon thought for a moment, then nodded.

"Yes."

"Very well," Danitus said with a bow.

"And, Maktus, we need our militiamen ready," Del Alzon added. "The Samanian might attack again. And if we learn anything from this, it would surely be that we need to be better prepared for this sort of thing."

Maktus bowed. "Sure thing, Mayor."

Del Alzon winced at the title. He turned to Yager and his wife.

"And what to do with you?"

"You best choose yer words wisely, Del," Yager said, stepping in between Del Alzon and his wife.

"Relax, Yager," Del Alzon said. He could see the woodsman's wife wrapping a hand around her husband's wrist. "Truly, I think I fear your wife more than I fear you. After watching her work with the bow. Although, I suppose her being a she-elf explains it."

"So?" Yager said curtly.

"Husband," his wife whispered, certainly meant for only the woodman's ears, although Del Alzon heard it.

"We will have to continue to praise her place in our town, in what she did today," Del Alzon said. "I never thought I would see an elf in my lifetime. Truth be told, never really thought they existed."

"My little laddie, as well," Yager said.

"Ma," came a tiny voice just as Del Alzon spoke those words. "Da!"

"I told you to stay in the house," Yager's wife said as she bent down and opened her arms to receive a frightened little boy running as fast as he could. She lifted him up, and the boy hugged his mother tightly, nestling his face in her neck. "You silly boy."

"Trebor is his name," Yager said. "He's a good lad, even though he has a hard time listening to his mother."

Yager looked at his son over his shoulder, and the boy retreated farther into his mother's arms.

"Nice to meet you, Trebor," Del Alzon said.

His mother shook him gently and the boy finally looked up. His hair was as blond, almost white. He looked much like Yager, with high cheekbones and a strong jaw, only a little slenderer. And his eyes, an exact copy of his mother's, piercing and mesmerizing. His ears were pointed, but not as pronounced as his elvish mother's were.

"How is it you are married to an elf, Yager?" Del Alzon asked.

"It's a long story," Yager replied, "but, rest assured, Arlayna saved my life when I was ready to give it up. And to save my life, she sacrificed much."

"Your family is safe here, Yager," Del Alzon said, putting his hand on the woodsman's shoulder. "I give you my word. You and your wife and child will always be safe here."

"Thank you," Arlayna said, putting her boy down, bowing, and pulling the hood of her cloak back up over her ears. "May El bless you and keep you. Say thank you, Trebor."

The half-elf boy stepped forward, squishing the dirt nervously with one of his feet and looking at the ground.

"Look the man in the face, lad," Yager said with a smile, nudging his son forward a bit.

Trebor looked up at Del Alzon with those blue eyes, eyes at which Del couldn't help smiling, and said, "Thank you, sir."

Del Alzon crouched down, gently grabbed the boy's arms and said, "Oh, my boy, you are very welcome."

Trebor smiled and then backed away, hiding behind his mother's legs.

"He's a shy boy," Arlayna said.

"No matter," Del Alzon replied, standing and noticing the blacksmith dwarf standing by, looking about as the crowd began to disperse and go about putting their town back together.

"And what about you, master dwarf?" Del Alzon asked.

"What about me?" the dwarf asked, his voice hard and gruff and not much like the voices of the other dwarves with whom Del Alzon had ever spoken.

"There's a lot of repairing—and rebuilding—to do," Del said.

"Aye," the dwarf said with a simple nod, "that's an understatement."

"Would you be willing to help with those repairs?" Del Alzon asked. "Maybe lead those repairs? The resourcefulness of your people is legendary, is it not?"

"Aye, it is," the dwarf replied. He waited a moment, not saying anything and just looking about. Then he gave another simple nod. "Aye, I suppose I'd be willing to help."

"And are you from the north or the south?" Yager asked.

The dwarf shook his head. "Neither."

"What do you mean?" Arlayna asked. "You were born in the cities of men?"

"No." The dwarf continued to shake his head. "Not that neither."

"Then, where are you from?" Del Alzon asked.

"I'm from the west," the dwarf said. "West of Gongoreth. The city of Hapstadt, capital of Hügelstan, the dwarvish country of Nothgolthane."

Del Alzon looked to Yager, and then to Arlayna. They both shook their heads.

"I wouldn't expect you to know of it," the dwarf said. "Most in the east don't. And it seems less and less people from my country and Gongoreth travel your way."

"And your name?" Del Alzon asked.

"Hmm," the dwarf groaned. It seemed the new mayor's question struck a sensitive chord with the dwarf. "Haven't gone by my real name in some time. A little boy once called me Tank. He meant to say *clang*, for the sound my hammer made, but he couldn't quite get the word out right, and it stuck. So, you can just call me Tank."

"All right, then, Tank," Del Alzon said, "I will put you in charge of building and rebuilding."

"Sounds fine," Tank said. "Thanks."

"That was Kehl," Del Alzon said, "but, unless my eyes betrayed me, it didn't look like him at first."

"Thieves magic," Arlayna said, "without a doubt. Petty but effective for what a thief or assassin might need."

Something must have happened. Kehl had more men under his command than Del thought, especially after he killed the Samanian's brother and destroyed his camp. He wasn't really a thief by trade, but using thieves' magic. He would have to be wary of the man. He would keep coming back until one of them was dead.

Del Alzon turned around and looked about Waterton. *His* town. *His* home. *His* people.

"Never thought I would find a home," he muttered to himself. "Feels good."

"That fat, piece of ..." Kehl could feel the heat in his face. He turned to Albin. "What happened?"

"I don't know, Kehl," Albin said. A large welt had begun to rise on his cheek. The cut on his shoulder bled freely. And he limped, the broken shaft of an arrow still protruding from his leg.

"That she-elf bitch," Kehl replied as he looked at his own shoulder. The tomigus root had taken away some of the pain, but he had to be careful not to drink too much of the tea. He chewed on some kokaina leaf. That seemed to help as well.

"Yeah," Albin replied, "without her, they didn't have a chance. Her and the fat merchant."

Kehl wanted to punch something, kill something, destroy something. He looked to Albin. For a moment, the thought of ripping his throat out crossed his mind. Kehl shook his head. No. Albin had proven a loyal servant. That would be foolish.

"How many of the men from our guild remain?" Kehl asked.

"Of the dozen we took," Albin replied, "eight."

Kehl nodded. Losing four in that fight. That wasn't too bad.

"And the others?" Kehl asked. He felt woozy. He could feel his consciousness waning. "The ones we hired?"

"I'm not sure, Kehl," Albin said. "We hired fifty men, at least. Many of them are dead."

"Do you agree with A'Uthma, Albin?" Kehl asked.

"About what, Kehl?" Albin said.

"These thieves and assassins," Kehl continued, "in our guild?"

"What about them?" Albin asked.

Kehl dropped to a knee, putting a hand out to steady himself against an elm tree.

"Are they loyal?" Kehl asked. "Can I trust them?"

Albin thought for a moment.

"Yeah, Kehl," Albin finally said, "I agree with A'Uthma. I think we can trust them."

Kehl nodded. His breathing slowed. His eyelids felt heavy.

"Good."

"Kehl, you all right?" Albin asked.

"I'm going to pass out, Albin," Kehl said. "Before I do, I need you and our guildsmen to do something."

"Sure, Kehl. What is it?" Albin asked.

"Kill the men we hired," Kehl muttered. He almost toppled over, but Albin caught him. Kehl crouched, and his servant crouched with him.

"Did you say kill them?" Albin asked.

"Yes," Kehl replied. His speech began to slow, slur a bit.

"I'll do whatever you ask me to do, boss," Albin said, "but can I ask why?"

"We can't trust them," Kehl said. "They will go and tell people ignorant militiamen from Waterton beat us. They'll go telling people about some bitch she-elf. We don't need the publicity right now."

"You got it boss," Albin said.

Albin gently laid Kehl down. Kehl's vision began to blur.

Can I trust Albin? he thought. *I suppose we will see.*

He saw Albin gather the guildsmen to him. Kehl watched as Albin spoke to them. It seemed commanding, harsh at moments. Then he saw his guildsmen nod. Some looked to him, but as they did, Albin barked at them, and they again paid attention to him. Then he saw the words mouthed on Albin's lips.

"Kill them all."

18

Erik walked through a small copse of white-barked ash trees to find his companions waiting. As soon as Balzarak saw him, the dwarf smiled and commanded the party to move out. As they hiked onward, the rain grew harder, and the air grew cooler. Erik felt goose pimples rise on his skin and his bones shake under his armor.

"This isn't the way we came, is it?" Wrothgard asked.

"No," Turk replied, shaking his head.

"Where are we, then?" Switch asked.

"I don't know," Turk said.

"Bloody great," Switch spat.

"We are still south of the ravine," Balzarak said, "but north and east of the main entrance to Orvencrest, that much I can tell."

"So, where do we go, General?" Wrothgard asked.

"We continue west," Balzarak replied. "We should eventually find the great ravine. If we follow it, we will eventually come across the land bridge we crossed before. At least, I hope."

The mountain steepened and, with the heavy rain, temporary rivers began to wash down the mountainside. A curtain of rain obscured any clear vision, and the ground became so saturated that Erik found himself walking on dirt that was only half solid.

"By An's beard!" Demik exclaimed as he took a step and sank knee-deep into the sodden earth.

"We must find shelter soon before we are washed away by the mountain," Balzarak said, as he gave Demik a hand to pull himself out.

"Or before we all die of a fever," Turk added.

"Agreed," Wrothgard replied, his teeth chattering and his hair and beard a matted mess of water and dirt, evidence that he had slipped and fallen several times already. "But where?"

"If we can find a cave," Balzarak said, "or even an overhang or thick copse of trees, that might suffice."

The rain hardened into a steady stream of water until all Erik could see in front of him was a sheet of gray. Rain washed down his face so that he could barely open his eyes, and every time he tried to breathe, water washed into his mouth, causing to him to constantly cough.

Through heavy downpour, squinted eyes, and now waning light, Erik saw something large and round and gray ahead.

"A rock," Erik said more to himself than anyone else. "Shelter."

Erik hurried on, passing everyone else and doing his best not to slip along the wet earth, until he reached what he had seen. He could hear his companions running after him, calling after him, but the rain drowned out their voices.

"Damn it," Erik muttered, "damn this mountain!"

"What is it?" Turk asked.

"I thought it was a boulder," Erik said, chin to his chest, "signifying at least a bit of shelter."

"By the gods," Wrothgard said.

"What the ..." Switch began to say, but his voice trailed off.

"It's a dead troll," Erik said, kicking the body.

His foot broke open the skin, already decaying. Gas hissed from the wound, and Erik gagged at the smell. Maggots spilled from the troll's body, wriggling violently in the cold rain. Erik stepped on them angrily, twisting his foot as he tried to kill them.

"It's been dead a while," Turk said.

Threhof knelt by the beast.

"Wolves," the dwarf said, stroking his wet beard.

"Huh," Switch said, standing behind Threhof, "those wounds look more like they were made from a bloody cougar."

Threhof shook his head.

"A cougar would have bitten the back of the neck," Threhof explained, "trying to break its neck. There wouldn't be all these other wounds."

Erik walked to the front of the troll, to see what Threhof was talking about, and indeed, bite and claw marks riddled the front of the beast, from its face to its feet. The wounds were black and no longer oozing blood. The troll's face looked bloated, as did its stomach, arms, and legs.

"This was done by a pack. Cougars are lone hunters. Besides," Threhof continued, "even though a large enough cougar could probably take down a troll, it normally wouldn't try."

"Why?" Erik asked.

"Too much of a fight. Too risky," Turk interjected. "With food so plentiful in these parts of the mountains, why risk life?"

"And this troll is uneaten," Threhof added, nodding at Turk's comments.

"Wouldn't a pack of wolves eat a troll?" Wrothgard asked.

"Aye, they would," Threhof replied, "but if wolves truly killed this troll—and I believe they did—they weren't normal wolves."

"What kind of wolf was it then?" Erik asked.

Threhof just looked to Balzarak and the rest of the dwarves with worry evident in his eyes.

"We need to find shelter," Balzarak said. "Now."

"What about these flaming wolves?" Switch asked.

"That is why we need to find shelter," Balzarak replied.

Erik gave the dead troll a shove on the shoulder with his boot and watched as the body began to slowly slide down the mountainside. Standing and watching, he felt his feet sinking into the mire, and as he set off again, it felt as if the mountain, clinging to his boots, was trying to hold him back. He walked only a few paces when he looked back, and over his shoulder he saw the troll disappear from sight, consumed by the mountain.

They hiked until the darkness created by the rainclouds made telling time difficult, eventually finding a small shelter formed by several large boulders that had fallen and stacked together in ages past. It didn't look to do much in the way of keeping out the rain, water escaping through small spaces where the rocks met, but inside, they found a small den. Dug into the side of the mountain by some long-gone animal, the floor of the den sat higher than the ground outside, so it was relatively dry and comfortable and warmer, even without a fire.

"We will be hard pressed to find any dry wood for a fire," Wrothgard said.

"It's warm enough in here for now," Turk said as they all piled into the small den, sitting practically shoulder to shoulder to fit and help each other keep warm.

"Are we going to fall asleep and find ourselves awakened by a pack of troll-hunting wolves wondering what we are doing in their home?" Switch asked.

"Nothing has lived here for a while," Demik replied.

Looking around, Erik agreed. He was no expert in the matter of animal dwellings but could see no evidence of recent occupancy. Weeds and creepers grew over the walls, and there were no old bones or scat like he assumed would be in most inhabited dens.

"I wonder why," Switch grumbled, "who's bothered about a few troll-hunting wolves wandering about."

Erik moved himself to the very back of the den, as small as it was. As he leaned his head back, listening as his companions talked and the rain outside continued to fall, his eyes began to close.

"I sorry."

Bofim's voice broke Erik's sleep, and when he opened his eyes, he saw that it was dark outside.

"What?" Erik asked.

"I sorry for your brother," Bofim said. He sat next to Erik.

Erik, at first, pursed his lips and felt his face grow hot, but then he calmed down.

"Thanks," Erik replied.

"Bim was like brother to me," Bofim said. Erik could see that the dwarf's eyes were red. "It very hard to lose both Mortin and Bim."

Suddenly, Erik realized that he had to accept what Turk said, that he wasn't the only one who had lost someone close. Tears began to fall from Bofim's eyes. Erik put a hand on the dwarf's shoulder.

"I am sorry too," Erik said in as comforting a tone as he could muster. Bofim just nodded.

"I wish I could say something like, don't worry, now they're in heaven being applauded as warriors," Erik said, "but right now, I just don't know."

Erik looked at Bofim and shrugged, and the dwarf looked back at him, as if he understood.

"Now more important have faith than ever before," Bofim said.

"I suppose," Erik replied, feeling his own tears welling up in his eyes. "It's just hard."

"I know," Bofim said. "We all know. We all lose someone at some point. Never easy. Pain is always there."

Erik just shook his head, holding back his tears.

"Be strong," Bofim said. "Have hope."

Erik wished he could be like the dwarves, to have hope in the face of despair. Although, the look on Bofim's face ... the looks on many of the dwarves' faces said their notion of hope at this moment was simple pretense.

After Bofim moved away to sit with the other dwarves, Erik removed as much of his armor as the small space would allow. He wouldn't hope for dry clothing by the morning, but perhaps it would be a little less wet. He watched as Turk continued to tend to Bryon.

"How is he?" Erik asked.

"Not good," Turk replied. "The cold and rain aren't helping. I am using all of my ability to try and stem fever and further infection. If we could have a fire, it might be better, but there is no chance of that tonight."

The darkness of night consumed the makeshift den, and silence fell on the company of men and soldiers, only to be broken by the sounds of Switch rifling through his haversack.

"Ah, that is good," Switch said in the darkness of night, smacking his lips.

"What is?" Wrothgard asked.

"The sailor's apple rum," Switch replied.

"Be easy with it," Turk said. "We can't have you drunk and hung-over in the morning."

"A man has to drink," Switch replied, "sitting next to naked dwarves and their little, hairy pricks."

"Nothing little over here." Dwain laughed.

Switch just groaned, and then they could hear him smack his lips.

"When you are done," Turk said, "let me have some. It might help Bryon, warm him up."

Switch never replied, and the cave fell into silence until Wrothgard spoke.

"We were attacked by a cave bear that you say should never have come that close to dwarvish settlements and then you spoke of wolves that aren't *normal*. What's this all about?"

"The cave bear," Threhof replied, "is an anomaly. It could be because of General Al'Banan's men if he has a large force camped in these mountains. It could have been driven by hunger. Who knows? But these wolves ..."

Threhof fell silent and, even though Erik couldn't see the dwarf's face in the darkness, he guessed he wore a look of worry.

"They are not so uncommon in the deepest parts of the mountains," Dwain said, picking up the explanation. "They are bigger than what you men have probably seen and far, far more intelligent. We will even train them and use them as guard dogs and hunting dogs. Even more so in the north, yes General?"

"Aye," Balzarak replied. "Gray wolves. They can be loyal, much more loyal than a dog, and their intelligence means they are even more adept fighters. But as their intelligence grows, so does their corruptibility."

"Corruptibility?" Wrothgard asked. "How can a wolf be corrupted?"

"Do you mean someone who is evil trains them to do evil things?" Erik asked.

"No," Balzarak replied. "They become evil, minions of the Shadow."

"How?" Wrothgard asked.

"More intelligence means a greater understanding of good and evil—right and wrong," Balzarak replied. "Those that have been corrupted, we call them winter wolves because of their white fur, but at certain times of the year, the more common gray wolves also have white fur. However, there is one thing that separates the winter wolves from the others—they have red eyes. That is how you tell them apart, that and the fact a winter wolf will go about terrorizing and killing for sport, aligning themselves with powerful evil forces. It could have been gray wolves that killed that troll, cleansing what they see as their lands of a pest, but more likely, it would have been winter wolves, scaring whatever they can. Whether they were gray wolves or winter wolves, they undoubtedly know we are here."

Dwain and Threhof seemed to argue for a little while in their own language, speaking rapidly so Erik couldn't understand most of what they said. But what he did understand was that there was a disagreement between the two as to whether or not the wolves that killed the mountain troll were just gray wolves protecting their territory, or actual winter wolves, simply killing for sport.

"They are uncommon here in the south," Beldar said, seemingly trying to help resolve the argument. "It is concerning, if the troll was truly killed by winter wolves."

"Very," Balzarak agreed. That was enough for silence to descend once more.

A crack of thunder rattled the small cave as Erik heard the sound of the rain falling heavier and faster. Erik sat there as the snores of his companions rose, each one in succession until they were a chorus of noise. The smell of sweat and the infected puss coming from Bryon's wound caused his nose to curl. He wanted to step outside, despite the rain, and breathe some fresh air. But then he caught a familiar smell, through the stink of bodies huddled together. Apple rum. Switch was there, staring at him. No. He was staring at Erik's haversack. The scroll.

Erik could see the thief's eyes, even in the darkness. He had positioned himself so that he pretended to sleep on his side, back to the cave's entrance and facing Erik. He feigned a snore. Erik saw his mouth move, heard the man lick his lips. He thought Erik was asleep.

Erik repositioned himself, acting as if it was normal movement during slumber. But he moved so that he could get to his dagger. He felt it buzz against its hip. It was ready. He touched the handle with his left hand. The thief would come slowly, quietly. Erik inched the blade from its sheath, exposing just a bit of the steel. He moved again, freeing his right arm that was partially stuck underneath Turk.

Erik blinked. The thief was closer. Was this the night? When one of them would die? He moved again.

"Erik, what are you doing?" Turk grumbled, half asleep.

"Sorry," Erik replied, "can't sleep."

"With you moving about," Turk said, his voice slurred with sleep, "neither can I."

"Sorry," Erik said again, and when he looked to the thief, the man's eyes were closed, and he had inched back closer to the wall. Turk had foiled his plan. He knew Erik was awake, and he would not try to take the scroll now. It would be too risky. Nonetheless, Erik didn't sleep.

19

Their leader stood at the entrance of the tunnel. His neck stretched, he sniffed the air, smelling their recent presence before he inspected the ground. He could see their footsteps. They would be easy to track. They always were. They always thought they were so clever. Fools.

She had called on him, she needed him, but it had been a long time. Many winters had passed since she beckoned him to her side, since he had killed for her, since he had feasted on the flesh of dwarves and men.

More of the pack arrived, sniffing and grunting, but keeping their distance from him. They knew their place. His mistress had called him, and, in turn, he had called his ... his followers. He once had many who would only think to do his bidding, but he knew they all wouldn't come. Distance separated many of them, time, and death.

He waited a little longer, and as the others got impatient, he sensed that no more would heed his call; there were enough. He turned his head and looked into the red eyes of each of the four. It was time. He sniffed the path again and then, neck stretched once more, he howled at the gray sky. With a long, steady pace, he set out toward their scent. He had no problem finding his way ... no problem following his kill. Their time had come again.

They traveled a day and a night, not stopping to rest nor eat as the scent became strong. The stink of their prey was heavy in this place, and he knew they were congregated together. Weak. Hiding away.

He saw it, boulders leaning together, forming a shelter, probably used by their scrawny cousins. They were there. He growled at his comrades—he would go first—they understood. Two would follow, and other two would wait, to ambush them when they ran, to take them one by one.

His red eyes peered through the fog. He saw them, their shadows, huddled together like sheep. So frail. So helpless. So insignificant. Fools. Fools for the taking.

20

The rain had stopped. There was a chill in the morning air despite the close proximity of everyone in the den. Looking outside, beyond the boulders stacked against each other, Erik could see a heavy haze hanging just off the ground, a thick fog that masked everything outside the small cave.

Erik looked about the small den. Everyone else was asleep, even Switch. An eerie, uncomfortable silence hung as thick as the fog outside. A wolf's howl—too close for comfort—snapped the uneasy quiet, and Erik decided he preferred the stillness. He patted his mail hauberk, lying next to him, and contemplated putting it back on.

Rather, he crouched low, unable to fully stand in the small den, strapping Ilken's Blade to his belt and moving towards the cave's entrance.

Erik heard two more howls, one more distant, perhaps a response to the first one. The first howl sounded like it was just outside, beyond the boulders that made up the den's entrance, and the hair on the back of Erik's neck stood up. Then he heard soft footsteps. Someone or something was out there, creeping through the thick fog.

Erik shook Turk's shoulder, the dwarf sleeping soundly.

"Who?" Turk said groggily, rolling over to see Erik crouching over him. "Erik, are you alright?"

"There's something outside," Erik said, keeping his eyes trained on the fog just outside the cave.

"I am sure there is," Turk replied with his typical smile. "It is the morning on a secluded mountainside."

"No," Erik said, "something more than just a mountain bird or rabbit. I heard two howls ... one was close by."

Turk sat up quickly. He told Demik and Nafer to get up, and as they began to stir, so did Switch and Wrothgard. While he waited, Erik peered into the gloom and saw a shape move in the mist of the mountain morning. It seemed to stop just outside the mouth of the den. As Erik gripped the handle of his sword and drew Ilken's Blade, the fog swirled, and a snout appeared in the entrance of the cave, followed by a wolf's head and body until, as the mist swirled about the beast's long, strong legs in swirling eddies, the animal stood completely inside the den.

Erik could hear the wolf sniffing. It didn't see him yet, but nonetheless, it crouched low, ready to pounce, and he heard the rumble of a growl. Its white fur, turned gray with the incessant rain, clung to its body, but the beast was still larger than any wolf Erik had ever seen; it was as big as a small horse. Then, as the beast turned its head, he saw them ... red eyes.

"Winter wolf!" Erik yelled. His call inside the den sounded as if it had been blown through a mighty trumpet.

Everyone in the den immediately got to their feet. Those who were already awake grabbed weapons, and those who had still been dozing were scrambling around, seeking to focus.

The wolf threw its head back and howled. The cry was deafening in the small space and was answered by more howls and yelps. Erik knew there was a message in that howl.

The wolf launched itself towards the nearest person—Beldar. The dwarf threw up an arm as the wolf's powerful jaws wrapped around his forearm. Beldar groaned loudly as dagger-like teeth dug into his flesh but still punched out, striking the wolf in the head. Dwain moved to help Beldar, but another winter wolf leapt through the fog and tackled him to the ground. Before the beast could bite down on the dwarf's throat, two arrows thudded into the creature's meaty shoulder. It yelped and jumped back.

The den became a mass of chaos in such a small space. The growls and howls of the wolves drowned out the shouting. Erik couldn't move, stuck towards the back of the den as Turk shoved Bryon behind them—too weak to fight—and the rest of the mercenaries crowded in front of him.

Erik smelled blood. Dwain. Threhof. Wrothgard. Gôdruk. Even Balzarak. They all suffered wounds at the teeth and claws of the wolves, the animals—as big as they were—adept at moving in small spaces.

"We have to move outside!" Wrothgard yelled, blood smearing his face and claw marks etched deep into his unarmored chest.

The wolves' attack seemed to intensify, and Erik watched as the first one, leaping out of the way of two more arrows loosed from Switch's bow, jumped against the den wall and behind most of the mercenaries, just in front of Erik. The second one isolated Beldar and Dwain, both already injured, driving them towards the front of the cave.

"They're trying to isolate us," Erik said. He had seen wolves, and even sheepdogs, do it back home. It made for an easier kill or round up.

The wolf in front of Erik paid no attention to him, rather nipping at Turk and Demik. Erik slashed Ilken's Blade across the beast's flank. Even Dwarf's Iron did little to wound the creature, but it turned its attention away from the dwarves and towards Erik.

He watched as both Beldar and Dwain disappeared into the thick fog that hung just at the entrance of the den and realized what the wolves wanted to do.

"They're trying to drive us outside!"

Like the dragon, Erik saw intelligence in the wolves' eyes, and as the one in front of him growled before turning away to leap at Threhof, he couldn't help thinking there was a malevolent mirth in that snarl. Both Threhof and Thormok tried defending themselves, but the wolf was too fast, and again, Erik saw the beast slowly leading them to the entrance of the den. Out from the fog, as Thormok stood at the entrance, a muzzle appeared, its sharp fangs clamping around the dwarf's ankle, and dragging him outside.

"There's more outside!" Wrothgard yelled.

"They're going to kill us, one by one," Erik said, "if we don't do something."

Both winter wolves ran outside. Balzarak yelled something in Dwarvish—a command to follow.

"Be ready," Turk said.

Erik was still shirtless and only had time to grab his shield. He left an unconscious Bryon behind and followed his companions outside. When he passed through the cave's entrance of fallen, leaning boulders, he looked to his left. Thormok lay there, face down in the mud created by the torrential rain. Balzarak and Gôdruk stood in front of him, both yelling and cursing. Threhof lay on the other side of the den, lying face up, blood covering his face. He cradled his left arm with his right. Five wolves surrounded Dwain and Beldar, the fur on their backs bristling as they growled and yelped.

They attacked. One wolf easily dodged Turk's attacks only to clamp down hard on the dwarf's leg. As it pulled Turk to the ground, it swiped a clawed foot across his chest, leaving four neat, red lines from shoulder to belt. At the same time, it jerked the dwarf's leg side to side. Any more, any harder, and his leg would surely break.

Erik rushed to the aid of his friend. He kicked the wolf hard in the ribs. He should have heard bone cracking under his boot. The beast should have run away, whimpering with its tail between its legs. The kick only made the wolf jerk harder. Turk cried out. Erik stabbed with Ilken's Blade. The sword barely pierced the tough hide, but it was enough to give the animal reason to drop the leg and turn his attention towards Erik.

The winter wolf snapped. Erik blocked the attack with his shield. Turk, limping and bleeding, got to his feet and attacked with his battle-axe with little effectiveness. The tip of Erik's sword nipped the wolf's snout, and he cut a forelimb when the beast swiped its claws at him. But when the wolf leapt at Erik, its front feet landed squarely on his shield, pushing him to the ground. As he felt the full force and weight of the wolf, he found it difficult to breathe as he ducked behind his shield when the wolf bit at his face. He felt scratches along his legs as the beast breathed down on him, baring teeth already stained with blood, teeth that belonged on a dragon, not a dog. Its breath was thick and putrid, and as it growled, Erik thought he heard a voice.

Turk and Nafer came running. Demik was there too, knocking the wolf off Erik, causing it to back away. Erik surveyed the mountain outside the cave. Wrothgard was alone, fending off a wolf, his back to the trees. Beldar and Dwain as well.

"Don't you see," Erik said, "they are trying to divide us. We need to come together, with our backs to the cave."

"You are right, Erik," Demik said.

Demik yelled, called to their companions in Dwarvish, telling them to gather in front of the den, next to Balzarak and Gôdruk who both still stood over the unconscious Thormok.

Wrothgard tried to push past the wolf in front of him, but any which way he ran, the beast cut him off. It was the same with Dwain and Beldar. The rest were able to gather together. Nafer grabbed

Threhof's collar and pulled him into the cave. Switch fired two more arrows at the beast that had cornered Wrothgard, but it was as if it didn't even feel the attack.

Erik jumped over the swiping claw of one wolf and rolled under the biting maw of another, coming up to his feet, dropping his shield, and grabbing his sword with both hands. The beast that held Wrothgard at bay growled at the soldier, its flank towards Erik. He lunged forward, hard, the steel biting deep into the wolf's hide. It yelped and jumped, and that was all the time Wrothgard needed to run past the beast. As the winter wolf yelped, the two that cornered Dwain and Beldar turned, giving them enough time to run to the mouth of the small cave.

Erik felt his dagger twitch, and the moment he touched it, he sensed another voice inside his head. At first, it consisted of growls and barks and yelps, and then they turned into a language, one Erik didn't understand, but he had heard it before. In the entrance hall of Orvencrest. There was more than one voice, and he couldn't help thinking he could hear the wolves communicating with one another. His dagger twitched again only harder.

They are coordinating an attack. They are focusing on you.

Erik felt a sharp pain at this ankle as his face smacked hard into the ground. He looked back through one eye as mud caked his face and saw a wolf's jaws clamped around his foot, dragging him back, away from the cave.

He heard the voices again, in that dark language. They were laughing wickedly. Then, another voice, a commanding voice, cut through the others. And he could understand.

The wolf let go of his foot, and Erik stood despite the pain. The wolves circled him as he stood. He could hear his companions yelling, even see them run to him through a sidelong glance, but every time they got close, two or three wolves would break from the circle and push them back.

You will be the first to pay for the mistress' pain. You will be the first to feel the wrath of the Shadow.

Erik scanned the wolves, growling and drooling, and focus returned to the one he knew was their leader. Erik sought to slow down his heart and compose his thoughts.

I don't fear the Shadow.

For a moment, the wolves stopped growling. They just stared at him. The voices in his head stopped.

How can you hear me?

That was the leader of the wolves. It snarled and crouched low; its jowls quivered with anger, revealing deadly fangs.

No matter. Today, you will learn to fear the Shadow ... and you will learn to fear me.

Even in the deepest, darkest places.

Before Erik had finished his response, his dagger, glowing an emerald green, appeared in his left hand.

"Erik, what are you doing?" yelled Wrothgard.

One of the wolves attacked. Erik sidestepped it only to feel another attack from behind. He turned, bringing his sword hard across the wolf's shoulder. His steel bit deep, but he felt yet another attack and turned again to see another wolf lunging at him. He jabbed, the tip of his blade punching a small hole in that wolf's chest. But as he struck at one wolf, another would attack. He would turn and attack only to turn again and have to dodge claws and teeth. He finally turned to face the second wolf that had entered the cave.

You will be the first to die.

In response, Erik thought he heard more laughter. The wolf he faced growled and stepped forward. Erik felt a tickle in his left hand, knew his dagger was ready, and lunged. The-wolf pushed back onto his hind legs, dodging the attack. That was what Erik wanted. He thrust forward with his dagger and, even though a small blade fell well short of the wolf's exposed chest, the dagger began to change, glowing a bright green.

The blade elongated, as did the handle, until Erik held a long spear with a broad blade of greenish metal. Even as the wolf seemed surprised and tried to back away, the spear grew and grew until the spear's tip punched through the animal's chest and through its shoulder blade and the beast growled and howled and cried, shaking violently, trying to free itself from the deadly shaft. As it did, Erik heard bone break and flesh rend.

When he retracted the weapon, he once again held a dagger in his hand, and the wolf lay on the ground, dead. Erik stood ready, feet planted firm for the next attack, the dagger by his side as his heart beat as slowly as if he was sleeping. Erik's companions stopped trying to come to his aid. He could see them, just standing and staring through a sidelong glance. They stopped yelling, and the rough, archaic voices of wolves stopped flowing through his mind as well.

Another wolf leapt at him, and Erik stepped away. This time, his dagger glowed a bright gold. The handle remained the same, but the blade went slack, as if the steel had melted, but then it grew into the barbed tongue of a whip, coiled on the ground next to Erik's foot. Erik twirled the whip around his head and snapped it, the crack thundering before it fell by his feet again like a loyal dog.

The winter wolf moved to attack again, but Erik struck with his whip. He had never used one before, and the type some farmers had for their animals were shorter. But he instinctively knew what to do, his dagger leading him through the motions. He snapped the whip again, this time at the wolf. The tongue of the whip wrapped around the wolf's legs, and Erik pulled the beast to him and onto its back. The animal whimpered at his feet, knowing it's stomach and neck were exposed, and it tried in vain to free its legs. Erik brought his sword down hard onto the wolf's neck, and its head rolled away from its body.

Erik heard the leader growl and snarl before rushing him. His minions didn't follow him. Erik held his dagger up, and it flashed a bright, silvery light, which subsided to reveal a glowing, wide shield. The winter wolf hit the shield with all its weight and force, but Erik felt naught but a minor jolt as the wolf bounced away.

Wretched creature.

Standing shaking its head, the leader's voice dripped with hatred, and Erik smiled as his dagger returned to its usual form.

Primitive creature, you sicken me. Your taste, your smell, your sight, everything about you makes me wretch.

Erik smiled again and shared his thoughts.

Sounds like the words of someone who knows they've been beaten.

You, who try to rule Háthgolthane as if it was yours to rule, and yet, you are but a speck in its history books. You have upset the mistress. You have aroused an ire you for which you will one day pay. You will pay for your treachery, and as the fires burn on the backs of your children, the last thing you will see is my teeth sinking into your neck.

"The dragon?" Erik said out loud. He shook his head. "She's dead."

He heard laughter.

You can't kill her, especially with fire.

Erik watched as the bodies of the two dead wolves caught fire—one a green fire while the other a golden fire—and burned away. The winter wolf leader seemed surprised by that, and Erik laughed.

Insolent creature. Your kind has no length to it. You are young, and you will die young. Do not forget me. One day, as you die, you will see again; know that the pain is just the beginning.

The winter wolf growled at Erik and, for a moment, Erik thought the beast might attack again, but he just howled. The other two remaining wolves howled back, and after the leader had turned and fled into the mountain forest, they followed.

Erik sighed and felt his shoulders hang low. He sheathed his golden-handled dagger. He felt a tickle at his side.

Thanks.

Erik picked up his shield. The hide that covered it hung in tatters. Some of the wood had split, and he could see that iron rivets along the edge of the shield had come loose.

"Can you imagine an army of those beasts?" Erik asked of no one in particular—perhaps the forest in front of him—and shook his head. He added, "Led by a dragon, nonetheless."

Erik heard footsteps. He turned to find Switch and Wrothgard running to him.

"What, by all the gods, was that?" Wrothgard asked, grabbing Erik's left arm and inspecting him.

Erik just shrugged. "A much appreciated gift."

"Are you all right?" Switch asked.

"I'm surprised you care," Erik said, looking at the thief coldly. He knew he didn't. Switch had to show concern. He eyed his dagger now with the same intent that he eyed Erik's haversack.

Erik looked down to see a bloody boot. It didn't feel all that bad. It certainly wasn't broken. Just a bad scratch, perhaps. The others parted as Erik neared them. He couldn't tell if they were scared, worried, angry. But then he saw Balzarak and Gôdruk.

Balzarak knelt next to Thormok, who still lay, face down, in the mud. Turk tapped the general on the shoulder and, when Balzarak looked up, made a motion as if to ask him to move. Balzarak complied and stepped away from Thormok. Turk then knelt beside the fallen dwarvish warrior, put his hands on the dwarf—one on his neck where blood continued to spray from a gaping wound and one on his shoulder—and bowed his head.

Erik walked up behind Turk. He could hear his dwarvish friend muttering in his native language. As Turk spoke, he began to glow. At first it was just a faint aura of golden-yellow, but as Turk continued to pray, it grew brighter and brighter. As the light around him grew, the rain above him seemed to part, flowing around him as if someone was holding a leafy branch over his head. Both dwarves had been soaked by the rain, but now, they were completely dry, as if not a single drop of rain had touched them.

Thormok had lain motionless for many long moments, but now his back moved, his sides, as if he took long, deep breaths. Turk's chanting grew louder, quicker. But then, he slowed. He looked tired. His breathing became more and more laborious. Erik didn't know why, but he felt compelled to touch Turk, to put his hands on Turk's shoulders as Turk had put his hands on Thormok. And so, against his own intuition, Erik did. He put his hands on Turk's shoulders, and immediately, he felt energy—like the shock one might feel when lightning strikes just a little too close, but only a thousand times more so—flow through his body. He had no idea what he was saying, but Turk's words overtook his mouth and he said them in unison with the dwarf. And then he felt it—pain. Pain stabbed his neck, his arms, his inner thighs, his face. A stabbing pain like a thousand daggers; like teeth, biting into his flesh.

Then, Erik felt weak, like the breath had been stolen from his body. He could barely stand as his legs wobbled and his knees buckled. And then he fell. His hands slid off Turk's shoulders as he collapsed, and the feeling was gone. The energy. The pain. The chant. It was all gone, and Erik found himself staring up at a gray sky as rain fell upon his face.

Erik looked to his side and saw Turk lying there, next to him, eyes closed.

"What was that?" Wrothgard asked.

Turk then sat up.

"I'm sorry, General," Turk said. "I couldn't save him. We couldn't save him."

Erik sat up as well, and as he did, he saw Balzarak drop to his knees and fall upon Thormok, his cousin. Thormok lay motionless. His back didn't rise with breath. Nothing. Balzarak cried and cried, and Thormok didn't move.

Turk stood. As he did, he turned and offered Erik his hand, who wobbled when he stood and found himself light-headed.

"What was that?" Erik asked.

"Healing," Turk said. The dwarf turned to follow the others—everyone but Balzarak and Gôdruk—back into the cave.

"Wait," Erik said. "Healing magic?"

"Not magic in the sense you are thinking," Turk replied, turning to face Erik.

"What other sense of magic is there?" Erik asked.

"Ever since I was a little boy, I knew I had this gift," Turk replied. "My father had fallen ill—a serious fever of some sort—and it was just he and I. He asked me to pray for him. He was afraid. He wasn't getting any better. So, I did, and as I did, the room lit up, and my father sat up, feeling as good as he ever had, as if he had never been sick."

"So, it's not magic?" Erik questioned.

"It's a gift," Turk replied, "from the Creator. The gift of healing. Every time I bandage a wound, every time I care for any of you when you are sick or wounded, I use this gift. I feel your pain, and I pray for An to take it away."

"So, what about Befel?" Erik asked.

"My gift has its boundaries," Turk said. "I cannot defy death. Truth be told, this was beyond my limits." Turk spread his hands as if to present Thormok to Erik. "But, I felt I had to ..."

Turk trailed off as he seemed to be stuck in his own thoughts.

"Drake then?" Erik asked. "Could you have healed the miner?"

Turk shook his head.

"No. Again, he was so broken," Turk replied. "And, there is an element of willingness that needs to be there as well. If the person is unwilling to be healed, I can do nothing."

"And Bryon's wound," Erik asked, "the dragon wound?"

"That is a difficult one, indeed," Turk replied. "Dragons use dark magic, and their poison is black. I am fighting against darkness when I try to heal him. The healers in Thorakest will be able to fully tend to your cousin."

Erik thought for a moment.

"What I felt, when I put my hands on you, is that what you felt?" Erik asked.

"Perhaps," Turk said. "I have no way of knowing what you felt. What I do know is, I believe you have the gift as well. My strength was waning, and when you touched me, it grew again. I thought, for a moment, I ... we would be able to save Thormok, but he was beyond saving. My gift, like I said, has its limits."

Erik didn't follow Turk into the cave. He looked at Balzarak and Gôdruk as they cried over their kin, and Befel's face came to mind. He hadn't forgotten what he looked like.

Now they know. Now they know how I feel.

Erik walked into the cave, only to meet Turk there, as if the dwarf had been waiting for him.

"You have a lot of hate in your heart right now," Turk said.

"What do you mean?" Erik asked, shaking his head.

"You have a vengeful heart," Turk reiterated. "It will bring you to ruin. One of the greatest qualities you have, Erik Eleodum, is your ability to follow your heart. But if your heart is leading you astray ..."

Turk shook his head, turned, and walked to Bryon near the back of the den. Dwain and Threhof were there, as was Wrothgard, all waiting for Turk to tend to them.

21

They sat under the large boulders that leaned against one another, forming the entrance to the den. The night was crisp and clear and, in this spot with its natural cracks between the large rocks, allowed for fire and ventilation.

"What was that?" Wrothgard asked. "What just happened?"

"Bloody wolves," Switch replied.

"No," Erik said. He looked at Switch, who looked angry, and then at Balzarak, who sat motionless in front of the fire. "Winter wolves."

Balzarak just slowly nodded.

"Damn the gods," Switch hissed.

"They are minions of the dragon," Erik said. "Minions of the Shadow."

"Aye," Turk said.

"Evil wolves serving a dragon and some evil deity?" Switch said, almost exasperatedly. "Really?"

"Yes," Erik said.

"What an excellent guess," Switch said.

"It's not a guess," Erik said. "They told me."

"Who?" Switch asked.

"The wolves," Erik replied.

"Oh, so now you speak with wolves?" Switch asked.

"I don't know," Erik said, and he couldn't help seeing Balzarak staring at him. "I heard voices in my head, and when I responded, it was the wolves."

"I just want to go home," Switch hissed. Then he looked at Turk. "And what about you?"

"What about me?" Turk asked.

"What are you? Some kind of wizard?"

"I'm no wizard," Turk replied.

"But you can supernaturally heal people?" Switch said. "Sounds like a wizard to me. I tell you what, I am getting really bloody tired of all these surprises. Evil wolves. Dragons. Magic daggers. Magic dwarves."

"It's a gift," Turk replied. His face was growing red. "I have a healing touch. It is why I am always the one to bandage your wounds. It is why your wounds heal faster than they should. It is why you don't have the scars you should have."

Everyone, dwarf and man, touched parts of their bodies—ribs, arms, legs, chests—where Turk had tended them.

"My gift is why Bryon isn't dead," Turk said.

"Did you know about this?" Switch asked Demik.

"Don't speak to me as if I am some simpleton fool, thief," Demik hissed. He looked ready to fight Switch. But then, the dwarf shook his head. "Yes, I knew ... partially. I, at least, had an idea of what he could do even though he never really told me. But what a truly blessed gift."

"Bloody blessed indeed," Switch sneered, standing. He walked towards the cave's entrance, sitting just outside, seemingly ignoring the wet ground.

"Where are you going?" Demik called after the thief, but Erik put a hand on the dwarf's shoulder.

"Let him go," Erik said. "Leave him be. It's not worth the fight."

"How is your arm, Threhof?" Erik asked.

"I doubt I'll ever be able to use it again," Threhof replied, cradling his arm close to his body. Turk had wrapped the arm in cloth and then tied a sling for the dwarf, it took some time, Turk being fatigued by his attempted healing of Thormok. Erik could tell Threhof was still in a lot of pain. He grimaced often and moved side to side, trying to find—in vain—a comfortable position in which to sit. It reminded Erik of Befel when he had first hurt his shoulder.

"You never know," Erik replied. "You seem to be in fairly good hands."

Turk smiled and nodded at the compliment.

"Do you see what this has caused?" Threhof asked Erik.

"What are you talking about?" Erik replied.

"This thing, desired by the Lord of the East. Look at the devastation. Mortin. Bim. Thormok." Threhof looked all around, and when his eyes met Erik's, he added, "your brother. All because of this scroll, this family heirloom."

"Threhof," Balzarak said, almost scolding him.

"No, General, I am sorry," Threhof said. His voice rose a little, although he was more pleading than arguing. "The pain this thing has caused, and we mean to just hand it over to the Lord of the East, a sworn enemy of the dwarvish people whether we want to admit it or not."

"Don't give us this speech as if it is because of the scroll that you left Thorakest, dwarf," Erik said, his voice cold and hard.

"What other reason is there?" Threhof asked, almost hurt by the question.

"Gold," Erik accused.

"The lost city is more than just gold," Threhof hissed, pointing an accusatory finger at Erik. "History. Honor for our people."

"And gold," Erik added.

"Stop this," Balzarak said. "Threhof, we are not taking the scroll. Erik will do as he was bidden to do, and we will keep our word. That is what honor is."

"Do not lecture me on honor," Threhof said, moving to the back of the cave away from everyone else. Erik could see he was favoring his arm, and that he was in a lot of pain. He hoped it was the pain that was making Threhof inconsolable.

"You needn't worry about dwarves trying to take the scroll from you, Erik," Balzarak said, chancing a quick glance at Switch, his back to the fire.

Erik nodded.

There was a long silence, men and dwarves passing water skins and wineskins, passing dried meat and dried fruit, simply welcoming the drying warmth of the fire.

"They called the dragon their mistress," Erik said, breaking the silence.

"Who?" Dwain asked.

"The wolves. The winter wolves," Erik replied. "They kept calling someone their *mistress,* and I finally figured they were speaking of the dragon."

"Dragons are evil. Winter wolves are evil. But working together," Dwain said, shaking his head.

"Is that so hard to imagine?" Balzarak said slowly. "Is it so hard to imagine that the Shadow has a hand in all this? That the Shadow rules over a dragon, who in turn rules over more minions of the Shadow, who might even rule over more minions of the Shadow?"

Dwain just stared at Balzarak.

"If the cursed ones are present," Balzarak said, "the dwomanni, we know the Shadow is present."

"Are they just simply evil dwarves?" Erik asked.

"Aye," Balzarak replied. "Evil and twisted and bent by the Shadow, turned against their own people, taught to love the darkness. That is what happened to Orvencrest—the Dwomanni. That is what is happening to the Southern Mountains."

"Are they allied with the Aztûkians as well?" Wrothgard asked. "Are they allied with Patûk Al'Banan?"

"No." Balzarak shook his head. "The dwomanni are xenophobes. They hate anything that isn't them and will only serve something that isn't dwomanni if it is powerful enough to bend them to their will. They despise men, but they hate us even more so."

"They were there, in Orvencrest," Erik said.

"Once, maybe," Dwain said, thinking Erik had asked a question.

"No, they were there," Erik said, "when we were there. They were serving the dragon."

"Well," Wrothgard said, "the dragon is dead, so what does that mean for the dwomanni?"

Erik knew differently but said nothing. Balzarak just shrugged.

"These are dark times," Dwain said. "Makes me glad I am nearer the end of my life than the beginning."

"Sometimes, ignorance seems easier, doesn't it?" Demik said to Erik in his native language.

Erik didn't answer for a while, and then nodded.

"I think at first, yes, ignorance is easier," Erik replied, also in Dwarvish. "I have often thought that, as a farmer, I knew none of this ... this world. My father probably wouldn't believe me if I told him everything I have seen. Everything I have experienced. But, given what I know now, would I still want to be that ignorant farmer, toiling away at the earth, unaware of all of this around me?"

"And," Demik said when Erik didn't answer his own question, "would you want to remain that ignorant farmer?"

"I would trade all this to have my brother back," Erik replied.

"But, despite that, no, I don't think I would want to be an ignorant farmer living out all of my days knowing nothing of the world around me."

"And why is that?" Demik asked.

"I have been tested," Erik replied, "my faith has been tested, beyond what I thought I could handle. I am plagued with dreams every night—dreams of my tortured family, dreams of the dead, dreams of darkness. I have lost my brother. My relationship with my cousin has almost turned deadly. And through all of that, my faith is stronger—mostly my faith in the Creator, but also my faith in myself, my faith in others. It is because of these trials that I have become the man I am. It is because of these experiences that I will be the man I will be, and, hopefully, that will be a good man."

"Those are wise words ... coming from a man," Demik said with a smile, and he and Erik shared a quiet laugh.

22

Erik sat outside the space where his companions had built a fire, relishing the chill in the air for a moment. He sat there, head back against the rock, eyes closed. He held the scroll case, the Lord of the East's treasure in his hands. As he decided to sit outside, and Switch decided to move farther back into the old den, he thought it prudent to take the treasure with him.

"Just one more day," he said, thinking of Befel.

He sat there for a while, watching the stars and the blackness of the mountain forest, listening to the wind pass through tall branches and sucking in the smell of wet pine needles. Then, the hair along his arms and the back of his neck rose. He knew something watched him, hidden in the darkness of the forest. Then he saw them. Those red eyes.

Are you going to try me again?

No reply ran through his head. It wasn't the leader. He wouldn't hang back in the darkness of the mountain night.

Then why are you here? To scare me? Foolish dog.

He heard growling at that, and the hair on his arms and on the back of his neck seemed to stand a little taller. He shook his head again.

Keep growling, I know you won't attack. You're just watching us. And you'll keep watching us until we reach Thorakest. And then you'll scamper back to your hidey hole somewhere just wishing and hoping and praying that one day you'll meet me again.

Erik smiled when he heard another growl. A pretend show of strength.

I hope we do meet again, someday, because that will be your last day.

Erik heard, in the far distance, a deep, long, angry howl that was unmistakably the leader's. And the eyes were gone.

"You should come inside," Turk said.

Erik hadn't seen his friend there.

"I will in a moment."

"Didn't you hear that howl?" the dwarf asked.

"I did." Erik nodded. "I'm not worried about it."

"Do not tempt the Shadow," Turk said. "It is a powerful force."

"I understand," Erik said. "I just really appreciate the chilled air and the stars."

"All right, Erik," Turk said, concern evident in his voice. "Just be careful ... and don't be too long."

Erik closed his eyes and could sense that Turk wasn't there anymore.

When Erik fell asleep, the dead were there, waiting for him. This time, two dead wolves waited for him too, one scarred and bent and broken and the other pink and red, its fur all burned away. They snarled and snapped as he moved past them, but he still sensed their animal instinct to accept him as their leader.

Erik wandered through the mountain forest for a while until he came to a wide field of waist high grass. The dead were always behind him, threatening, cursing, spitting, but there were no altercations, not like in the tunnel of Orvencrest, and then he saw it, the hill with the single willow tree.

"It's been a long while," the man sitting under the tree said as Erik sat down next to the man to await the rest of his dream.

When Erik awoke, he knew he had talked to the man about different things, new things, but he couldn't remember now. Something else had happened in that dream, but he couldn't grasp, as if it was being dragged back into his subconscious. It seemed important but remained elusive.

"Did you sleep out here?" Turk asked, coming up beside him.

"Yes," Erik said, standing and stretching. "I meant to come in last night, and I suppose I was just too tired."

"You must be more careful," Turk said.

"I wasn't worried." Erik shrugged.

"I suppose I knew you wouldn't be," Turk replied with a smile. "Be careful not to get overly confident, Erik."

"How is Threhof?" Erik asked, getting to his feet.

Turk shook his head. "Not good. He struck a fever last night. His arm is infected. I am doing what I can, but I am tired. It takes a lot out of me, you know."

"Then we must hurry back," Erik said, turning towards the den. "I am sure Thorakest has other healers, yes?"

Turk nodded. "Aye. And far better than me."

23

Patûk's men marched slowly. As they moved deeper into the mountains, the trees and creepers and bush becoming so thick, at one point, Patûk could no longer ride and had to dismount and lead his warhorse, Warrior.

More of his men joined them as Bu's scouts brought word that they were marching.

"How many do we number now?" Patûk asked Captain Bu, who rode next to him, astride a destrier the general had hand selected for his new officer of officers.

"We numbered six thousand when we broke camp," Bu replied, "and maybe two thousand more have joined us."

"How many men does Captain Kan have?" Patûk asked.

"Close to one thousand, my lord," Bu replied.

"So we have another four thousand away," the general said.

"Yes, my lord," Bu replied.

"And trolls?" Patûk asked.

"Two dozen, my lord," Bu answered, "but ..."

Bu stopped. General Patûk Al'Banan gave his captain a hard look.

"What is it, Captain?" Patûk Al'Banan asked. "It isn't wise to withhold information from me."

"Two of our trolls are gone," Bu replied.

"Is that so odd," Patûk replied, "that little more than wild animals driven more by their stomachs than anything else would leave?"

"They are well trained, my lord," Bu replied. "My scouts ... they found the remains of one of the trolls."

"The remains?" Patûk asked.

"Yes, my lord," Bu replied. "It hadn't been eaten, but it had been chewed upon. Disemboweled. Tortured even."

Patûk stopped Warrior, pulling back on his horse's reins so hard that the animal began to stamp backwards.

"Tortured?" momentarily, Patûk looked taken aback. "Something tortured a troll?"

"Yes, my lord."

"Antegants?" the general asked. "I know they roam—sparingly—these parts of the Southern Mountains."

"I don't think so, General," Bu replied. "I think antegants and trolls avoid each other. And if not, I don't think an antegant would chew upon a troll."

Bu sounded as confused as Patûk felt.

"Wolves? A cougar?" Patûk asked.

"I thought of those too, sir," Bu replied, "but they all avoid trolls. A pack of wolves, especially the ones that grow up in these woods, might be able to take down a troll, but at what cost?"

Patûk shook his head. He looked over his shoulder. He hadn't realized his whole column of men had stopped, waiting for him to move once again. He nudged Warrior's side, replacing his usual heel with an elbow, prompting the destrier to walk on.

Patûk Al'Banan wondered if something followed them. Perhaps dwarves. Agents of Golgolithul. Agents of Gol-Durathna even. But why would they bother with trolls. He didn't like this place. He didn't like these mountains or these forests. Patûk shuttered.

"There are men that live in these mountains," Patûk mumbled to himself, so softly, his captain could not hear him. He dipped his chin to his chest. "Certainly, they wouldn't bother to kill a troll, let alone torture it. But I wonder if they would know anything about this, of such a thing that could torture a troll."

Patûk Al'Banan lifted his head.

"Men live in these mountains, yes?" Patûk asked Bu, although he knew the answer.

"Yes, my lord," Bu replied.

"Do you know where, in these cursed mountains, they live?" the general asked.

"Yes, my lord."

"Would it be worthwhile to question one of these ..." Patûk thought for a moment, "mountain men what could have done such a thing to a mountain troll?"

"Yes, my lord, I do," Captain Bu replied. "These men—and their families—have lived in these mountains for generations. I do believe the only creatures that might know more about these mountains than them are the dwarves, my lord."

"Then lead us, Captain," General Patûk Al'Banan said. "Lead us to these mountain men. Lead us to the answers we seek. And, then, lead us to General Abashar so we might join forces."

24

Once they left the den, Erik found the company of dwarves and men moving at a pace much faster than he had expected. Balzarak and Gôdruk had buried Thormok and spent a little more than a moment praying over their fallen kin. And Threhof seemed more than willing to push the pace to get home to Thorakest.

"Do you recognize any of this?" Erik asked Turk.

The dwarf shook his head. "No. I don't think we are anywhere near the way we came."

"At least it isn't raining anymore," Erik said, and as he spoke, the sky darkened with gray clouds, and they let loose their contents on the mountains.

"You were saying," Turk said.

It must have been about midday when Erik suddenly stopped and looked, almost causing Wrothgard to run into him.

"Did you sense something? Wolves again?" Wrothgard asked, the tension in his face already obvious. Erik shook his head, still looking around.

"I recognize this area," Erik said.

"I don't think that's possible," Dwain said, moving up beside them. "We didn't come this way, so unless you have somehow been here before you met any dwarves, I think that would be quite impossible."

"No," Erik said, shaking his head, "I don't know why, but I recognize this place."

He looked around, taking in the trees, the rocks, the steepness of the mountain, the pattern of the moss and grass. He was certain he had never been here before, but it was somehow familiar. How could that be? Then he understood. He had spent all morning trying to remember his dream. It seemed so important when he woke and yet, until now, he couldn't remember a thing.

Now the images came to him, a cluster of dwellings near here, a dozen or so, each separated by a league. But what was so odd about these dwellings, these stone and thatch homes with little more than primitive stables and an outhouse besides a single room hut? That was it. In this land of dwarves, they were occupied by men. Men and their families.

"Do men live in these mountains?" Erik asked.

"Aye," Dwain replied. "Rarely, but a few. Some call them wild men, mountain men, homesteaders, whatever you want to call them. They are men who shun society and wish to brave the harsh life and many dangers of the uncharted parts of the Southern Mountains. Why do you ask?"

"There is a settlement of men near here," Erik said.

"Flaming sheep's guts," Switch cursed. "And how would you know that? Oh don't tell; you saw it in a dream?"

Erik nodded. "Aye."

"Oh, to the Shadow with you and your dreams."

And what about these men and their families? Besides the fact that they lived in the remotest parts of the Southern Mountains? Erik closed his eyes to concentrate. He tried to remember, to relive his dream. And then it came to him.

"That's it," he muttered.

"What, Erik?" Turk asked.

"They were attacked," Erik explained, "in my dream. Winter wolves ravaged each dwelling, one by one, eating man and woman and child. There are a little less than a dozen such dwellings near here, and each one will receive a visit from those monsters."

"If there truly are homes near here, may An have mercy on them," Balzarak prayed, touching an index finger and thumb to his forehead and then heart.

"We can have mercy on them," Erik said, "with the Creator's help, we can save them."

"What are you talking about?" Dwain asked.

"They are near here. I know this area. I spent ... it must have been hours here ... in my dream," Erik said. "It would take the rest of today but—"

"What are you talking about, Erik?" Wrothgard interrupted.

"You are speaking as if we truly know these mountain men dwell here," Beldar said. "You are a good man, a noble man, Erik, but you are asking us to trust a dream."

"We are tired," Balzarak said, "and we are injured. Look at Threhof. Look at your cousin."

"It would only take a day," Erik said. He found it hard to voice why this was so important to him. "What is another day? We go to each home and offer to take them with us, back to Thorakest. I am sure your king would welcome people forced from their homes by something so evil."

"Another day could spell the end for Threhof and Bryon," Balzarak said. "Turk?"

"It is true," Turk said with a nod of finality.

"We are talking about lives," Erik said. "We saw those beasts, eye to eye. Can you imagine what they would do to unsuspecting men? Their wives? Their children?"

"And for that, I am sad, but ..." Balzarak began to say, but Erik cut him off with a raised hand.

"You are sad, but not sad enough to do anything about it," Erik accused.

"You wish to sacrifice more for men," Threhof said. "More dwarvish blood for men, for the Lord of the East."

"What would you have us do?" Dwain replied with as much sternness in his voice as he could muster. "Would you have us traipse around these mountains, hoping to find wild men—wild men, let me emphasize. And when we do find these wild men—ones who have settled here because they wish to abandon society—you expect them to willingly go with us?"

Erik shrugged. "I don't know."

"Clearly not," Dwain replied.

"Cousin," Bryon said, "I don't feel well. In fact, I have never felt this badly. My whole body aches and burns."

"They will die," Erik said. "And we can help. Is it not enough if we even save one family?"

Why was he so convicted of this? Why was he so certain this was something they needed to do? How did he know these attacks were even truly going to happen? Because, in his dream, the old man from the hill spoke to him—even though the hill wasn't there, in the dream forest. It was just his voice, telling him ... no, asking him to help these families. Pleading with him, even. Because he saw the winter wolves, their muzzles red with the blood of innocents. They laughed at Erik and howled.

"Listen to me," Erik said. He walked to the front of the party, even in front of Balzarak, "I know we are tired, and I know we are burdened with injury and fever and loss of loved ones. But I know that those things, those ... those minions of the Shadow are following us. I saw and heard one last night and that was *not* a dream.

I know that they are going to take revenge for their losses on anything and anyone they can. I know that there are men out there—my people, whether they have shunned society or not—oblivious to the fact that they are going to lose their lives and families in the most horrific way possible if we do not do something. It will take a day. We lose only a day for just trying."

Erik heard grumbling, saw Threhof shaking his head as Beldar and Dwain spoke with him. Erik knew they wouldn't agree. And he didn't blame them. They were all tired and hurt and sick ... and so was he.

"I go with you," Bofim said. "I trust you, Erik. You lead. I follow."

Demik stepped forward.

"Me too," he said.

It was the last person, other than maybe Threhof, Erik ever expected to put his trust in him, but there Demik stood, ready to follow the young man.

"I didn't think, in my lifetime, I would ever hear myself say this about a man," Dwain said, "but I trust you as well, Erik. And yes, even if we save a single family, by An, even if we save a single person from those creatures, it is worth it. I am with you. Let's find these families and offer them safe passage, with us, to Thorakest."

"And what makes you think the guards of Thorakest will just welcome wild men into the city?" Threhof asked.

"As Erik suggested, can you imagine King Skella not welcoming those in need, especially those chased from their home by winter wolves, into his home?" Dwain replied.

Threhof simply shook his head.

Erik watched as Dwain looked to each one of the other dwarves.

"General," Dwain said to Balzarak, "you are my commander, and I will follow your orders, but you know this is right. I believe we all do."

Balzarak nodded slowly, reluctantly.

As soon as Balzarak relented, Erik turned to Wrothgard.

"And you, Wrothgard?" Erik asked. "What say you?"

"Truth be told, Erik," Wrothgard replied, "I am tired, and I am scared. I never thought I would say this, but I want nothing more than to be in a warm dwarvish city, lying in a warm dwarvish bed, waiting to eat some warm dwarvish soup, but you have proven a man of integrity and leadership, despite your years. I am astonished, really, at how much you have grown since I have known you. And, even though I have many years of experience over you, I could see myself following your lead, my friend. So, if you say this is a worthwhile cause ... if you say this is something worth postponing our comfort, possibly even giving our lives for, then I will follow you."

Erik smiled for the first time in a while. He gave Wrothgard a quick bow. The soldier's words made Erik's hair stand on end, to hear this man say something like that. Erik never thought the day would come when such a man would pledge allegiance to him.

"This doesn't mean, however," Wrothgard added, "that I am not still your teacher and privy to giving you switches when you screw up."

Erik bowed again, a smile still on his face. He looked about the mountain. He could hear Switch grumble and curse as they waited for Erik to find the way, and the thief's complaining only made Erik laugh silently. His mood was improving.

"This way," Erik finally said, pointing to a small hillock covered in berry bushes and shrouded by tall pines growing at the top of much larger hills on either side of it.

"You know the way, my friend," Balzarak said. "You lead us."

Erik led the company up the hillock, through the thick copses of berry bushes—some of which had little, pricking thorns that only made Switch complain more—and through a heavily forested area of the mountain. They had walked only for a while when Erik stopped. He stuck his nose in the air and sniffed. He could smell them, sense them. He knew they had been here, the winter wolves. He couldn't quite put his finger on it. Was it wet fur? Their putrid breath? Their feces? Or just the scent something so evil leaves behind.

"What is it?" Balzarak asked.

"They've been here," Erik replied.

"Men?" Threhof asked.

"No," Erik said. "The wolves. The winter wolves."

"Weapons," Balzarak muttered, and Erik could hear the subtle clatter of men and dwarves readying their weapons.

They slowly walked only a couple dozen more paces when Erik knelt and squinted. He saw something, just behind two white-barked pines.

"A home," Erik whispered. "Move slowly, quietly."

It must've taken them some time to travel the short distance from this point to the home, but winter wolves were stealthy and cunning. To simply walk, bumbling and loud to a home might spell disaster as they walked into an ambush.

The home was a simple thing, with a base made of uneven river rock, walls of warped wood made from several pine trees whose stumps still jutted from the ground, and a thatched roof that now smoldered and smoked and slowly burnt away. An opening lay gaping where a door once stood and smoke seeped from there, as well as the single window, shutterless, and the many holes in the thatching.

"They've been here all right," Switch spat. "This is flaming folly, Erik. We're bloody done. We've found the Lord of the East's trinket. We're a day away from safety."

Erik ignored Switch. He moved slowly towards the gaping doorway.

"He acts as if he didn't hear a word I said," Erik heard Switch say.

"He does that," was Bryon's reply.

"I'll go in first," Erik said to his companions. "Be ready."

He didn't wait for a response. Rather, he drew his sword, readied his tattered and broken shield, and walked slowly to the dark hole that was once a door of the home. He could smell fire and wet fur as he got closer. He could smell rotting food. He could smell blood and filth. The smells of death.

"Even in the deepest, darkest places," he whispered to himself as he passed the threshold of the home, stepping into smoke-filled darkness.

It took a moment for his eyes to adjust. Erik crouched low, shield in front, sword at the ready, just in case, in those few, tenuous heartbeats while he focused, there was something still in there that might attack him, but there wasn't.

A pile of old thatching from the roof smoldered in one corner of the home, red heat snaking its way along the straw and leaving behind black and gray ashes, threatening to spread the fire to the wooden walls. Scattered logs from underneath the home's kettle had apparently started the fire, with one wall already blackened. What little furniture there was in the home looked broken and scattered. And then Erik saw them.

Three beds lined one wall. Bodies lay in those beds. Erik's stomach knotted. He stepped forward. Just two steps. A blanket covered the larger bed—the adults, the parents, perhaps—and an arm dropped from under that blanket, all bloody and bruised and broken. It hung there, from its shoulder for a moment, just by a tendon and some skin, until the strain became too much and the arm—now unattached—fell to the floor.

Erik felt himself gag. He stepped back. He didn't know how many bodies, how many people lay in the home. He didn't care. They were dead. Chewed on. Eaten. The scenes at a mining camp, burned and destroyed many months ago, rushed back to haunt him, the vision of women and children, faces frozen in fear, raced through his mind. And now this.

Erik spat the last of the vomit from his mouth, and his stomach settled.

"May the Creator welcome you with open arms," Erik prayed as he stood just inside the doorway. "I am sorry, but I *will* avenge you. I promise."

He turned to walk out of the home, but he didn't feel good about his promise.

25

"Erik, are you alright?" Turk asked.

"I'm fine."

"What did you find?" Wrothgard asked.

Erik just shook his head.

"Can we go now?" Switch hissed.

"We must hurry to the next homestead," Erik said, "before the same thing happens to them."

"Flaming sheep guts," Switch cursed. "What makes you think we'll find anything different?"

Erik shrugged. "I don't know. We may not."

"We probably won't," Switch added, "so let's turn around and head back to Thorakest with that scroll and our treasure."

"Go," Erik said.

"What?" Switch asked, a weird look of confusion strewn across his face.

"Go," Erik repeated. "Go. Any of you. Go if you wish. I won't go back until I know every family has been checked on."

"Give me the scroll then, and I'll gladly go," Switch said, extending his hand.

Erik didn't respond. He just glared at the thief with a steely gaze.

"We are with you," Balzarak said. "You lead. We follow."

They walked perhaps a league, no more, when they came to another homestead, one that looked similar to the first. Only, this one was intact. They hid on a hillock, amongst a thick copse of pines, watching the home. Out front, in front of a closed door, stood a young man chopping wood. He looked to be about Erik's age.

Another man, a little younger than the first, walked around the corner of the house, a bundle of un-chopped wood in his arms. Just off to the side of the house sat a small garden where a boy went from plant to plant, picking berries and tomatoes and long, green squash and placing them in a basket.

"Shall we go down there?" Wrothgard asked.

"We'll just scare them," Erik said.

"The longer we wait, Erik, the more time we give those beasts," Turk said.

Erik looked at his dwarvish friend over his shoulder and nodded. He stood and stepped out in front of a tree. The boy in the vegetable garden dropped his basket and yelled something. The other two boys looked to Erik. The one chopping wood said something to the youngest one, who promptly ran inside. Then, he turned to face Erik, axe in hand. The other boy dropped his wood, save for a single piece, which he held as if it were a club. The door to the home opened again and an even older boy with a boar spear stepped out, followed by a large man—gray beard and dark hair—holding another axe.

They started calling to Erik, yelling and showing their weapons.

"Are they speaking Dwarvish?" Erik called back to his companions.

He could make out some of the words but couldn't string together a full sentence.

"Aye," Turk said, stepping out from their hiding as well. "At least, some form of it. Sheathe your sword, Erik."

Erik complied while Turk called to the men, who continued to approach them. He heard Turk speak of *peace* and *friend*. The mountain men seemed to ease a bit, but they still held their weapons ready.

"Follow me," Turk said as he strode up to the gray-bearded man.

Erik stood behind Turk as he spoke to the man. They seemed to understand one another, but the mountain man didn't look none too happy about what Turk was saying. Erik's understanding of Dwarvish was so new, and this dialect different enough, that he could only pick a few words and phrases here and there and eventually, just stopped trying to understand them altogether.

"I told him we have a whole company of men and dwarves waiting for us," Turk said to Erik. "That will, hopefully, prevent them from killing us. I explained what we found at the first homestead. I told him we would escort them to Thorakest and help them, whether they want to live there, or somewhere else. This man, Angthar, doesn't seem too worried."

"Tell him they should be," Erik said.

"I did," Turk replied. "He says that is a risk they take living here in the mountains."

"He clearly doesn't understand," Erik said.

Erik could see Angthar watching them as they spoke, and Erik could also see the man's face contort into a pensive, concerned look.

"Winter wolf," Erik said to Angthar. "Se understand? Winter wolf. Dey athen se."

Angthar stared at Erik as the young man told him in his best Dwarvish that the inhabitants of the last homestead had been eaten.

"They are evil," Erik said. "Minions of the Shadow. Tell him, Turk. Tell him."

Erik raised his voice. It wasn't from anger. He certainly wasn't upset with Turk, but he had hoped that Angthar would understand his sincerity through his voice and his tone since he probably couldn't understand a thing Erik said.

The boy holding the piece of wood as a club looked up at Angthar and took a step back, stepping behind the large man.

"Da," the boy said.

Angthar was the boy's father. Erik understood. And he saw an opportunity. If he could scare the man's children, maybe he could convince him the right choice was to leave.

Angthar looked down at the boy, a head and half shorter. The man reached around the boys shoulder, pressed the boy into his body and patted him gently.

"Waten her," Angthar said. He gathered his boys and ushered them into their home.

It was a long while, but finally, the door opened again. This time, Angthar exited the home with a woman wearing a dull blue dress slightly tattered at the bottom. Gray streaked the edges of her hair, but she still looked to be at least a dozen summers younger than Angthar. The boys were not with them. As she walked closer to Erik and Turk, she pulled a simple white shawl tightly around her shoulders.

"You speak Westernese?" the woman asked.

"Yes," Erik replied.

She smiled. "My husband recognized the language, as you spoke it to the master dwarf here. It has been many summers since I have spoken it." She smiled again. "I met my husband many summers ago when he visited Venton. That's in—"

"I know where it is," Erik said.

"Yes, well, if you speak Westernese, I assume you would," the woman said. "My name is Alga. We have seen some things lately.

Odd things. Deer dead, but not eaten. Mountain troll scat—we hardly ever see that. And we haven't seen any cougars. They stay away from our homestead, but they are common around here. And we see shadows, movement in the forest. It doesn't feel right."

"Because it isn't," Erik said. "Winter wolves—evil wolves—have been stalking these parts."

"You have seen my boys," Alga said. "I have another, younger one in the house, along with my two daughters. And I have another, my oldest child. She is married to a man, Lethgo, who lives in the next homestead. She has two little ones of her own."

"So, will you go with us?" Erik said. He could feel himself losing his patience. He was trying not to. "Time is short."

"I married Angthar and moved with him to his homestead, master soldier, because I was tired of the city, tired of people. This is our home, and we love it here. We have prayed that An protect us, and so far, he has," Alga explained. "But we also know, it is foolish to ignore An's promptings that sometimes come through other people. And as much as I love the seclusion of this forest and these mountains, I love my family more."

Alga looked up at Angthar. She nodded to him with a smile, wrapping her arms around one of his and drawing herself closer to him. He nodded back.

"We will go with you, granted you take those in the next homestead with you as well," Alga said.

"That is our plan," Erik said. "We mean to visit all of them."

"There are eleven in total that we know of, including ours," Alga said. "You have already been to one—may their souls find peace in An's presence."

Turk whistled, and the rest of the company emerged from the forest. They packed up what few possessions Angthar and Alga had and made their way to the next homestead.

Each homestead carried on in the same way, but each one, as the number of mountain men and their families grew, seemed quicker to relent. Two homesteads, that of Alga's daughter and the next one, half a league from hers, were small, younger families. But the rest were large with at least four children, some with grandparents and grandchildren, and one even with a weathered, old great grandmother and an infant baby.

One home had only a single inhabitant, an older man perhaps a few summers older than Erik's father. He refused to go with them. Erik pleaded with the man, as did Turk. Even Alga and her daughter pleaded with him. He simply refused to go, caring little for leaving his home despite warnings of the dangers that evil wolves, mountain trolls, and anything else posed him.

"That is the last homestead," Alga whispered to Erik, pointing beyond two wide-trunked, gray-barked pines. "Just through there and down in a valley. It is a smaller family, I think, with but two boys and a girl."

Erik nodded. He looked back at Wrothgard and Balzarak. The man and dwarf nodded back. Now, with some two score mountain refugees with them, stealth became less and less a reality for the company. So, most of them would hang back with the mountain families while Erik and Turk, and sometimes Alga, would go up to the homestead and speak with the master of the house, whom, in all but one instance, was the eldest man.

Erik, Turk, and Alga crept through heavy bush until they reached the two, large pines. The ground immediately sloped downwards and amidst a clearing, stood the last homestead, perhaps almost a hundred paces away. When the home came into view, Erik could hear a quick and sorrowful gasp from Alga.

"Look," Erik said to Turk.

A small company of men surrounded the home. A large, long-haired man knelt, hands tied behind his back, while another man, hair close-cropped and gray, stood before him, hands crossed behind his back, pulling his purple cloak away from his steel breastplate. Enough trees had been cleared from the homestead that a sun spilled into the clearing and Erik could see the insignia on the breastplate as clear as day.

"A striking cobra," Erik hissed.

The older man standing before the presumed owner of the homestead struck the mountain man hard with the back of his gauntleted hand. The mountain man rocked back before falling forward, straight onto his face. Another man—dark hair cut short as well—in a leather breastplate emerged from the home with an older woman, her hands also tied behind her back, her forehead bloody and bruised. He pushed her to the ground, next to the now unconscious man. Erik heard a muffled scream and turned to see Turk clasping a hand over Alga's mouth. The woman didn't struggle with the dwarf. Rather, she melted into his arms and sobbed, quietly.

"We are too late for them," Turk said.

"Please, no," Alga pleaded. "They are good people."

Erik's hand went to his sword handle. He felt a tickle at his hip as if his dagger was ready to come to his aid once again, as well.

"Erik," Turk muttered.

When Erik looked to the dwarf, Turk shook his head.

"We can't just leave them," Erik whispered.

"Think of the lives we have already saved," Turk said. "To attack these men—and we know they are well trained and well-armed—in our current state, with Threhof injured among others, would not only be folly for us, but it would also forfeit the lives of all these other people."

"Please." Alga cried. "Please. You can't just leave them."

"Think of your family," Erik said. "Think of all these families. I curse myself for not coming sooner, but all the cursing in the world will not save your family if we were to attack former Eastern Guardsmen."

They turned to leave when Erik faced the homestead one last time.

"May the Creator welcome you with open arms," Erik prayed. "May you find peace in the Creator's presence."

They slowly crept back to the company. When they reached the dwarves and men and mountain refugees, they found a man tied up and gagged, lying in front of Switch, who had that usual malicious smile on his face. The man had on a leather breastplate emblazoned with the cobra, coiled and ready to strike.

"Look what we bloody found," Switch said. Erik looked from the man to the thief and thought something about that smile seemed false, like it was pretense.

"One of Patûk's spies," Wrothgard added.

The spy looked up at them, seemingly staring at Switch more than anyone else. He groaned loudly against the cloth stuffed in his mouth, but Switch backhanded the man, and he shut up.

"We saw the rest of their force surrounding the last homestead," Erik said. Then he lowered his voice to a whisper, "This family is lost."

"What do we do with him?" Bryon asked.

"There will be others," Wrothgard said. "They might have even seen us."

Erik looked to Balzarak. The look the general gave him might have seemed indiscriminate to most, but Erik knew its meaning.

"Kill him."

The man shook his head with wide eyes. He tried speaking, looking to everyone with pleading eyes, and then finally staring at Switch. Erik couldn't help thinking there was recognition in those eyes. Switch winked, and the spy's eyes went narrow, and now, rather than fear, there was anger.

Wrothgard brought his sword down onto the back of the man's neck. It killed him instantly.

"It was too quick for this prick," Switch said, spitting on the man and kicking him, but again, there was something in the way Switch spoke that Erik didn't trust. As they readied to leave, he saw the thief staring off into the forest, in the direction of the homestead they couldn't save.

As Erik followed his gaze, he saw the quick shuddering of a branch but nothing else. When he looked at Switch, the thief gave him a wink and a nod and then clicked his tongue as he fell into line with the rest of the mercenaries and mountain men. Erik couldn't help shivering.

26

It took longer than expected to return to the trail that would hopefully lead them back to Thorakest. Switch and Wrothgard lagged behind, just in case any Golgolithulian soldiers or spies had seen them, while Nafer and Demik ran ahead. Their task was to make sure they didn't wandering into any Golgolithulian traps or have another encounter with the winter wolves. Then there were the mountain trolls and even antegants to consider.

"We have to camp," Wrothgard said as the sunlight began to wane over the trees.

"Just a little further," Erik said.

"Erik," Wrothgard replied sternly, grabbing the young man's arm, "we have a woman that has probably seen ninety summers, and a babe who hasn't seen one. We must stop. You wanted to save these people, and they are trusting us. Pushing them through the night in these mountains won't save them, and might kill some of them."

Erik thought for a moment. He looked back at the group of homesteaders. They looked hardy enough, but they also looked tired. It wasn't a physical fatigue that Erik saw, it was an emotional one. They had all left most of their belongings and their homes and put their lives in the hands of men and dwarves they didn't know.

"Trust?" Erik muttered, "Not in me."

"Yes, in you," Wrothgard replied. "These people ... they don't know you, and yet, look at them. Forty or more and they follow you. Not us. Not me. You. Do not break that trust. Do what is best for these people."

Erik thought only a moment longer before putting a hand up.

"We will camp here for the night."

"Blood and guts and flaming sheep piss," Switch cursed. "We could at least go another couple leagues."

"Not with an old woman and an infant, Wrothgard is right," Erik replied. He thought the thief was going to protest again. He looked as if he was about to, but he didn't. He just walked away, as he normally did, cursing as he disappeared for a while.

The night was uneasy. The children were anxious and scared, and the adults were apprehensive at best. To allow everyone to get close enough to the warmth, they had to build a half dozen fires, which spread the homesteaders out farther than Erik would have liked, so he and his companions took turns walking the perimeter of the encampment. They had tried finding the most open and flattest part of this mountain, but that proved the wettest, without trees to block the previous days' rains and without a slope to drain the water properly. Erik knew he would get no sleep that night, and for that, he was thankful.

As darkness descended, Erik realized the homesteaders were growing more restless about being out in the open, and the children were picking up on their parents' concerns. Erik went to speak to Alga, squatting down beside her next to the fire where she and her family sat. With her daughter's head on her lap, Alga ran her fingers through the child's hair as she leaned against her husband. She looked at Erik over her shoulder.

"We need a distraction. Would you tell the children, and their parents if they wish, to gather around me?" Erik asked. "Tell them I wish to tell them a story and maybe play them a song."

She nodded with a smile and called to the other homesteaders. Most complied, even the old great grandmother, and Erik went on to tell the children a story—through Alga as his translator—that his grandmother once told him, of a warrior and an elvish maiden and how the man had won the maiden's heart. Then he told the story he heard Rory tell, of a sailor who had sailed to a faraway, magical island and found a six legged horse that could fly and a lizard that laid golden eggs. Turk asked if he might tell a story and spoke of an ancient dwarvish knight who slew a dragon and saved a good king from certain death.

With both the children and their parents seeming enthralled in their stories, Erik retrieved his haversack and, digging through it for a moment, pulled out his simple, wooden flute. He sat, cross-legged, in front of the crowd of homesteaders and put the flute to his lips, thinking of his brother, and did not play yet.

Befel's face seemed so clear in his mind. He had been so afraid it would fade with time, but this night, it was clear, as if he stood there, in front of Erik whose heart began to race. He felt tears at the corners of his eyes, his cheeks and ears grow red and hot with anger. Then he wanted to laugh.

Now he saw the farm. He heard the mooing of cows and the clucking of chickens. He heard children laughing. He smelled fresh cut roses and orange blossoms. He felt the warmth of a hearth fire. He felt the soft touch of a woman's hand on his cheek. He felt the loving embrace of his mother. He smiled. He played.

Menacing gray clouds, full of thunder, rolled overhead. A boy looked out from his window, scared as the rain began to fall hard and fast. Lightning flashed through the sky, followed by the boom only a heartbeat later. His room shook. The whole world shook. And he cried. The earth couldn't drink all of the rainwater, and it spilled over the wooden planks of his home's porch. He cried some more. More lightning. More thunder. More rain. And the sky grew so dark.

Then, he found himself huddled next to a brother and two sisters. His mother and father hugged them, assured them they would be okay. The storm broke, and the rain subsided. The lightning and thunder faded away into the distance. And the parting cloud left the waning light of day.

The boy was now in his mother's lap, in her arms, holding him so tight. They were in a rocking chair. The room was dark. It was night outside. But he was safe. She rested her cheek atop his head and, as she held him and as they rocked back and forth, she sang to him. Her song was sweet and soft, and nothing in the world—no amount of rain, thunder, lightning, nothing—could harm the little boy in that place.

With only a single, magical flute, Erik did his best to convey this image through his music. When he opened his eyes, he saw men and women holding their children tightly. They didn't hold them out of fear, but they embraced them lovingly. They all went back to their campfires, and Erik could see the children quickly settled and fell asleep.

As he put his flute back in his haversack, he felt a gentle tap on his shoulder. He turned to see Alga and Angthar there, and the man bowed.

"We believe," Alga said.

Erik shook his head. "I don't catch your meaning."

"We believe," she repeated. "We believe An sent you. We thank you, and we thank An. You have delivered us."

"No yet," Erik said with a mirthless smile.

She patted his mailed chest, over his heart, her smile genuine.

"We believe," she repeated and returned to her fire with her husband.

27

Erik hadn't expected to fall asleep, but he did ... and his sleep was dreamless. That was probably why he awoke a little confused, especially when he saw that it was still nighttime. The multiple campfires were still burning, the crackle of blazing wood mixing with the other sounds of night in a mountain forest. He sat up and looked around. Everything else was still. Even one infant who had constantly cried and fussed was silent. Was he in one of his dreams? But he knew he wasn't.

He heard the rustling of a bush or a branch, hoping it was just a rabbit or a fox or night bird, but then he saw movement on the other side of the camp. He stood, fastening his belt and sword around his waist and tapping his golden-handled dagger. He didn't see Switch, so he dug in his haversack to retrieve the cased scroll, and he stuffed it under his belt. This was just the kind of opportunity Switch would want to steal the treasure from him.

Erik slowly walked to where he saw the movement. He peered past a tree and saw the shadow of something, someone, moving through the forest. He sighed, relieved it wasn't a winter wolf. But who could be traipsing through the forest at night, knowing what dangers lay nearby? A mountain man needing to relieve himself? Fool if that was the case.

Erik followed the shadow, slowly, relying on the training his mentors had given him. He felt as if he walked for a long time, even though he knew he hadn't. Then, the shadow disappeared.

Damn it,

He felt his heart quicken as he heard hushed voices. Silently, he moved toward where sound came from and found the shadow again, in between two large red-barked pines. Another shadow joined it. Erik crouched, listening intently. He didn't know what they were saying, but he recognized the language—Shengu.

Erik peered closer. He recognized one of the shadows. Was that …

"Switch," Erik mouthed in a whisper.

"What are you doing out here?"

The voice startled Erik, although it wasn't loud enough to alert anyone to their presence. He turned to see Threhof, his face barely visible in the intermittent moonlight of the canopied forest. He saw the pain on the dwarf's face, though, and the sweat that was heavy on his brow glistened in the dim light. He breathed heavy, but shallow.

"What are you doing?" Erik replied.

"I followed you," Threhof whispered.

"Why?" Erik asked.

"I saw you take the scroll," Threhof said.

"Have you been spying on me?" Erik asked.

"What are you about, Erik?" Threhof asked. "We trusted you."

"Wait ... what?" Erik asked, confused at first. "Do you think I mean to do something with it?"

"Do what is right," Threhof said. He raised his voice slightly.

Erik looked over his shoulder at the shadows. They had stopped talking. He thought the shadowy figures looked in his direction.

"Be quiet," Erik said in a whispering hiss.

"Do what is right," Threhof continued, "and hand it over to the dwarves."

"Shut up and get down," Erik said, squatting while he still watched the shadows. They drew weapons, one of them—the shadow that wasn't Switch—holding a long sword that glimmered in the dim moonlight.

"I will take it if I need to," Threhof said, his voice now fully raised.

"You're delirious," Erik said, "from fever."

"Erik." It was Switch's voice, and it sounded surprised.

The other shadowy figure said something in Shengu.

"Is this what you're doing?" Threhof yelled. "Selling us out to easterners?"

Threhof drew his sword. Switch stepped out from behind a tree, just a few paces away from Erik and Threhof. The other man, wearing a leather breastplate and holding his long sword, stood next to him.

"I should have known you would betray us," Threhof said, looking at Erik.

"He thinks you're a traitor." Switch laughed. It was the genuine, malicious laugh of the thief. "You're a fool, you little bearded prick."

Now Threhof turned his attention to the thief and lunged forward, but he was in no condition to fight. He was injured, his arm still slung to his body, and fevered.

"*Threhof, stop!*" Erik shouted, but it was too late.

Switch easily dodged the dwarf's attack and, with the flick of his wrist, a thin bladed knife thudded into Threhof's thick neck. That, alone, wouldn't have stopped the dwarf, but the other man, capitalizing on the dwarf's surprise, plunged his long sword hilt deep into his belly and up into his heart. The dwarf let out a deep gasp and fell back, dead, when the swordsman retrieved his weapon.

"You're a dirty bastard," Erik hissed.

"No denying that," Switch said with a smile. "Now hand it over."

"No," Erik said. "You'll have to kill me."

"Suit yourself," Switch said with a shrug of his shoulders.

He flicked his wrist, and Erik moved to the side as another thin bladed knife whizzed past his face. The other man came at him, and Erik easily blocked his attack, only to feel yet another thin knife digging into his shoulder. It wasn't a grievous wound, but it surprised him enough to give the other man time. He drove his shoulder into Erik's stomach, sending him back. Erik dropped his sword. They wrestled for a moment, Erik trying to keep his eyes trained on the thief. Erik finally kneed the man in his crotch, and he rolled away with a groan. Erik stood, retrieving Ilken's Blade.

He had seen Switch in battle but wasn't prepared for an actual fight with the thief. He was much more adept than Erik thought he would be, attacking with two blades, slashing precisely and quickly. Erik felt a cut on his arm, along his chest, and along his abdomen; he immediately regretted not taking the time to don his armor. He pushed back equally as strong and had Switch on his heels when the thief's accomplice tackled Erik from behind. Falling on his face, Erik felt a hand digging underneath him, felt that hand grip the scroll case and pull hard.

Erik tried to get up, but the man on top of him pushed his face into the dirt. Erik couldn't breathe, and for a moment, he panicked before he felt the tickle. He worked his hand and arm free enough to grab the dagger and swung up with a backwards stab. He caught flesh, and the hands on the back of his head released. He rolled over to his back, seeing the man on top of him grasping at his thigh, and he plunged the golden-handled dagger into the man's belly, the steel easily passing through the leather armor, which—as Erik could fully see it now—had the symbol of a coiled cobra ready to strike emblazoned on it.

Erik stood, pushing the dead man off him and lifting his sword once again. Switch stared at the scroll case, holding it up to the moonlight.

"Here's to my future," he whispered.

He was so engrossed in the Lord of the East's treasure, he didn't even seem to notice Erik slowly approach him, still staring at the case. Erik lifted his sword high, and Switch turned, just as Erik brought the blade down.

Instinctively, Switch lifted an arm to block the blow, screamed as Ilken's Blade easily passed through bone, severing Switch's left hand just above the wrist. The stump sprayed blood across Erik's face as Switch clutched the scroll case close to his body with his other hand and turned to run.

Erik gave chase and was able to briefly follow the thief, but the nimble Switch disappeared. Erik wanted to keep following him, but even a one-handed Switch would be dangerous, especially in the dead of night. Erik felt sick. The scroll was gone. Threhof was dead. They had failed in their mission ... and Befel's death was all for naught.

28

Patûk Al'Banan's lip curled. Pavin Abashar had let his hair grow long, and it looked ridiculous, gray and thinning, he had tied it back in a knot. He was a ghost of the soldier he once was, not that he was ever much of a soldier. He held that haughty look he always had, a tilt of his head with a feigned air of confidence that looked more like a smirk.

The two antegants standing to either side of him—still half a head taller than him even astride his warhorse—were off-putting as well. Mountain trolls were bad enough, but these were hideous. One of the creatures had hooves where feet should have been, the other had splotches of gray scales all over its chest and arms. And both had a single, gnarled horn above their one, grotesque eye. These were not the antegants that often dwelled amongst men.

"General Al'Banan," Pavin called, his voice much louder than it needed to be in the wide-open meadow that led into the mountain forest, "so good to see you after so many years."

"Has it been so long?" Patûk replied.

"Long enough," Pavin said. "I see you have finally come to your senses."

"How so?" Patûk asked.

"You wish to join forces," Pavin said with a smile. "You wish to align yourself with me. It's about time."

"You misunderstand," Patûk replied. "I come to accept your willingness to serve me."

The smile on Pavin's face disappeared. Then he laughed.

"Truly?" he said with the pretense of bewilderment. "You are not the commander of the Eastern Guard anymore, Patûk. You cannot simply command things and make them so."

"I outnumber you," Patûk said, "and am more powerful than you. It would be folly to resist."

"We can work together," Pavin said, "and together we can thwart the usurper and work to his overthrow."

"I am not so interested in Golgolithul anymore," Patûk said. "And I have no interest in working side by side with you."

"You say you outnumber me," Pavin said. "My scouts tell me you number thirteen thousand, but four of that is away. I number twenty thousand. And I haven't spread myself thin like you."

"You lie," Patûk said.

"Do I?" Pavin replied. The look on his face said he was telling the truth, but Pavin was an adept liar. "You see, your harsh tactics and cruelty and regimented ways are your undoing. Men don't want to serve a tyrant. It's why they flee the east. It's why they flee your ranks."

"Twenty thousand of your whelps aren't worth a thousand of mine," Patûk replied.

"Just like old Patûk," Pavin said with a laugh. "And what will you do, with your men and my men, if not overthrow the Lord of the East?"

Patûk smiled. It was an idea that consumed his thoughts, his dreams.

"Rule my own kingdom," Patûk said.

To that, Pavin broke out in a fit of laughter. Several of his officers and advisors, also horsed and standing by behind General Abashar, joined in the laughter.

"And which kingdom will you rule?" Pavin asked. "Are you going to build your own castle? How will you populate your country? I don't see any female soldiers."

"I will conquer Hámon," Patûk said.

"Now I have heard everything." Pavin laughed. "Surely you jest."

"Will you join me or not?" Patûk replied.

"But you don't wish me to join you," Pavin said. "You want me to serve you. No. I don't think so. I think I will kill you, and then your men will serve me."

Patûk felt his face grow hot. He had expected as much from Pavin. He was always a fool. But he didn't want to kill the man. He had value, and as foolish as he was, he was a decent leader, and if he did command twenty thousand men, they would serve Patûk well.

The two antegants that stood next to General Pavin moved forward, one carrying a large club studded with iron spikes and the other carrying a double-headed axe that most men would barely be able to carry with both hands.

"The trolls?" Captain Bu asked.

"No," Patûk replied. "We need to save our resources. In fact, it pains me, but I must kill these two creatures."

"You, General?" Bu asked.

"Yes, Captain," Patûk replied. "Be ready, just in case, but I must kill these creatures myself, as a show of strength. Do not worry, Captain Bu, I have survived much worse odds."

Patûk heeled Warrior, his great warhorse, and the horse took several steps forward. He heard the antegants laugh. They looked to one another, said something in their own language, and stared back at Patûk.

Patûk drove his heels into the sides of Warrior, and the warhorse lunged forward at his command. The antegant holding a club swung its weapon at the general, but he easily ducked the attack. Horse and rider knew each other so well, and Warrior moved without him having to direct the animal, turning so that Patûk could jab the point of his sword into the side of the antegant's neck. Blood immediately spurted from the wound, spraying the general across the face. As the antegant turned, the general brought his blade across the front of its throat and more blood gushed as it dropped its club and clutched at its neck. Patûk took the opportunity to jam his blade into the singular eye sitting above the humanoid's wide nose.

Now the other antegant attacked, swinging its double-headed axe wildly about its head. Warrior backed up, so that the wide blades missed, then reared up on its hind legs, kicking out with its front hooves. Both iron-shod hooves struck the antegant in the face. It staggered backwards, groaning, and as it took its attention away from the general, he attacked, slashing his sword across the antegant's face and then jamming the blade, hilt deep, into its throat.

Pavin's men were silent. Patûk rode up next to the other general, sheathing his sword so that he looked less threatening, although from the looks on Pavin's officers' faces, he knew the show of peace did little good.

"I don't want to kill you, Pavin Abashar," Patûk whispered, "but I will if I need to. I need able-bodied officers. Serve me and share in my dream of creating a new kingdom, one that remembers the Golgolithul of old. Join me, and you will be well rewarded."

"It is folly," Pavin replied, also in a whisper.

"You don't understand," Patûk said. "I will have, soon, a weapon ... a *most* powerful weapon."

"What powerful weapon?" Pavin asked.

"Bu!" Patûk called. His captain rode up next to him. "Do we have word? Has our spy recovered the weapon?"

"Yes, my lord," Bu lied. They expected to get it but did not yet have it.

"My sources tell me this weapon is mighty, powerful," Patûk said.

"A trebuchet is powerful," Pavin said, "and both Hámon and Golgolithul have many of those."

"It is worth a thousand trebuchets," Patûk said.

Pavin seemed to think for a while.

"You seem very sure of yourself," Pavin said. "But it could all be an act."

"Golgolithul is actively trying to create a vassal in Hámon," Patûk replied. "One of my officers, Kan, is in Hámon now. They are a fragmented, feudal kingdom. Between your men and mine, we number almost as many men in their combined armies. There are several more defectors like us out there. If we can convince them to join us, we will outnumber the soldiers of Hámon. With our men, and this weapon, the fight will be short."

"You cannot be sure of any of that," Pavin said, but his resolve was weakening.

"Their nobles are not stupid," Patûk replied. "If we offer them the opportunity to keep their titles and their lands, they will relent."

"And what is this weapon?" Pavin asked.

Patûk didn't know, but he wouldn't let Pavin Abashar know that. It was powerful, world changing. That was what his spy in the Lord of the East's courts said. The usurper had convinced mercenaries that they were seeking a lost dwarvish city for some family heirloom. But, no, it was a weapon he was searching for. And then his other spy, his mercenary infiltrator, had sent word—a letter—that they had found what the Lord of the East wanted. He had given up hope on his spy, the thief from Goldum. He figured he had either died or decided he would keep the dwarvish treasure for himself. Either way, Patûk didn't really care. He knew it was a long shot that mercenaries heeding the call of the usurper would find some hidden, fabled dwarvish city. But apparently they had. And with the help of dwarves, nonetheless.

Patûk felt gooseflesh on his arms. A powerful weapon. And then he remembered the last thing the letter had said about the weapon. It had been protected ... a Dragon. Patûk shook his head. Superstitious foolishness, no doubt. A fabled creature from the past, one that probably never actually lived. And then the general remembered the earthquake he had felt, the unusually hot wind. He shuddered.

"All in due time, General Abashar," Patûk said with a smile. "I will reveal this weapon all in due time."

"And you will be King Patûk Al'Banan?" Pavin asked.

The words sent more goose pimples along the general's arms.

"Yes," he replied, "and you will be Duke Pavin Abashar. We will offer our officers and our loyal men titles and lands. Think of your men, General. Think of your future. Think of the whole reason we left the Eastern Empire. And if we control Hámon, we can stop Golgolithul's expansion west. We can control the west, and with that, we can reclaim what is ours in the east."

Pavin Abashar looked down at the two dead antegants and then up at the sky as if the heavens would give him inspiration. Then he slowly nodded and turned his eyes back to Patûk.

"All right, General Al'Banan," he said, "We will follow you, but at the first sign of deceit—"

"I am many things, Pavin," Patûk interrupted, "brutal, cruel, hard ... but one thing I am not is deceitful. I always keep my word."

"Then I must accept your word," Pavin said. "Lead the way, General."

Patûk rode back to his men with Captain Bu.

"Keep an eye on him," Patûk said.

"Yes, my lord," Bu replied.

"Over time, we will gain the loyalty of his men," Patûk said. "This much I know. As that happens, he may begin to rethink his loyalties."

"And if he does?" Bu asked.

Patûk smiled, looking almost fatherly for a moment.

"You know what to do," he said, and the look was gone.

Patûk watched as Pavin explained what he was doing to his men, and they seemed excited. A good sign. He heard voices behind him and saw Ban Chu, Bu's corporal, speaking hurriedly to the captain. Bu now turned to the general.

"Sir," Bu said, whispering.

"Why are you whispering, Captain?"

"He has it," Bu replied in the same quiet tones.

"What are you talking about?" Patûk asked.

"The treasure," Bu said, "the thing the usurper wanted. Our spy, the thief, has it."

"Truly?" Patûk said, trying to quell the excitement in his voice.

"He is close," Bu explained. "Apparently, the mercenaries he traveled with are not even a half-day's ride away. Shall I have him brought here?"

"No," Patûk said. "We will meet him away from Pavin. I want to find out what this thing is, first. Bring Ban Chu with you, and Li."

"Li, my lord?" Bu asked.

"Yes," Patûk replied. "He seems like a worldly man. Supposedly this treasure is some scroll. Who knows what language it is in, what symbols it has. I would think Li might know how to decipher such things if anyone does."

"How is a rolled piece of parchment a weapon, my lord?" Bu asked.

"I don't know," Patûk said with a shrug, "but I trust my spies in Golgolithul. One of them is a member of the Soldiers of the Eye."

"That is why you attacked The Messenger," Bu said. Patûk could sense the smile on his captain's face. "So, you could kill some of them, regardless of the cost in our men's lives, and have your spy infiltrate their ranks."

"You are learning, Bu," Patûk said, looking at his captain. Indeed, the man was smiling. "What seemed like folly to most, even to the

Black Mage, was a well-executed plan, one that was set in motion a long time ago."

"I still don't see how a piece of parchment could be used as a weapon," Bu said.

"Perhaps it is directions on how to build a weapon," Patûk said, as much to himself as to Bu, "or maybe it is a map to locate a weapon. Whatever it is, Bu, it is in our possession now, and our purpose is at hand. Revenge will be mine."

29

"Continue to lead the homesteaders," Erik told Wrothgard early the next morning. "Dwain recognizes where we are now."

The dwarf nodded in agreement.

"What are you doing?" Wrothgard said. "This is folly. If Switch is working for Patûk, there is no way we will ever see that scroll case again. It is gone."

"Switch couldn't have gone far," Erik said, although he didn't completely believe himself. "If we return to the civilized world without the Lord of the East's treasure, we might as well kill ourselves."

"I cannot believe it of him," Wrothgard said, shaking his head.

"I can," Bryon said through labored breaths. He grew paler every day. "He's a bastard. I even caught him stealing from the dwarves in Thorakest when he knew it would be the death of us all."

"Balzarak and Turk will go with me," Erik said. "Wrothgard, I suggest you take charge along with Dwain."

Both man and dwarf nodded in agreement.

"I'm going also," Bryon said, trying to straighten his back despite the severe grimace of pain on his face.

"Not a chance," Erik replied.

"You can't tell me what to do, little cousin," Bryon said.

"This time, I can," Erik replied. "Look at you. You are barely clinging to life right now, Bryon. You need to get help in Thorakest. You'll do us no good tracking Switch. You will slow us down and be weak if it comes to a fight."

Bryon looked like he wanted to protest, but he didn't. He simply opened and then closed his mouth.

After Threhof had been buried—the other dwarves simply accepted what Erik said about Switch killing him when Threhof was trying to help Erik—it was time for Erik to leave, to follow the thief into the forest with Balzarak and Turk. As Erik turned to move away, Bryon put a hand on his shoulder.

"Take my sword," his cousin said, handing Erik his sheathed blade.

Erik took it, hugged his cousin—something he hadn't done in a long time—and left.

It took Turk only a small amount of time, in the early morning, to find Switch's trail. Erik saw the blood, and the severed hand. They took a moment to inspect the other man that had been with Switch.

"A spy," Balzarak said. "You can tell by his armor and his boots."

They followed the trail for half a day, finding the places where Turk said the thief had rested for a time. Then they found discarded cloth, soaked still in blood, and the remnants of a fire.

"He cauterized the wound," Erik said, remembering the way in which Bo the gypsy had sealed the wound on Befel's shoulder.

Then, at about noon, Turk held a hand up. He pointed to his ears and his eyes, and then pointed beyond several trees.

"There's a small clearing," he whispered in Dwarvish. "I hear voices."

They inched closer, and Erik could hear the voices as well.

"Shengu?" he whispered.

Turk nodded.

Erik saw Switch. He held the stump of his left hand close to his chest. He looked worn and tired, sweating profusely. He saw two other men wearing leather breastplates—spies—and he saw another two men wearing steel breastplates. They were both older, one with a glaring scar running down his face and through an eye. The other, he remembered this man from the last homestead they couldn't save; he had a hard jawline, close cropped, gray hair, and looked powerful and mean.

"Patûk Al'Banan," Erik whispered.

Balzarak nodded this time.

Then, Erik saw him, another man he recognized. He wore loose fitting robes, had a baldhead, and a close-cropped, black beard. His lazy eyes stared at something the group of men had spread out on a tree stump.

Cho's seneschal. What is he doing here?

"What are they looking at?" Turk asked.

Erik chanced to lean forward. He saw a scroll case lying on the ground, next to the tree stump. The cork that sealed it was gone. His eyes widened with a mixture of shock and horror. They had opened it.

"The scroll," Erik said, "the treasure for the Lord of the East. They opened it."

Li pointed to something on the scroll, then looked at Patûk Al'Banan. They seemed to argue, only briefly, as the other men just stood and watched. Switch swayed back and forth, and sweat poured down his face.

Patûk Al'Banan sucked in a deep breath and then began to speak, but it wasn't Shengu. Erik didn't know what language it was, but he recognized it. It was the language his brother had spoken in the tunnels of Orvencrest. It was the language that had consumed him and taken control of him. It was the language that he heard when the dragon spoke in his mind as if she had spoken Westernese. It was the also the language of the winter wolves, an evil language that belonged to the Shadow.

As Patûk Al'Banan spoke, reading from the scroll, the sunlight in the forest clearing seemed to dim. Erik wasn't the only one who noticed it as both the dwarves and the other men started looking around. Erik felt a tremble in the earth below his feet. He heard a distant rumble, like thunder, even though there were no clouds to be seen. His stomach knotted. He knew what the sound really was.

Erik's thoughts went to the dragon, and he heard her voice in his head. She laughed as he felt heat; her presence. She wasn't dead. Not at all. She was barely hurt, and she was coming for them. These fools had no idea what they were doing.

Erik smelled the rot of the dead. He heard them, amongst the trees, their feet shuffling, smelled their rancid breath as they laughed.

"He has to stop," Erik said. "He doesn't know what he is doing."

"What?" Turk asked.

"This is no family heirloom, some scroll of lineage," Erik said. "I don't know how, but it is tied to the dragon. Somehow the scroll is calling to her; she will rise again and wreak havoc on the world if they finish reading. We have to stop him."

Erik drew Ilken's Blade and his cousin's elvish sword, holding it in his left hand.

"Erik, wait," Balzarak said.

"There's no time," Erik said, and he jumped out in front of the tree behind which they hid. "Stop!"

Patûk Al'Banan stopped reading and turned to face Erik. The

sunlight returned, the unnatural heat dissipated, the stink of the dead disappeared, and the earth stopped rumbling. The general said something Erik didn't understand. He would have to learn Shengu.

"By the bloody Shadow," Switch said, although his words were labored and somewhat slurred.

"*Do not read that*!" Erik warned, pointing the elvish blade at the scroll. It hissed as he moved it.

"Erik of Waterton," Cho's seneschal said. The others looked at the man, and he returned that lazy-eyed response. "Truth be told, I didn't expect you to live a week after you left Aga Min. How interesting?"

The seneschal steepled his fingers in front of his face.

"You left Aga Min to join traitors," Erik said.

"No, my boy," the seneschal said. "Aga Min is gone, destroyed like Aga Kona. I chose a path that offered life."

"Enough," Patûk Al'Banan said, speaking perfect Westernese. "Thief, I thought you said you were alone."

"I thought I was," Switch said with a shrug.

Patûk Al'Banan growled and drew his sword.

"Kill him," he said.

The dwarves joined Erik. The two men wearing leather breastplates came at them, and Turk and Balzarak engaged them. Erik made for Patûk Al'Banan, but the older soldier stood in his way, his own sword drawn. Erik didn't really know how to fight with two swords, Wrothgard had forced him to train with his sword in both hands. The older, scarred soldier attacked with perfect strikes, but Erik parried and blocked them. As the soldier lunged at Erik, he saw a small opportunity and jabbed Ilken's Blade into the man's hip. He growled and turned, just as Erik brought the elvish blade down hard.

As he was about to give the man a matching scar on the other side of his face, Erik felt something stick in his shoulder. One of Switch's knives. It wasn't really enough to hurt him or enough to throw off his attack, and the elvish blade seared through the soldier's steel, sinking into the flesh of his chest and cutting through several ribs. He cried out in pain, falling backwards.

"Bao Zi!" Patûk Al'Banan yelled, jumping in front of the old soldier.

Patûk Al'Banan was the most adept warrior Erik had ever seen. His movements were crisp and precise, and a part of Erik felt that if the old general wanted him dead, he would have run him through the moment he jumped in front of the other, older soldier. He found himself back on his heels as each blade stroke from the eastern general came hard and fast, making anything Wrothgard had ever done seem novice. Turk and Balzarak tried to help, to come to Erik's rescue, but the two soldiers clad in leather breastplates consumed their attention, cutting them off every time they tried to break away. The general clearly had the upper hand.

Erik's shoulders ached, and the tip of Patûk Al'Banan's sword found a space between his armor. He felt blood trickle down his arm and chest.

I'm going to die.

Erik could see Switch trying to sneak up behind him, and if the thief had been completely healthy, he might have, but he was slow and weak from losing his hand, and the grip he had on his backwards-curved blade was shaky at best.

While Patûk Al'Banan continued his onslaught against Erik, Switch attacked. Erik felt the wind move behind him and side-stepped. The thief's knife caught Erik's pant's leg but only cut cloth. Erik kicked out, catching Switch's shin and, at the same time, brought Ilken's Blade down on his back. The thief went down with a muffled cry, tumbling into the general, who continued to come at Erik.

"You fool!" Patûk Al'Banan yelled as Switch caused the old soldier to trip. It was all the opportunity Erik needed.

As Patûk Al'Banan regained his balance and stood, Erik brought Ilken's Blade down hard. He knew the general would block his blow with adder-like speed. He counted on it. Patûk Al'Banan's sword barely moved as Erik brought his blade down as hard as he could.

"Looks like you need more training," Patûk Al'Banan sneered. "Too bad you won't receive it. You could have been a decent swordsman."

Patûk Al'Banan laughed, but then his eyes went wide. Steam rose up and shadowed his face, and the smell of burning meat and heated metal hit Erik's nose. The general looked down at his chest. The elvish blade sat there, hilt deep, melting through steel, flesh, and bone. Erik's attack with Ilken's Blade had been a ruse, giving him enough time to jab upwards with the magical blade.

The look on Patûk Al'Banan's face was one of disbelief. This was a great warrior. Erik knew that he should be the one who was dying. If it hadn't been for the fool thief, he would be dead. But the one thing that Wrothgard hadn't taught him, but the past two years had, was take an opportunity when it presents itself, for it may never come again.

"I should have died by the hands of a greater man," the general hissed. "You are a lesser man."

The general should have died at the hands of some other mighty warrior, or fighting a hundred soldiers, or maybe even fighting a dragon, but he died at the hands of Erik, a farm boy who hadn't seen twenty summers. Erik retrieved his sword with the sickening spitting of searing meat. He heard the two men who fought with the dwarves cry out when Patûk Al'Banan fell to his knees.

"Today," Erik said, leaning forward so that his nose was almost touching the general's, "you are the lesser man."

Much to Patûk Al'Banan's credit, and his resiliency, he reached up and grabbed Erik's neck, squeezing with all his waning strength as his breaths became slower and more labored. Erik didn't hesitate, even though the move did take him by surprise. He jammed Ilken's Blade into the general's exposed armpit, and the soldier released his grip and slumped to the ground, dead.

Erik turned his attention to Switch, who had started to scoot backwards and tried to stand.

"Mercy, Erik," Switch said, almost crying. "Please, mercy."

"Are you worried about tomorrow now, thief?" Erik asked. "All your talk about not giving a wit for what comes tomorrow or what happens after you die. Are you worried now?"

"Please, Erik," Switch said. "They forced me. I'm sorry. I wasn't thinking straight."

"You are worried, aren't you?" Erik added. "Now that it's your time."

"Son of a whore," Switch cursed, but still looked frightened, tears filling his eyes, "please."

Erik had heard enough. He brought Ilken's Blade down hard, and the thief went limp.

"Erik!" Turk called.

The young man turned to see Cho's former seneschal and the two leather breast-plated men trying to run. One of the men had the other older soldier over his shoulder, the injured man still breathing, albeit slowly. They didn't bother with the scroll, which was still lying on the tree stump.

Erik gave a quick chase. Instinctively, he swung out with the elvish blade and caught the lazy-eyed seneschal on the shoulder. The heat burned away some of his robe, catching the rest on fire. The man screamed as the fire spread over the whole of the thin, shimmery material. He tried to strip the robes off as quickly as he could, and Erik swung again, the broad side of the elvish blade hitting the man in the face. The seneschal's ear melted away, and his cheek and eye drooped as skin charred and cracked. The scream he gave was gut-wrenching.

The easterner not carrying the older soldier stopped. He leapt in front of the seneschal, sword out in front of him, staving Erik off from running the screaming, lazy-eyed man through. The easterner grabbed the seneschal—rolling about on the ground as much of his body was burned and disfigured—and quickly slung him over his shoulder, keeping Erik at bay, and ran. Erik wanted to give chase again, but when he saw his dwarvish companions were not behind him, he stopped.

"What are you doing?" Erik asked, walking back to his companions.

"They are unimportant," Balzarak said. "The scroll is what is important. The language Patûk Al'Banan was speaking ..."

"It was evil, wasn't it?" Erik asked. "I remember it from Orvencrest."

"Yes," Balzarak replied.

"What does this scroll do?" Turk asked.

"I dare not read it," Balzarak said. "I wouldn't know what most of it says anyways."

"It's connected to the dragon somehow," Erik added. "I could sense her presence when the general was reading from it."

"This is not something that should fall into the hands of the Lord of the East," Balzarak said.

"Then perhaps we should take it to Thorakest," Turk suggested.

But, to Erik's surprise, Balzarak shook his head.

"No," he said, "this is something that, if connected to the dragon, no one should have. It is evil. It was made by evil. And only evil will come from it."

"Then what do we do with it?" Turk asked.

"Destroy it," Balzarak said.

The dwarf picked up the scroll. It was a long piece of parchment, tanned and worn by time. The top half was script, line after line of writing, whatever Patûk Al'Banan was reading. The bottom half looked to be a map of sorts with writing underneath it. It almost looked like a list, and Erik presumed that they were directions or instructions. Balzarak grabbed the scroll with both hands and tried to rip it in half, but the parchment remained intact.

"What, by the Creator?" Balzarak grunted as he struggled against the scroll. "It is as if it is made of steel."

Balzarak laid it back on the tree stump and nodded to Turk. The dwarf swung his battle axe down at the parchment, but just before the steel bit into both paper and wood, a glossy barrier appeared above the scroll, and Turk's weapon bounced back, throwing both it and the dwarf through the air several paces and to the ground with a hard thud.

"Turk," Erik said.

"I am fine," the dwarf replied, brushing himself off with a confused look on his face.

"We'll burn it, then," Erik said, and without another word, touched the elvish blade to the scroll.

At first, the blade flared to an almost blinding purplish white, but then the metal dimmed, as it had in the tunnels escaping Orvencrest. It was as if the parchment was sucking the magic away from the sword. It did nothing to the paper, and Erik found himself pulling the blade away, but struggling to do so, as if the scroll held on to it with a firm grip. The sword looked like a normal, steel sword for a few moments, and Erik's heart stopped until the purplish glow returned, and he could feel the heat it produced.

"I don't think we can destroy it," Erik said.

"Roll it up," Balzarak said, "and place it back in its case."

"The Lord of the East will know we opened it," Erik said.

"He may," the general said, "but we must worry about that later. We must rejoin our companions. I am sure, despite being dead, Patûk Al'Banan's men will soon join the rest of his force, and they will be close on the heels of our company and moving fast."

Erik did as Balzarak asked, and before they left, he stared down at General Patûk Al'Banan. He looked regal almost, even in death. His jaw was hard. His body even harder. And for a moment, Erik wondered if the man did indeed deserve a more glorious death. Then he remembered Aga Kona and the women and children. He thought about what Master Cho's seneschal said, about Aga Min being destroyed as well. More women and children. This man was a monster, as evil as they came.

You deserved a worse death. We will see what you look like in my dreams as you begin to rot.

Then he looked at Switch. He looked thinner than before, pale and sickly. The gash that ran from his shoulder to hip exposed bone and intestines and even those looked sickly. There were moments when Erik actually thought this man was a true companion, maybe even, in a weird way, a friend. It was all a ruse, all pretense to get even more gold than he already had and, despite all they had been through, Erik didn't feel any remorse for the thief as he had for Drake and Vander Bim.

"Erik, we have to go," Balzarak said and Erik turned, nodded, and followed his dwarvish companions.

30

Bu rode Warrior, Patûk's old warhorse. He was surprised when the animal let him mount it. It was mean and angry and bit at anyone who wasn't Patûk. But he had just stood there when Bu slung Bao Zi over his own horse, tethered the reins to Warrior's saddle, and then mounted the destrier.

When they reached the camp, now ever growing as more of both Patûk's and Pavin's men showed up, Bu called for their healers. Some were just hedge witches and some were trained surgeons, but all were expendable.

"Listen here you gutter shite," Bu said to the closest healer, grabbing the man by the front of his shirt and pulling him close, pointing to Bao Zi, "if this man dies, I will cut off your balls, open up your stomach, rip out your intestines, and hang you with them."

"But sir," the man said with a shaky voice, "he is mortally wounded."

"Save him," Bu simple replied.

As the healers carried Bao Zi on a litter, the old soldier reached up and grabbed Bu's wrist, pulling him down. Even near death, the man was incredibly strong.

"I serve you, my lord," Bao Zi whispered into Bu's ear. "I serve you."

Bu stood as they carried the man away and, even though he felt silly for it, gooseflesh rose along his arms. Li still rolled about on the ground, his face marred—left ear gone, left eye gone, left cheek a blackened, cracked mess—and much of his chest and back burned. The two fingers on his right hand had melted together, but he still clutched something, a rolled-up piece of parchment. Bu crouched down.

"I've never heard you so excited," Bu said as the seneschal rolled about.

"It burns," he groaned in a long, pained, wheezing tone. "Please, it burns."

Bu thought the man had started to cry.

"I am sure it does," Bu said. "What is that in your hand?"

"The scroll," Li replied, good eye closed, body shuddering with pain. "I convinced General Patûk to let me create a copy before he began reading it."

"Did you now?" Bu asked. "With what intention?"

Li didn't answer. He just breathed heavy and shook. His flesh had turned a bright red, and much of his chest had begun to blister.

"You are false," Bu said. "An opportunist indeed. What does the scroll do? I somehow believe you could read it."

For all of Li's excitement, still rolling about and crying, Bu was calm.

"Help, please," Li whined.

"Tell me what the scroll is, first," Bu replied.

"It is an ancient spell," Li replied, eye still shut. "It has to do with dragons. What exactly, I don't know. Part of it is a map ... to a weapon —a sword. The wielder becomes powerful. That's all I could decipher."

Bu stood. Dragons? Did they still exist? Did they ever exist? And a sword. History was full of stories about powerful wizards who commanded dragons, full of stories about powerful warriors who slew dragons.

"Healer," Bu said to a single surgeon standing by, "get this man help."

"Yes sir," the surgeon said.

As Li was placed on a litter, Bu leaned in towards him.

"Before the tomigus root and dream milk take your senses, know this," Bu said, "you now serve me. You are alive simply because you are useful. If I find you to be false, like you were with old Patûk, the pain you feel now will pale in comparison to the horrors I will put you through before being merciful and ending your life."

Bu pushed Pavin Abashar to the ground, right hand wrapped around the general's throat. The general squirmed and struggled, but Bu was too strong. No one else was in the tent, save for Sergeant Andu and Ban Chu, who Bu had made a lieutenant. Ban Chu was loyal to the death to Bu, and Andu was a broken dog and wouldn't say a word.

"I am now in charge," Pavin struggled to say. "Patûk is dead. It is the natural course of succession."

"Listen here, you worm," Bu seethed, pushing hard against Pavin's throat. The general's face started to turn purple, and his eyes began to bulge. "I am in charge. You now follow me. You will tell your men such, and my men."

Bu let up on the general's throat a bit so he could respond.

"The nine hells I will," he replied.

"Wrong answer," Bu said, pressing down now even harder.

Pavin kicked and gurgled and clawed at Bu, but Bu simply squeezed and smiled. Just as Pavin was about to pass out, Bu released his grip.

"You now serve me," Bu said, "as do your men."

He held out a hand. Ban Chu gently placed something that looked like a small, white worm in his open palm. He presented the little worm-like thing to Pavin. The general's eyes widened.

"You know what this is, don't you?" Bu asked.

"Brain demon," Pavin muttered.

"That's right," Bu replied with a smile, "and if I am nice, I'll simply drop it in your ear. If you struggle more, I'll stick it up your ass."

Brain demons, starting life off as helpless, white larvae, were beetle-like insects that seemed to seek out the brains of whatever host they had infected, burrowing into the skin or finding their way into whatever orifice they could. As they grew, thus growing barbed legs and large, sharp pincers, they caused a tremendous amount of internal pain, especially as they made their way to the host's brain. The farther they had to travel to get to the brain, the more pain they caused. Once they reached the brain, as they ate away the fatty organ, they then caused insanity.

"Who do you serve?" Bu asked, inching the little white larvae closer to Pavin.

"You," Pavin whispered back, voice shaking.

"Who do your men serve?" Bu asked.

"You," Pavin replied again.

"And when we conquer Hámon," Bu said, "which I still intend on doing, who will be king of Hámon?"

"You," Pavin said.

"Good," Bu replied, closing his fist and squeezing the brain demon larvae until it was nothing but a green smudge in his hand. It was a costly sacrifice. Brain demon larvae were expensive as the faraway Feran Islands were their natural habitat, but it was a necessary one, and Bu had more larvae if Pavin decided to go back on his pledge of allegiance.

"My lord," Ban Chu said, "should we follow the men who attacked us?"

Bu shook his head.

"To Hámon, for now," Bu said. "We have a copy of the scroll. We don't need them anymore. And I will have my revenge all in due time."

"On the Lord of the East, my lord?" Ban Chu asked.

"No," Bu said, shaking his head. "Well, yes. I still intend on conquering the east as Patûk had. But my first act of revenge will be on that little prick who killed Patûk."

"How, my lord?" Ban Chu asked.

"That fool of a thief," Bu said. "He said a name when they attacked."

"What was the name, my lord?" Ban Chu asked.

"Erik Eleodum," Bu said with a smile. "Erik Eleodum. That was the man's name. That is who will feel my revenge. He and all he loves will know my wrath."

31

Erik and the two dwarves caught up with the rest of their company again as they began to cross the land bridge. Dwain was already on the other side of the ravine, helping the mountain folk as they stepped to the other side. Bryon was over there too, one arm draped around Demik. Wrothgard was on their side of the ravine, helping the mountain people onto the bridge.

"We recovered the scroll," Erik said.

"Good," Wrothgard replied as the last homesteader walked out onto the bridge.

"They had opened it," Erik added.

"Who?" Wrothgard asked.

"Switch and the men for whom he betrayed us," Erik replied.

"Was it truly Patûk?" Wrothgard asked.

"Aye," Balzarak said. "Erik killed him."

"Truly?" Wrothgard asked.

"Yes," Turk replied, "and Switch."

"Do you think the Lord of the East knows ... will he know it has been opened?" Erik asked.

"Most definitely," Wrothgard replied, "but it is a risk we must take. We did not open it, and I believe the punishment for not returning it would be much harsher than having opened it."

"It's not some recording of family lineage, Wrothgard," Erik said.

"What is it then?" the soldier asked, and Erik explained what had happened and what they suspected the scroll was and did. Wrothgard's skin turned pale, and he shook his head.

"We can't worry about that now," he said, trying to appear positive. "We have to move. Patûk's men, regardless of his death, are close. I am sure they will want revenge. We must move quickly."

Clouds had once more formed overhead, and a light rain was falling when Wrothgard, Erik, Turk, and Balzarak crossed the land bridge. When they reached the other side, the rain fell harder and faster, and Erik could tell there was unease and tension in the homesteaders. They had only traveled a short distance, when Alga came rushing back to Erik, worry evident on her face.

"We have to stop," she said. "The old one is not well, nor is the mother and her infant."

Erik looked up to the sky as large raindrops plopped against his face.

"And one of yours," she added. "The man, I believe the one who is your cousin. He has a fever, and it is getting worse."

"Where do we camp, General?" Erik asked.

"This is what I feared might happen," Balzarak replied.

"We are at least a day from Thorakest," Turk added.

"We need to find a place for the four of them," Balzarak said. "The rest of us will have to bear the weather, but they cannot."

"How are you doing, cousin," Erik said, walking up to Bryon.

"I don't feel ... don't feel well," Bryon said, and he looked it, his face ashen, and he had lost weight.

"Turk," Erik said, "can you go with them, tend to them throughout the night?"

"I will do what I can," Turk said.

"I hope we haven't trusted you in vain, Erik," Balzarak said.

"Me too," Erik added.

The sky always seemed so clear after a storm, as if it had washed away all the dirt, given the sky a clean slate. There were the stars, and Erik poked at them, laughing inwardly. He remembered a night like this one. He sat behind his father's barn, watching the stars. His father hadn't come home yet, and when he did, he cursed Hámonian nobles for their treachery in the marketplace. That was the night Erik decided he would go with Befel and Bryon on this fool's journey.

He could go back to his farm now. He could pay off his father's debt. He would be the one to inherit his father's land, and then he could buy more. He could probably even buy the Hámonians' lands. He could marry Simone and buy the largest farmstead possible and still have enough money left over for the next dozen generations of his family. He had found fortune and, in some respects, he assumed, fame. Would the Lord of the East herald him as a hero? He had done everything he had set out to do—and against what odds. He wasn't yet twenty summers.

Erik shook his head. He couldn't go home ... not without Befel. His throat went dry, and he put his face in his hands.

"Just one more day," he muttered. "What will Mother think? What will Father do? Beth and Tia—what will they think of me?"

He stared back out at the darkness through wet, blurry vision. He remembered his dreams.

Are they even there, still? Or are Mother and Father dead? Are Beth and Tia sitting in some cell, somewhere in Hámon, slaves?

Erik hugged his knees to his chest. He looked at all the people huddled close to the mountain slope, trying to sleep. He turned his head so that he could watch the darkness.

Erik watched the pinks and purples of an early morning finger across the sky. He had sat there all night, thinking of his mother and father, sisters and brother. He could have sat there forever with their faces in his head, remembering sitting on his mother's lap, playing with his sisters, working with his father, following his brother around wherever he might go. But the ensuing light and the sound of early morning birds told Erik he had to move. He stood, stretching out his stiff muscles, trying to shake away the weariness of two sleepless nights. He heard someone crying.

"What happened?" Erik asked as he came to a small crowd—as much of a crowd that could be afforded on that mountain ledge—gathering where Bryon had slept that night.

"It's the old woman," Dwain said. "She passed in the night. She didn't have a chance, really. She was too frail to make this journey."

"This is all my fault," Erik muttered angrily.

"What was that?" Erik hadn't noticed Alga standing next to him, her arms tightly wound around her husband's arm. She pressed her body close to him. Her eyes looked sad and red-rimmed as if she had been crying. Despite that, she smiled at Erik.

"This is my fault," Erik repeated. "This poor old woman. She died because of me."

Alga's face scrunched up and twisted. She looked to her husband, and he looked back at her with a questioning, raised eyebrow. Alga said something to him in their native tongue. It was just different enough from Dwarvish that he could only pick out a word here and there, not enough to understand what she said. Angthar shook his head, shot a quick glance to Erik, and then said something back. She nodded and looked to the young man.

"She would have died anyway," Alga said. "It is because of you that this woman—who would have died either way—was able to pass without much pain, surrounded by her family and her people.

"We believe in you, Erik," Alga said. "My husband and I. You have displaced our family, taken us from our home, changed all of our dreams and goals, and we followed you because we trust you. The Creator sent you to us, this we do not doubt. Believe in yourself."

Erik watched a little longer while the homesteaders prepared the old woman and prayed over her once she was buried in a shallow grave. Then it was time to move on, but first they made a litter for Bryon as well as the mother and her infant. Bryon argued at first about being carried, but took little convincing, and he soon relented.

As they grew closer to Thorakest, Erik could feel something, someone, watching them from the other side of the ravine. Winter wolves? Trolls? Traitorous Eastern guardsmen? Dwomanni? It didn't matter.

Maybe I'll just stay in Thorakest. Will I even have a family to return to? And if I do, how to I tell Mother Befel is gone? And what of Simone? Surely, she's married someone else by now. I could just stay here, with the dwarves.

Erik took a deep, long breath and let the air slowly escape his lungs. The sun had reached its apex, and the day was warm; a pleasant change if there was no danger to their journey. The cliff that protected the pathway from the giant ravine grew taller, and Erik remembered leaving the comforts of Thorakest to embrace the wilds of the Southern Mountains.

"Halten!"

The cry came from the front of the train of people. Erik followed Turk to the front of the line. When he passed by Alga, she had a worried look on her face. Her husband held their littlest daughter and son in his great arms. As they neared the front, Erik heard arguing in Dwarvish.

Balzarak and Dwain argued with another dwarf, a stranger with bright red hair running straight down the middle of his head. He looked a haphazard fellow as did his armor, all pieced together in no particular arrangement. Blue and purple inked tattoos covered the shaved sides of his head and migrated to his neck and across his forehead and even to his cheeks. He looked young, compared to the other dwarves, with a close-cropped beard and no moustache, and his face looked almost as red as his hair.

"It's a tunnel rat," Turk said. "It's the name given to the young warriors who are chosen to explore the unknowns of the mountains, and, in times of war, lead initial assaults."

"Sounds dangerous," Erik said.

"It's very dangerous," Turk agreed. "Their lives are short. It is a great honor."

"If his job is to explore undiscovered tunnels," Erik said, "what is he doing here?"

"I know as much as you do," Turk replied, "but him being here concerns me."

The tunnel rat wasn't alone. Four dwarves stood behind him, all dressed the same, all carrying short handled spears and short swords.

"More tunnel rats?" Erik asked.

Turk nodded.

Erik heard a hiss and looked up to see a giant rock lizard, clinging to the side of the mountain with its wicked-looking black claws and staring at them. Its tongue flickered in and out a few times, and it opened its mouth wide, hissed again, and then snapped its maw shut. The lizard wore a thick, leather collar, a long leashed attached to it. Another dwarf, all clad in armor made of soft leather, held the leash and stood atop the mountain slope, staring down at them.

"Do tunnel rats normally have lizards with them?" Erik said, pointing upwards.

"Sometimes, yes, but that dwarf isn't a tunnel rat."

"How do you know?" Erik asked.

"The tattoos on the dwarves' heads and faces give them away as tunnel rats," Turk explained.

"But that one is a wearing a helmet," Erik said, and Turk nodded; explanation given.

Looking around, Erik saw more lizard handlers walking along the tops of the mountain peak that shadowed the entrance to Thorakest. He heard a low growl and looked up above the tunnel rat, the rocky wall above the city's entrance, and saw yet another dwarf standing there. This one was clad in full plate mail, although it was difficult to fully see him as the sun shone behind him and cast a dark silhouette around the dwarf. But nonetheless, Erik could see that this dwarf also held a leash, but this one was tied to a great brown bear that growled again and bared its massive fangs.

The conversation grew decidedly heated as the volume of both the tunnel rat's and Balzarak's voices raised. Finally, Balzarak threw his hands in the air and turned around. He saw Erik and let out a concerned sigh.

"The whole city is on alert, Erik," Balzarak explained.

"Why?" Erik asked.

"Fréden Fréwin has left the city, defecting and taking others with him," Balzarak said. "In addition, there have been sightings."

"Sightings?" Erik asked. "Sightings of what?"

"It is as we thought," Balzarak said. "Sightings of *them*."

"The—"

"Do not speak their name here," Balzarak said. "King Skella is a good ruler, and I now know that I was wrong about you when we first met, but it is not safe for you to return to Thorakest."

"What about the homesteaders?" Erik asked.

"It is not safe because you possess the scroll the Lord of the East wants," Balzarak said with a mirthless smile, "not because you are a man. They will be welcomed in Thorakest as long as they wish, I will make sure of that."

"What do we ... do I do then?" Erik asked.

"I need to make sure you find your way to Fen-Stévock," Balzarak said, "as much as it pains me to say so."

"If we are not safe in Thorakest," Erik asked, "then how will we be safe on dwarvish roads, or some other dwarvish city?"

"The main roads of Drüum Balmdüukr are as traveled as any other road in the world," Balzarak explained.

"And as treacherous?" Erik asked.

"Aye," Balzarak replied, "but no one will know who you are ... or what you carry."

"And what will be our route?" Erik asked.

"Go via Ecfast," Balzarak said.

Erik remembered Turk and Wrothgard having a conversation about Ecfast. It was the route Wrothgard had originally planned on taking, having a token that would permit him entrance into dwarvish lands.

"The captain of Ecfast is a dwarf name Khamzûd," Balzarak explained. "He is a distant relative of mine and loyal to King Skella. He will welcome you, make sure you are safe, and see you are on your way to Fen-Stévock without unwanted intervention."

Erik thought for a moment.

"Do you trust me, Erik?" Balzarak asked.

That gave Erik more cause for thought, but then he looked the dwarf in the eyes. Erik nodded.

"Yes."

32

Escorted by a dwarf named Forgrim and his company of tunnel rats, it took less than a day's travel to reach the underground road that led one way to Thorakest and the other to Ecfast.

"Erik," Balzarak said, extending his hand, "I wish you success and the Creator's blessing."

"Thank you, General," Erik said, "although, I am worried about Bryon. He is getting worse. You said that the surgeons in Thorakest could heal him, but now we are not going to Thorakest."

"I can take him to Thorakest with me," Balzarak said.

"Will he be safe?" Erik asked.

"He will be in the direct care of the King, my friend," Balzarak replied. "And I will make sure he is safe. I will guard him myself if I must. And when he is well, I will have a host of dwarvish warriors escort him home."

"Did you hear that?" Erik said to Bryon, but his cousin lay on the litter, unconscious. Erik rubbed his cousin's shoulder. He snored softly, breathing slowly. "I will keep your sword for now. Do not worry. I won't steal it. You'll get it back."

"I suppose it's just you and me, Wrothgard," Erik said, looking at the soldier.

"Do not forget about us," Turk said. "Demik, Nafer, and I intend on seeing this through. We started this together. We will finish this together."

"But Thorakest is your home," Erik said.

"Thorakest is in my heart, Erik," Turk said, "and you are my friend."

"We come too," Bofim said. "Beldar and me."

"You're an extraordinary man, Erik Eleodum," Balzarak said, "to earn the respect and fellowship of dwarves such as these. I have this for you."

The general retrieved a circlet from his haversack. It looked much like the one he wore upon his brow, only this one was silver and centered by a sapphire. He handed it to Erik.

"Wear this when you reach Ecfast," Balzarak said. "It will let Captain Khamzûd know you are a friend of dwarves ... a friend of mine. And keep it from here on, a token of my gratitude and our friendship. You will find it a friend, even in the deepest, darkest places."

Even in the deepest, darkest places

Erik remembered his grandfather had once uttered the same words. He bowed as he took the circlet and placed it on his head.

"An be with you," Erik said in Dwarvish.

"An be with you," Balzarak replied.

Erik stood in a wide field. The grass was waist high and brown, as if it was dead, but it wasn't. The sky was reddish pale, and the sun seemed to be a minute version of what it should have been. He looked over his shoulder, half expecting to see a hill with a large weeping willow on top of it. It wasn't there, but he had still been to this place before.

This was another place in his world of dreams, only something about this place spoke of nightmares. More than the undead, more than dark forests, this was a place of distortion, of altered realities. As Erik walked, he felt his sword, Ilken's Blade, at his hip. No dagger. His dagger had told him it couldn't come to this place.

All was quiet as the tall, brown grass fluttered in a breeze, but it made no sound. What should have been a cool wind seemed more like the fanned flames from a fire. As flies buzzed in front of his face, the annoying sound of their wings was barely audible. Then, a long, screeching cry broke to quiet. Millions of insects rose up from the grass in a chorus of hissing. A flock of black birds flew overhead, bobbing and weaving through the pallid, red sky as if joined invisibly. They rose and dove, and then, with a screech that hurt his ears, flew into the ground, each one hitting the ground with the sickening sound of breaking bone and splitting flesh. When Erik walked to where the birds' bodies should have been, he found nothing.

Erik felt the ground rumble under his feet. Like a sheet tossed by his mother as she put it out to dry, it seemed to sway and roll and, when he looked up, off in the distance black clouds had built up, with purples, pinks, and whites flashing through their darkness as thunder followed. A blinding lightning bolt struck the ground, so bright Erik was forced to close his eyes, and when he opened them again, he saw a small mountain range, as black as the clouds, and Erik felt compelled to walk towards them.

But with each step he took, the mountains never seemed closer. He just stayed in the same spot until, ahead of him, a man suddenly appeared, his back to Erik, walking in the same direction in front of him.

"Hey!" Erik called. "What's your name?"

The man never turned around, and he didn't answer; Erik hadn't expected him to. Then came an all too familiar smell, that of rot and decay, and he knew they were there. He could hear them. The other man must have sensed them too, and he began to run, only, he never gained any distance.

"Don't run!" Erik called. "That's what they want! Come to me! Stand and fight them!"

But the man didn't hear Erik, or he ignored him. Then, Erik saw them, an army of the undead. Some of them were mere skeletons, loosely held together by barely strings of ligament. Others were recently deceased, skin intact save for the yellow and blue and black decay.

Erik heard the man scream, and the undead laughed. He stopped walking, drew his sword, and readied himself. The other man ran faster, but he went nowhere. There was another screeching cry, a loud thunder bang, and a bolt of lightning struck the tallest, black peak of the distant mountain range. The earth shook. The air heated up. And Erik could only think of a dragon.

This must be her realm.

The earth shook again, and this time, the undead came. They ran as fast as they could, moving wherever they wanted to, and the man in front of him didn't stand a chance. Their boney hands slashed and ravaged his body, pieces of flesh and muscle flying into the air, and Erik smelled new death. Then they saw him.

"Bring it on," he said, with the hint of a smile on his face.

They came, and he cut them down, one after another. An endless stream of the undead. A whole army of the undead. But Ilken's Blade did its work.

Erik felt like he had been there for hours, and for the first time, he felt fatigued in this place of his dreams. His shoulders and back ached. Several skeletal fingers made it past his defenses and scratched his skin. One even drew blood but nothing like they had done to the man in front. He heard another cry, this one behind him, and he spun around.

"By the Creator," Erik muttered in Dwarvish, seeing a dwarf rush to his side, battle-axe gripped in two hands and naught but a pair of stitched pants on his body.

The dwarf threw himself into the fray of undead, and the scene gave Erik renewed strength. They fought the undead together and, even though their enemy kept coming, harder and faster, they fought. Erik felt blood run from his body, but it didn't matter. When he felt his strength wane, the dwarf would cry out, and he would jump into the fight again, reinvigorated.

Finally, there was another screeching cry, another thunderclap, another blinding flash of lightning, and the undead were gone. The mountain range was gone. The clouds were gone. But the dwarf was still there.

"Who are you?" Erik asked in Dwarvish.

The dwarf dropped his battle-axe and put his right hand over his left breast.

"Baptized," was all he said.

When the dwarf removed his hand from his breast, Erik saw a brand, raw and red and new.

Bofim had been certain the underground roads of Drüum Balmdüukr were safe and well-traveled, but as Erik walked, he saw few people. A dwarf here or there, but that was it. The well-lit road and uniform walls were monotonous after a while, but he needed to keep going. He needed something to take his mind off the scroll—shoved into the front of his belt—and off his brother, the dwarves, the mountain folk, and his cousin. So, he left his companions behind, keeping going as they slept in a small barracks that were built specifically for travelers into the wall every five leagues or so. Like his dream the last time he slept, he moved onwards, but this time, he progressed.

The part of the tunnel he was now in wasn't as straight as before, and it continued to curve slightly to the left then the right. Erik took several more steps and then stopped, pressing his back hard against a wall so that someone would have had to be only several paces away to see him. He listened, intently, remembering the tracking lessons both his father and the dwarves had taught him. From the direction he had come, the sound was ever so slight, but he heard them; whispers and light footsteps. They were getting closer. He felt gooseflesh rise along his arms and a tingle at the back of his head. They were closer still, their voices seeming a little more rushed, their footsteps faster as they sought to catch up with him. And then they came into view.

Six dwarves rounded the slight curve in the tunnel, almost running, but when they saw Erik, pretending to drink from a water skin, they slowed to a leisurely walk. Erik hung his water skin back on his belt and gave the dwarves a slight nod and a smile. They returned the gesture, although he felt as if they eyed him cautiously.

"Good day," Erik said in Dwarvish.

"Good day," one of the dwarves replied, seeming surprised Erik spoke their language. Bofim had explained it wasn't so strange to see men traveling this road, the one they called Handelstrat, but bid Erik be careful since it wasn't too common. He figured it might calm these dwarves if he spoke to them in their native language.

"Are you traveling to Lagern?" Erik asked, speaking of the small dwarvish town that many used Handelstrat to reach.

"No," the same dwarf said, stopping only for a moment to speak with Erik, "further."

"I'm going to Lagern. Perhaps I could travel with you?" Erik lied with a feigned smile, "until we reach it."

The dwarf gave the other five a concerned look. One whispered something, inaudible and in a different language—one Erik thought he had heard before—to the one speaking.

"No, thanks," the dwarf replied. "Don't mean to be rude. We are in a rush."

"No problem," Erik said, lifting his water skin again as a salute and then pretending to take another drink.

Then, the smell broke into his senses. It was so slight, he almost missed it, but it was there, nonetheless—the stink of rot. It wasn't necessarily pungent, more like the rotting spot on an apple that was otherwise good, but it was there. However insignificant, it was the smell of death.

Erik let his water skin drop, its strap still attached to his belt, as his hand withdrew Ilken's Blade just as a broad-bladed short sword swung towards his face. His blade of Dwarf's Iron easily swatted the short sword away, knocking it out of the dwarf's hand. He meant to jab at the attacking dwarf, but one of the other ones swung a club at him, and he had to move quickly to get out of its way. As Erik looked to each of the six dwarves, they quickly surrounded him, weapons ready, darkness in their eyes.

The first one came at him again, jabbing with that short blade and reaching for the scroll case in his belt at the same time. Erik moved, stepped aside, bringing his blade across the dwarf's ribs. He cried out as the clubber attacked. Erik gripped Ilken's Blade with two hands, chopping the club in half and then removing the dwarf's head from his neck. The smell of death intensified.

Erik felt something smack against the back of his leg and turned to see a dwarf yielding a quarterstaff. But before he could attack, the short sword jabbed at his face. He dodged another clubber, swatted away the quarterstaff, jerked away as another hand reached for the scroll case, and felt the tip of a dagger graze his hip. The dwarves closed in, and as they chuckled, they reminded Erik of his dreams ... the dead.

Ilken's Blade shattered the quarterstaff as the dwarf tried to block Erik's attack, and the sword sunk deep into a meaty shoulder. Blood sprayed the wall as Erik removed his blade and then jammed it into the dwarf's belly. Intestines spilled when Erik ripped his weapon away to block the edge of an axe, but then he slipped on a slick of blood and went to one knee.

The dwarf with the short sword tried to take advantage of Erik's position, but he blocked another attack and swiped at the dwarf's leg, exposing muscle. Erik brought his blade down hard with a mighty grunt, but the dwarf with an axe blocked him. Standing, Erik squared off with the axe wielder. The dwarf giggled devilishly, taunting Erik in that language he thought he had heard before. As the dwarf spoke, Erik heard distant laughing. The dead. The torches that lined the walls seemed to dim a little. It was the language he heard in the halls of Orvencrest. It was the language Patûk Al'Banan spoke when he read the scroll. It was the language of the dwomanni, the language of the Shadow.

"The Shadow is not welcome here," Erik said, swinging at the dwarf and missing.

"The Shadow is already here," the dwarf chided. "Give us the mistress' treasure, and we'll let you live."

The dragon. She sent you.

And as he thought those words, he heard a distant, familiar laugh.

Erik blocked two more axe attacks before driving his blade, hilt deep, into the dwarf's belly. Even as he died, the dwarf reached for the scroll case stuck in Erik's belt. He pulled away quickly, swatting the dying hands to the side. He watched as the three remaining dwarves closed in on him. The dwarf with the short sword limped forward, clutching at his leg wound with one hand.

"Are you ready to meet the Shadow?" the dwarf asked. "Your brother met him."

Erik laughed.

"No, he didn't," Erik replied. "But you will. I hope you enjoy eternity rotting in darkness."

"I look forward to it," the dwarf hissed, smiling and exposing already rotting teeth.

Just then, a hand axe thudded into the dwarf's chest. He reeled back with a cry and died before he hit the ground. Erik turned to see

Bofim and Beldar rushing to his aide. They made short work of the remaining two dwarves, Beldar demolishing the face of the axe-wielding dwarf with a ball and chain, and Bofim removing the other dwarf's head with his axe, but only after chopping off one arm at the shoulder and the other at the elbow.

"What are you doing here?" Erik asked.

"You had been gone a while," Beldar replied. "We felt like something was wrong."

"It is a good thing we did," Bofim added.

"Aye, that it is," Erik said. "They were just waiting for the right time. I saw others on the road, but these ones ... I smelled them. They wanted the scroll, the Lord of the East's treasure."

"What do you mean?" Bofim asked.

"They kept reaching for the scroll case, and they smelled rotten," Erik replied. "And then they spoke a language that I have only ever heard in two other times. Balzarak said it was the language of the Shadow. The language of the dwomanni."

"Hush, Erik," Bofim said, not in a scolding manner but one of caution. "Not so loud here."

Beldar bent down to the dwarf that had carried the short sword, ripping open his shirt.

"What are you doing?" Erik asked.

Beldar ignored the question, exposing the dwarf's left breast and a large mound of scarred skin like a burn that had been cut and disfigured. Erik remembered the dwarf in his dream and how he had touched his left breast. Beldar gave Bofim a concerned look.

"What is that?" Erik asked.

"Baptism," Bofim replied.

Erik then remembered an argument between Threhof and Turk. Turk had mentioned the word, baptism. He had said he had been baptized, but Erik had no idea what that meant.

"It is the symbol of a warrior, Erik," Beldar explained. "Everyone's baptism is a little different, but after each one of us survives the test ..."

"Is it a dream?" Erik asked. "A vision? A field of dead grass with a red sky and purple lightning and black clouds? And a mountain range that is as black as coal?"

Beldar and Bofim just stared at him for a while. Then, they argued, still speaking in Dwarvish, but so quickly and softly, Erik couldn't hear what they said. Then, Bofim stepped forward.

"How do you know that?" he asked.

"I've been there," Erik replied.

"How?" Bofim asked.

"I don't know."

"It doesn't matter right now," Beldar said. "But yes, you are right. After we survive the test—the vision—we are branded on our left breast. To mutilate the symbol of baptism is to denounce not only your status as a warrior, but your people. The mutilated mark of baptism is usually the mark of an exile. There is only one reason a dwarf would choose to mutilate their mark."

"The dwomanni," Erik said.

"Yes," Bofim replied. "The Shadow."

33

Andragos was not having a good day. He stood waiting in the hall of the Lord of the East, disgusted at the sight of the naked men and women who caressed each other, lounging in the luxury of the ruler of Golgolithul. The Lord of the East finally appeared from behind his curtain, followed by his two witches, and sat in his seat. Andragos' displeasure increased; he hated those bitches. They were both beautiful, although he suspected it was some sort of enchantment. As far as he could tell, they were almost as old as he was.

One of them, Kimber, wore a black dress that hugged her waist, two strips of cloth barely covering her breasts. Her hair was crystal white, her skin was pale, and her eyes blue and piercing. The other one, Krista, who wore a white dress that looked identical, but her hair was as black as ebony, her skin a deep brown, and her eyes an emerald green. They stood on either side of the Lord of the East, each resting a hand on his exposed shoulders, as he wore simple, black leggings that plumed at his ankles and covered his navel.

Much to Andragos' further chagrin, the Lord of the East's other advisor appeared from behind the curtain as well. He was a weathered, old man, small and bent, his back twisted at an unnatural angle. His olive skin and almond shaped eyes gave him away as a man originally from the Isuta Isles, although Andragos knew he had been living in Háthgolthane for at least a hundred years. His thin, white hair spilled haphazardly over his black robes and his equally thin beard, also a pure, snow white hung in tangles.

He chooses the council of this foreigner over mine, Andragos thought, guarding his mind in a place where others could easily read the thoughts of a lesser man.

"You summoned me, Your Highness," Andragos said.

"Yes, I did," the Lord of the East said. "I am upset, Andragos."

"Oh, and why is that?" Andragos asked, but his visions had already spoken to him.

"The scroll has been opened and read," the Lord of the East said.

"Yes, Your Highness," Andragos said.

"These mercenaries now know what is on that parchment," the Lord of the East said. "They know of the power it has."

"It is doubtful," Andragos said. "It is unlikely they could even attempt to read the language in which it is written."

"They have betrayed me," the Lord of the East insisted.

"As I suspected," Andragos replied evenly. "It is why I thought we should use the Soldiers of the Eye for this task. We can't trust mercenaries."

The Lord of the East, who had been lounging in his chair with one leg over an armrest, unslung his leg and leaned forward. The light in the hall dimmed, and Andragos felt his ruler scanning him, scanning his mind.

"You have grown powerful, Your Highness," Andragos said, "but might I ask why you think it prudent to try and read my thoughts."

"You forget your place, Andragos," the Lord of the East said.

"Apologies," Andragos replied, "but, perhaps if you would heed my counsel a little more."

"Your counsel was appreciated, my old friend," the Lord of the East said as he stood, "but I am in a new season and, therefore, in need of new counsel."

When the Lord of the East—Syzbalo—was just a boy, Andragos was his teacher, his counselor, his doctor, his everything, but in a few short years, these two bitches and this old foreigner had replaced him as the Lord of the East's chief counsel. Andragos was a black mage—the names men had given him for an age were true—but the magic these new advisors gave the ruler of Golgolithul was different, darker than anything Andragos had ever touched. They knew things, discovered things, and they had twisted the Eastern Emperor's mind.

"Did you know what the Dragon Scroll was?" the Lord of the East asked, stepping down from his dais onto a lower step.

"I had heard of it, yes," Andragos replied, still keeping his tone flat despite his worsening mood.

"Then why not mention it to me?" the Lord of the East asked.

Andragos didn't answer.

"Do you see, Andragos," the Lord of the East said, "Melanius came to me with its whereabouts the moment he learned of it. My sweet Kimber and Krista advised me on how to find it, where it might be, even helping draft the map. And it has been found. All you did was issue the instructions."

"I have often wondered how such things ... the location of a lost dwarvish city and the mystery behind such a powerful weapon lost by time, could be so easily discovered," said Andragos.

"You are a fool, Andragos the Black Mage," Melanius, the old, Isutan advisor croaked, pointing a long, bony finger at the Messenger, "if you think such information came so easily. There is a price. A high price."

"Clearly," Andragos replied, irritated that this man, a wizard as he was, would speak to him in such a way. Was he even needed anymore?

Kimber glared at Andragos as she turned and spoke to Krista in an ancient tongue that predated Old Elvish; Andragos wondered where they learned such a language.

"Why don't you speak your mind out loud, witch?" Andragos said.

Kimber turned her head quickly and hissed.

"Your necessity is waning, mage," she said, her voice a snake's whispering hiss.

"Your time is nigh at hand," Krista, added, her voice the same as her twin's.

"We are strong," Kimber said.

"We are powerful," Krista added.

"The gods smile upon us," Kimber said.

"They have given us the mysteries we desire," Krista said.

"You speak in a witch's riddles, full of your own self-importance," Andragos said, "which is nothing more than nonsense."

"Show him," Krista said.

The Lord of the East turned and made eye contact with Melanius. The old, broken wizard nodded his head.

"Follow me," the Lord of the East said rising before turning. Following the witches and wizard, he disappeared behind his curtains.

Andragos did as he was told, pushing aside the heavy curtain and stepping into the Lord of the East's private quarters. The ruler of Golgolithul walked along a path, lit by magical light, followed in a single file by the witches and wizard who had waited for the master to lead the way. Andragos followed, and beyond the path, the space behind the curtain was pitch black, but he knew what terrors waited in the darkness. This wasn't the first time he had been behind the curtain, but it had been a long time.

The Lord of the East stopped in front of a small platform, square and made of pure gold. He stepped up onto it, everyone else, including Andragos, joining him. The ruler of Golgolithul snapped his fingers. The space around them shimmered and, only for a moment, Andragos' vision went black, and when it returned, they were in a wide, dark room barely lit by several torches and smelling of disease and death.

"The dungeons, Syzbalo?" Andragos asked.

The Lord of the East didn't reply. He simply led them down a hallway that ended in a single cell, iron bars old and rusted, no door in them—just thick, iron rods. A single torch burned faintly outside the cell, leaving most of the cell dark. Andragos could see feet poking out from the darkness.

The Lord of the East lifted a hand, and the iron bars of the cell disappeared. He stepped inside, and the witches and his new advisor followed.

"Do you want to know how we have discovered the mystery of Orvencrest," the Lord of the East asked, "and the dragon scroll?"

Andragos stepped forward. The Lord of the East started speaking in a language—one different from what the witches had spoken—that Andragos hadn't heard in years.

Shadow tongue.

"Yes," Kimber said, turning to face Andragos, her blue eyes glowing in the darkness of the cell. Krista's eyes grew equally as brilliant, becoming gleaming emeralds.

Andragos stepped forward even more and gasped.

"Is that?" he started to ask.

"Yes, Andragos," the Lord of the East replied.

A dwomanni leaned against the wall, chained and bound. It looked as if it was sleeping, although Andragos couldn't quite see in the darkness. The Lord of the East snapped a finger, and a ball of red light appeared, floating in front of them. The dwomanni hissed, putting an arm in front of his face.

"What is your name?" the Lord of the East asked of the dwomanni, speaking in the Shadow Tongue.

"You know my name," the dwomanni replied in the same language, its voice raspy and angry.

"Tell me again," the Lord of the East said. "And put down your damn arm."

The dwomanni put its arm down. Its skin was a pallid gray. Its eyes were glassy, seeming to be blind, but the way it looked about, Andragos could tell it could see. As it snarled, its face flat and head hairless, it bore teeth that had been shaved to points. It was a sickly-looking thing, smaller than any dwarf Andragos had ever seen and barely bigger than a gnome.

"Tarren," the dwomanni replied. "Tarren Red Hair, Captain of Shadow Horn's Guard."

"Little good you did as a captain, no?" the Lord of the East said, and Andragos could hear the chiding mirth in his master's voice. "And why are you here? What have you confided in me thus far?"

The dwomanni hissed again and squirmed a bit, but both witches started chanting, and the dwomanni's back arched and he grimaced in pain.

"Curse you bitches. The dwarves hid a powerful weapon from us, a millennium ago," Tarren Red Hair confessed, "when our mistress reclaimed lands and gold that were once hers. It was a spell that could control the mistress or allow her to control others of her kind."

"Dragons?" Andragos asked. "A spell of dragon control. That is what the dragon scroll does?"

The dwomanni hissed again.

"The dwarves tried to use it themselves," Tarren Red Hair continued, "and that is why she destroyed them and burnt their flesh. While she has slept, we have protected her, her offspring, and searched for the scroll, but the dwarves are crafty whores, aren't they?"

"But when the mercenaries found the scroll," Andragos said with realization, "they awoke the dragon."

"The mistress is awake?" the dwomanni said with a hint of glee. Clearly, he hadn't known. He cackled. "You are all doomed. She and her mate will lay waste to your lands and enslave your people, the ones she doesn't feast on. Your cities will burn. Your lands will burn. The world will burn."

The witches looked at Andragos and hissed. The Lord of the East waved them off.

"But the scroll is incomplete, isn't it, Terran?" the Lord of the East said. When the dwomanni didn't answer, the witches chanted again and, again, the twisted creature jerked and writhed in pain. "Isn't it?"

"Yes," Terran said. "The dwarves separated the weapon."

"And what are we missing?" the Lord of the East asked.

"The dragon sword," Terran replied, "and the dragon crown."

"You are a cursed thing, aren't you?" the Lord of the East chided. "Your whole race is. When I rule, I will wipe you and your kind from the world."

They left the dwomanni screaming and cursing as the Lord of the East snapped his fingers and the iron bars to the cell reappeared. As torture, he left the ball of light in the cell, and as the dwomanni's screaming intensified, so did the light.

"It is doubtful the dwarves tried to use this weapon ... this spell for themselves," Andragos said.

"Doubtful, but still possible," Melanius said.

"More than likely they hid it so that it could not be used," the Lord of the East said, "but now, with this little wicked creature in our possession, we not only found out where the scroll was, but we know how to find the dragon sword as well. He was able to give us detailed information about the scroll. It is from Terran that we constructed the map to Orvencrest. And it is because of him we know the sword lies in the keep of Fealmynster, north of the Gray Mountains, guarded by an ancient mage."

"And this is your plan?" Andragos asked as they stood in the main room of Fen-Stévock's deepest dungeons. "You wish to find the three pieces of this weapon and rule all the world?"

"It is my destiny, Andragos," the Lord of the East said. "It is my future, one I wish you to be a part of, my old mentor."

For a moment, the Lord of the East's little charm worked on Andragos. He felt the gooseflesh on his arms, the excitement of being needed and wanted. But it quickly wore off. Syzbalo was a powerful mage in his own right, but not that powerful. Andragos would be a powerful ally, but despite Andragos' many inequities, Syzbalo knew the Black Mage had seen what such power could do, had done. The Messenger remembered the time before the Long Peace, and a time even before that.

Andragos steeled his mind, knowing that the Lord of the East's witches and new mentor were always searching it. He had to go home and prepare.

34

Ecfast was more than just a dwarvish outpost. A myriad of peoples gathered there during the day, trading and requesting passage into the lands of the dwarves. Erik saw ogres, men, and gnomes. He even saw the cat-men he had seen at *The Lady's Inn,* in Finlo—five of them, all an array of different cats, and they bartered with the ogres and spoke in a language of purrs and meows and hisses.

A tall dwarf, all clad in plate mail with a dark red cloak trailing behind him approached the mercenaries, helmet tucked under an arm and smile evident under his thick, red beard. He spoke to the

Turk for a moment and then motioned for the companions to circle up around him.

Turk produced a piece of rolled parchment for the other dwarf to read. Then he turned to Erik.

"Show him," Turk said.

Erik retrieved the circlet Balzarak had given him and handed it to the dwarf. His eyes widened a bit as he handed the circlet back to Erik.

"Friends of the General of Fornhig and Keeper of the North are always welcome in Ecfast. Turk Skull Crusher tells me that all of you speak Westernese," the dwarf said in a voice that carried only a little bit of an accent, "so I will speak to you in that tongue. Welcome to Ecfast. You are honored guests. I am Captain Khamzûd Tall Tree, the Captain of Ecfast. You will stay here for a day and then we will send you off to be on your way."

Khamzûd Tall Tree bowed low and then added:

"You are free in this place to do as you wish within our laws, but know only a few things. The main gate to the Liha marketplace stays closed so, if you wish to go there, you must first ask the guard to open the door. Secondly, the main gate to Ecfast opens at sunrise and then closes at sunset. It does not open at any other time for any other reason, on orders from King Skella."

Ecfast seemed a simple structure. The middle of the outpost lay open, rising up four stories. The various rooms and quarters sat on the south side of the outpost. Dwarves leaned against the railings of each level, staring down at Erik and his companions. Walls sat along the north side of the outpost, centered by wide stairs. As they moved into the center of Ecfast, Erik saw that the stairs led down to the foyer in the front of the outpost, where the main doors sat. Two inner watchtowers raised the height of the outpost, one on each side of the main doors, and bear handlers stood in front of the double doors, large, thick leashes tied to the collars of huge, brown bears.

That night, the dwarves of Ecfast pulled more than a dozen long tables into the main center of the outpost, and that is where they ate dinner. Erik found it a joyous occasion and, once the guards of Ecfast knew he could speak their language, it became even more fun, with good food and good conversation. After dinner, and after the tables were put away, Erik and Wrothgard took to training.

"No one drank ale or wine," Erik commented on one of their breaks.

"I suspect they wouldn't," Wrothgard replied.

"And why not?" Erik asked.

"Ecfast is a major outpost," Wrothgard replied. "As you saw, many people come through this place for a number of different reasons, and not all of them come under the banner of peace. Naturally, they must have their wits about them."

"When you were a soldier," Erik said, "did you not drink a lot? Even in the field?"

"When I was young," Wrothgard said with a smile, "I drank enough to make up for all my years. But when I grew older and wiser, and when my skills improved and I was given more responsibility, I realized it was to my detriment to do so."

"I see," Erik said.

"Now, that isn't to say I never had fun," Wrothgard replied, his smile growing wider, "but in order to be an effective soldier, you must always be aware, be at your sharpest."

They trained late, stopping only as the doors closed at sunset. A myriad of people milled about hurriedly, noisily trying to make a last minute sale of their goods and wares before they had to leave for the night. Erik watched the waning sun of the Southern Mountains spill through the front doors of Ecfast and thought the sun looked a little different here. He looked to the sky, and this didn't have the same vibrant pinks and purples and reds it did back home.

He looked the other way and studied how the dwarves had carved the outpost straight into the mountainside. Watchtowers jutted from the stony cliffs, and guards stared down, watching the road that wound through the mountain ... and watching him.

"Onbreg!"

Erik heard the call as he and Wrothgard finished their morning training session and the sun began to rise. With a large creaking, the front gate opened, and as before, a diverse group of people spilled into the front gates, meandering through the outpost and into the marketplace.

It was noon when Erik gathered with his mercenary companions in front of Ecfast's gates.

"It will be hot," Captain Khamzûd Tall Tree said, mopping his brow with the back of his hand.

"Aye," Wrothgard replied before turning to the dwarf. "Your kindness and hospitality are appreciated. And, we know that you must go back to your business and tending to us takes attention away from your duties."

Captain Khamzûd Tall Tree bowed.

"Last night," he said, "a messenger arrived from Thorakest with word from King Skella which concerned you."

Erik, for a moment, thought the captain might demand the Lord of the East's treasure, or even try to stop them. What did that mean about Bryon? Was he dead?

"King Skella has ordered we give you each two horses," the captain said as they heard a clatter of hooves behind them. "They are well trained, from the King's personal stables."

Several dwarves led a train of fourteen horses to the mercenaries who began loading bags onto seven of the horses which had not been given saddles and bridles.

"You men must have made a good impression with His Highness," said Captain Khamzûd Tall Tree smiling, "to receive such a gift."

Erik held the reins of a white quarter horse. Khamzûd came over, directly to Erik, and extended his hand.

"Each passing moment, word comes to us from all over Druum

Balmduukr," the captain said. "It seems these are becoming dark times with the emergence of ancient enemies."

Erik shook the captain's hand but looked at the dwarf with confusion. Khamzûd Tall Tree explained, "Further word has come to us, that of a man who has found a great treasure lost to the dwarves, a treasure that will help the dwarvish people immensely, a man who is a true friend to the dwarvish people, a man who is a hero to the dwarvish people. They call him Erik Wolf's Bane, Erik Troll Hammer, and Erik Dragon Slayer. Truth be told, I have no idea where you could have gotten such names, Erik Eleodum, but if you are a friend to the dwarvish people, and you have, in a way, contributed to the health of my people, then I do hope our paths cross once again."

Erik felt goose pimples rise along his arms. A hero? Wolf's Bane? Troll Hammer? Dragon Slayer? If they only knew. If they only knew what thing he carried back to the Lord of the East. If they only knew that a dragon he supposedly slew—and most of the dwarves who heard that probably didn't believe a dragon lived anyway—still lived and had begun plotting her revenge, a revenge the dwarvish people would most undoubtedly feel first. If they only knew that the treasure he ... they found was guarded by the deepest, darkest evil imaginable, he wouldn't be so lauded as a hero.

"Thank you," was all Erik could muster.

Fame, right Befel. Fame and fortune, for your brother. Fame and fortune in the east. Didn't help you much did it?

Khamzûd bowed and then held up a hand. "Go with An."

"Go with An," Erik repeated.

Erik and his companions rode down the winding trail that led from the entrance of Ecfast to the foot of the Southern Mountains and, eventually, to Fen-Stévock. He looked over his shoulder, watching the dwarvish outpost fade with each step against a background of the bright blue noon sky.

I feel as if a part of me is gone. A part of me was lost in these mountains. A part of me died, maybe.

He thought of the farm again. He thought of Simone and his brother, his cousin. He was now the eldest, a status he never wanted. He was now a leader, something he never wanted. He was now rich by any standard, something he never wanted. He was now a wanted man, the dwomanni and who knew who else desiring him dead. Erik looked back at Ecfast one last time.

A part of me is gone, yes, but I think a new part of me has emerged as well.

35

Ranus and Cliens walked down the mountain path. They had to be careful because this was dwarvish territory, and the outpost of Ecfast was close. Cliens couldn't help noticing Ranus' posture. He was dejected and upset. They had trailed the mercenaries across the ravine, passing through the remnants of a battle that they had clearly won. They had even followed them through the thickest forest Cliens had ever seen. And then ... gone.

It irritated Ranus the most. He was a master tracker after all, hailing from the Shadow Marshes. He spent a whole day trying to find their tracks, all the while Cliens had noticed oddities within the mountain forest. He had never felt so unnerved. He heard voices on the wind, saw odd glimmers at night, and felt as if someone closed a hand around his throat when he closed his eyes. He finally had to pry Ranus away and convince him to return to the Plains and that was slow going. They ran into a cave bear, a pack of red-eyed wolves, and more of Patûk Al'Banan's men, hiding for what seemed an eternity each time.

Then they found them again, walking out of the entrance to Ecfast. Cliens had hoped they might rest and resupply at Ecfast, but seeing their target again offered a better option; supplies could wait.

"Fortune smiles on us," Cliens said nudging Ranus' arm.

His friend refused to turn and look, just shaking his head and grumbling.

"Look, my friend," Cliens said, grabbing Ranus' shoulder hard and pointing to the group of mercenaries, "it is them. I recognize the younger one although his beard looks thicker."

Ranus finally relented and looked. He stopped, and Cliens didn't need to see his face to know his eyes widened with excitement. Cliens was a little surprised that this was the mercenary group from Finlo, the group that had traveled with the dwarves of Drüum Balmdüukr.

"All is not lost," Cliens said.

Ranus communicated by hand signals: How do we know they succeeded?

"Few have survived. It must have been a hard journey," Cliens said. "And we don't. But they have as best chance as any, and are they now not on the road to Fen-Stévock?"

Should we take them now? the next set of hand signals asked.

"No," Cliens replied, "we will follow them. It isn't wise to start a fight right in front of dwarvish guards."

"We will attack tonight," Ranus said, now using his language of hisses and clicks.

"Very well," Cliens said with a smile.

Erik and his companions hadn't traveled long along the road from Ecfast when it split into three distinct directions: west, east, and north.

"The road west leads to what was once Aga Min," Wrothgard said, "and the one east to the Yerymann Steppes and, eventually, Crom and Bard'Sturn. North is Fen-Stévock."

"North it is, then," Turk said.

Some of the road, after it split and continued north, was simple packed dirt and hard ground—lined with flagstone and markers—but other parts were paved with large, flattened rock and it was well-traveled. Constant traffic consumed the road, and along the subsequent roads that crossed this main one. Even at night, there was little need for a fire, with all the campfires from other travelers giving off more than adequate light.

"Where do you think they're going? All these travelers?" Erik asked the first night they camped along the road.

"Some to Crom," Wrothgard replied. "Some to Ecfast. Most probably to Fen-Stévock. I am sure we will pass those on foot in the morning."

The farther north they traveled, the more diverse the people became on what Wrothgard referred to as, the Merchant's Road. Erik thought Finlo full of different people, but that was no match for the people of the east. He also saw different animals used to transport both persons and goods, large, gray animals with tusks and trunks, Wrothgard called elephants, and brown, hairy animals with a large hump on their back and funny looking faces, called camels according to Wrothgard. They almost scuffled with one group of travelers, even though they passed one another on opposite sides of the road.

"What was that about?" Wrothgard asked.

"Alfingas," Demik spat.

"Goblins?" Erik translated.

"Aye," Turk said.

Erik couldn't help thinking the goblins were ugly creatures. About as tall as the dwarves with flat noses and gray-green skin, they had pointed ears and wide mouths that, when they yelled at them, Erik could see were filled with sharp, pointed teeth. Their eyes were small and beady and had a reddish tint to them that reminded Erik of the winter wolves.

"Goblins and dwarves just don't get along," Turk explained.

"Most creatures don't get along with goblins," Demik said. "They are the runts of society."

"How long until we reach Fen-Stévock?" Erik asked.

"A day, two at most," Wrothgard replied. And then he added, "Not soon enough."

Ranus and Cliens followed at a distance, both covering their heads with scarves of cloth in case one of the mercenaries looked back and recognized them. Dusk was close at hand, and they had started seeing the signs of eastern life and small villages. Cliens had been devising a plan on how they would take the Lord of the East's treasure from these mercenaries—and their lives if necessary—when he heard a grumble come from his friend. He had stopped, and Cliens almost ran into him.

"What is the matter with you?" Cliens asked. But then he saw them.

A group of half a dozen goblins stood a dozen paces from the road. They were normal travelers, with two small ponies and a hand drawn cart, but they glared at Ranus and Cliens. Cliens saw that Ranus had dropped his scarf away from his face.

"Not now. Put your scarf back up. We don't have any time to worry about a group of stinking Alfingas."

His plea fell on deaf ears. Ranus and his people hailed from the Shadow Marshes. So did goblins. And it was goblins, supported by Golgolithul, that destroyed Ranus' village, killed most of his family, and displaced many of his people. The truth was, it was a rare sight to see one of Ranus' people in the Shadow Marshes anymore, all because of goblins.

"They are looking at us," Ranus clicked and hissed.

"We are looking at them," Cliens replied, knowing goblins hated Ranus' people as much as they hated the goblins.

Goblins were a common sight on the trading roads that led to Fen-Stévock—that was the problem with the east—and Ranus' people were not.

"They will follow us," Ranus said, "and kill us in our sleep."

"You don't know that," Cliens said. By the Creator, he didn't want a fight this night, especially before they were supposed to steal away this treasure.

"What you looking at?" one of the goblins called, speaking in Shengu. His voice was raspy and gravelly and, well, ugly.

Ranus hissed.

"Nothing," Cliens replied.

"Don't understand what he said," another goblin said. "Still has some of the marsh stuck in his throat. Or maybe a rat turd."

Ranus growled, and the goblins laughed.

"Keep walking," yet another goblin said as they stepped closer to Ranus and Cliens.

"We plan on it," Cliens said with a smile and a nod.

The last goblin to speak was bigger than the others. He wore battle scars on his face, a wide glaring one across his flat nose. One of his pointed ears folded over, causing him to squint with one eye. The handle of the sword he wore at his side looked well made, leather bound and strong. He watched Ranus and Cliens with suspicion as he stepped to within a pace of the two.

"Let's go," Cliens said, taking Ranus' arm.

The other goblins laughed, and they were close enough that Cliens could hear them whispering in their native language. Clearly, they didn't think that either Ranus or Cliens understood them. Both of them did.

"Shut up," the one who must have been the leader said, and the other goblins complied. "Watch them ... closely."

"What do you want us to do?" one asked.

"Just follow them," the leader said. "When they bed down, bring me a souvenir."

"A tongue?" another goblin said, almost with childish excitement in his voice.

"They shouldn't have looked at us," the leader said.

Ranus looked at his companion, and Cliens knew that look. It was the *I told you so* look he gave him frequently.

"All right," Cliens said, "but this is a waste of time."

They both turned, Cliens with his sword drawn and Ranus with his two-pronged spear. People moved away from the road, seeing the fight about to ensue. Certainly, they were a common sight here, being far enough away from Fen-Stévock for any constables to patrol the area.

"Don't worry," Cliens said in the goblins' language, "we won't ever look at you again. No one will."

Goblins were formidable foes in large groups. They swarmed their enemy and wore them down by sheer numbers. One might even call them brave, if they considered soldiers throwing themselves into the waiting spears of the adversary with reckless abandon brave. But individually, goblins were not very good warriors. They were strong for a creature as slight as a small woman and no taller than a dwarf, and there were certainly stories of goblin heroes, but normally a goblin in a small group or by himself was not much of a threat to a well-trained and much bigger combatant.

Ranus leapt over the group of goblins, his legs strong. He jabbed his spear into the back of one, drawing a knife and slicing the throat of another. Cliens yelled, causing one of the goblins' ponies to rear up and run away. That spooked the other pony, knocking over another goblin. Cliens took the opportunity to run him through. Another one charged, and he was an easy kill.

The goblin leader grabbed his remaining companion by the scruff of the neck and threw him into Cliens. It took the man by surprise, and he found himself on his back with the goblin on top of him. He was heavy for how he looked, and Cliens couldn't lift his sword. He dropped his weapon and wrapped his hands around the goblin's neck. Looking up, he saw the goblin leader training his blade over the two, and Cliens moved to the side as the leader ran his blade through his companion.

"You are scum," the goblin leader growled in his own language.

Ranus, who squared up to the remaining goblin, simply growled as Cliens got back to his feet. Both he and Ranus stepped forward, ready to engage the goblin, but he noticed a crowd growing. Even without constables patrolling the area, and the relatively loose laws of Golgolithul, too much attention was never a good thing.

"We should go," Cliens said.

Ranus didn't move.

"Ranus, people are noticing," Cliens added. "We should go."

Now it was the goblin growling, angrily.

"Watch your back, swamp monster," the goblin hissed as Cliens and Ranus backed away from him, pulling their scarfs over their faces again and leaving the scene.

"Don't worry about him, Ranus," Cliens said.

Ranus just shrugged.

"Let's find this thing for Gol-Durathna and the General Lord Marshall and get home," Cliens added. "We've both been gone too long."

36

Bryon woke up to see the face of a dwarvish woman hovering above his. The features were hazy at first as Bryon tried to blink the sleep from his eyes, but they soon came into focus. She had a pleasant face, not necessarily a pretty one, but compared to the dwarvish men ... Bryon would rather wake up to her than one of the several surgeons that had been treating him. Bearded and angry looking—always angry looking.

The woman dabbed Bryon's forehead with a dry towel. He could feel the sweat that had collected at his neck and in his armpits and at the small of his back. As consciousness took a firmer hold of him, he could feel the heat. It wasn't the room, though. That much he knew.

It was him. He was hot, burning up as if he was lying in the hot sun in the middle of summer.

And then there was the pain. Bryon had forgotten about the pain which raged through his whole body but centered in his chest. It felt as if someone stabbed him over and over with a knife that was as hot as an iron from the forge.

Bryon tried to move, but couldn't. He told his body to move, and it didn't listen. He commanded his body to move, but it was unresponsive. The dwarvish woman put a gentle hand on Bryon's bare chest. She smiled and shook her head ever so slightly. She said something in her native tongue, and at that moment, Bryon had wished he had paid attention to Erik's language lessons.

The pain built and built, and Bryon groaned louder and louder until he was screaming. There was no other way to voice the situation, but the dwarvish woman put two fingers to his lips and hushed him gently as if he was a crying babe. She said something to him, but he didn't understand. He shook his head, and he felt tears role down the side of his face. She said the same thing again.

"I don't understand you," Bryon murmured, shaking his head.

"Pain," she said. Then she repeated, "Pain."

Bryon began to weep. It was too much, and he had never felt anything so terrible. He managed to nod his head.

Still smiling, the woman left his side for a moment and returned with a tall, thin bottle. She uncorked it and put the bottle to Bryon's lips.

"Drink," she said.

Bryon opened his mouth. The liquid was cool, cold almost. It was sweet at first, but slowly turned sour and tart. Bryon wanted to stop drinking—in fact, he tried—but the dwarvish woman kept the bottle to his mouth. As he drank more, the liquid became hot and bland, losing its entire flavor. It began to burn his throat, and his stomach twisted, and he wanted to stop drinking, but the woman made him continue. Finally, she showed Bryon the empty bottle, patted him gently on the arm, and turned to move away.

"Wait," Bryon muttered, weakly grabbing her wrist. The pain still seemed to swell through his body, and whatever he drank didn't do anything. He thought maybe it was sweet wine, or something like it.

"Wait. It still hurts. Please. Whatever god is out there, please. The pain. Make it stop. Please, make it stop," he said but the women simply smiled, took her arm from his grasp and patted his hand before she left the room.

Bryon cried and moaned and pled for his pain to subside; he just wanted it all to go away. Then, he felt comforting warmth, emanating initially from his stomach. It felt like a blanket held tight on a cold night, or the gentle embrace of a beautiful woman under the stars. Bryon smiled. The warmth spread to his chest and his back as the pain subsided there and the warmth spread to his arms and his legs. Now he felt numb—his neck, the back of his head, his cheeks, his lips. Then there was only darkness.

When Bryon woke again, he felt well enough to lift his head and look around the room. There were no other beds, just the one in which he lay. A small table sat in one corner with a candle burning faintly on it, and another one on a table next to his bed. Most of the room was dark, but despite the shadows, he knew he was the only person there.

Where am I now? Is this Thorakest?

He could move, and for that, he was glad. The pain was mostly gone, lingering in his chest and head, but it was manageable, and certainly no worse than he had dealt with in recent weeks. He put his hand to his chest, where it hurt, and felt padding. It was a patch, a bandage that covered his wound. As he pressed on it, a surge of ache throbbed through his whole body, and he clenched his teeth.

The dragon wound. How long until this damn thing heals?

He laid his head back again, welcoming the envelopment by his pillow. It was soft and warm and seemed to wrap itself all around

Bryon's face so his vision became tunneled. He watched the shadows cast by the candles dance along the ceiling of the room, and it reminded him of the candle in his room back home. His stomach immediately tightened, and he sat up quickly, despite the discomfort it caused in his head and chest.

Leaning on both his elbows, Bryon found his breathing quicken. Sweat poured from his brow. He closed his eyes tight, shook his head, and then opened them, watching the swirling grays and purples and reds dance about in his vision before disappearing quickly as his vision refocused.

Does home hold so many bad memories?

He slowly rolled to one side, swung his legs over the edge of his bed, and pushed himself into a sitting position. He hadn't realized he was naked and, even though he was the only one in the room, he pulled his blanket over his lap. The floor was warm to his feet, and he thought he might walk around a bit. Bracing himself with both hands set firmly at the edge of the bed, Bryon tried to stand, but immediately felt dizzy and sat back down.

For a moment, pain raged through his head, and he grimaced and held his breath, which only made it worse. As soon as he started breathing again and relaxed his face, his headache went away. He found a small cup sitting on the table next to his bed. He lifted it and put it to his nose. It smelled indiscriminate, and in the faint light he couldn't really tell what color it was.

Are you water? Or, are you some drink that is going to make me pass out again?

Finally, he shrugged his shoulders and took a sip. Water. Just a sip ended up not being enough, and Bryon drained the contents of the cup, immediately wishing for more—perhaps a whole pitcher.

They'll be around soon, I hope, to refill my cup. Maybe I can ask them for a pitcher then.

He made one last attempt to stand before relinquishing to the fact he would have to remain sitting. He finally lay back down and closed his eyes and tried to fall back to sleep but couldn't. Every time he closed his eyes, he would see home, his mother, his sisters ... his father. He would hear the low moan of mooing cows and the baaing of sheep. He heard the buzzing of bees collecting nectar in the early morning and the gentle cooing of a dove. His mother loved that sound and would sit outside in the morning, just as the sun peeked over the horizon, and listen to them, drinking her tea and eating buttered bread. He always found them annoying sounds, a sign that work was just moments away. But now ... now he wanted to be there. He wanted to be home.

"You're a damn fool," he cursed, and his voice echoed off the walls of his room.

He tried thinking of the work, from sunup to sundown. He tried thinking of the blisters on his hands and of biting flies and stinging ants. He tried thinking of the smell of pig food and horse manure and hearing his father curse and yell and scream as orange brandy consumed his senses. But he couldn't. He couldn't remember how his muscles ached when he worked, or the feeling of pestering insects, or the smell of manure. He couldn't even think of some of the colorful curses his father would come up with.

Instead, he smelled fresh baked muffins, juiced oranges, and the sweet bitterness of squeezed rind. He heard his sisters giggling and remembered how the sound would bring a smile to his face. He felt his mother's hand on his cheek, soft and gentle. He even heard his father ... he heard his father tell him what a good job he had done. He felt the clamp of a strong hand on his shoulder, the embrace of a strong arm as his father hugged him.

Bryon propped himself up again, leaning on his elbows and shook his head.

When, by the Creator's beard, was the last time that happened?

He rubbed his eyes with the back of one hand, surprised to find tears.

When was the last flaming time my father ever said something bloody nice to me?

He shook his head. Fool. Idiot. Naïve whelp.

When was the last time I was happy to be home? When was the last time my father was sober enough to hug me?

But then, he remembered with great clarity the day before he left home. His mother had baked fresh muffins, and his sisters were playing in the back of the house with dolls and a little play hut he had built them—a thatched roof, wooden porch, and even a washing basin he had made from one of his mother's old sewing thimbles.

He had already completed his work in the fields for the day, and his mother had squeezed fresh oranges and he drank two cups worth of the sweet juice. He had decided to do more work, tending to the horses to make sure their shoes were all right and they were groomed. That's when his father grabbed him, led him to the fields he had just worked, and put his arm around Bryon. He squeezed Bryon and told him how proud he was. He had already started drinking, but it was too early in the day to be drunk.

He said he was proud of me,

Bryon sat up in his bed and watched the tears fall into his cupped palms.

You old bastard. You old drunk bastard.

He had forgotten those memories of home, pushed aside by the sour ones of the fighting, the yelling, the drunken, cursing rants that assuaged his guilt for leaving as he did. Then he remembered the sight of a young man, about his age, tilling a field with him, pulling weeds and digging ditches and planting seeds. Befel.

Bryon had gotten a late start and knew that he would never finish in time, causing his father to be furious again. So Befel came to help; despite all the work he also had, he agreed to help Bryon, work with him, side by side. The cousin he had so despised for the last two years.

Befel always comforting Bryon when his father got too drunk, when the cursing was especially mean. It was Befel, coming over to Bryon's house when he just couldn't stand being around five sisters anymore, just to be with Bryon. It was Befel, jumping into a fight to back up Bryon, even though Bryon had started it. It was with him whom he played wooden swords. It was Befel with whom he went riding. It was Befel with whom he shared his deepest secrets, his hopes, and his dreams. And now he was gone.

"I'm sorry, Befel," Bryon cried. "I'm so sorry. I'm the bastard. I'm no better than my father. I'm worse. I'm so sorry."

He sat there and cried, thinking of all the time he had spent with Befel, thinking of all the fits of laughter from his sisters he had missed in the last two years, thinking about all the batches of muffins and pitchers of orange juice he had missed, thinking about all the hugs—those coveted hugs—from his father he had missed.

"Just one more day, cousin," Bryon sobbed. "I wish I had just one more day. Just one more day to tell you I'm sorry. Just one more day to tell you how much your friendship actually meant to me. Just one more day ... one more day to tell you I love you."

37

The tall grass tickled at Erik's fingers as he walked through the meadow. The sky was clear and dark, faint purples and reds floating overhead as the sun descended in the west. Erik had never been here at dusk, as the light of the day waned and dared to disappear.

Erik saw the hill in the distance, with the great willow tree sitting atop it. The tree looked like a shadow, dark and ominous, in front of the setting sun. The light breeze that always seemed to exist here had picked up, briskly fluttering the tops of the tall grass, whipping Erik's hair about his face, and pulling and pushing the branches of the willow tree as it pleased.

Erik walked towards the hill expecting to hear the voices, the hissing curses and maniacal laughter he so often heard when he was here. He expected to smell the rot and the death and feel their hot breath of the dead on his skin. But they weren't there, and he heard nothing but the flutter of a brisk wind through tall grass.

As he approached the hill, he saw the shadow of a man standing at the hillock's foot, but as he neared the solitary figure, he saw that it wasn't one of the walking dead. It was a man standing there.

"I normally see you sitting under the tree," Erik said, speaking to the shadow even though he was clearly too far to hear.

As Erik got even closer, though, he realized this wasn't the man he normally saw in his dreams, sitting under the willow tree and staring out onto the meadow. In fact, Erik could now see that man sitting as he normally did. No, this other man was broad at the shoulders, slightly shorter than Erik. As he came into view, Erik could see his sandy hair kept short in the back and around his ears. He wore plain clothing, wool pants, and a cotton, stitched shirt.

The man turned around and Erik stopped. His breath and his heart stopped. The world around him stopped.

"Befel," Erik whispered.

Befel just stared at Erik; his pale face held no emotion. He stood straight and still, and now Erik moved to run to his brother as Befel turned back around to face the tree.

"Befel!" Erik yelled and ran to his brother. His heart went from not moving at all to slamming against his chest.

Befel didn't respond, remaining facing away from Erik, unmoving, stoic almost.

"Befel!" Erik cried again. He ran so hard his feet got tangled and he fell, hitting the ground hard. As he skidded along the ground, Erik felt dirt cake on his cheeks and forehead. A strong gust of wind blew over the dream meadow, and the grass whipped hard against Erik's face.

He pushed himself to his knees and over the tops of the grass, saw

Befel, still standing there. He got to his feet and continued to run to his brother.

Erik finally stopped, just paces away from Befel.

"Befel," he said. The smile on his face made his cheeks hurt. "Brother."

Befel didn't move, as if he didn't hear Erik, didn't see him or even sense his presence.

"He can't hear you, Erik."

Erik recognized the voice. It was the man sitting under the willow tree.

"What do you mean?" Erik asked.

"He cannot hear you," the man said again. "He has passed from this world. You know this. You saw him die."

Erik felt tears well up in his eyes and trickle down his bearded cheeks.

"He is getting ready to take the caravan home," the man under the willow tree said. "He is waiting to join many others, including your grandfather."

Erik was close enough to touch Befel, and he reached out, putting his fingers on Befel's shoulder. Befel turned around and looked at Erik with blank eyes as blue as they had always been. But they saw nothing.

Erik's stomach knotted, and a lump caught in his throat. He couldn't help himself. He hugged Befel, squeezing his brother as hard as he could, weeping the whole time. Befel didn't move. He didn't hug back. He didn't push Erik away. He just stood there and stared straight, eyes still blank.

"What cruel place is this?" Erik cried, releasing his brother, "that my own brother doesn't recognize me. Won't recognize me."

"One more moment," said another voice, not of the man under the willow tree. Erik turned to see another figure, clothed in a black cloak, a cowl pulled low over his face so that it was hidden, standing next to Befel. He remembered this person, from another dream, deep in the forest. He remembered this person leading people onto a carriage. He remembered the person cursing others to doom.

"That is what you wished, yes? One more moment with your brother. You cried it, over and over. You prayed it. You even commanded it—such boldness—of the Creator, that he gave you one more moment with your brother. This is your moment. Do with it what you will."

"What good is a moment with my brother if he doesn't recognize me?" Erik asked.

He could see the cloaked figure's shoulders move as he shrugged.

"What good would one more moment do you if he did recognize you?" the cloaked figure asked. "What would you say to him?"

"I would tell him I love him," Erik said, straightening his shoulders a little, wiping tears away from his cheeks.

"Did he not know you loved him when he died?" the cloaked figure asked.

"I don't know," Erik replied. "I suppose he did. I would tell him how much I appreciated him."

"And he didn't know that?"

"I would talk to him about our family. About my mother and father and sisters," Erik replied.

"And how long would that take?" the cloaked man asked. "Do you see, Erik, that a moment is not enough time? Do you see that a day is not enough time? Do you see that even a year, a lifetime, is not enough time?"

"So, I am a fool," Erik muttered.

"No," said the man under the willow tree. "You are no fool, just a man who misses his brother."

"Will my brother ever recognize me?" Erik said.

"You will not see him again," the cloaked man said.

"For a while," the man under the tree added. "Probably for many years. But you will see him again. And when you do, he will recognize you. And the lifetime that you've been apart will seem like just a moment."

"Come, Befel," the cloaked man said.

Befel looked at the cloaked man and nodded, allowing the man to lead Befel to a carriage that had appeared in the meadow, amongst the tall grass.

"Befel," Erik whispered.

Befel continued to walk, slowly, towards the carriage.

"Befel!" Erik cried. "Befel! I love you!"

Befel stopped, just before the carriage, and turned to face Erik. He didn't smile, didn't show any emotion at all but, for a moment, his eyes met Erik's. Erik knew, then, that his brother recognized him, and he smiled as Befel stepped onto the carriage and as it rolled away.

"Come, Erik," the man under the willow tree said. "Come, sit next to me and watch the sunset."

Erik climbed the hill and sat down under the tree. The wind was cool on his face as it dried the tears that rested there.

"I was here, in another dream," Erik said, "but everything looked dead and dull. There was a man there. And a dwarf."

"Ah, yes," the man under the tree said. "The Shadow tries to mirror everything the Creator does, but it is always twisted, distorted, ugly. That you were there, in that place, makes me wonder ..."

"Wonder what?" Erik asked.

The man only chuckled and shook his head with the slightest of smiles.

"A conversation for another time, perhaps," the man said.

Erik stared out at the meadow of grass, the sun setting, and the carriage gone.

"I've never seen a sunset here," Erik said.

"It is a rare thing," his companion said, "that someone is here when the sun sets. But it is a wonderful sight, unlike any other sunset you will ever see."

And it was. The colors were nothing like Erik had ever seen. Golds and silvers and coppers. Reds and purples and pinks and blues. Yellows and oranges and greens. It was as if all of the colors of the world had been painted across the sky. And when the sunset subsided and the nighttime took hold, the sky sparkled with stars, constellations Erik had never seen before. They shined so brightly, it almost looked like daytime across the meadow.

"Beautiful," Erik said, keeping his eyes on the sky.

"Yes, it is," the man next to him said. "Beautiful and everlasting, just like life."

Erik looked to the man sitting next to him, and the man looked back. Where did he know him from? Erik shook his head and looked back at the stars, smiling at his constants.

Erik woke and sat up. It was night, but traffic could still be seen traveling along the road to Fen-Stévock. He rubbed his face and stood, his companions still asleep. Then, his hand went to his belt. The scroll case wasn't there, and for a moment, his heart stopped. He looked about, feeling underneath his blanket on which he slept and under his haversack. Then, he remembered he had put it in his haversack, not worried about Switch or Threhof or anyone else trying to steal it anymore. He retrieved the treasure and held it, staring at it in the moon and starlight.

You are becoming obsessed with this thing.

He stuffed it in the front of his belt, feeling the obsession he had over it. He could not get the scroll out of his mind, nor the smell of the dead as Patûk Al'Banan read the words on the scroll, nor the voice of the dragon inside his head. What exactly was on that scroll? He knew it was evil. He knew it had to do with the dragon and the dead and the dwomanni. But a part of him wanted to know for sure.

A finger tickled the small cork that sealed one end of the case, knowing it had already been opened. He was probably already destined for punishment for that from the Lord of the East, so what would be one more look?

But then what? Perhaps in his mind he understood the language of evil, what Balzarak had said was called the Shadow's Tongue, but he doubted he could read it. But in the halls of Orvencrest, when the evil that resided there had taken over Befel's body and Befel spoke those words, Erik understood. Maybe the same thing would happen if Erik read the words. Would he recognize the characters on the page? There was only one way to find out.

He tickled the cork again, grasping it with his thumb and forefinger, wiggling it just a bit ... Another thought entered his mind. What if a man with a good heart controlled a dragon? Could a thing of pure devastation be used for good? Could not a sword be used for sin or righteousness?

If Erik controlled a dragon, he could wipe the dwomanni from existence. He could use it to support rulers that were good and depose rulers that were wicked. Slavers and thieves and assassins and murderers and rapists would fear the punishment of their crimes so much so that they would turn from their malicious ways.

A smile crept across Erik's face as he wiggled the cork toggle a little more. Then he felt a pinch, a painful poke at his hip from his dagger.

You toy with something you know nothing about Erik.

I simply wish this could be used for good.

You have no idea what is on that scroll, what true devastation can come from this thing.

Do you know?

Yes.

Tell me!

Men become drunk with the thoughts of power, It turns good men evil, heroes to villains, and righteous rulers to tyrants.

Erik grunted with frustration. What did his dagger know? But it did. It helped lead him to the scroll. It trusted him. Did it choose poorly, trust wrongly?

"No," Erik muttered, shaking his head. "I don't want to be a savior. I don't want to be some hero. I just want to go home and hope that my family and Simone are still there and alive."

He pushed the cork back into place, pushed the scroll case farther into his belt and patted his golden-handled dagger.

Thank you.

He felt a gentle tingle along his hip.

Erik decided he would try to go back to sleep, but as he was crouching down to lay down once again he saw a shadow move off to the side of the road. It shouldn't have been such an alarming thing, there were lots of shadows along the Merchant's Road as people camped for the night, but this was different. There were two of them, moving stealthily as if stalking something, stopping for a moment before moving again. They got closer, and Erik reached down and shook Turk's shoulder.

"Huh, what?" the dwarf said, still groggy with sleep.

"Wake up," Erik whispered. "There's someone out there."

Turk sat up, rubbing his face.

"There are a lot of someone's out there," Turk grunted.

"I know, and if this is a false alarm, I'm sorry," Erik said, "but if there is anything I have learned on this journey, it's to listen to my gut which is saying there is something out there that has its sights set on me ... us."

"All right, Erik," Turk said, still with a hint of irritation in his voice as he sat up straighter and grabbed his battle axe.

Erik woke Wrothgard and Beldar and Bofim while Turk woke Nafer and Demik. It had been a few moments, and Erik hadn't seen the shadows for a while. Demik decided to make a fire since they were all awake.

"Well," Wrothgard said, "I suppose at least we'll get an early start."

Erik wondered if he was being foolish when he saw them again. They were closer. He stood, one hand on Ilken's Blade, the other on Bryon's elvish blade. Then he felt something disturb the wind as it passed by him, a sudden whiz as if a large bumblebee had fluttered by his face.

"What, by the god," Wrothgard said, standing quickly with his hand grasping a small dart that had stuck in his neck where it met his shoulder.

It was a tiny thing, and Wrothgard pulled it, barely drawing blood, but when Wrothgard moved to stand, he stumbled and fell to a knee.

Erik drew his swords.

"It's a froksman's dart," Demik said, inspecting the tiny weapon as Wrothgard sat on the ground. He looked, drowsy, almost drunk.

"A froksman?" Erik asked.

"Frog men," Demik explained, "from the Shadow Marshes. Not meant to kill, but to slow down, put a man to sleep, as you can see."

Erik felt another dart whiz by his face. This one bounced off Turk's shield just as he raised it. Then one hit Beldar, and the dwarf fell back, tripping over his saddle. He groaned as whatever poison on the dart began to take hold of him.

"Show yourself!" Erik yelled.

The answer given was another dart. This one scratched his cheek, and Erik could immediately feel numbness on that side of his face.

Bofim was next to Erik, but when a dart hit him in his exposed forearm, it took just a bit more time than it took Wrothgard for him to go to both knees, woozy and fighting unconsciousness.

Erik leapt into the darkness beyond their camp, the purple light of his magic sword casting weird shadows. That's when he saw them, two men he recognized from Finlo. The recognition was only because of the froksman—the frog man. He was an odd-looking thing, with the torso of a man, but the wide, wedge shaped head of a frog, eyes set atop. His hands were webbed and, even though Erik couldn't see them, he suspected his feet were too. His companion, who was simply a man, was broad shouldered and bald, with a close cropped, black beard that still looked somewhat wild. Erik only recognized him because he was with the froksman.

Erik charged them. He could hear footsteps behind him and knew at least Turk followed. Erik had his eyes trained on the froksman, with his poisoned darts, but suddenly, a flash of bright light blinded him, and he felt himself stumble. When his vision returned, both men were past him, making their way towards the camp. Turk was on his knees, also blinking wildly.

Why wouldn't they attack? Why wouldn't they have tried to kill us?

But then Erik saw the two men in the middle of their campsite. The man had kicked Demik in the stomach as he tended to Wrothgard, and the froksman held up a hand, a cloud of dust swirling around Nafer so that the dwarf couldn't see anything. The froksman then leapt into the air, higher than any man could have jumped, and landed behind Nafer, kicking out and shoving the dwarf across the fire to the other side of the campsite, where he tumbled over haversacks and saddles and fell to his face.

Then, both the froksman and the man began rifling through their things, tossing clothing, cooking implements, anything about.

What in the world ...

Realization hit Erik like a fist to the face.

"They're looking for the scroll!" Erik yelled to Turk as he rushed back to their campsite.

By the time Erik and Turk reached their campfire, their things had been torn apart. Nafer and Demik were back on their feet, and both the man and froksman had to turned to face them. Erik saw the froksman lift a hand.

"Cover your eyes!" Erik yelled just as another flash of blinding light consumed the space.

Nafer hadn't covered his in enough time, stumbling backwards, blinded, but the others had. The man said something to the froksman in a language Erik hadn't heard before, and the froksman replied with a series of clicks and chirps and hisses.

"They're Durathnan," Turk said. "That is probably why they want the scroll, so the Lord of the East doesn't get his hands on it."

The froksman flicked a small knife at Erik, and he blocked it with his elvish sword, attacking the frog-man at the same time with Ilken's

Blade. The Durathnan man engaged Nafer, dodging arching swings from the dwarf's wicked mace and returning the favor with precise swipes and slashes from his sword. Erik tried to close the distance between him and the froksman, but as soon as he got near, the creature did a backflip away, landing near their horses. He hissed and untied the reins of one of the animals, sent the horse running away into the darkness with a slap on its rump.

"Damn it!" Erik yelled, charging the froksman.

This time, the froksman leapt over Erik, and he heard the creature land behind him. Before he could turn, Erik felt a foot kick him in the back, and he lurched forward but managed to retain his footing. When Erik turned, the froksman was fending off Turk with a two-pronged spear while Nafer and Demik were fighting with the Durathnan man. He thought that two dwarves would have made easy work of one man, but this was clearly no ordinary fighter as his movements reminded Erik of Patûk Al'Banan.

He easily countered Demik's sword strikes, blow for blow, while dodging Nafer's mace, only to push him back with swings of his own. There were a few times when Erik thought the man could have certainly killed one of them but chose not to.

They're simply after the scroll. Perhaps we should just give it to them. Gol-Durathna is a goodly nation, isn't it? A friend of dwarves?

A tingle at his hip told him that wasn't a good idea, and as Erik rushed in again to help Turk, the Durathnan yelled something to his comrade and pointed to Erik. The froksman looked at him as well. They knew. They realized he had been carrying the scroll case, and now both of them, ignoring the dwarves, made for Erik.

Another flash blinded everyone, save for the Durathnan and the froksman, and when Erik opened his eyes, blinking wildly, the Durathnan was on him, pushing him to the ground. Both his swords were on the ground, out of reach, and the man was reaching for his belt. Erik kicked up, catching the fleshy part of the man's groin. He groaned loudly and rolled to the side, but as Erik sat up, the froksman jumped on him, shoving his shoulders to the ground and bringing one of the points of his two-pronged spear until it touched Erik's face.

The froksman grabbed the scroll case with his long fingers as Erik instinctively reached for it as well. Even though his attacker was stronger than he looked, Erik struggled with the creature until he found one of the blades of the two-pronged spear pointed at his eye. With a deep sigh, he let go of the scroll case.

The froksman jumped to his feet, grabbed the Durathnan's arm, and made for the horses. Erik turned onto his stomach, pushing himself up and grabbing his swords. The froksman cut several more reins, the horses fleeing into the night, before grabbing one for him and one for the Durathnan. Erik's companions were next to him.

"We can't let them get away," Demik said.

"No, we can't," Erik replied.

As the froksman turned his horse and lifted his heels to spur the animal on, Erik threw the elvish blade at him. The blade was a whirl of purple light as it flew steel over handle until thudding deep into the horse's ribs. The animal crumpled to the ground in a heap, its legs flailing for only a moment. The froksman flew from the saddle, tumbling head over heel. He came up, visibly angry, and turned to Erik who saw another flash before he felt something solid hit him from the side. He flew through the air, knocking all the air from his lungs when he landed. He sat up gasping, blinking wildly. When his vision returned, the froksman and Durathnan were gone—with the scroll—and Turk was kneeling in front of him, Demik's head in his lap, Nafer standing over them. The froksman's two-pronged spear was lodged in Demik's chest.

"He pushed you out of the way," Turk said, fighting back tears. "The froksman blinded you and then threw his spear at you, and just before it struck home, Demik knocked you out of the way."

"No!" Erik yelled, scrambling to his knees and crawling to Demik.

Demik's breathing slowed.

"Why?" Erik asked in Dwarvish. "You fool. Why would you do that?"

Demik groaned and turned his head towards Erik. His eyes were closed, but for a moment he opened them halfway and smiled.

"You are my friend," he said.

"But ..." Erik began, but something caught in his throat.

"There is no ... no greater honor ... than to give your life ... give your life for a friend," Demik said, still smiling, eyes now closed, breathing slowing. "I choose to ... to give my life ... for you, Erik."

"You fool," Erik said, tears welling up in his eyes. "I am just a stupid man."

But Demik shook his head, the smile still on his face. Then he grabbed Erik's wrist and pulled him close.

"Go," Demik said. "Retrieve the scroll. It is ... it is too important."

"Go," Turk said. "I will tend to Demik."

Erik looked up at Nafer. The dwarf nodded back.

Almost all of their horses were gone, only five remaining. Erik and Nafer mounted and rode hard in the direction the Durathnan and froksman fled.

Will you help me? Will you lead me?

He felt that all too familiar tingle at his hip.

38

General Bu led over thirty thousand men out of the Western Tor and into the plains of Southland. Even from a distance, he could smell the South Sea, and the masts of ships made slash marks on the horizon. There were few homes along the Western Tor of the Southern Mountains, but the small communities that did exist came out to watch the general's army march by. A mixture of fear and wonder painted everyone's face and, even though General Bu Al'Banan—a name he had started calling himself, convincing his men and Pavin Abashar's men he was the late general's son—kept his face forward as he led his men, he couldn't help cracking a small smile.

As Bu and his army neared the city of Finlo, which he had no intention of entering, the city's militia had seen them coming and rushed to create a human wall between the shops and homes and the army.

"What do we do, General?" Pavin Abashar asked.

"Nothing," Bu replied.

"If they attack?" Pavin asked.

"They won't," Bu replied. "Look at them. They're scared. Just keep marching. We will turn north at the Sea Born Road."

As they reached the ancient road that once went from Finlo all the way to Gol-Durathna, a group of five men, very diverse in both appearance and clothing, rode quickly to the front of Bu's long train of men, several well-armed militia behind them.

"Shall I have them moved?" Pavin asked.

"No," General Bu replied. Then, he looked to his left, Li—all bandaged and wearing a scarf that covered most of his face. "Who are these men?"

"The Council of Five, the ruling council of Finlo," Li said, his voice slightly muffled by both his injury and the scarf he wore.

Bu put his hand up, stopping the march of his army. He heeled Warrior forward, motioning for Li to follow him. One of the five men—a man with dark brown skin and a large bushy beard wearing brightly colored robes of orange and yellow and green and a flat turban—rode forward to meet the general.

"My name is Amman," the man said. "I am the speaker for Finlo's Council of Five. Who are you, and what are you doing with this large force of men in our city?"

"I am not in your city," General Bu replied.

"You are traveling through Southland," Amman said. "What is your purpose for such a show of force? And who are you?"

"You would be wise to watch your tone," Pavin Abashar shouted from the front of the troop column, "when speaking with General Bu Al'Banan."

Bu gave an irritated look over his shoulder, making eye contact with Lieutenant Ban Chu. The Lieutenant nodded back and inched his horse forward.

"Bu Al'Banan?" Amman said with an air of apprehension. "I know of Patûk Al'Banan, former General of the Eastern Guard. But I have never heard of you."

"I am his son," Bu replied.

"By what proof?" one of the other council members asked, a man with gray hair, a long mustache, pasty pale skin, and a simple brown tunic.

"By proof that I say so," Bu replied, "as do the thirty thousand men who follow me."

"We need more than that," the long mustached man said.

"Will it matter when I have you drawn and quartered?" Bu replied. He turned his attention back to Amman when the gray-haired man's face went even whiter than it already was. "We are heading north. That is all you need to know."

"We have no allegiances or alliances with any nation or kingdom," Amman said, "and as such, have no reason to care that General Bu Al'Banan, son of Patûk Al'Banan, passes through the country of Southland. However, with such a large force of men following you, and so many in Háthgolthane and beyond opposed to your father—peoples and nations that are incredibly powerful—your presence here could bring us trouble ... trouble we do not want or need. Where is your father?"

"Dead," Bu replied.

"Truly?" Amman asked.

Bu cursed himself inwardly. It was an ill-advised response.

"Our lord Patûk Al'Banan was tragically taken by an outbreak of the pox," Li intervened. "We once numbered forty thousand, but that scourge ravished our men. It is a tragedy, that such a man as General Al'Banan would leave this world so. Truly, he deserved a glorious death in battle."

"Truly," Amman said, and Bu couldn't tell if the man believed his seneschal.

"The wonderful city of Finlo has always treated my father kindly," Bu added.

"As such, you must lead your men away from our lands immediately," Amman replied.

The general had every intention of leaving Southland as soon as possible. He knew Patûk detested the coastal city, which meant so did he, and the late general had even less love for a people who claimed they held no allegiances or alliances, which meant so did he. And, in thinking about a stance of neutrality, Bu didn't think it possible. But this insect of a man, trying to command him, General Bu, son of Patûk ... no, he couldn't have that. Now Bu Al'Banan decided he would stay just outside of Finlo for a day or two, camp his men along the countryside of Southland.

"As much as I wish to lead my men north, immediately, I have many mouths to feed, and we will need to camp here for a day or two," the general replied, speaking with a feigned politeness.

"No, you cannot," Amman replied. "This is unacceptable."

"I am truly sorry," Bu said, putting a hand to his chest and giving a bow that was entirely too low, "but there is no other way. We will camp but two days, after which, we will continue our march north."

"This will not stand!" yelled another of the council, this man with fiery red hair and a leathern jerking.

"Oh no," Bu replied. He knew Ban Chu and Pavin had ridden up next to him. "And what do you plan on doing about it?"

"We have our militia," the red-haired man said.

"They will be dead within the hour," Bu said. "All of them. And then I will set my men loose upon your city. They will rape every woman and plunder every shop. And after I have skinned each one of the members of the council alive, feeding your skin to street dogs while you watch, I will put fire to your beloved city, surrounding it with my soldiers, so that not one wretched soul will escape."

Amman moved to speak, but before he could, General Bu put a hand up.

"Or, you can ride away and let us camp here for a couple days, unharassed," Bu added.

The general could hear the other men protesting, but Amman hushed them.

"What assurance do we have that you will not unleash your men on our city?" Amman asked. "What assurance do we have that law will remain?"

"My men will do as I tell them," Bu said, "and we have no interest in making trouble within your city. But my men do not fall under your law. If they cause lawlessness, I will take care of it. You will not. It would be great folly if your militia men attempted to discipline even my lowly soldiers."

While they camped that night, what must have been every whore and butcher and brewer streamed from Finlo and into Bu's encampment.

"Let's see that pompous bastard complain when his tax coffers fill with my men's coin," General Bu said as he stood in front of his tent, hands clasped behind his back, watching his camp.

He had seen Patûk stand in such a way, surveying everything before him with an emotionless stare. He knew Patûk had a penchant for spiced wine, but never too much, so when a brewer passed by offering drink, Bu just glared at him. He never saw the general eat in front of his men, so when a butcher passed by, he simply nodded to Ban Chu, and his new lieutenant hurried the man along. And he was certain the general had lain with women before—in fact, he heard him talk about it, but Bu didn't even know if the general would have enjoyed it. So, when several whores came by the general's tent, as beautiful as they were, Bu told them to piss off and service some soldier, for that's all they were good for.

"Said truly, my lord," Li said. "You have brought them much financial gain."

"The Council of Five are fools that hide behind a pretense of lawfulness," Bu spat. "I have been in Finlo before. Lawlessness rules that city."

"That they are," Li agreed. "Anyone knows that the true law here is the glimmer of gold."

"Who do they think they are, to challenge me so?" Bu asked, almost ignoring his seneschal.

"They must challenge you, my lord," Li said.

"How do you mean?" Bu asked.

"Would the citizens of Finlo trust the Council, or their laws, if they didn't at least show a moment of force?" Li asked. "Today, they would let you pass by, unabated, and tomorrow they would find themselves out of a job and new men serving as the Council."

Bu nodded.

"How are your injuries?" he asked.

"Every movement hurts," Li replied. "My face is scarred. My skin is cracked. My speech is slurred."

"But you still have your wits?" Bu asked.

"Yes, my lord," Li replied.

"And the surgeons are tending to you?"

"Yes, my lord," Li replied, "although, I fear drinking too much tomigus root tea, or drinking too much dream milk, lest I become completely dependent on them."

Bu nodded.

"And what do you make of your translation of the scroll," Bu asked, "the one those mercenaries are to return to the Lord of the East?"

"It is called the Dragon Scroll, my lord," Li replied. "Part of it is a spell that gives the reader the ability to ward off dragon fire and dragon magic. The other part is a map and directions to the Dragon Sword."

"And, tell me again, what this Dragon Sword does," Bu said.

"The wielder, with the spell, can control or even kill a dragon," Li said.

"That is power," Bu muttered.

"But it is incomplete," Li added.

"As you have said," Bu replied.

"And I have no idea where the missing piece is," Li added. "It was clearly ripped from the bottom of the parchment."

"Do you think the missing piece could be with the Dragon Sword?" Bu asked.

"Perhaps," Li replied. "It is a good notion. Or at least some indication as to where to find the missing piece."

Bu nodded again.

"Might I ask," Li said, "what was your surname before you became the long, lost son of the late Patûk Al'Banan, thus making you Bu Al'Banan?"

Bu never knew how to take any of Li's questions. There was always a hint of derision and sarcasm in his voice. But he shrugged.

"I don't know," Bu replied. "I was a gutter shite, a fatherless gutter rat. I am no one."

"You *were* no one," Li said, and Bu turned to look at the man, who dared to allow his scarf to drop from his face in the confines of Bu's tent. The cracked skin on his face was red and glaring, his left eye permanently closed, the left side of his mouth drooped slightly, and his hair patchy over burnt skin where his ear once sat. "You are now Bu Al'Banan, son of General Patûk Al'Banan, leader of thirty thousand free men."

Bu smiled, and gooseflesh rose along his arms.

"My spies report we have men coming into our camp," Ban Chu said as Bu met with his officers in a larger meeting tent.

"Yes, I can see that," Bu replied.

"No, General, men who want to join your army," Ban Chu clarified.

"How many?" Bu asked.

"Several hundred, General," Ban Chu said.

"Truly?" Bu said. He didn't mean for his surprise to be so evident.

"Yes, General," Ban Chu said.

"I say we let them join," Pavin said as Bu met with his officers.

"Lieutenant?" Bu asked.

"I agree," Ban Chu replied.

Both men's responses were met by a cacophony of disagreement from the other officers. Bu finally put his hand up, silencing the men in his tent.

"We will welcome these men," Bu said. "They want to be a part of a new nation. I cannot blame them for that. Set them to do servant tasks. They must prove themselves. But, if I know the east, we will need every man willing to fight in the coming months and years."

Bu Al'Banan knew many of his officers walked away from the meeting disgruntled, upset about his decision. They still held on to eastern ideas of purity, but the man who, at the moment, mattered the most, Pavin Abashar, supported him. Pavin would take care of the officers who dissented too much. And anyone who continued to oppose his decision ... Bu would use them as an example of what happened to people who decided to cross him.

39

From the corner of a street at the edge of the city, Kehl and A'Uthma watched as all the whores and merchants flocked to the encampment that had been established outside Finlo. When he had returned, yet again defeated by that fat pig Del Alzon, the Samanian decided it was time to return home, taking with him what knowledge and wealth he had gained from Finlo and Háthgolthane. He would build a slave empire there and return to finally kill that fat bastard and burn his city to the ground, enslaving all its inhabitants in the process.

Kehl couldn't get his mind off the she-elf. He groaned, thinking about her, feeling his manhood stiffen. It wasn't because of her beauty—despite her almost white hair and pale skin, she was beautiful—that aroused him. It was the very idea of having an elf in his stock, a creature many believed didn't exist anymore, perhaps never existed, and there she was, in that dung heap of a city. She, alone, would make him a king. He wouldn't even have to sell her. He could chain her and charge people to come see her. Men would pay a fortune to lay with her.

"Who is this general?" Kehl asked, looking back at the encampment.

"The son of some revered soldier from Golgolithul, Im'Ka'Da," A'Uthma replied. "He has frightened the Council of Five."

"The most successful general is a fool compared to the tacticians of Wüsten Sahil, A'Uthma," Kehl said.

"Truly, Im'Ka'Da," A'Uthma said.

"The arrogance of these Háthgolthanian dogs," Kehl said. "We need to leave this place and soon."

"I agree, Im'Ka'Da," A'Uthma said. "Men are even begging to join this soldier's army."

"Why would a man beg to serve this man?" Kehl asked.

"I have heard that he means to march on Hámon," A'Uthma replied.

"March on Hámon?" Kehl asked.

"Yes, Im'Ka'Da," A'Uthma replied. "March on Hámon and take it."

"He means to be king of Hámon?" Kehl said. "Truly, what arrogance. I wish him a slow death. Should we slip into his camp and place a brain demon in his ear?

"It is a tempting notion, Im'Ka'Da," A'Uthma said, "but this man commands thirty thousand, and I have heard his tent is well-guarded."

"Do you doubt my ability to infiltrate?" Kehl asked, turning and glaring at his lieutenant.

"No, Im'Ka'Da," A'Uthma said, bowing low, "but it is said that he has a mage from the east, scarred from using too much magic, with him. Would your disguises work around such magic?"

"Perhaps not," Kehl replied. "Set our thieves to watching this encampment. They anger me. Any man that ventures into Finlo, have him castrated and raped before they slit his throat."

"Your will be done, Im'Ka'Da," A'Uthma said.

"Have we procured a ship to sail back to Saman?" Kehl asked.

"Not yet, Im'Ka'Da," A'Uthma replied.

"Do we not have enough money?" Kehl asked.

"I am increasingly finding that men are unwilling to sell to us ... as Samanians," A'Uthma said.

"These worthless dogs," Kehl seethed and slammed a fist into the wall of the building next to which he stood. He wanted to destroy something, hurt someone.

A groan erupted from beneath a pile of rags as a homeless man shifted in what Kehl suspected was a drunken slumber. He drew a knife, stepped to the man, stood over him, and plunged his weapon into flesh over and over again until all he felt, or heard, was wet, pulverized meat. He stood and breathed. He didn't feel any better.

"These Háthgolthanian dogs aren't worth the dung on our boots, A'Uthma," Kehl spat.

"You speak truly, Im'Ka'Da," A'Uthma said.

Kehl groaned and thought for a moment.

"Before I kill every man, rape every woman, and enslave ever child of Waterton," Kehl said, "I will burn Finlo down. I don't even want its riches or its people. I simply want to wipe it from the maps."

"A denizen of disease-ridden filth, Im'Ka'Da," A'Uthma said. "It could not be destroyed too soon."

Kehl breathed and calmed himself.

"Send Albin to buy a ship," Kehl said, taking a deep breath to steady himself. "They will sell to another Háthgolthanian, and I trust Albin."

"Yes, Im'Ka'Da."

"Are those men from our guild," Kehl asked, pointing from the shadows at a group of four men walking to the camp.

"I believe so," A'Uthma replied.

"Didn't you tell our people they were not to go anywhere near this camp?" Kehl hissed.

"I did, Im'Ka'Da," A'Uthma said with a low bow.

Kehl watched as the four men walked about the camp. But rather than drink or pilfer or thieve, they met with a soldier and seemed to talk to him for a long time. When they had finished talking to the soldier, they all four touched a fist to their breast and bowed to the man.

"They mean to join this army," Kehl whispered, narrowing his eyes and seething quietly.

Three of his men stayed in the camp, but one made his way back to the city. Kehl jerked his head, commanding A'Uthma to follow him. They slunk through the shadows of the city's alleyways. The city streets were almost vacant and quiet. As this one man wandered into a side street that would eventually lead to Kehl's secret hideout, the Samanian snuck up behind the man and wrapped his arm around the man's throat, pulling him back into the shadows.

"What are you doing?" Kehl hissed as he released the man, pushing him to his knees.

"Who ... Kehl?" the man said, realizing it was Kehl who had grabbed him. "What's the meaning of this?"

A'Uthma backhanded the man across the face.

"Answer your leader," A'Uthma commanded.

"I was just enjoying the revelry," the man replied, rubbing his face.

"You lie," Kehl hissed.

"Now see here ..." the thief began to say, but another hand across his face shut him up.

"You were there to enlist in that general's army," Kehl accused. "You dog."

"No, no," the thief said, fear evident in his eyes. He knew what was coming.

As Kehl stood straight, the thief's hand went to a short sword at his belt. A'Uthma punched him while Kehl drew a razor-sharp scimitar, removing the hand from its wrist. A'Uthma clapped a hand over the man's mouth, muffling any screams. Kehl then slashed his blade across the thief's chest repeatedly. Blood poured down the thief's front. Kehl nodded to A'Uthma who beat the thief until he could no longer even lift his head.

"I hope your friends stay there, in that camp," Kehl said, "because if they come back into the city, their punishment will be far worse."

Kehl drew his sword again, and in one, quick motion, removed the thief's head from his shoulders.

Kehl stood still in the room, trying to press himself into the wall. The Council of Five sat around a round table, arguing. He knew he didn't look like some Samanian. The disguises left behind by the thief Toth worked well and even his own men didn't know it was he at first. His voice and face had been changed, but nonetheless, he was still nervous, spying on the Council of Five.

He did it, from time to time, disguising himself as a servant so he could eavesdrop on their meetings, find out ahead of time what parts of the city they were getting ready to pressure or inspect or increase security in. It helped him learn of militia movements, shipments coming in and from where, a number of things that might help a slaver and his band of thieves. With this army camping on Finlo's doorstep, Kehl thought it prudent to find out what the Council of Five had to say. They didn't look very happy after speaking with this General Bu Al'Banan.

"*Martial law—that's the answer!*" one of the council members yelled, slamming his fist against the table.

"I agree," another said. "It is time to rein in our people. We have been too lax. They are all lawbreakers. Clean up the alleyways. Bar ships coming in from Wüsten Sahil and the Feran Islands."

"How will this help?" another asked.

"We are no longer respected," the first said. "It is evident. Look at the way General Al'Banan has treated us ... treated our city."

"What say you, Amman?" asked the fourth council member, standing and looking at a man yet to speak, one that could have been taken for one of Kehl's countrymen. Amman seemed to think for a while. Kehl knew that Amman was the speaker of the council. He had, at least for this cycle, the final say on the matters of law. Finally, he stood, placing his hands on the table in front of him and leaning forward.

"Martial law," Amman said. "Immediately. Close the docks for a week. Those ships that don't want to leave, burn them."

Amman then looked at Kehl, pressed hard against the wall and looking, to the Council of Five, like some young serving boy with barely a hair on his chin.

"Boy, my wine cup is empty," Amman said, "and my pitcher bare. Go get more wine."

Kehl bowed and rushed out of the room. He walked past the kitchen, where the wine was kept, and out the front door of Finlo's legislative building. When he reached the shadows of an alleyway, he pulled the disguise from his face. It still hurt, but he had finally gotten used to the pain.

"We must leave," Kehl said in a rushed tone when he met with A'Uthma.

"We don't have a ship," A'Uthma said. "And some of our slavers and thieves aren't ready."

"I don't care," Kehl replied. "We'll steal a ship, and those that aren't ready we will leave behind. The Council of Five is imposing martial law."

A'Uthma didn't offer any other argument.

Kehl knew that the commotion at the dock was because of the dead militiamen. He had killed them quietly, but one had still managed to cry out. He finished off the last sailor on this ship and threw his body overboard. The body thudded against the wooden dock, bringing even more alarm from the militia.

"We must hurry," Kehl said. He knew nothing about sailing, but some of his men did.

"This whole dock is closed!" one of the militiamen shouted. "Get off your ships, now!"

"Piss off," one sailor shouted from a ship docked directly across from Kehl's newly acquired boat.

His curse was met with different cursing, and Kehl watched as several pitch-smeared torches flew over the side of the boat. The wood quickly caught fire. The flames blazed high, and most of the sailors on board had to jump into the dirty sea. Those who chose to try and escape via the dock met their demise at the end of a sword, and those in the water fared no better, meeting their end via a crossbow bolt as soon as they emerged for air.

"Let's move," Kehl commanded as the militia set fire to yet another boat.

Some of his men began using long poles to push the boat away from the dock while others unfurled the single sail. Kehl heard a scream as a crossbow bolt struck one thief in the chest. Another squirmed about on the ground, another bolt slashing a wide wound across his face. Kehl knew the man would be blind, at least in one eye, and nodded to A'Uthma. His lieutenant picked up the injured man and threw him overboard.

"If you want to live, don't get hurt," Kehl said as some of the other Finnish thieves stared on in disbelief.

He didn't lose any more men, and they certainly gave worse than they got as they returned fire with their own bows and crossbows.

"Finnish pricks," Albin spat.

They watched as the coastal city grew smaller and smaller, two large oars first propelling the ship and then, as the wind picked up, the sail billowing and speeding them out into the open ocean.

"Most of these men are nothing more than dogs," Kehl whispered, "expendable and worth little more than the dirt on my boots. But you, Albin, you are worth any Samanian, and when we reach our home, you will enjoy the pleasures on offer to a citizen of Saman."

Kehl continued to watch until Finlo was nothing but a speck in the distance. Then, he retired to the main quarter, where his woman waited. He would relish in the pleasures of his homeland, even as they traveled there.

40

Andragos watched the bowl of water intently. He saw this new general—a man named Bu—leading a column of many thousands of men, north, towards Hámon. What was he calling himself? Bu Al'Banan, the legitimate son of Patûk Al'Banan. Andragos knew that Old Patûk probably had a dozen or more children out there somewhere, but none of them would have been legitimate. And this fool didn't even look like Patûk.

The old soldier had always worn that stupid pompous look on his face as he tried to present a facade of humility, but Andragos knew better. He had been as prideful as the rest of them, even more so. He didn't blame him, necessarily, he'd been successful, talented, a true tactician and leader. But he had left, defected, and before his death, wished to be his own king.

"Insolence," Andragos grumbled.

Many could be kings. So why weren't they? Why wasn't he a king? His powers were great. He could simply speak a word, and thousands would follow him. Duty. Loyalty. Andragos clutched at the sides of the bowl, some of the water spilling out. Stupidity.

This new man, the so-called son, however, wore a different look. There was nothing fake about that stern look he had. This man, this Bu, had no pretense about him. And as Andragos watched him through his water, he could tell that this man could be even more dangerous than Patûk.

To think, Patûk Al'Banan was finally dead. He wished he could have seen it, at least known how. His magic wouldn't tell him. The rumor was the pox. When word eventually reached the Lord of the East, Andragos knew he would laugh, internally at least. He would present a façade that he didn't care.

Pox? Andragos thought. *What a comical way for such a warrior to die.*

But he didn't believe it. Did this Bu kill him? Andragos shook his head. No. As he watched this General Bu ride in front of a column of men, he knew that this man took Patûk's last name because, in a way, he looked to the general as if he were his father. He had Pavin Abashar with him. What a fool.

Pavin Abashar was always arrogant and never sought to hide it like Patûk did. But this new general, he must have commanded respect for Pavin to follow him. Andragos could see how Abashar might follow Patûk, but some upstart general?

Andragos continued to stare at his magical bowl of water. He saw another retinue of men, heavily armored and led by a rich carriage. A well-respected nobleman rode in that carriage followed by three thousand men. They were on a collision course with General Bu Al'Banan ... and with their deaths.

If Pavin counseled him right, and if Patûk had taught this Bu anything, the general would offer this noble, the honorable Barde Bik, the chance to surrender the gold he carried, gold meant for the king of Hámon, a chance to surrender his men to Bu, his horses and carriages. The general might even offer Barde the opportunity to go home unscathed, but that was perhaps unlikely.

But Barde Bik would spit in Bu's face, and all the men that followed him to Hámon would die. Bu would torture Barde—this much Andragos knew if Patûk had truly trained him—and then send his body back to Fen-Stévock as a message. And the Lord of the East—his lord—would scoff at the message, forget the loyalty and sacrifice that Barde Bik gave to him and his country. Syzbalo would wait until this Bu and Pavin Abashar and any other defector—Dimrûk Lu-Fan was another Andragos could think of who commanded a decent number of men—had established his own kingdom before concerning himself with the west. Fool.

Andragos threw the bowl across the room. The water splashed across the wall, and his vision disappeared. The Lord of the East was always consumed with his witches, his new advisor, and his foolish new endeavors. If his father could see him. How disappointed he would be.

"My lord," Terradyn said, running into the room and Raktas following him, "are you all right?"

"I'm fine," Andragos replied, rubbing both of his temples with his forefingers.

"My lord," Raktas said, "beg your pardon, but you do not look fine."

"Patûk Al'Banan," Andragos grumbled.

"What about him, my lord?" Terradyn asked.

"He is simply a thorn, my lord," Raktas said.

"Once, yes," Andragos said, standing up and turning to see his two personal guardsmen. "But now, even in death, he is much more."

"My lord?" Terradyn asked.

"He is dead," Andragos said.

"Truly?" Raktas asked.

"But his protégé and Pavin Abashar march on Hámon as we speak," Andragos explained.

"To what end, my lord?" Terradyn asked.

"They mean to conquer the Kingdom of Hámon," Andragos replied.

"How?" Raktas asked. "Patûk was an excellent tactician, and he had zealots that followed him, but now that he is dead, and Pavin Abashar is anything but a tactician, how can they conquer a kingdom?"

"Firstly, this new man—General Bu—who leads the former Patûk's men, he is well-trained. I can tell the late general trained him personally. Secondly, Hámon is feudal and fractionalized," Andragos said. "Thirdly, Patûk Al'Banan's forces and Pavin Abashar's forces number thirty thousand. And other defectors will undoubtedly come to join them in the near future. Men like Dimrûk Lu-Fan and Captain Fluker—men on whom Lord Syzbalo has turned his back—will welcome the opportunity to serve Pavin, or this new General Bu, and openly fight against the Eastern Empire, bringing yet another three or four thousand fools under their command. What they command now is more than enough to bring the Hámonian nobles to submission and overthrow King Cedric."

"What should we do?" Terradyn asked.

"What can we do?" Andragos replied. "I cannot crush a whole army, even as powerful as I am. And Syzbalo—the Lord of the East—does nothing, spending all his time with those bitches. Patûk, even in death, will eventually be much more than a thorn in our side, and when that day comes, I will bear the brunt of the Lord of the East's condemnation."

"Why put up with it?" Terradyn said in a hushed tone. Even in Andragos' personal quarters—which were protected by powerful magic—the walls of Fen-Stévock had ears, and the Lord of the East was a powerful mage in his own right.

"A day may come soon, Terradyn, when I will not," Andragos whispered, more to himself than to his guard.

41

"General," Captain Kan said, meeting Bu Al'Banan as he reached the lands of Hámon. Bu couldn't help sensing a bit of apprehension in the captain's voice. Captain Kan and Bu had always gotten along, even when Bu was a simple spy. The captain seemed to recognize his worth and treated him with at least that much respect. But Captain Kan was as loyal to Patûk as Bu was, and Bu could tell that the death of Patûk and his ascension to general and commander of thirty thousand men could possibly cause tension between the two men. Bu truly hoped Kan would accept him as his general. Kan was a good leader, a good soldier, and commanded the men's respect.

"Captain," Bu said with a quick bow.

"Lieutenant Ban Chu," Captain Kan added. "General Abashar."

Both men also bowed.

"How have you been, Captain?" Bu asked.

"Well," Captain Kan replied with eyes that spoke of distrust, "but not, apparently, as well as you, it seems, General Bu Al'Banan."

"Can I expect your loyalty, Captain Kan?" Bu asked.

"Al'Banan?" Kan asked, ignoring Bu's question.

Only men that Bu trusted—Li, Ban Chu, Pavin, and Andu—stood in the tent with Kan.

"I thought it would make the transition to general easier," Bu explained. "If the men believed I was Patûk's son, they would more readily accept my lead. It was Li's idea. It has seemed to work thus far."

Kan looked at the disfigured and burned seneschal with the same suspicious eyes that Bu found himself looking at the man with most times.

"And why was the title of commander not passed on to General Pavin Abashar?" Kan asked, eyeing the general. "By the god of the east, why wasn't I considered?"

Bu shifted, ever so slightly, nervous and a bit uncomfortable and trying not to show it. He gave Pavin a sidelong glance and the general returned the glance, fear evident in his eyes. They knew why the general relented control.

"You would have been the first choice, Captain," Bu replied. "But we needed someone to lead, lest we lose command of thirty thousand men, and as for Pavin ..."

"Truth be told," Pavin said, interrupting Bu, "General Bu offered the title of commander to me, but I turned it down. He is as adept a leader as any—I have had enough time to see that much—and, even though I am still an ambitious man, I am no spring chicken anymore."

"Do you wish to be Commander, Kan?" Bu asked. Kan smiled, only slightly. "I will pass this title to you, right now, if you wish. You are right. It should have been rightfully yours."

Li looked at Bu, with his one good eye, in disbelief, as did Ban Chu. Pavin didn't show any emotion. He knew what Bu was doing, and Andu shifted uneasily. He was always nervous, a man with a broken spirit.

"I would be lying if I said I didn't desire this," Kan said, and then shook his head, "but no, you are Commander General. You have led the men this far with success, and to change leadership right now would cause turmoil. I trust I will receive due reward for my loyalty and support when we conquer Hámon?"

"Yes, of course. You will be Duke Kan Schu," Bu replied. "Now, what news?"

"As we speak," Kan explained, "a delegation from Fen-Stévock makes its way to Venton, having requested an audience with King Cedric."

"Have you tried to stop them?" Pavin asked.

"I would, my lord," Kan replied, "but my men only number a thousand, and theirs over three thousand. I believe in my men, but I am sure the vassals of Hámon would come to the Stévockian's aide. It would be folly. I am sorry, General Al'Banan."

"No need for apology, Captain," Bu said. "We will intercept this delegation."

"And when we do, General?" Pavin asked.

"Offer them the opportunity to turn over all their gold and carriages and horses and then return to their home country," Bu replied with a smile.

"You know they won't accept," Pavin said. "Surely, Patûk taught you that much of Eastern officers."

"Of course, they won't," Bu replied. "And yes, Patûk taught me that much and more. So, we will make an example of them ... to both the Eastern Empire and to the vassals of Hámon. This is what happens when you cross General Bu Al'Banan. Who leads this delegation, Captain Kan?"

"Lord Barde Bik, my lord," Kan replied.

"Unfortunate," Bu said with a scowl.

"Indeed," Kan replied. "You have heard of him?"

"Yes," Bu said.

"He is actually a good man from a good family," Kan said. "I hate it when such men must die. I hope you will make sure his death is quick and as painless as possible. A show of humility and compassion to the people of Hámon."

"Yes, of course," Bu said. "Li, Ban Chu, Pavin, what do you think?"

All three men nodded.

Bu marched his army for another day, and when they finally neared the walls of Venton, they could see Barde Bik's camp settled outside. Ban Chu's spies had brought word that the Stévockian delegate had already been meeting with the king. It was no matter, just another anthill Bu would have to deal with. As the army neared the city, General Bu could hear the yelling and screaming of men and women as they ushered their families inside the city walls. With the fearful shouting, he saw a cloud of dust as a large retinue of about two hundred horsed men raced towards his column. He held up a fist.

His army stopped and waited. It was only a moment before the entourage of horses and men reached him. He saw Barde there, a short, broad shouldered man with almost all gray hair, save for a bit of Golgolithulian black sprinkled in here and there. Many of the men with Barde were Golgolithulian soldiers, but among them was a large, blond-haired man, fat and clearly uncomfortable on his wide saddle. His beard was splotchy, and his robes spilled out over his hands and feet, and he wore a simple golden circlet about his head.

"Lord Bik," Bu said with a quick bow.

"How dare you speak to a simple lord before addressing the King of Hámon," another man, one who wore a woman's paint on his face and clothing that billowed out at his elbows and knees, said, his face red and angry.

"Who are you?" Bu asked.

"Jackson," the man replied, "steward to King Cedric."

"Well you're not the king then, so I will make sure to kill you first," Bu said.

"What insolence!" the steward shouted.

"Who are you?" Barde Bik asked. "Why should I bother speaking with you?"

"I am Bu Al'Banan, son of Patûk Al'Banan," Bu replied, "and as to why you should treat with me, well, because I command thirty thousand easterners."

"Patûk had no sons," Barde Bik said, "at least legitimate ones that he would have cared enough for to train as a replacement. Clearly, your claim is a pile of troll scat, but I care not. Call yourself whatever you want. I know Pavin Abashar, and I know Kan Schu, and you must be a worthy leader if they choose to follow you. As for easterners, despite their number, they are all defectors, traitors to the east."

Bu laughed. He liked this man. It was a pity he had to kill him.

"My men hold allegiances to the true eastern rulers," Bu replied, "and true eastern ways."

Now it was Barde's turn to laugh.

"Foolishness. Rulers rise and fall and everyone under their rule must change and adjust," Barde said. "It is the way things are. In reality, I care not about your agendas or allegiances. What do you want here in Hámon?"

"I mean to conquer the country of Hámon and stop eastern encroachment into the west," Bu replied. "It was Patûk's dying wish."

Barde let out another short laugh.

"What a noble cause you have, General," Lord Bik said.

"Noble cause!" the king shouted. "How do you plan on conquering my kingdom?"

"Do you not see the army behind me?" Bu asked.

"Pittance," the king said, his cheeks and chins jiggling as he spoke. "I command more men than you."

"No," Bu replied, "you have vassals that respond to you simply because you give them lands and money. What happens when I give them more land and money? What happens when I show those without the fortune of being born *noble* that loyalty and fealty and hard work can earn them such a title?"

The king laughed, but then he looked around him and the soldiers and knights that surrounded him looked at the general with wide eyes. They were considering Bu's offer.

"Jackson," the king said, "take me back to the castle."

Jackson lifted a hand. The horsemen—all wearing mail hauberks and conical helms—snapped their long lances into their shoulders and sat up straight at attention. The king glared at Bu angrily, his cheeks puffing red, but pulled on his horse's reins, the animal groaning under the man's weight, and made his way back towards Venton. Jackson followed him, and as soon as they passed the last of their horsemen, the whole company turned and, in a great cloud of dust, followed the monarch back to the city and to the confines of his castle. Barde watched, over his shoulder, shaking his head.

"This is who the Lord of the East has you treating with?" Bu asked. "This is disgraceful. You are a good man, from a good family."

"It doesn't matter," Barde replied. "If Patûk Al'Banan has truly trained you, you know that. General Abashar, you understand this."

Both Bu and Pavin nodded.

"Join me," Bu said.

Barde Bik shook his head.

"You know I cannot," he replied.

"Why not?" General Pavin Abashar interjected.

"What would you have me do?" Barde asked. "Should I join you while the Lord of the East has my sons tortured and my wife and daughters raped by the whole of his army?"

A man facing the maw of a lion with a spear at his back. This Barde Bik had honor. He was a man who loved his family. Bu knew of men who would readily sacrifice their families for life. It was truly a pity he had to die.

"I will honor you with a quick death," Bu said.

"And I will do the same for you," Barde Bik replied.

The battle was short; Lord Bik's army was outnumbered ten to one. It commenced with General Bu Al'Banan jamming his blade into the back of Barde Bik's neck. A quick death—his promise. Most of Lord Bik's soldiers chose death over surrender, even though Bu Al'Banan offered mercy—service in his army—to any Golgolithulian men who yielded at the beginning of the battle. The general suspected that many of the soldiers had the same concern that Barde Bik had. They all had families back in Golgolithul. Capitulation meant certain torture and death for those they left behind.

The battle had spilled into the civilian lands of Venton, even though none of the men at arms or knights that owed King Cedric bothered to leave the protection of the city walls to protect their citizens. It was collateral damage, and Bu hoped that rather than anger the people of Hámon against him, the lack of protection its king offered would spur the people towards allegiances to Bu.

"No one leaves the city, Captain," Bu said as he stood, surveying the battlefield, the burned homes, the dead, and the gathering crows.

"Yes, my lord," Kan said with a quick bow. "Are we laying siege to Venton?"

"Not yet," the general replied. "Send men—emissaries—to Bull's Run and the other manors of Hámon. Tell them to let the Hámonian nobles know what has happened here ... what is about to happen."

"My lord," Kan said with another bow.

"What allegiances do you hold with King Cedric?" Bu Al'Banan asked the nobleman seated on a palfrey next to the general.

"I hold the allegiance any vassal should owe to their king," the nobleman said. "He grants me land and title, and I return the favor with support, especially in times of war."

"So, should I expect you to march your army towards Venton any time soon?" Bu asked.

The nobleman lazily picked at his lacquered fingernails, pretending to care little for his conversation with Bu Al'Banan. His attitude reminded Bu of Li, and part of it infuriated him while the other part made him smile.

"Should I worry about you marching on my manor any time soon?" the nobleman asked.

"Count Alger," Bu replied, "I have no need to march on those who swear loyalty to me, and I have no desire to take any more Hámonian lives. If I am to rule this kingdom, I need both its people and its nobles to endorse me."

"And what do you offer Hámon's people and nobles in response to such allegiance?" Count Alger asked.

"More land, more title, even lands in the east," Bu replied. He could tell that Count Alger was about to give him a rebuttal, so he held up his hand and continued, "I will also offer them the opportunity to expand beyond the dreams of any Hámonian. Look at what I have done, my lord. I am but the son of a defected eastern general. Unlike my father, I never held position in the eastern armies, and here I am, commander of thirty thousand men and soon to be newly crowned King of Hámon. Those who follow me will be a part of a thriving kingdom and no longer a simple footnote in history. We will expand and conquer and become an empire in our own right, and those who choose to follow me from the beginning will reap the greatest rewards."

Count Alger seemed to ponder Bu's words for a long time. He was considering the general's offer.

"You know the castle will fall," Bu said with finality.

"And what will become of King Cedric?" Alger asked. "Will his head wind up in a basket underneath an executioner's axe?"

"I'm not sure ... yet," Bu replied. He didn't really think Alger cared what happened to the king but simply asked because he was supposed to care. "Do you think the Hámonian people would look kindly on mercy?"

"Mercy," Alger scoffed. "Most see mercy as kindness. I see it as weakness."

Bu shot the count an angry look.

"You, however, are clearly not weak," the count quickly added. "The people and nobles of Hámon might look kindly on a merciful act. The House of Elefante has ruled Hámon for many generations. Cedric may not be the greatest of rulers, but Hámon has prospered under his rule."

"Very well," Bu said. "Assuming the siege on Venton doesn't take his life, I will spare it. I may even give him a title of nobility in my court."

Count Alger nodded with a look of agreement and then looked over his shoulder.

"Acwel," he said.

"Yes, my lord," Count Alger's seneschal said.

"Ready our men," the Count said. "We are going home. Tell them that we will not be sending an aide to King Cedric of House Elefante."

"Yes, my lord," Acwel replied.

Two of Bu's horsemen led a wagon towards the general as he made small talk with the count.

"My lord," one of the horsed soldiers said as they neared the general.

"Excuse me, Count Alger," Bu said and then turned to his soldier angrily. "What is it?"

"This farmer wishes to leave the city and return to his farmstead," the soldier said.

"I said no one leaves the city," Bu replied.

"Yes, my lord," the soldier said, "but he was very persistent and had started causing a small uproar among some of the other farmers trapped within the city."

Bu nodded and rode to the man leading the wagon. He was a broad-shouldered, ruddy fellow wearing a wide-brimmed straw hat with a couple holes in it. He had two girls with him, one almost upon her womanhood and the other quite a bit smaller. They both had sandy blonde hair, and the older one sat next to, whom Bu presumed to be, her father. The back of the wagon was packed with barrels and bags, and the two horses that pulled the wagon looked far more expensive than any farmer in the east would have owned. The man glared at the general with angry eyes.

"No one leaves the city," Bu said to the man.

"Not good enough," the man replied. His older daughter nestled even closer to her father while his younger daughter glared at the general with the same angry eyes that her father stared with.

"Do you know who you are speaking ..." Bu began to say, but the farmer cut him off.

"I beg your pardon," the farmer said, but before he could continue, Ban Chu rode up to the side of the wagon.

"You will address General Bu Al'Banan as *my lord*," Ban Chu said.

"Nope," the farmer said with a shake of his head, "I only have one lord, and he's not it."

"Yeah," the younger daughter said, standing up in the back of the wagon, "he's not our lord."

Ban Chu's hand went to the handle of his sword.

"Tia," the farmer hissed, "sit down and be quiet."

The little girl crossed her arms across her chest and did as she was told, but with a look of defiance. Bu liked this little girl, this little Tia. She had fire.

"Lieutenant Chu," Bu said softly, "it is all right."

Ban Chu nodded and backed his horse up.

"We are not vassals of Hámon, General," the farmer said. "We are free farmers, north of here. There are several of us in the city."

"Free farmers?" the general asked.

"Aye," the farmer replied, "for the last two hundred years."

"And to whom do you hold allegiance?" the general asked.

"The Creator," the farmer said. "To be honest, General, I don't really care who rules Hámon. We come here to trade and sell our goods, buy seed for the next year, find workers when the need arises, and for a fair price."

Bu had never heard of a *free farmer*. They didn't exist in the east. Every farmer was a serf for whatever lord or family that owned the land on which they worked.

"How fair have the prices been?" Bu asked.

"Not very," the farmer replied.

"Maybe we can change that," Bu said.

"That would be appreciated, General," the farmer said.

"You and the other free farmers in Venton may leave," Bu said, "and I will remember our conversation."

The farmer gave Bu Al'Banan a quick bow and then snapped the reins of his wagon.

"Tell me about these free farmers," Bu said to Count Alger.

"A nuisance," Count Alger replied. "Little more than peasants, and you see how they act, even towards men of a higher station."

"Are they successful?" Bu asked.

"Their farmlands have rich soil," Count Alger said. "I have assumed several of these *free farms* as my lands have expanded and our farms on those lands are very plentiful."

"When the dust settles," Bu said, "we will have to look north to these farmlands."

42

Sitting with almost twenty other men at a large round table, Del Alzon was not sure who most of them were. They were the aristocrats of Waterton, men who had never bothered to come by his fruit stand or mingle with the *common* folk of the border town. Yager was there, his newly appointed head woodsman. So were Danitus and Maktus. Along with these *aristocrats*—the word left a sour taste in Del Alzon's mouth—were dignitaries from Southland—Finlo and Dûrn Tor—and Gongoreth. He hoped his discomfort wasn't visible.

In reality, Del's mind was on the death of Simon, the former mayor of Waterton. The man couldn't keep his mouth shut and had started sowing discord from inside his jail cell. Men who had initially pledged allegiance to Del had started to rethink their positions. It was Del Alzon's last nefarious act. He knew a man, one talented in the ways of mysterious deaths. This man found himself the newly appointed jail guard when the man who had been there for years *fell* from his horse and sustained a serious broken leg. The next day, the newly appointed guard discovered a very unfortunate scene inside the former mayor's cell—a private cell due to his former status. He had hung himself. Perhaps the weight of his former iniquities was too much to bear. Overnight, those questioning their loyalties to the new mayor, Del Alzon, became supporters once again.

"The egregious attack on Hámon cannot be allowed to stand without military response," said Amman from Finlo's Council of Five. He brought Del Alzon back from his thoughts and into the present.

"And what would you have the city of Waterton do?" Del Alzon asked. "This new army consists of thirty thousand zealots, trained to eastern standards. Waterton has three hundred militiamen who run scared when a rat farts."

The aristocrats of Waterton murmured angrily at that, but as Del Alzon glared at them, they quieted.

"What about the armies of Gongoreth?" Amman asked.

"What about them?" an armored man, all in plate mail, asked. His voice was deep and commanding, and his dark beard and tanned skin were a stark contrast to his bright blue eyes.

"Well," Amman said, and then stopped, seemingly taken aback by the curtness of the Gongorethian knight.

"You are affected by trade that comes through Southland, are you not?" asked one of the aristocrats Del had allowed to stay on his council, a man named Hammond.

"Somewhat," the knight replied. "But Southland, nor Háthgolthane, are not the only sources of trade for the west. And a Gongorethian army has not been east of the Blue River in over two hundred years. What would the response be by Golgolithul? Gol-Durathna? Nordeth even?"

"Sir Charles," Del Alzon said, "is there no help you can offer?"

Sir Charles, the Gongorethian knight, seemed to think for a while. Two other knights stood behind him, along with half a dozen men-at-arms and several advisors. They each took turns whispering into the knight's ear.

"I cannot justify sending a whole army to help restore the Kingdom of Hámon to its previous ruler," Sir Charles said, "however; the city of Waterton and the country of Southland have always been kind to my lands in the County of Law. So, I will send five hundred men-at-arms to Waterton, for protection, and another five hundred to Southland."

"That is most generous," Amman said, even though the look on his face told Del Alzon he thought otherwise. Del knew the Council of Five wanted an all-out war against this Bu Al'Banan, all without having to lift their own fingers and risk their own lives.

Bu Al'Banan. Del Alzon knew of Patûk, even though the old general had left the service of the east when Del was just a young soldier. His was a superior tactician, a spectacular leader, and a cruel man. But no one ever knew of a son. A man like Patûk probably had at least a dozen bastards all over the world, but he never married—as far as Del knew—and if he had, one might wonder if he would ever have time to raise a son and teach him how to be a soldier. Del Alzon suspected this Bu was just using the name of the former general to gain loyalty, respect, and fear.

Del Alzon shook his head. Patûk Al'Banan was dead. Many wondered if the man would ever die. And from the pox nonetheless. Another lie, Del Alzon suspected, but who could have killed a man such as Patûk Al'Banan? There wasn't a sane man in all of Háthgolthane with the balls to challenge old Patûk. Kehl, the Samanian, probably would have challenged him. Stupid Samanian pimps, they would fight anyone.

Whoever killed Patûk, Del Alzon thought, *is not only a man of tremendous skill, but a man with the biggest balls I've ever heard of.*

"My men will come to Southland by way of the South Sea," Sir Charles of Law said. "It would be bad form to have them marched through the Abresi Straits and so close to Hámon. And I doubt any of the other nobles of Gongoreth will give such an offer. Háthgolthane has been a source of much pain for Gongoreth, and its peoples need to learn how to take care of themselves."

"Will King Buxton approve of such a move?" Del Alzon asked.

"Let me worry about King Buxton," Sir Charles replied. "I am in good relations with the king, and I think he will see my logic when I explain my reasoning. He may even send some of his royal soldiers to Waterton, although I doubt he'll send any to Southland. He has little love for sea ports."

Ammon seemed even more perturbed at that.

"And what of you, Countess?" Amman asked.

A woman in her middle years, wearing a wide headdress of purples and blues that hid her hair and a large dress that required the help of several servants when she sat looked to the speaker of the Council of Five with lazy eyes and pursed lips. They were painted purple, like her headdress, and heavy black paint marked the outlines of her eyes, contrasting her very pale skin.

"I can help," she replied, "but not as much as Sir Charles. My resources are spread thin, as of late, with some efforts to expand west of our lands. My main concern is that the supposed son of that pompous ass, Patûk Al'Banan, will set his sights even farther west. If he is anything like his father—and who knows if he really is the son of old Patûk—he would do that. Patûk Al'Banan thought he was indestructible, and if he trained this upstart general, then so does he. I will send two hundred men to you, mayor, and I will send a hundred with Sir Charles to Finlo. I am sorry, but it is all I can do."

"If it is all you can do ..." Amman began to say, but the glaring look the countess gave him caused him to stop and look away.

"Countess Elaine," Del Alzon said, "it is more than enough."

"And what of you, Del Alzon?" another man asked, a diplomat from Dûrn Tor.

"What of me?" Del Alzon replied.

"Can we trust you, the newly appointed mayor of Waterton?" the man asked, a husky fellow with a great, gray bushy beard. "Your ascent to leadership seems very fortuitous, and you are a defected easterner, just like Patûk Al'Banan and these thirty thousand men that now serve his son."

Del Alzon felt his blood boil.

"I am no defector, Rufus," Del Alzon said with the slightest hint of a hiss. "I served my time in the eastern armies and was given leave ... honorably discharged. The only similarity between Patûk Al'Banan and me was our eastern blood. And I don't know this Bu. Who, by the nine hells, even knows if he is an easterner?"

"We have an invested interest in what happens in the east," Sir Charles said, "but it isn't critical for our survival. The moment it seems our presence is more of a nuisance, or the moment General Bu Al'Banan decides to set his sights farther west ..."

The knight spread his hands, matter-of-factly.

"Our chief concern is the safety and survival of Gongoreth," Countess Elaine added.

"Understood," Del Alzon said, and Amman and Rufus both nodded, reluctantly.

Del Alzon sat in his room, drinking a tankard of ale. Some young servant had tried to stand next to him and hold his cup, but Del dismissed him. He didn't need to be waited on hand and foot and wondered if that was truly what the previous mayor of the broken, run down border town of Waterton actually required. He shook his head and finished his drink.

"It seems you have had a hard day."

The voice, speaking in Shengu, came from the shadows. Del

Alzon rose so quickly from his chair that he knocked it over. He turned to face the corner of his room. His sword wasn't anywhere near him, so he held his heavy tankard in one hand and balled his other hand into a fist.

A slight man with an angular face and close-cropped, black hair stepped from the shadows. A sword, sheathed, hung from his belt, and he raised his hands, showing himself as not a threat.

"Peace," the man said.

"Says the spy slinking in the shadows," Del Alzon replied in Shengu.

"My name is Ban Chu," the man said, keeping his hands up and visible, "and I am the chief scout to Lord Bu Al'Banan."

"Chief scout?" Del Alzon scoffed with a smile. "Is that a fancy name for spy?"

The man shrugged.

"Lord Bu Al'Banan, huh?" Del Alzon said. "Is that what he's calling himself these days? This supposed son of General Patûk Al'Banan. You know that any intelligent man knows that's just hog's piss. When will he be King Al'Banan?"

"As soon as King Cedric of House Elefante abdicates, of course," Ban Chu replied.

"And what does this Bu's chief snake need or want with me?" Del Alzon asked.

"Please," Ban Chu said with a feigned hurt look on his face, "can we dispense with the name calling?"

"Very well," Del Alzon replied.

"Lord Bu Al'Banan wishes to extend to you an offer," Ban Chu said. And when Del Alzon replied with a questioning look, the scout continued, "His power will only continue to grow, but he knows already men conspire against him."

Del Alzon wondered if this Ban Chu knew about the meeting he had just had.

"He wishes to offer Waterton vassalage," Ban Chu continued, "and as such, he would make you a lord—a duke. You would be

Duke Del Alzon of Waterton. This would give you more land, title—"

Del Alzon's sudden fit of laughter cut Ban Chu off, and the scout gave the mayor a questioning look, one that was a mixture of irritation and hurt.

"Did I say something funny?" Ban Chu asked.

"What makes you think I want to be a duke?" Del Alzon asked. "What makes you think I want lands and extra money?"

"Who wouldn't ..."

"What makes you think I want anything from you or that jumped up prick who leads thirty thousand idiots, the so-called son of a whore who turned his back on his country," Del Alzon hissed, his tone turning from one of jollity to anger. "Waterton is a free city—always has been, always will be. It's why I came here. I wanted to be free, beholden to no man. So, if you think I'm going to bow down to some rat turd for land and money, you're dumber than a pig's fart."

"It's free for now," Ban Chu offered, eyes level and voice indifferent.

"Get out!" Del Alzon yelled. He hadn't wanted to lose control of his emotions, but he had had enough of this Ban Chu.

"Watch your back, fat man," Ban Chu said with a condescending smile on his face.

Del Alzon turned and grabbed his sword that was leaning against a small table. He turned back to face Ban Chu, his weapon gripped tightly with both hands, only to find the spy gone. Del Alzon groaned angrily. Spies. Worse than thieves and gypsies.

"Watch my back," Del Alzon repeated. "Always do."

"We need to build a wall," Del Alzon said to Maktus.

"A wall?" Maktus asked. "Waterton has never had a wall."

"It's time for change," Del Alzon said.

"How much change is too much?" Maktus asked.

"I don't know," Del said with a shrug. "But we need to do it."

"Do you think it will deter travelers and adventurers?" Maktus asked.

"I don't give a pig's ass if it does," Del Alzon replied. Maktus stopped as they walked through the city, looking at Del Alzon with concerned eyes.

"What's going on, Del?" Maktus asked.

"We need to be prepared," Del Alzon said. "I feel the days of being neutral are over."

"It will take money," Maktus said.

"We will raise it," Del Alzon said.

"It will take manpower," Maktus added.

"We will employ everyone we can," Del Alzon replied.

"It will take time," Maktus finally said.

"That ... we don't have."

43

Bryon rolled to his side. His pillow was still wet. Tears. Sweat. He stared at the door to his room then closed his eyes and tried to go back to sleep but couldn't. He pushed himself up and sat at the edge of his bed, staring at the floor for a long while, rubbing his feet along a rug made of bear fur. It was soft and warm. He craned his neck to the side, and it responded with several loud pops. Stretching his arms, his shoulders and back crackled as well.

He was glad to be in a normal room, away from Thorakest's infirmary. His surgeons had finally moved him the previous day. Even though he still felt weak and he still looked a little pale, he had healed well enough. As he stretched, he could still feel the ache in his body, and a part of him wondered if it would ever go away. His dreams hadn't stopped.

Dreams of dead men, fields of burning grass, and, always, a dragon, up close or in the distance. Bryon rubbed the wound on his chest. There were only four little scars left, from where the dragon had scratched him, but from time to time he could still feel it, feel the excruciating pain. Had that wound connected him to the dragon in some way? And then he wondered if his dreams were similar to Erik's. He heard his cousin talking about dreams of the dead.

He had mocked them off as foolishness, childish, until he had them ... until he saw Fox's face, black and rotting and crawling with maggots. He smelled him. Heard him. And then the dragon, the things she said. He didn't know how he understood her, but he did, and the curses she cried made him shudder.

Bryon finally stood. He kicked the pile of his clothes to the side and walked to the washbasin, dipping his hands in the cool water and cupping them, splashing it up against his face. The water ran down his face and neck, over his shoulders and chest, and down his legs, causing a quick shiver. He cupped more water and poured it over his head, washing his hair. Dirt dripped away with the water and swirled about in the basin as a brown cloud.

A quick knock thudded against Bryon's door. He brushed the wet hair clinging to his face away and went to the armoire. He put on pants as another knock came and opened the door. A young dwarvish woman stood on the other side of the door. Her cheeks blushed. She looked at her feet and folded her arms in front of her.

"His Maj ... Majesty, the King," she stammered, and Bryon couldn't tell if her stuttering speech was from embarrassment or from a lack of understanding of the Westernese language.

"In Ervendwarfol, se wen wishen," Bryon said. He had tried becoming more efficient at the dwarvish language as he stayed in their city.

She nodded.

"His Majesty, the King, he wishes to have audience with you," she said in her native language. "I am to take you to his private chambers."

"Very well," Bryon replied, also speaking in Dwarvish. "I will get dressed and meet you outside this door."

Minutes later, Bryon followed the dwarvish woman through the castle of Thorakest and they eventually entered a chamber warmed by a large fire roaring in a simple fireplace. Shelves, floor to ceiling and filled with books, consumed the wall to Bryon's left and, directly across from him, stood a wall covered by drawings of maps and castles and sketches of dwarves and humans and creatures he had never even thought of. In the middle of the room was a large, round table, and King Skella, General Balzarak, and Gôdruk sat around it.

Bryon bowed when he saw the king, and Skella returned the favor with a slight nod of his head. The dwarvish woman walked to the king, whispered something into his ear, turned to Bryon, gave a short curtsey and smile, and left.

"Please," King Skella said, "have a seat."

Bryon found a chair waiting for him, next to Balzarak.

"It is good to see you again, Bryon," the king said. "It seems you have embarrassed my great granddaughter, however, by answering your door bare chested."

The look on the king's face was stern and sincere.

"I-I'm sorr—" Bryon began to say as he moved to stand again and bow low, but the king cut him off with a smile and a wave of his hand.

"I only jest," he said in his typically, grandfatherly voice. "You are tired and weary and didn't know I would send a woman as beautiful as my great granddaughter to fetch you. Please, have a drink, Bryon."

A stately looking dwarf, regaled in fine livery of yellows and reds walked to Bryon's side, lifted a metal pot from the middle of the table, and poured a light brown liquid into a small cup, offering it on a saucer to Bryon. Bryon grabbed the saucer, as the cup looked hot—steam rising from its contents—and nodded to the serving dwarf.

"Please," King Skella said, offering a hand and motioning for Bryon to drink, "tell me what you think of the tea."

"It reminds me of home," Bryon said after sipping, "of my mother."

"That is good, then, yes?" the king said.

Bryon just shrugged but perhaps it was more from habit.

"Does home hold so many sour memories?" the king asked.

"No." Bryon shook his head. "And yes."

"And how can it be both?"

Bryon waited a moment to answer, not sure even what he might say.

"I'm not sure what I will find when I get home," Bryon finally said. "I never really wanted to return until now. What will my parents say? How do I look my uncle and aunt in the face after ...?"

Bryon's voice trailed off.

"The loss of your cousin," King Skella said.

Bryon nodded.

"Hold on to the good memories," King Skella said, "and try not to think of the things that might be, or that might have been, as hard as that is. How are you feeling?"

"Much better, thank you," Bryon replied.

"You were near death," King Skella said. "It was a close one. My surgeons worked day and night to fix you up."

"I owe them much," Bryon said.

"Yes, you do," King Skella added, "but I feel, more so, you owe General Balzarak and your cousin, Erik, for getting you here. I understand the apprehensions behind coming back to Thorakest, but had you gone with Erik, you would be dead."

"I know my cousin didn't mean any disrespect by not returning," Bryon said.

"I know," King Skella said. "Balzarak has already briefed me. It was probably the wisest course of action. I would have honored my agreement, but I cannot say the same for others in my city. Thorakest, much to my sadness, has become a dangerous place lately."

"How come Your Majesty?" Bryon asked.

"My own mayor, Fréden Fréwin," the king explained, "has led an uprising against me. As much as we have never gotten along, I never thought in all my years he would try and turn my own people against me."

"He is dead then?" Bryon asked.

Balzarak shook his head, a wistful expression on his face.

"He stole away with a group of loyalists," Balzarak said, "and he now makes the Wicked Spire his residence, a mountain with three peaks that rises up from the Plains of Güdal. It was a former kingdom of the ancient dwarves. Our scouts say dwarves from all over Háthgolthane and beyond, those disenchanted with their leaders, are heeding his call to join him."

"I can't believe it," Bryon muttered.

"Aye," Balzarak said. "Dark times. That accompanied by ..."

The general shot King Skella a look, one of fear, and Bryon couldn't help seeing it.

"You were there in Orvencrest," the king said, turning to Bryon, "so, you know what lives there?"

"The dwomanni?" asked Bryon with a questioning look.

"Yes," King Skella said. "And that is a dangerous secret every dwarvish king must keep. A secret that, I fear, is no longer only known to a few."

"Your Majesty?" Bryon asked.

"A young dwarf was executed in Strongbur just a month ago for conspiring against the duke," King Skella said. "Many thought he was conspiring with men. The duke and I knew the truth."

"He was conspiring with the dwomanni," Balzarak said.

"And you knew of the dragon, as well?" Bryon asked.

"I did," King Skella said. "Another former secret. She was asleep for a thousand years. I should have known that the treasure the Lord of the East sought was the Dragon Scroll."

"The Dragon Scroll, Your Majesty?" Bryon asked.

"It is a spell, Bryon," the king explained, "a powerful weapon kept secret and hidden by the dwarves ever since the fall of Orvencrest. The caster of the spell becomes invincible against a dragon's fire, at least for a time. But with only the scroll, the spell is incomplete. With it, one needs the Dragon Sword and the Dragon Crown. Once someone is in possession of all three, they can control a dragon, even the most powerful of dragons."

"That sounds frightening," Bryon said, visions of their time in Orvencrest flashing through his mind.

"It is more than frightening, Bryon," King Skella said, "and the last time it happened, the world almost ended. It is a good thing Erik didn't bring the Dragon Scroll here."

"I often wonder," Balzarak said. "Is it a better idea to deliver it to the Lord of the East?"

"Both are evil," King Skella said. "Let the hunger that such power creates consume the Lord of the East. While Syzbalo searches for the Dragon Sword and Dragon Crown, we dwarves can be ready. For if the Dragon Scroll was here, my people would become drunk with the thought of such power. It would be chaos. And I do believe that Erik and Wrothgard and yourself would be in great danger, even more so than they are now."

"We found lists of names, as well," Balzarak interjected. "The lost clans."

"Lost, yes," King Skella said, "gone and dead, hopefully."

"Your Majesty?" Balzarak said.

King Skella looked to his servant, Nordri, who stood in the corner of the room and, in turn, he walked to the wall full of books. The serving dwarf scanned the shelves only for a moment before stopping at a book, thick spine worn and weathered. He gently lifted the book from its resting place, blew years' worth of dust away from its cover before wiping away what his breath could not catch. He handed it to the king with a bow.

"Few know of these families," the king said, thumbing through several pages of the book. The pages were yellowed and brittle. Some of them were torn and chipped. "Few know of these stories. Even fewer know of their fate, those who could not escape Orvencrest."

"Your Majesty?" Bryon said.

"There are times, Bryon, when certain mysteries are better left mysteries," the king replied. "I do not like keeping my people in the dark, but knowledge is a powerful tool. It can be a powerful weapon, and what people might do with that, the knowledge ... Well, we have seen the passing of many ages and the destruction of many people over the pursuit of knowledge."

"I don't understand," Balzarak said.

"Is it better to let dwarves like Fréden believe a dwarf spy in Strongbur is working for men," the King said, "rather than let him know he was, in fact, working for the dwomanni? Is it better to let people believe dragons were some fanciful tale so many years past, or let people know they truly do exist and could destroy a whole city with a single breath?"

"People—men, dwarves—seem to delight in ignorance," the king explained. "What would people do with the knowledge that a lost dwarvish city is out there?"

The king waved his hand as if to present the whole room, the whole world, perhaps.

"Look at the Lord of the East," King Skella said. "Look at the lengths he went to in finding this city or, rather, something hidden within its treasures. Look at the death it has caused. Look at my friend, Fréden Fréwin. That knowledge has consumed him enough for him to rise against his own king. His own people. What will my people do now they know dragons truly exist? The dwomanni exist? Even worse, that dragons can be controlled."

The air in the room seemed to hang still. The warmth of the fire left, and Bryon held his breath.

"Yes," the king continued. "What would my people do if they knew those who were not destroyed in the tragedy of Orvencrest were enslaved by the dwomanni? That their descendants are probably still enslaved by the dwomanni, a thousand years later?"

"We should rescue them," Balzarak said urgently, leaning forward.

"Exactly what every righteous and self-respecting dwarf should say," the king replied, "and exactly why it has been kept a secret. Exactly why it must be kept a secret."

"Your Majesty?" Balzarak questioned.

"Should we send all of our armies into the depths of the earth in search of these lost souls?" the king asked. "I mourn for them daily, but it would be folly, and the dwarvish people would soon meet their final demise, that we are sure of. The dwomanni are powerful. And now that they have made their presence known, I fear for our future."

King Skella sat back in his chair and took a sip of his own tea. Balzarak just stared at the king, mouth open. King Skella put his cup of tea down and smiled mirthlessly.

"And, all this mystery, is to my foolishness, I suppose," the king said. "What good has it done us? Our people once again will know of the dragon—Black Wing is her name in your language, Bryon."

"She's not dead?" Bryon asked.

"Dead, no," the king said, shaking his head. "She is probably in the process of seeking out her mate, Shadow Tooth. It has been millennia since they have been together. The havoc they will wreak upon this world, I shudder to think of it."

The king flipped through several, yellowed pages, the paper creaking as they moved from one side to the other.

"Yes, it is all in this book," King Skella said. "There is a copy of it in your grandfather's library, General Balzarak."

Balzarak looked at the king hard as if a part of him didn't believe what Skella had just said.

"An age ago, this book came to Thûrkzan, son of Thûrkbrand the Second and descendant of Brumber the Second," the king explained, "around the time Orvencrest was about to fall."

"I've heard of Brumber Steel Fist, but who is Thûrkzan?" Bryon asked.

"A king of Orvencrest," King Skella explained. "He knew his city was about to fall, knew it was doomed, and so he collected all the information, history, and genealogies he could and sent it to Thorakest."

"Why didn't he just ask for help?" Bryon asked. "Why didn't he ask for reinforcements?"

"There are several pages at the end of this book written by Thûrkzan," King Skella replied. "He talks about that. He speaks to his desire to send his whole army to Orvencrest. That was a dark time, you must understand. The forces of the Shadow were strong, and hope was a sparing commodity. But after consulting with his advisors, he decided that sending their armies would have not only spelled the end of Orvencrest, but of Thorakest and another city called Throdukr as well. So, Thûrkzan did as he was asked. He copied the book so that the north would also have knowledge of what happened, studied it, and passed it on to his son when he was ready to become king."

The king sighed and clicked his tongue, tapping his fingers on the yellowed pages of the book.

"The families, the clans lost in Orvencrest?" Balzarak asked. "The stories and poems and battle songs? The genealogies?"

"All in this book," King Skella said. "All—Stone Hammer, Blood Axe, Red Steel, Bone Breaker, Fire Beard—regretfully and thankfully, in this book."

The king took another sip of his tea.

"I, too, know of the pain," King Skella finally said to Bryon after Balzarak and Gôdruk had left. "I know, too well, the pain of losing my own blood. Of losing my brother. I can still hear the cries of warriors dying around me. I can still smell that scent of battle. I can still feel my brother's body as I held him. I can still see his eyes as life slowly flickered away.

"My brother bled in my arms, his breathing slowing, his skin paling, his eyes closing. He lay there, and there was nothing I could do. The Prince of Thorakest, and there was nothing I could do. All I could do was kneel there, his head cradled in my hands, and rock back and forth, weeping as more dwarves died around me."

The king placed an elbow on the table, made a fist, and rested his chin on his knuckles.

"Just one more day," the king muttered. Bryon didn't know if the king meant for him to hear what he had said, but he had nonetheless. "Just one more day, Skalli. All I want is just one more day with you."

The king stood from his seat and walked towards the door. As he neared Bryon, he put his hand on the man's shoulder.

"If you never let go of that pain Bryon—what I know you feel about your cousin—it will destroy you. The hate you feel will never give way to any other emotion. You will never know joy. You will never know peace. You will never know sorrow; only a painful hate that will eventually be your undoing."

The king patted Bryon's shoulder and left the room.

44

Bu drove his sword hilt deep into the man's belly. His sword—Patûk Al'Banan's sword—slid easily through the count's hauberk. He stared at Bu with wondering eyes—amazed, perplexed, curious, confused. That look, one of a man as he died, always sent shivers down Bu's spine. He lusted for that look, more than he did so for a woman. The count, one of the few Hámonian nobles that actually came to the defense of King Cedric, took one last look at the battlefield, staring at all his dead soldiers. Bu didn't know his name. He didn't care.

"The Shadow take you," the man said with a gurgling hiss as blood filled his mouth.

Bu simply nodded. He respected defiance in the face of death. He pushed a little harder, even though his sword had nowhere to go. The count groaned, and then his head fell back, and Bu retrieved his blade.

Another battle was over, again finished far quicker than he had expected. The fields in front of Venton once looked green and lush, but blood now glimmered everywhere in the noonday sun. Smoke rose from burning wagons and the campfires that died in harmony with the men. Crows and the peasants of Hámon had already started picking at the dead, the birds for supper and the people for loose coin or other things of value. Walking about the field, Bu saw four dead Hámonians for every one of his men.

Only five nobles heeded the king's call, and four of them surrendered when they knew the battle was lost.

"The city is ours," Pavin said, riding up next to Bu.

"Have Andu bring me Warrior," Bu commanded, and General Pavin Abashar gave him a quick bow.

The keep of Venton was unimpressive. It sat towards the back of the city, surrounded by a short curtain wall. Other than a few storage buildings and a nondescript chapel to some deity of whom Bu had never heard, the keep building was the only structure within the walls, a square building that rose eight stories. Compared to Fen-Stévock, this was nothing. The east could have easily conquered Hámon.

Warrior's hooves clattered on the stone stairs as Bu rode up to the front double doors, which were quickly opened by Hámonian guards who didn't dare make eye contact with the general. With Pavin, Ban Chu, and Li behind him, Bu rode through into the main hall of the keep, which was about as lavish as he expected.

He assumed that, by Hámonian standards, it was decorated richly, with several large tapestries hanging from the walls, a purple rug leading from the doorway to the throne, painted columns on either side of the rug, and a giant hearth and fireplace built into one wall. The many windows in the room provided ample light, but still, a fire raged in the fireplace, and every sconce held a lit torch.

Towards the rear of the room opposite the fireplace, Bu saw a set of narrow stairs. As he rode along the rug that led to the throne, on which King Cedric still sat, Warrior stopped to relieve himself. The warhorse must've known how his rider felt about the room. The gasp coming from the king and two aristocrats that stood to one side of his throne made Bu smile. A woman, younger and blonde and voluptuous, standing on the other side of Cedric giggled. Bu smiled wider.

King Cedric wanted to say something, but he had lost, and he just sat and stewed as Bu neared the throne and as his men spilled into the keep.

"King Cedric," Bu said, dismounting and stepping forward.

"Bu Al'Banan," the king replied. "I suppose congratulations are in order."

There was no belief in his words or on the king's face, just frustration. His nobles and citizens had abandoned him. He had been overrun in no time at all.

"I understand the ways of the feudal west, after a loss in battle, are to imprison nobles and then ransom them off to some nearest of kin," Bu said.

The king nodded with the slightest hint of a smile.

"The ways of the imperial east are different, King Cedric," Bu said, and the small smile on the king's face disappeared. "We execute men such as you, in front of your people, to discourage ideas of revolt or resistance."

The king's face blanched. Despite his plate mail and the open-faced helm he wore with a crown welded to it, this man was no warrior. He was a coward.

"But ... we are not in the east, so what shall we do with you?" Bu asked.

"My lord ..." began one of the king's advisors. He was a portly man, much like the king, with brown ringlets in both his hair and his beard. His yellow robe was no doubt meant to look like gold, and he wore rings on each of his fingers, even his thumbs. But before the man could get past his insincere introduction, Bu's sword was out of its scabbard and, up under the man's jaw, was lodged firmly in his skull.

A scream echoed throughout the hall, and Bu thought it had been the woman standing next to the king, but she simply looked on with wide, inquisitive eyes; it was the other advisor who had screamed in such a feminine manner. He was a slight man with a thin ring of hair around an otherwise bald head. He wore a woman's paint around his eyes and on his cheeks. Bu stepped forward, the king slinking back in his throne, and removed the other advisor's head from his shoulders.

"These were your advisors?" Bu asked.

The king nodded, tears in his eyes.

"No wonder you lost," Bu added. He wiped his blade off on the robe of the first dead man. "You will stay in the keep ... as my guest."

Bu turned around, sheathing his sword, looking to Pavin, Ban Chu, and Li and then turning around again. Li had counseled him extensively in the formalities of western nobility over the last few days, and Bu finally realized why Patûk had kept him around.

The woman just stared at Bu. There was a boldness in her brownish hazel eyes. She was a pretty woman. The paint on her lips and cheeks and around her eyes, but she would be pretty despite that. And she was curvy, with round hips and large breasts. She looked like the king—her father—but only slightly.

"Your nobles abandoned you, Cedric," Bu said, folding his hands behind his back and making sure to refrain from using the title of king. "But I doubt they trust me either. Your notions of nobility in the west are confusing at best. I would just kill the lot of you, but I know that will not sit well with your people, if I mean to rule them."

Bu could see the irritation work its way across Cedric's face. The princess looked at her father, then at Bu, inquisition still on her face.

"We need something that will help the nobles of Hámon accept me as their ruler," Bu said.

"They will never accept you," Cedric hissed, his frustration finally boiling over.

Ban Chu stepped forward, his sword halfway out of its scabbard. Bu caught his hand and shook his head. His lieutenant bowed.

"You see, Cedric," Bu said, "my men follow me because they respect me. Your men follow you because ... well, I don't know why they do. Yes, your nobles will accept me, especially once I marry your daughter."

Cedric stood quickly.

"You cannot!"

"Truly?" Bu replied with a smile on his face. His eyes met those of the princess. They gleamed with mischief. He could see in her eyes she was cunning and bold. She was nothing like her father.

"This is preposterous," Cedric said.

"No, this is the way of the west, is it not, Li?" Bu asked.

"It is, Your Majesty," Li replied, and his change in title made Bu smile again.

"How would he know?" Cedric said, pointing to Li, who wore a cloth mask over his face and a hooded robe so that only his eyes were visible.

"He is my steward and my seneschal," Bu said. "Yes, I will marry your daughter; you will live, and your people will recognize me as their king. Princess."

Bu extended his hand to the princess, and she took it without hesitation. Cedric tried grabbing her arm, but she shook him off.

"Ilsa," she said.

"Princess Ilsa," Bu said.

"Queen Ilsa has a much better sound to it," Ilsa said.

"Yes, it does," Bu replied.

In the west, according to Li, a woman could be stoned or burned for lying with a man before she was married. Certainly, that was true with a princess. But Ilsa was relentless in the bedroom, and Bu knew this was not her first time. He breathed heavy as he felt the sweat pool around his body. She traced a lacquered fingernail along Bu's chest, stopping at his nipple before pinching it. He winced, and she giggled, burying her face in her pillow.

"Are all western women as aggressive as you?" Bu asked.

"Are all eastern men as out of shape as you?" Ilsa retorted and then laughed.

"Three times, woman," Bu huffed.

"It's a slow night," Ilsa said. "Sorry."

"By the gods," Bu said and then sat up when he heard a knock on the door.

He stood, wrapping one of Cedric's old robes around his waist.

"I always wanted to have a tussle in my father's bed," Bu heard Ilsa say, more to herself than him, and then giggle.

Bu opened the door to Li. His seneschal bowed.

"Aren't you going to cover yourself?" Bu said to Ilsa.

"Why?" she replied. "I am their queen. If they stare, have their eyes plucked out."

She had fire, Bu had to give her that. He shrugged and let Li in. He wasn't wearing his cloth mask, and when Ilsa saw his disfigured face, she gasped and pulled the bedding up to her chin. Ban Chu followed the maimed seneschal, followed by Bao Zi, who walked gingerly with bandages still on his face.

"I am glad to see you doing better," Bu said.

Bao Zi simply bowed, ever so slightly.

"What is it, Li?" Bu asked.

"I have been looking at the scroll I copied," Li said, folding his hands—thus covering his crippled right hand—inside of his robes.

"Yes," Bu said. He caught his soon to be wife wriggling underneath the covers of the bed, biting a finger seductively. He felt himself become aroused and didn't much care about what Li had to say at the moment.

"I have translated more of my copy of the scroll," Li said.

"You discovered the missing piece?" Bu asked.

"No," Li replied.

"Then why are you here?" Bu asked.

"I have discovered where the Dragon Sword is located," Li replied.

"Oh," Bu said, his interest now peaked.

"In my travels, I had heard of a wizard from Gol-Durathna," Li explained. "It is a story that is over a hundred years old, but the myth speaks of this wizard practicing dark magic. Just that alone would be enough to have him banished from the northern kingdom, or worse. But the stories surrounding him say he was also experimenting on people, testing his spells on live subjects, peasants that lived near his lavish estates."

"What does this have to do with the scroll and the Dragon Sword?" Bu asked as his interest waned again and Ilsa began moaning while she pleased herself.

"General Bu," Li said in a whisper, leaning forward, "this wizard found his way to a village called Fealmynster, north of the Gray Mountains. It is there that he enslaved all of its inhabitants, has employed giants to build him and protect a large keep, and found the fabled Dragon Sword. If I have discovered this truth hidden in the scroll's inscriptions ..."

"So has the Lord of the East, and if he gets his hands on this ..." Bu said, looking to the ground as he thought of all the possibilities.

"It would be a disaster, my lord," Li said. "You must find it before he does—or his lackeys. Once he gets his hands on that scroll, he will waste no time in sending the Black Mage after this weapon."

"Patûk was right," Bu said introspectively. "This is a powerful weapon." He looked up at Li. "As soon as I secure my rule here, in Hámon, I will leave for Fealmynster."

"Bu, my lover," Ilsa said, almost pouting.

"We will speak on this more in the morning," Bu said, ushering Li, Ban Chu and Bao Zi out of his room with as much haste as he could.

He turned to face Ilsa, uncovered and waiting for him on the bed.

She smiled mischievously. He dropped the robe wrapped around his waist and smiled. Who would have thought a little gutter shite from the alleys of Fen-Stévock would be a king. He felt powerful, the world would be his, and the east would pay first. Then the rest of the world.

Bu married Ilsa the next day. Her father gave him her hand at spear point. She could have cared less. The priest of Freo—the Western goddess of love—hadn't even finished pronouncing them as husband and wife, and him as King of Hámon, when Ilsa dragged him back to their bedchamber. She was as power hungry as Bu, and it both excited and worried him.

The very next day, he sat astride Warrior, ready to travel north, to the Gray Mountains.

"Why must you go?" Ilsa asked. Bu couldn't help thinking the tears in her eyes and the sadness on her face were feigned.

"Because I refuse to sit on a throne and hide behind those I rule like your father." His words were hard, but he couldn't help seeing a small smirk amidst Ilsa's tears.

Bao Zi and Andu would go with him while Li, Ban Chu, and Pavin would stay behind. He trusted Ban Chu. Li would be worthless on the road and had proved himself a worthy steward, and he was sure that he had scared Pavin into submission—and he would prove a good leader in Bu's absence. Another dozen men, all knights of Hámon, sat on their warhorses in front of him outside the walls of Venton. Bu had commanded the twelve wealthiest and most powerful nobles of Hámon to give him one warrior each to travel with him.

"Sir Garrett is the best knight of all Hámon," Count Alger said, sitting on his palfrey next to Bu.

Bu gave the count a hard look.

"Your Majesty," Alger added quickly.

"You will find that I award those who are loyal to me," King Bu Al'Banan said, "beyond their imaginations ..."

"I don't know, Your Majesty," Alger said. "I can imagine quite a lot."

"But to those who cross me," Bu said slowly, intentionally, turning slightly to look at the count. "I am not some dickless king who will sit on his throne and turn a blind eye to insubordination. Do not cross me, Alger. Do not test me."

The look on Alger's face was one of true fear, as much as he tried to hide it behind those lazy eyes and that nonchalant look of his.

Bu nodded to Bao Zi.

"We move," Bao Zi said in his deep, gravelly voice.

"Watch my wife," Bu said to Ban Chu before he rode completely away from the city. Then he nodded to Alger. "And watch that one. Stay the course. We stick to the plan."

Ban Chu bowed as Bu led the twelve Hámonian knights north.

"What is our course?" Bao Zi asked. The man almost never spoke.

"First, I find this Erik Eleodum's family. I am told they are wealthy free farmers north of here," Bu said, "and we kill them. This man's family will pay for Patûk's death. And then we head north. Li has drawn us a map. We will follow it."

"Very well, my lord," Bao Zi said with the slightest hint of a smile touching the corners of his mouth.

45

"I don't understand why a froksman would be working for Golgolithul," Nafer said in Dwarvish.

"Why is that?" Erik asked.

"The Eastern Empire destroyed most of their lands," Nafer explained as they followed the trail of the two *men* who had stolen the Lord of the East's scroll. "Enslaved them. And those that weren't killed or enslaved by the east, the goblins took care of the rest."

Erik felt a tingle at his hip.

"They are close," he said.

"How do you know?" Nafer asked.

Erik felt a stronger tingle.

"I just do."

As they rounded the next bend, Erik could see the giant walls of Fen-Stévock in the distant north. They were tall and black, and even from a league away, they looked larger than anything Erik thought a man could build. The sun had just begun to rise in the east, and the walls seemed to drink up the light. Villages dotted both sides of the Merchant's Road as they neared the capital city, most of which looked much like Stone's Throw, small communities that had gathered for common commerce and protection, hoping to capitalize on their proximity to Golgolithul's largest city. In front of the city walls sat a sprawling municipality, Nafer called it South Gate, and he and Erik had reached its southernmost borders. This made tracking the two thieves all that much harder, but Erik's dagger led him, and he followed.

South Gate was poor at best. Erik dared a small smile as he rode past run down tavern after tavern and whorehouse after whorehouse. Bryon would have loved it there.

The people looked little better than the primary institutions of this suburb of Fen-Stévock. Those who weren't hocking their wares or goods or food along the street were begging and fighting. Erik kicked out at several men and women who became too interested in their horses.

Erik felt another tingle at his hip, and then a sharp pinch. He gave out an involuntary yelp.

"What is it?" Nafer said, but then leaned forward in his saddle and pointed. "There they are."

The froksman had covered his face and head with a scarf, and the passersby seemed rather unaware of the humanoid, more intent on drinking or selling or talking, but Erik could tell it was him. And his companion, the bald, stout man, stood next to him.

They had stopped by a small stall right in the middle of a busy side street of South Gate. The reins of their horses, Erik's horses, were held firmly in their hands while they drank something.

"A water break," Erik suggested.

"Aye," Nafer replied. "They must've assumed they lost us once they reached South Gate. We should hide the horses and go on foot. Look at all the people. It would be hard to ride fast through here."

They rode into a nearby alley and tethered their horses to the back of a shop. Erik paid a beggar boy a silver coin to watch their horses, but he didn't expect them to be there when they returned. He didn't really care. All that mattered was that they retrieve the scroll.

"Hurry," Nafer said, "we have to get to them before they enter Fen-Stévock."

Sneaking back into the main thoroughfare in the shadows, Nafer and Erik crouched behind an abandoned cart, watching their two targets drink and catch their breath. Nafer leaned forward, trying to eavesdrop. He could not understand the clicks and hisses the froksman made but could make out what the man said. Halfway through their conversation, Nafer's eyes widened.

"They aren't working for Golgolithul," Nafer whispered.

"Who, then?"

"Gol-Durathna," Nafer replied. "They mean to stop us. I heard mention of King Agempi and the General Lord Marshall."

"Who?"

"The head of all of Gol-Durathna's military," Nafer replied.

Perhaps that would be better. Gol-Durathna was a kingdom known for its compassion, and an ally to the dwarves of the Gray Mountains. The kingdoms that would become Gol-Durathna led the charge against Golgolithul at the Battle of Bethuliam and deposed the original Stévockians. Erik wondered if it was a good thing, maybe some sort of divine intervention that these two had stolen away this scroll that had to do with the dragon. But they had mortally wounded Demik.

Stay the course.

Erik touched his dagger.

But, surely, their king is a better man than the Lord of the East.

Power corrupts even the most righteous of hearts. Stay the course and retrieve the scroll. If you do not, many will die.

I understand.

"Wha' you doin' back here?" a man said, coming up behind Erik and Nafer.

"Minding our own business," Erik said. "Now go away."

He hadn't bothered to even turn and face the man, but a large hand clasped on his shoulder and stood him up. When he turned, he looked straight into the burly chest of a very large man. A year ago, Erik would have been terrified, but now, he was simply annoyed.

"We don't want trouble," Erik said, looking up at the dirty, bushy-bearded face of a resident of South Gate.

"A lil' whelp and a dwarf sneak behind my cart means you wan' trouble," he slurred, the stink of ale on his breath.

Nafer stood and turned, and as he did, the man pushed Erik. He was strong, but Erik could have stood his ground if it wasn't for him stepping on a broken wheel. He fell back, rolling over his head and coming to his feet with Ilken's Blade instinctively drawn. But now he was out in the middle of the street, and when he looked to the bald man and the froksman, they saw him. They glanced at one another briefly and then at Erik before they threw down their cups and mounted their horses.

"Hurry!" Erik said, and he knew Nafer was close on his heels as he ran after them.

They couldn't gallop in the busy street; they could barely move. It looked as if they were about to dismount as Erik and Nafer caught up to them, pushing past a throng of citizens that had just begun to crowd the road, when Erik felt the earth underneath his feet roll. Most ignored it, but Nafer felt it too by the look on his face. The look the man and froksman gave one another said they felt it too. The bald man heeled his horse hard, but Erik felt another shake of the ground, this time much stronger.

Everyone felt this one, and people started yelling and running about, mostly shouting in Shengu, but Erik heard one man yell "Earthquake!" in Westernese. As another shock hit the suburb of South Gate, toppling some unstable carts, the people became even more scared, crowding against each other frantically and pushing each other out of the way. A hot wind blew through the street of the suburb, wafting up the smells of sewage and trash and sweat, and the air felt heavy and constricting.

"That's no earthquake," Erik said, staring at Nafer intently, "that's the dragon."

Erik heard that roar again, like the distant rumbling of thunder even though there were no clouds in the sky. The air grew hotter.

"Nafer," Erik said, both swords drawn, caring little that people would see the magic sword, "she's close."

Nafer just nodded.

The horse that the bald man rode reared up as the people in the street became more frantic, throwing its rider to the ground and falling over itself. The froksman stopped to help his comrade.

"It's a dragon you fools!" Erik yelled and knew the man heard him because he looked up.

The froksman held out his hand to his companion and the bald man took it and pulled himself up onto the animal.

"Do you want to lead her all the way to Gol-Durathna?" Erik yelled.

"There's no such thing as dragons!" the man yelled over the din of frightened people, more earthquakes shaking South Gate, and the people so out of control that the city guard began running through the streets clubbing people and trying to maintain order. "You're the fool!"

The two Durathnans tried making their way through the street, and were able to push past people, but slowly. They caught the eyes of several eastern soldiers, who made their way towards the pair just as Erik and Nafer did. At that same moment, another quake caused the ground to roll as if it were a sheet Erik's mother was laying over a bed. The buildings on either side of the street creaked, the wood and stone cracking, many of them crumbling and tumbling to the ground. People screamed as they found themselves buried under the rubble and now, the city guard seemed more interested in saving themselves than trying to maintain order.

The next shock caused the ground to crack, the earth swallowing buildings and people alike. Erik looked to the south and, as thunder rumbled and the ground rolled uncontrollably, he saw an explosion, flames and smoke billowing up into the air, seeming to almost touch the sun.

Her roars and crashing of buildings were now so loud that Erik ducked and the people around him covered their ears. To them it was just a noise, but Erik understood.

I will reduce the lands of men to rubble. I will make you pay for your treachery.

46

She felt it. It was close as she soared over the land, reveling in the feeling of the air passing over her. It had been so long since she had flown so high, watching men—like insects—below her scream and run, listening to their pitiful and futile cries for help. Fire Beard, the dwarf came into her mind, and she snarled. His last act, his last fruitless spell before he died, was to put her to sleep, causing her to go into a hibernation that lasted a thousand years. All for nothing. Soon the scroll would be hers, the spell would be hers, she and her mate would reunite, they would raise their son, control the others of her kind—hidden away like gutless fools—and destroy the world, bringing shadow and fire that would last an eternity. She would be a goddess and her mate would be a god.

She laughed and belched out a ball of fire, consuming a whole village below her. Watching them burn excited her, and a part of her wanted to stop and consume their flesh. But it was too close to stop. The spell. The scroll. That fool of a boy had lost it ... that much she knew. The voice reading the spell wasn't his. But it didn't matter. She would make him pay. He had injured her, and he had evaded wolves, killed several of his kind. He still didn't have the scroll, but she could feel him ... they were close to it. She could smell him, an odor that would be forever imprinted in her mind.

By the demon gods of old, how many men had populated the world? When she had last flown above the world, they were scarce, fractionalized. Now, there were so many of them. She belched and destroyed another village. They were like ants. There were millions of them. As far as she could see. At every corner of the world. The elves. The dwarves. Giants and gnomes. They were bad enough. But these men ... they were a disease. If she hadn't been asleep for so long, they would have never grown this powerful. They would have never grown so numerous. It was no matter. Soon, they would all die. They would satiate her hunger and then her and her mate would rule again.

She saw a city, far away. It was new and hadn't been there when she reigned before. It was gigantic by the standards of men, so many of them. And they were there, that wretched boy and the fools who had stolen the scroll.

She dove towards the ground and flapped her wings. The earth below her cracked and split as she doused every open space she could with flame. She screamed, and the weaklings that fled her wrath fell to the ground, dead from only the sound of her voice as she landed and vomited fire. Everywhere she looked, the land burned, and she reveled in the heat before she turned her head skyward and spit into the air.

She was growing stronger by the moment, and her powers were

increasing. Not just her body, nor her breath. She remembered a spell and cast it in her mind. Two giant golems—mounds of dirt and stone and mineral shaped like giants, with heads and bodies and legs and arms—rose up from the ground, as tall as buildings, and followed her. She conjured a different spell, and a black cloud formed over a small village. It flashed so brightly, even she had to turn away, and lightning spilled from the cloud, consuming the whole community. Within the flutter of a fly's wing, the village was gone—every building, every animal, every person. She roared and cast yet another spell. Wherever someone had fallen dead, wherever someone lay buried within a league of her, whether they had recently fallen or buried in some village cemetery for years, they rose. Their flesh fell away, and ligaments tightly bound their bones together as she commanded them to march.

Erik could see her. The smoke that trailed behind her blotted out the sun, and the morning light turned deep red, as if blood had painted the sky. Most of the buildings at the beginning of South Gate were gone, and she and her new minions were coming closer, two gigantic golems in her wake followed by the growing skeleton army. The golems looked like mounds of rock and dirt, but they had heads and bodies and legs and arms. One had a tree growing from its scalp as if it had been formed straight from the earth. Whichever way she turned, they followed, as if they knew what she sought and were helping her look, and Erik knew what it was she hunted.

"What kind of man would follow a dragon?" Erik asked.

He looked to where the bald man and the froksman were.

"Do you believe me now?" he yelled.

The bald man looked at him. Fear filled his eyes. It wasn't the kind of fear that a man had when he was about to die, either. Erik had become accustomed to that look. No, this was the look of a man who was frightened beyond death. This was the look of a man who was fearful for his people, his family, his children.

"Give me back the scroll," Erik said, walking closer to the two Durathnans. "She doesn't care about you. She only cares about the scroll."

There was something about the scroll—or on the scroll—that the dragon desired. Perhaps it was more of a driven need, but the scroll was powerful and dangerous, and she wanted to keep it out of the hands of men, and have it for herself.

"Give it to me!" Erik screamed.

As the light from her nearby shadow dimmed even further, the bald man gave Erik a look of uncertainty mixed with, for a moment, confusion. How did this young man, who looked like he hadn't seen twenty summers, know what this mythical creature wanted? But it was a look that was short-lived. He turned to the froksman, a look of resolution and anger in his face, but the froksman hissed and shook its head. With a brief nod of understanding, the man reached into the front of his belt, the froksman waiting behind him and holding the reins of two horses that would rather be somewhere else, and retrieved the scroll case, showing it to Erik.

"Never," he said in Westernese. "It goes with us to Amentus, where it will be safe and away from the evil that has consumed the east."

As the man turned to join his comrade, the air now grew blisteringly hot, and the space between Erik and the two Durathnans became hazy and distorted. A hot wind, greater than any fire or furnace, blew against his face and all sound stopped, as if Erik had gone deaf. He knew what was about to happen. He remembered.

A pillar of flame erupted from the dragon's mouth and consumed the space where the bald-headed man used to be. Anyone, anything, that was within a dozen paces was gone. Everything but the scroll case, which lay on the ground where the man once stood. But how?

Erik looked over to see the dragon, her wings flapping, holding her head high above what used to be South Gate. People ran about as the two giant golems around her, as tall as three-story buildings, crushed people with their feet. And the soldiers that followed her, the skeletons, struck out at any people who ventured near, their bones seemingly as strong as Dwarf's Iron and killing indiscriminately.

As he wondered how to reach the scroll, Erik considered his dreams had been different. These walking dead were not those who came to him in the nighttime, but nonetheless, they indiscriminately killed anything they came across.

Erik heard a horn blow as both the city guard and the regular soldiers of Fen-Stévock organized in front of a gate in the city walls. At least a hundred men stood there, ready to charge the dragon as she landed. Erik could sense her mocking laugh, and in a single breath, every soldier that had stood there, ready to fight, was gone. He saw the froksman run to the scroll case, but she knew he was there too. She knew it was there. Her tail whipped through the air, a crack of thunder following it, and struck the froksman. He flew through the air and landed somewhere among the ruins that was once South Gate. She stared at the scroll, and Erik's dagger stabbed at his hip.

Grab it! Before she gets it!

Erik knew that if he ran for the scroll, he would be dead before he took two steps. But just then, black clouds formed in the sky above him and two bolts of lightning struck the ground where skeletal soldiers marched and attacked. Bones flew everywhere as both the dragon and Erik turned to see the Messenger of the East leading his Soldiers of the Eye.

Andragos' hood was pulled back, and he didn't look like Erik had expected. He didn't know what he expected—a skull? A withered old man? A monster?—but this was just a man, with pale skin, straight, black hair, and handsome, masculine features. He lifted his hands, muttered something, and another bolt of lightning struck one of the earthen giants, the one with the tree growing from its head, and as the tree trunk and leaves caught fire, the thing crumbled to the ground, nothing more than dirt and rock again. Then, a bolt struck the dragon. It seemed to startle her more than harm her, and she tossed her head into the air and roared a fiery scream, but it was just the distraction Erik needed. He ran for the scroll case and scooped it up before pushing it into his belt.

The dragon breathed against the wall of Fen-Stévock as her skeletal minions and the remaining golem turned their attention to the Soldiers of the Eye. A pile of melted, molten liquid lay where a wall a hundred paces high and made of black stone and iron once stood. Then, she looked at Erik.

You!

Her deafening voice rang through his head as the spines along her back seemed to bristle and her wings rattled. A dozen more of the city guard marched against her, on the opposite side of Erik, and she disposed of all of them in another single breath.

"*Run, Erik!*" Andragos yelled, and even though he was a hundred paces away, his voice echoed over the din of the battle and the screams of the dying. Erik turned, but a wall of flame blocked his path.

You didn't think it would be that easy, insect?

Again, there was laughter in her voice. A sickening mirth mixed with a deep hatred, something Erik couldn't even describe. It was as if the dragon's voice portrayed her hatred of life itself, of all of creation. Nafer ran to his side, mace readied in both hands. What good would it do? Another of Erik's friends would now lose their life because of him. He would lose his own.

Again, there was a sudden silence, and Erik knew what was coming. He braced himself for the pain and the heat of death as he felt the explosion that said the dragon had breathed. Erik turned away and futilely shielded his face with a hand as Nafer stepped in front of him, ready to take the full force of her attack—as if that would help either. As images of his family flashed through his mind, he felt the intense heat, hotter than ever before, but there was no pain, no death.

He opened his eyes to see fire spraying all around him and Nafer, some invisible force blocking it from touching his skin. He turned to see Andragos, his eyes glowing a brilliant white as he chanted something, looking in Erik's direction. The fire stopped, and Andragos fell silent, almost collapsing before one of his bodyguards caught him.

As Erik looked around, the dragon roared with anger and whipped her tail, destroying men and her own skeletal soldiers alike. The whole of South Gate was now destroyed. What was once a city in its own right had gone, crushed and burnt in a matter of moments.

"Erik." The voice was Andragos', but it was little more than a whisper.

Erik turned to see the mage, standing on wobbly legs. His eyes had returned to normal.

"Read the scroll, Erik," Andragos said.

"But ..." he began to reply.

"Read the scroll," Andragos insisted. His voice sounded strained and weak. "It is our only hope."

Erik looked at the scroll case for a moment, remembering how he felt when Patûk Al'Banan had read it—the darkness, the evil. He pulled open the cork and removed the scroll, unfurling it. Even staring at the page made his stomach turn. The symbols on the page were no language he was familiar with, and he began to wonder how he would be able to read it, but then the ink moved and undulated until they formed letters from the Westernese alphabet. He still didn't understand the words, but at least he would be able to read them. He heard the sucking of breath again, the rattling of giant dragon wings.

"Hurry, Erik," Andragos urged him as skeletal soldiers made their way towards Erik.

Erik began to read. He had no idea what he said, but the world around him darkened. He felt distant as if he were outside his body watching himself. The ground began to shake as he chanted something in a language that sounded evil.

The Shadow Tongue.

He felt a tingle at his hip.

As the skeletal warriors reached the man and dwarf, Nafer

swung his mace, crushing skulls and shattering bones. Erik read as quickly as he could and, as his eyes moved down the scroll, the rattling of wings, the sucking in of hot breath, even the march of skeletal soldiers and the golem stopped. Whatever magic had knit the warriors of bone together failed, and they all crumpled to the ground. The golem slowly crumbled until it was nothing more than a hillock of dirt. And the dragon paced back and forth, in front of Erik.

She eyed him as she paced, but every time she tried to breathe fire, all she could do was gag. When she tried to fly, it was as if some invisible rope kept her tethered to the ground. When she lunged forward to snap, some magic wall stopped her from reaching Erik. The spell was controlling the dragon.

As it paced in front of Erik and Nafer, the whole of Fen-Stévock's city guard formed in front of the remaining city walls, led by Andragos' Soldiers of the Eye. Erik stared at the scroll and the words in Westernese began to change again, back to an ancient text that seemed to crawl across the old parchment on its own volition. Something felt wrong.

"The spell is incomplete," he said to Nafer. "We are missing two elements that complete the spell."

"What do you mean?" asked Nafer as he warily watched the still pacing dragon.

"It provided directions—a map and an explanation of what it did—but there is a sword," Erik said, and he felt his dagger tickle his hip, "and a crown."

The spell won't hold her for long.

"Erik, fall back into the city," Andragos said, his voice even weaker.

Erik shook his head and drew Ilken's Blade.

That won't do you any good. Unsheathe me.

"I know you are a powerful weapon," Erik said, "but this is a dragon."

Nafer looked at Erik with a cocked eyebrow. He hadn't realized he was speaking aloud.

Trust me. Tell your dwarvish friend to stand behind you and unsheathe me.

Erik sheathed Ilken's Blade.

"Nafer, get behind me," Erik commanded.

The dwarf looked at him for a moment, looked back at the dragon —who still paced and fought against the invisible shield that held her back—and smiled.

"Erik, what are you doing?" Andragos' urged as Nafer stepped behind Erik.

The force that held the dragon back began to lessen as Erik saw a spark in her nostrils as she breathed. She was able to spread her wings, and she roared, even though it sounded muffled. Erik could sense indignation coming from the dragon.

I will make you suffer.

Her voice cut through his mind with searing pain like a sudden headache. She sounded truly livid.

I will make you suffer. I will melt your skin from your bones but keep you alive while I burn all you love. I will force you to watch them scream in before I trap you in a world that is in between this one and death.

She sucked air into her mouth and this time was able to blow fire against whatever invisible force held her at bay. She was gaining strength, and the spell was weakening. Erik held his hand ready by his side while he continued to stare at the dragon, holding her evil gaze.

"Nafer, give me the dagger I carry on my hip."

As Nafer drew the dagger and handed it to him it was as if the small weapon infuriated her even more. She roared and beat her wings against the invisible force field and blew hot breath into the air, each time, the spell wavered and weakened until it finally dissipated completely.

The dragon looked first to the gathering soldiers in front of Fen-Stévock's walls. With a single breath, she obliterated a quarter of the men standing there waiting to attack her. Rocks flew over the walls, fired from siege engines within the city, but a single flap from the dragon's wings sent the missiles back into the wall, cracking stone. Gigantic bolts tipped with tar-smeared, burning blades sailed towards the dragon, but she breathed again, incinerating the arrows mid-air and melting the tops of the wall where the siege weapons had once sat. Then, she turned her attention to Erik.

The dagger felt different in his hand. It was changing, like it always did, but this time was different. Erik didn't know how, but it felt different. That familiar tingle wasn't there, and as the dagger shifted, it sent a shock up his arm. Normally, the transition to some other form was instantaneous, happening in a quick flash, but it was as if the dagger took its time. The blade elongated, as did the handle and crossbar, so that his dagger looked like a sword. When it was finished changing, it looked much like Ilken's Blade, but only golden, from hilt to tip. All of the jewels that had been set within the handle were still there and all of them—the differing shades of a rainbow—glowed with an indescribable brilliance.

The dragon stopped flapping her wings and breathing fire as she tilted her head and then leaned forward, inspecting. She squinted her eyes and then they widened as if she recognized something. And that thing infuriated her more than ever. Now the dragon wasted no time bellowing fire at Erik, but he knew what to do. He lifted his golden sword and, even though the force from the attack caused his heels to slide backwards along the ground, the flame split around him, leaving both he and Nafer unscathed. No longer a tingle, the sword vibrated in his hands.

Fight, Erik.

Erik took in a deep breath, held it for a moment, and charged. When he was within range, the dragon snapped at him. He had grown stronger and faster since training with Wrothgard, but it was as if he had a newfound strength and skills. When the open mouth reached for him—big enough to swallow him whole—he dove through the space between upper and lower teeth, rolling when landing and then standing, just underneath the dragon. She swiped at him, and he ducked, and then she dropped her body to the ground, trying to crush him, but he rolled away just in time. She reared up on her hind legs and flapped her wings. As they came forward, Erik held his golden sword in both hands and swung. The blade tore through the membrane of the appendage, leaving a gaping space that resembled a torn sail.

The dragon screamed and bit at Erik again. He lunged back, and as her mouth shut with a thunderous sound, just in front of his face, he brought his blade down on her scaled snout. Dark green blood sprayed across his face, and he could feel heat emanating from her nostrils. The darkness within the two holes began to glow orange, and he knew she was about to breathe fire. He rolled away as the fire came, drawing his blade across the underside of her jaw, removing several scales.

From the corner of his eye, he saw Nafer coming to his aide.

"*Stay back!*" Erik yelled.

The dragon turned her attention to the dwarf, but before she could give Nafer a fiery death, Erik ran to one of her feet, driving his blade deep into her flesh. She roared again, lashing out with her claws, and Erik drew his sword across the sole of her foot. She retracted it quickly, only to turn and swipe her tail at him. Erik did a somersault over the tail and then drove his weapon into its flesh, hilt deep. More green blood oozed that seemed to smoke and hiss when it hit the ground.

Erik thought the dragon was getting frustrated as her attacks seemed much more frantic, and he continued to wound her, although not mortally. Finally, he looked up at her as she stood over him.

"Men are stronger than you think!" he yelled at her.

Fool! You don't even know what you are doing. You have no idea what it is you wield, or why you are still alive, do you?

With that, she attacked again, snapping at Erik. He dodged her attack again, bringing his blade across one of her spear-like teeth. The fang sliced perfectly, falling to the ground and, as she lifted her head in pain, Erik jammed his sword upward, into the spot between her jaws.

The dragon staggered backwards, spewing fire in every direction before rolling on the ground; he had truly hurt her. Finally, she rolled to her belly, pushed herself up, and flew high into the sky until Erik lost sight of her.

47

Erik looked down at his right hand. He held his dagger once again, golden-handled and jeweled. He cocked an eyebrow. The power that he felt from this seemingly small weapon was like nothing he had ever felt before. He already knew it was something special, Ilken Copper Head knew that too, but now it had helped him defeat a dragon—again. But this time, he wounded it. This weapon a gypsy gave him had just helped him win a battle with a dragon. He wondered if it could even kill a dragon; perhaps she knew it could, and that's why she fled.

Erik knelt, picking up the tooth he had cut from the dragon's mouth. It was heavy and the length of his forearm. He was glad for gloved hands, for the tooth dripped with a green liquid that was no doubt poisonous. Nafer wrapped it in cloth and then retrieved several scales that he had cut from her body.

"Are you okay?" Erik asked in Dwarvish.

"Yes," Nafer replied. "How did you do that?"

"I don't know," Erik said with a shrug.

Erik felt a large hand on his shoulder. He turned to see Terradyn, one of Andragos' henchmen he recognized from Finlo, standing before him. His bald head was red—he looked angry—and the blue-inked tattoos on his scalp moved as he scrunched his eyebrows.

"Quick," he said, "we must go."

"Where are we going?" Erik asked.

"No time for questions," Terradyn replied. When Nafer didn't move, he turned to the dwarf and said, speaking in Dwarvish, "Now. I will not ask again."

The remnants of the Soldiers of the Eye met Terradyn, Erik, and Nafer as they made their way to the road that led into the main gate of Fen-Stévock.

"Where is Andragos?" Erik asked, not seeing the Messenger among his personal guard.

"No talking," Terradyn said curtly. Then, as they walked in between two columns of soldiers that marched in perfect unison, he gave Erik a sidelong glance. "And you will refer to the Messenger of the East as my lord."

A hundred men stood at the gates leading into Golgolithul's capital city. The portcullis hung at an odd angle, one of the chains broken and the iron lodged in between the gate's opening. Cracks in a wall that looked otherwise impenetrable and indestructible spider webbed throughout the structure. The soldiers at the gate parted for the Soldiers of the Eye, but Erik couldn't help seeing the looks of fear and worry on their faces. He had no idea how many of Fen-Stévock's protectors had lost their lives in the dragon's attack, but he saw just one fiery breath kill at least a hundred men.

The inside of Fen-Stévock had fared better than the suburb of

South Gate, but that wasn't saying much, since South Gate was completely gone. The attack outside the walls had still caused buildings to tumble and walls to crumble. The dead and dying, both military and civilian, littered the streets, and the stink of feces and urine and blood and death filled the air, a stink Erik had come to know well. The only sound that cut above the screams of the injured was the yelling of constables trying to regain order in the chaos.

As the Soldiers of the Eye marched Erik and Nafer through the city, they cared little for the wounded and dead that crowded the streets, stepping over the injured and stepping on the dead. One soldier swatted at a woman crying over a dead man with the butt of his spear and another simply nudged a weeping child, barely three summers old, to the side with his boot. And as if the dragon attack wasn't bad enough, the confusion and destruction gave rise to more chaos. Mass looting ensued with not a care who was watching.

The city guards were hard at work trying to stem the disorder, but the Messenger's personal guard cared not. One city guardsman even asked for help, his face smeared with blood. Erik couldn't understand what the man said, but he was frantic and breathing hard, and behind him a dozen or more looters were setting fire to overturned carts. Two other city guardsmen lay dead, trampled by the looters. The Messenger's man simply pushed the guard away and, as Erik looked over his shoulder, the looters converged on him, beating him with bricks and sticks.

As they marched closer to the center of the city, horns and bells rang out, and more of the city's defense people ran past them. It wouldn't be long until order had been regained, and Erik hated to think what would happen to those who had joined in the revelry of chaos.

The further they got from the entry to the city, the destruction grew less and less, as did the confusion. Eventually, Fen-Stévock looked like a normal city, its citizens wandering about, engaging in their normal, daily activities and either not caring or having no clue as to what had happened along the city's southern walls. But everyone stepped aside for the Soldiers of the Eye.

A wide moat surrounded the walls of the Castle of Fen-Stévock. Its keep, called the Black Thorn, rose high into the air, its stone black until it ended in a point. A single pole sat atop that point, and a flag bearing the symbol of the Stévockians—a black, gauntleted fist clenching a black arrow with a red tip and red fletching—fluttered in a mild wind.

They marched over a drawbridge, wide enough to hold several columns of soldiers at once, and Erik looked down at the water that filled the moat, But it didn't look like water; it was as black as the stone that created the castle walls. It moved in a fluid manner, like water, but it was slower, almost methodical. Little eddies formed here and there, and Erik caught the scent of something that smelled like burning hair. Even though he thought not a living thing could survive in such a seemingly inhospitable place, he saw movement in the water-like substance, as if something had poked a nostril through the surface only to descend quickly. He felt his hip tingle.

Do not talk to me in there. Do not acknowledge me. Mind both your mind and your tongue.

Should I not enter?

It seems you have little choice. Guard yourself. Nothing is as what it seems in this place.

More buildings stood on the other side of the wall and portcullis, but the keep dominated the center of the courtyard. It looked even taller on this side of the walls and stairs surrounded it, leading up to a great stone dais. That then led to a columned, open-aired walkway and eventually to the keep's door. At the foot of the stairs, two score of men stood, the symbol of an open hand centered by a lidless eye emblazoned on their leather breastplates. Their steel helmets and the long, steel blades of their spears glimmered in the sun that managed to escape through clouds of foundry smoke that billowed up from the eastern parts of the city.

Erik looked to the top of the great stone dais. The Messenger stood there, but how? Andragos had been in front of the city walls at the same time as him. But then Erik remembered he was a mage, not just any mage, but an immensely powerful one, capable of keeping a dragon at bay, even if only for a short while. But events had taken their toll, and the Messenger looked ragged, his hair tangled and messy, dark circles around his eyes, and his cheeks sunken and pale.

The soldiers escorting Erik and Nafer stopped and snapped to attention, the soldiers in front of the dais responding in the same way. The Messenger's henchmen met him as he descended the stairs, speaking quietly. Finally, they looked to Erik, pointing, and Andragos made for the man, slowly.

"Erik," the Messenger said with a forced smile, his voice sounding weak and shaky, "I had thought I might see you again."

"Really?" Erik asked, surprised.

"Yes," the Messenger said. He stopped for a moment, closed his eyes, and breathed deeply. Opening them, he continued. "Do you not remember me saying so in Finlo?"

"Yes, I suppose I do," Erik said.

"And you have gone from a simple porter to a warrior," the Messenger said.

"I don't know about a warrior," Erik replied, the slightest hint of a smile touching the corner of his mouth.

"And you have suffered much loss," Andragos added.

"My brother," Erik replied after a moment, any hint of a smile gone.

"Many give their lives in service," the Messenger said. "It is a hard sacrifice, if not a worthy—and necessary—one. You saw that first-hand. The destruction of a dragon."

"You ..." Erik began to say, wanting to ask what this was all truly about, wanting to ask how the Messenger knew what the scroll would do, and how he staved off a dragon, but Andragos put up a hand and stopped him.

"Perhaps another time, Erik," the Messenger said.

Again, Erik was struck by how Andragos didn't look how Erik

had pictured him. In Finlo, he had imagined the worst, a cruel if not evil visage that could cower a man with one look, but instead ... Here was a decidedly mortal-looking man, ragged and tired, but beyond that, Erik could see what the man looked like, could look like. He had expected an older man, or a thinner man, or even not a man at all, but Andragos was a man of middle years. He could have been his father's age, perhaps even younger. His hair, despite its current appearance, looked like it was normally well kept, and his sunken cheeks betrayed what Erik could tell was a strong face and frame, with dark eyebrows set around deep blue eyes. Even in its paleness, his skin looked perfect and soft.

Except for ... Erik saw the smallest hint of a scar. It was on the Messenger's jaw, just where it met his neck. Erik couldn't quite see it, among the folds of the cowl and cloak, but nonetheless, there was a scar there, red and glaring. As if the Messenger knew what Erik was looking at, he shifted so that the scar could no longer be seen.

"I must get you to your quarters," Andragos said.

"We have others ..." Erik began to say.

"Yes, I know," Andragos replied. "I have sent my men to retrieve them. They will be here tomorrow."

"Does the Lord of the East know we are here?" Erik asked.

"Undoubtedly," Andragos replied, "but, nonetheless, he'll want a formal introduction."

"Does he know?" Erik asked, pointing to the scroll case stuck in his belt.

"Also, undoubtedly, yes," Andragos said.

"What will happen?" Erik asked.

"Truthfully, Erik, I do not know," Andragos replied. "The Lord of the East is a hard man, unyielding and unforgiving. However, you saved our city from a dragon. I am sure that will mean something."

The worry on Erik's face must have been evident, as the Messenger smiled at him.

"Do not worry right now," he said. "Let me get you and Nafer

Round Shield to your quarters so you might rest. The eastern gods know I need a good rest as well."

Erik looked over his shoulder, saw the surprised look on Nafer's face, wondered how the Messenger knew the dwarf's name, and then remembered, he was the Black Mage.

48

The Messenger led Erik and Nafer to a row of houses situated on the other side of the keep. The courtyard they crossed, all contained within black walls, reminded Erik of Thorakest—vast and wide and a city unto itself. Workers from many different professions busied themselves with their daily tasks, metal workers, carpenters, farmers, or soldiers. Even with the powers he wielded, the Lord of the East's keep would be completely self-sustaining should the unlikely happen, and an army breached Fen-Stévock's walls and took the city proper. It seemed no one had ever planned for a dragon attack.

"You will stay here for the night," Andragos said, turning to Erik and Nafer.

They stood in front of a large, two-storied house with double doors as an entrance and two soldiers standing guard. Tall columns held up a wooden awning that extended just below the shuttered windows of the second floor and it looked like some place a visiting noble or aristocrat might stay.

"Is this a house for lords?" Nafer asked Erik, speaking in his native tongue.

"Yes, Master Dwarf, it is," Andragos replied in the same language with a wry smile. "At least, those who are visiting Fen-Stévock for any number of reasons."

Thick carpets and tapestries hanging from every open space on the wall decorated the inside of the home. Two baldheaded men wearing soft-looking robes quickly approached and bowed when Andragos led Erik and Nafer into the room.

"These are my lord's eunuchs," the Messenger said. "They will attend to your needs. They will show you your rooms and show you to the dining area when it is time. They will also make sure your things are cared for."

Both men bowed low again.

"I will be back in the morning to take you before the Lord of the East," the Messenger said.

"Will you be leading us to a warm welcome," Erik asked, "or to our execution?"

Andragos gave a forced smile.

"Most likely neither," the Messenger replied.

"Our friends out there," Nafer said, pointing to one of the walls, "Is it better they stay away?"

"Probably, but that is not possible. They will be safe, of that, I can assure you."

Andragos turned to Erik.

"Now, I also have matters of the state to attend to," he said with a smile. "Helping an emperor run an empire is a never-ending job. Raktas and Terradyn will stay with you. There is no safer place in the entire world, than inside these walls, but just in case, they will add to your safety. I will take that."

Andragos pointed to the encased scroll sticking out of Erik's belt. He looked down and pulled it, but then he hesitated. He had seen what it could do and now wondered what that could mean in the hands of a wizard. Then he looked at Andragos and gave it to him.

The Messenger turned to leave, but then stopped and turned back around.

"One last thing, before I go," Andragos said. "Do not go wandering tonight. The gates to the keep close, and there is nothing for you in the courtyard. Stay inside."

The look on Andragos' face was so stern and serious Erik took a step back.

"See you in the morning," Andragos said with a quick nod.

Erik sat at the edge of his bed. It was a giant of a thing, large enough to fit his whole family, and he had it all to himself. There were so many rooms just in this house: Kitchens, offices, libraries, storerooms, and bedrooms.

He found nothing about dinner appetizing and was still hungry. He didn't even touch dessert. He didn't drink any wine or ale, and the water tasted sour.

A tapestry bearing the crest of the Stévockians hung from the wall in Erik's bedroom—there was one in every room, a reminder of who owned this place to whoever slept here that they owed allegiance.

"They died for you," Erik said, thinking of the scroll that had saved his life and the lives of the citizens of Fen-Stévock. "Drake and Samus. Vander Bim. Mortin, Bim, and Thormok. Threhof. Befel. Switch even. Those people in South Gate. They all died for you—and for what?"

As he questioned what he had done, what had happened in just the last months, let alone the last two years, an image flashed through Erik's mind. Men stood before Erik, chanting, "Eleodum! Eleodum! Eleodum!" over and over again. Erik, wearing a dazzling suit of armor emblazoned with the symbol of a fist clenching a red fletched arrow, led an army into battle. He didn't know whom he fought, but he won, and his soldiers shouted his name again. The sky, clear and bright and blue, showered him with gold rain as blackened and charred skulls cracked and broke under the hooves of his horse.

Then, another image flashed in his mind. It was one of him and his family, his parents, his sisters, and, yes, his brother. They were on their farm, only it was ten times the size of their land now. A hundred men worked it, and even the Hámonian nobles were working the fields with the other hands. His mother wore a beautiful gown, and his sisters tied gold thread in their hair. His father wore high, hard leather boots and a high-collared coat of red and gold. He watched out over his fields and then looked at Erik.

"Thank you," his father said. "You are my favorite son and, because of what you have done, Erik, all of this will be given to you. These men will bow to you."

Then, Erik saw Simone. She also wore a gown, hers of silver and blue and glowing in the moonlight of a clear night. She was more beautiful than he remembered, her blonde hair like threads of gold, her skin pale and milky and soft. Two boys danced at her feet. They were his boys, Erik's boys. But, then, it wasn't just Simone there. He saw a dozen women—dark skin and pale skin, dark hair and blonde hair—all beautiful, all desirable. They were all his, all his wives, and two or three children from each one danced about them and sang and giggled as each one of his wives bade him to come to bed with them.

"Come, lay with me," they all said, sweetly, seductively. But the sweetest and most seductive was Simone. She stepped to him. He couldn't see any of the others. He could smell her, rose hips and mint and lemon grass. She pressed herself against him, and his face grew hot as he felt himself rise. She stepped back, not wearing a gown anymore, but a shift of soft, translucent fabric. She pulled it away, revealing herself fully to him. She laid back on a large bed, begging for him to join her. And then the rest of his wives were there as well, all of them naked in the bed, begging, desiring, waiting.

Erik shook his head.

"What, by the Creator, was that?" he asked himself. "Those are a fool's thoughts."

Erik had no desire to stay in Fen-Stévock, nor Golgolithul, let alone lead its armies. The day his father and mother wore a high-collared jacket and a gown would be the day they died, if that day hadn't already happened. And as for letting a hundred farmhands work his land while he stood and watched, Rikard Eleodum would never let that happen. Simone—he had often thought of what their life together might be like, of what their wedding night might be like—would never be happy if he took other wives. The thought of her made him ache.

He knew in other places, in other countries, men took more than one wife, but not in the valley in which his farmstead lay, especially with Simone as his wife. She wasn't the jealous type, but she was strong and could be stubborn, and any other woman trying to share their bed would likely find herself running home to her mother, broken and bruised.

And, yet, those thoughts still danced about in his mind. He looked to his dagger. He wanted to ask it but then remembered what it had told him.

There is something not right about this place. It feels like Orvencrest.

He shivered at the thought of Orvencrest. The darkness. The dead, just beyond the shadows. Their distant cursing and hissing and laughing. He scrunched his eyebrows, and it felt like a thousand ants crawled up his back. He saw the hair on his arms stand on end and decided he wanted to get out of this room, out of this house. He walked to his door, but then the Messenger's words rang loudly in his head.

"Do not go wandering about," he had said. "Those that wander tend to get lost."

Still, Erik opened his door.

Candles sitting in black iron sconces dimly lit the hallway. Nafer's room sat directly across from his, and Erik considered joining him but didn't. He walked down the hallway to where two sweeping stairways led down into the main room. Opposite the bottom of each staircase, at the far end of the room, a fire raged, but that proved the only light in the area. Erik felt drawn to the double front doors, something beckoning him. He quietly slipped down the stairs and soon stood before them, within arm's reach. He could open the door, get some fresh air, watch the stars overhead, and remember home. He smiled. He touched the round metal handle with a single finger, closed his eyes and opened the door.

The smell of fire and smelting metal and rotten flesh hit his nose. His eyes shot open, and there was no night sky, no stars. He wasn't even in Fen-Stévock anymore. The sky was anything but clear, the black, choking smoke of industry clouding any hopes of seeing stars or the moon. Erik saw a thousand rotting corpses. An army of dead men waited for him in a field of brown, dead grass.

How?

The dead laughed. Erik drew his sword, Ilken's Blade. It was with him, in this place. And he cut through them as they came. His steel touched the dead flesh, and they exploded into a thousand pieces. He saw his hill, in the distance as thunder and purple lightning raged behind him, and he knew a black mountain range loomed there. He made for his hill. The dead came, and he fought, sending each one of them into oblivion. He knew they would be gone. There was something about what happened when his sword touched them. They were gone and would never come back.

It felt like he had been fighting for hours. He must have destroyed a thousand dead men before he finally stood at the foot of his hill. Then, he saw them. It was a group of dead men that he recognized. Three of them were well decomposed, and two were fresh, some of their color still intact. Two of the dead men who were well-rotted looked like the slave boss who had attacked the gypsy caravan in the Abresi Straits. Dark, oily-looking beards clung to bony chins, and their black robes hung from their bodies in tatters. They both carried curved swords as well. The skin that still managed to stick to their bones was a darkened tan, and their eyebrows were thick, shadowing eye sockets void of any eyes. Another was Fox. He looked less and less like himself, but that red hair still managed to stick out from his head.

The general, Patûk Al'Banan, stood before Erik, fresh, his skin only pale with a few black spots. Death had already stolen his powerful muscles and jaws, and he looked a faint resemblance of the strong man he once was. And then there was Switch, even more gaunt and frail than ever.

"You can't win," Fox said, bugs crawling out of his mouth and into his eye sockets as he spoke.

"I've already won," Erik said.

Fox hissed and stepped forward. Erik swung Ilken's Blade. If the dead man had eyes, they would have looked surprised, for when Erik struck him, the result was different than before. Fox glowed as beams of light exploded from every part of his decaying body until he finally burst into tiny pieces that floated to the ground like snow. The two slavers came on, and the same thing happened to them as they disappeared from existence, nothing more than dust floating on a faint breeze. Patûk had none of the strength he possessed in life, and Erik easily dispatched him as well. He cursed as his body lit up, and then he too was dust.

Erik turned to Switch. He lifted his sword over his head, gripped tightly in both hands. Switch fell to his knees and began to weep.

"Please, Erik," the dead man whimpered, holding a hand up in front of his face.

"You don't deserve mercy," Erik said.

"No, I don't," Switch replied. "I'm a terrible bastard. I have been my whole life. I betrayed the only friends I ever had and now look at me. I'm sorry."

"You're just saying that because you're stuck here," Erik said, "wandering with the dead."

"No," Switch said through sobs, "I'm sorry. I truly am. I did you wrong. You trusted me, and I repaid you with treachery. If I could go back and do it differently, I would. I don't expect you to forgive me."

Switch looked up at Erik. He cried even though there weren't any tears falling from his eyes. His pale skin looked even sicklier, and his hair hung in knotted clumps, some of it already gone.

Erik lowered his sword and shook his head.

"I forgive you, Switch," Erik said.

The thief looked up at Erik, and he began to fade away, a translucent specter until he simply disappeared. The last thing Erik saw was the man's smile, and then he was gone.

Erik wanted to walk to the top of the hill and sit under the weeping willow tree, even though the man who was normally there wasn't to be seen, but something caused him to turn. When he did, he was back in the house, facing one of the household eunuchs.

"What are you doing, sir?" the eunuch asked, his voice deep and prying.

"Nothing," Erik replied, taking his hand from the door handle. "You startled me."

"My apologies, sir," the eunuch said.

"It's all right," Erik said. "I'll just return to bed."

The eunuch grabbed Erik's arm, and for a man who was pudgy, bald, and soft looking, his grip was surprisingly strong.

"You mustn't wander," the eunuch said. The tone of his voice deepened. "You might get lost in the night."

"Don't worry," Erik said, pulling his arm free of the eunuch's grip, "I won't."

He returned to the stairs and headed quickly to Nafer's room, knocking on the door softly. As soon as the dwarf opened it just a sliver, Erik pushed his way into the room.

"We need to leave this place," Erik said.

Nafer just stared with pursed lips and raised eyebrows.

"This place is evil, Nafer," Erik said. "It feels like Orvencrest. We need to get out of here."

"Right now?" Nafer asked.

"No," Erik said. "We'll wait until predawn. Better if we stay together?"

"Aye," Nafer replied.

Erik went into his room, grabbed his swords, his armor, and his haversack, and returned to Nafer's room, where they waited. It seemed a long while before they finally crept into the hallway slowly and quietly. They went down to the main hall and stood in front of the double door entrance. Erik looked to Nafer one last time. The dwarf nodded, and Erik opened the door. Then he remembered what his dagger had told him.

Mind both your mind and your tongue.

A dozen guards were waiting for them as they stepped from the house. Six of them pushed Erik to the ground while the other six held down Nafer. Terradyn and Raktas came running from the house, yelling at the guards holding the two. As they argued in Shengu, Erik could tell that the Messenger's bodyguards were angry and on the brink of fighting with the guards when one of them produced a letter. Terradyn read it, promptly crumpled it when he was done, and threw it to the ground, but he did nothing else. The bodyguards worked for Andragos, but the guards' instructions had come from someone higher.

The guards picked Erik and Nafer up and shoved them forward, leading them to the stairway that led up to the large dais of Fen-Stévock's keep.

"Keep quiet when you enter the keep," Terradyn said as they followed them and the guards.

"Do not look at the Lord of the East," Raktas added. "Look down, and do as you are told. And keep your thoughts away from him."

Standing in front of the stairway, Erik saw another small retinue of soldiers pushing Wrothgard and Turk. Erik felt a sudden elation and moved to run to his friends.

"Turk!" he yelled, but the butt of a spear to the back of his leg brought him to his knees, and the soldier that had struck him said something to him in Shengu that he assumed to be 'Silence.'

Erik looked on, past Wrothgard and Turk, but saw no Bofim or Beldar. He looked at Turk.

"They are safe," the dwarf said in his own language. He too was met with a spear to the back of his leg.

"And Demik?" Erik whispered.

Turk simply looked at him, his eyes red, and shook his head.

The guards stood Erik and Turk up and marched the four companions up the stairs. A walkway lined by columns led to the entrance of the keep, which stood open. Andragos was there to meet them, and a sharp look from the Messenger caused the guards to back away from the four mercenaries.

"I told you not to go out at night here," Andragos said, his voice hard.

"I would try to explain myself," Erik said, "but I think you probably already know why I thought what I did."

He met Andragos' eyes. There was understanding there, truth, and a bit of sadness. He nodded and folded his hands behind his back.

"As much as I understand, noncompliance in this place can mean a fate worse than death, Erik. That may be a cliché much of the time, but here it holds a savage truth. I do not know exactly what is going to happen to you and your companions, but you must follow my instructions, do you understand?"

Erik held Andragos' eyes, and there was truth. Erik nodded.

"Only speak when spoken to," the Messenger commanded, speaking more to all the mercenaries. "When the Lord of the East comes into the room, you will prostrate yourself before him. When he tells you to rise, you will come to your knees, but keep your eyes to the floor. When he asks you to please stand, you will do so, but keep your eyes down. Finally, he will ask you to look at him, which you will do. Do you understand?"

All four of the mercenaries nodded.

"Good," Andragos said. "Follow me."

He led them through the keep's entrance.

Windows on either side of the great hall gave the room light. Large fruit trees lined the walls, all in onyx planters. Trellises covered the walls instead of tapestries and paintings, each wooden framework covered with vines and crawlers, all with flowers of many different colors. Two great cats lay next to one of the planters, each white with black stripes and collars studded with diamonds and sapphires. They eyed Erik and the others as they walked by them.

Guards lined the wall as well, all of them clad in black armor, the symbol of the Stévockians emblazoned on their breastplates. Pointed visors hid their faces, and they stood motionless, holding tall, square shields and pikes. Despite not being able to see their eyes, Erik imagined they followed him as well as he made his way to the center of the keep.

A purple curtain extended from the high ceiling to the floor in the center of the keep, falling on a raised dais. Tall apple trees grew directly from the ground on either side of the dais, reaching higher than any other apple tree Erik had ever seen. In front of each of tree were pools of water, each with a fountain that spouted up so that it would fall back into the pool like rain. Men and women lounged around on chaises and rugs and pillows in front of the dais, some scantily clad in white, translucent robes while others were naked. Some of the men and women played flutes and lyres and lutes while others simply talked and giggled and caressed one another. Atop the dais, in front of the great curtain, sat three chairs, all well cushioned with low backs and low armrests.

The Messenger turned.

"Prostrate yourselves in the presence of the Lord and Emperor of the East, High Lord Chancellor of Golgolithul, Patron of Family Stévock, and Protector of Háthgolthane."

The men and women stopped talking and playing their instruments and lay on the floor, face down. The mercenaries followed suit. Erik heard shuffling he presumed to be the curtain followed by footsteps.

"Rise," a voice said in Westernese. It was soft, albeit commanding.

Erik pushed himself to his knees but kept his face to the floor.

"Please," the voice said, "stand."

Erik did as he was told, as did his companions. But he kept his eyes down. He could see, looking up ever so slightly, three people standing atop the dais.

"Look upon the Emperor of the East," the voice commanded.

Erik lifted his head. Three people stood on the dais. Two of them were women. One woman had almost white hair, with pale skin and piercing blue eyes. She wore a shear dress of black, two strips of material covering her breasts and meeting at a snug buckle about her waist. The rest of the dress billowed out and touched the floor. The other woman had black hair, dark brown skin, and emerald eyes that seemed to glow, and she wore the same exact dress as the first, only hers was white. Both were beautiful, with perfect noses and lips, high cheeks and round chins. They could have been twins if it wasn't for the different colors of their hair and complexions of their skin.

Between them stood a man, tall and lean, his bare chest showing a body used to training and exercise. A thick, red sash was tied around his waist, and he wore black pants of loose material, allowed to billow out before tapering back around the man's ankles. His black hair spilled down his back and over his shoulders, shadowing a slender face, a square jaw, and piercing, green eyes. He was handsome, beautiful almost, and Erik found it hard to take his eyes off the man.

"So, you are the ones who have succeeded in my quest," the Lord of the East said. "And yet, one of you isn't even one of the original men we called to Finlo."

He stepped forward. All four of the mercenaries kept their eyes on the Lord of the East but said nothing.

"And, yet, you have not really fulfilled your duty, have you? You looked at my treasure, even though my friend, Andragos, here told you not to."

They still said nothing.

"You disobeyed me," the Lord of the East said. "Do you know what happens to disobedience in my realm?"

"Your Majesty ..." Erik began to say, but the two women on either side of the Lord of the East hissed, cutting him off.

"Silence!" the Lord of the East shouted, and the walls shook with his voice. "Andragos, did you not instruct them in the etiquette of my court?"

"I did, Your Majesty," Andragos said with a quick bow.

"Clearly, they do not listen very well," the Lord of the East said.

"Please, Your Majesty ..." Wrothgard began to say, but this time, the women on either side of the Lord of the East held up their right hands. Wrothgard's voice stopped, and his face turned red, and then blue, as he struggled to breathe.

"Do you mean to explain to me what I already know?" the Lord of the East said. "Do you wish to explain to me that you lost that which you were commissioned to find? That a traitor among your ranks stole it and gave it to that defector Patûk Al'Banan? Or do you mean to tell me that you, by losing the Dragon Scroll and allowing Patûk Al'Banan to read from it, have brought a dragon down upon my city? Do you mean to tell me that the total destruction of South Gate and the lost lives of both my citizens and my soldiers are your fault?"

"I saved your city," Erik said.

The Lord of the East's women released his magical grip on Wrothgard. The man crumpled to the ground as the Lord of the East's glare bored into Erik. He felt a sharp pain in the back of his head and couldn't help feeling as if someone else was inside his mind. He felt heat burn through his body but stood resolute nonetheless.

The Lord of the East looked to Wrothgard.

"Stand!" he yelled.

Wrothgard stood quickly, even though his legs were still shaky, and he was having trouble breathing. The Lord of the East stepped halfway down the stairs that led to the platform on which his throne sat and fixed his eyes on Erik's

"If you had done your job," the Lord of the East said, "then you wouldn't have needed to save my city."

Erik just stood there and waited. Would the Lord of the East strike him down with magic, or would some guard run him through?

The Lord of the East softened his gaze and folded his hands behind his back.

"How is it you were able to read what was on the scroll?" the Lord of the East asked.

"When I opened it," Erik replied, "the ink began to move on the parchment until it was letters I could read and pronounce."

"Interesting," the Lord of the East said, looking down at Erik over his nose. "And what was this weapon you wielded to injure the creature? I only know of one blade that can harm a dragon."

Erik thought for a moment, but not too hard. He once again felt someone else inside his head, and then he couldn't help seeing the eyes of the two women who had stood next to the Lord of the East. They glowed, ever so faintly. They were trying to read his thoughts, but he wanted to protect—to save—his dagger.

"An elvish blade, Your Majesty," Erik lied, hoping Bryon would forgive him.

"An elvish blade?" questioned the Lord of the East. "Andragos, have you ever heard of an elvish blade being able to harm a dragon?"

Erik looked to Andragos. The Black Mage's face was unmoving.

"If it is a weapon from the Elvish Wars, then perhaps," the Messenger said. "The elves constructed many mighty weapons during those times."

The Lord of the East stared at Erik.

"Where would you have gotten such a mighty weapon, just a farmer turned porter?" the Lord of the East asked.

"My ... I found it," Erik replied, "on another mercenary that we killed."

"And how did you know it was an elvish blade?" the Lord of the East asked.

Erik didn't answer at first, and when he opened his mouth, the Lord of the East stopped him.

"Thorakest," he said, a mirthless smile on his face. "King Skella and his dwarves told you, didn't they?"

Erik nodded.

"And this is the blade you used to stave off the dragon?" he asked.

"Yes, Your Majesty," Erik replied.

The Lord of the East looked beyond the mercenaries and nodded. A guard approached the dais, both of Erik's swords in hand. He bowed and offered them to the Lord of the East. The emperor took them, first unsheathing Bryon's elvish sword. Erik noticed that, as the Lord of the East held the weapon, the blade seemed to dim and barely gave the slightest hint of purple glow.

"This doesn't seem that special," the Lord of the East said, "although I can feel its magic. This is the weapon you used against the dragon?"

"Yes, Your Majesty."

"Do not lie to me," he added.

"I'm not," Erik replied, desperately trying to think of what he said as the truth.

The Lord of the East sheathed the elvish sword and then drew Ilken's Blade, inspecting it in the light the windows of the hall allowed in.

"Dwarf's Iron," the Lord of the East said. "Did you claim this off of a dead adversary as well. Or are you such a friend of the dwarves that they made this for you?"

"It was made for me, Your Majesty," Erik replied.

"Ilken Copper Head," the Lord of the East said, looking at the runes on the blade. "A fine craftsman."

Sheathing Ilken's Blade, the Lord of the East nodded to the same guard. The soldier retrieved the blades from his master and promptly offered them to Erik.

"You obviously know that this scroll," the Lord of the East said, opening his hand and conjuring the scroll case to appear in his palm, "is no family heirloom or script of lineage. It is known as the Dragon Scroll. It is a powerful weapon. My first inclination when I discovered the scroll had been read was to have you all flayed alive if you ever dared return it to me ... but you stole it back, risked and lost lives, and did return it to me. For this, I am grateful. Your disobedience should award you death, but your loyalty, I think, has offset that."

"Thank you ..." Wrothgard began to say, but a hard look from the Lord of the East quieted him.

"Do not thank me yet," the Lord of the East said. "In order to clear your name, I have another task for you."

"Your Majesty," Turk said.

"This is not a request," the Lord of the East said, stepping down several more steps. "This is a command. And I care not whether you come from Golgolithul, the free lands of Western Háthgolthane, or the realm of Drüum Balmdüukr. Refusal will result in a painful, slow death."

All four mercenaries bowed. What choice did they have? The hands of the Lord of the East could reach them wherever they went. And if they could escape his grip, what of their families?

The Lord of the East walked back up to the top of the platform and conferred with the two women. As he did, Erik couldn't help noticing a look of irritation cross Andragos' face.

"Part of this scroll is an incantation," the Lord of the East explained, "and part of it is a map."

A small space parted in the purple curtain that hung down on the dais, and an old man with tanned skin, scraggly, white wisps for a beard, almond shaped eyes, and a crooked back emerged. He wore a heavy black robe that covered both his hands and feet, but Erik could hear shuffling as he walked to the Lord of the East.

Andragos' eyes widened, and the look of irritation on his face grew to one of anger. He glared at the old man with contempt.

"Your Majesty," Andragos said.

The Lord of the East shot the Messenger a hard look and the Black Mage backed up a step.

"I know what I am doing," the Lord of the East said.

Some internal quarrel between the two most powerful men of Golgolithul? Erik thought.

"Melanius here has studied the map," the Lord of the East said. "There is a second and a third piece to this puzzle that is the Dragon Scroll. As you saw, Erik Eleodum, the incantation on the scroll has enough power by itself to subdue the dragon—any dragon—for a time, but eventually the spell wears off. To truly harm the dragon, one must wield the Dragon Sword and to completely subjugate the dragon and control it, one must wear the Dragon Crown. It seems that the ancient dwarves separated these pieces. To what end, I do not know. Can you imagine, the ability to control a dragon?"

The Lord of the East seemed to trail off in his own thoughts for a moment, staring into nothing, thinking of all the possibilities a ruler could think of if they controlled a dragon. As he did, Erik remembered his dagger. That, so far, had been the only thing that could harm this dragon. And then, the Lord of the East looked back at the mercenaries.

"The empires of this world encroach onto Háthgolthane, and no one is willing to stand against them. Enemies from Wüsten Sahil, Nothgolthane, Antolika, even farther east and to the south, see the treasure that is Háthgolthane," the Lord of the East said. "Not Gol-Durathna or Gol-Nornor, not Drüum Balmdüukr or Thrak Baldüukr, not Hámon or Nordeth or Southland. Only I am willing to spill my countrymen's blood to stem the tide of invaders. To wield such a weapon would stop these invasions."

"You will find the Dragon Sword," the Lord of the East continued, "and return it to me. As payment, I will not only let you live, but I will make you heroes of the east."

"And what about the Dragon Crown?" Erik asked.

"You will let me worry about that piece," the Lord of the East said, "but it is a more complicated task. The sword is hidden away in the Keep of Fealmynster, north of the Gray Mountains. It is guarded by a powerful wizard, once a citizen of Gol-Durathna, now since exiled for his dabbling in the darkest of magic. As we have discovered through exhaustive research, you need a key to enter Fealmynster. The map leads to Fealmynster, but without the key, the map is useless."

"How do we find the key?" Erik asked.

"You will meet one of my agents in a town called Eldmanor in two months," the Lord of the East said. "Are you familiar with it?"

"Yes, Your Majesty," Erik replied.

"By that time, we should know where to find this key," the Lord of the East said. "Once you find the key, travel to Fealmynster, and you will retrieve the sword and bring it to me. Should you fail ... well ..."

The Lord of the East just stared at the mercenaries.

"We understand," Erik said.

"It is the middle of summer," the Lord of the East said. "You have until the end of the next summer to return with the Dragon Sword before I assume you have all died, and I send soldiers to kill your families ... even in the confines of Thorakest. I have assassins everywhere. My agent will travel with you, as well. Should you deviate on your journey, my agent will kill you and then torture your family."

"How will we know who your agent is?" Erik asked.

"You'll know when you see him," the Lord of the East said.

The Lord of the East looked to the two women and the old man who had joined him on the dais, and they turned to the great purple curtain that hung from the ceiling. Two men—at least, Erik assumed they were men—clad in heavy black robes from hood to foot, appeared from behind the curtain and pulled it aside, just enough so that the Lord of the East and the other three with him could pass through. As the curtain opened, it seemed that darkness spilled out, as light might spill through an opening when the door of a brightly lit inn was opened. Erik tried to peer into the darkness, to see what was on the other side of the curtain, but it was so dark, the shadows looked to swallow up the Ruler of Golgolithul.

"Come, follow me," Andragos said, and the mercenaries did as they were told.

As they followed the Messenger of the East out of the keep, Erik heard a voice in his head. It was the Lord of the East's, clear and succinct.

Do not fail me, Erik, for if you do, I will be waiting for you ... even in the deepest, darkest places.

49

"They wouldn't even let me bury his body," Turk said, his eyes red-rimmed as they followed the Messenger of the East and his Soldiers of the Eye through the city of Fen-Stévock.

Nafer put his arm around Turk as they walked at a brisk pace, everyone moving out of the way for the entourage of soldiers. Fen-Stévock was so expansive, this part of the city—along its northern edges—looked as if nothing had happened just a day before, and everyone had almost forgotten that Demik was gone, dead by the spear of a froksman.

"He's still out there, Nafer," Turk said, "lying on the ground, thrown to the side like trash. How many people—how many of our people—has this country thrown away like trash."

"Careful with your words, dwarf," the Messenger said, understanding them even though they spoke in their native language. "You are still in that country ... and that country has ears everywhere."

Turk didn't care. His friend was gone having given his life for Erik, and Turk turned to look at the man he now called a friend. Erik looked worn but hard, certainly not the same young man he had met in Dûrn Tor. It wasn't that his beard or hair was longer, or that his muscles were bigger. No. He wore a look of resolution and determination. He had seen so much death, like all of them, killed so many men, lost so much. They were all different. And for a moment, Turk didn't think of Demik and thought of their new journey.

He could steal away to Thorakest, and King Skella would protect him. He could live the rest of his life in safety, comfort, and as a hero to his people. He and Nafer. But then, what honor would that bring? How would he serve the memory of his father that way? And what of the dwomanni, or Fréden Fréwin? Was he so cowardly that he would live out his life in safety—if that were even possible anymore in this world—only to leave his children to suffer the evils that had started to spread?

He would not leave Erik, and he would honor Demik. His friend gave his life for this man, so he would follow him, even to the northernmost reaches of the world, past the Gray Mountains. Then, as they passed through the Gate House of North Gate, Turk saw something out of the corner of his eye. It was a familiar face, but one he hadn't seen in months. It must have been his imagination. There was word he had joined the traitor mayor Fréden Fréwin, but there was no way Belvengar Long Spear would find himself back in Golgolithul.

With Soldiers of the Eye marching intently in two lines on either side of them, they passed through Green Glen, Small Hill, and Meadowburg, all suburbs of Fen-Stévock and cities in their own right.

"That is North Hills," Wrothgard said, pointing to another town situated around a land of rolling hillocks and grasslands. "I used to live there."

As they passed by North Hills, Turk saw him again—Belvengar. It wasn't a mirage or his imagination. He was there, behind a building, staring from the shadows. He watched them and must have seen Turk staring back as he slunk deeper into the shadows.

"Are you all right?" Nafer asked, putting his hand on Turk's shoulder.

"I saw Long Spear," Turk said.

"What?" Nafer said, exasperated.

"Belvengar," Turk said. "He was watching us, from behind a building."

"Long Spear?" Nafer asked. "What is he doing here? He hates the lands of men."

"I don't know," Turk replied. "Keep an eye out for him. As much as he might side with Fréwin, it is not like him to slink in the shadows like some thief."

Nafer nodded.

"I am glad to be leaving these lands," Nafer said. "After having been home, I miss it."

"Aye," Turk agreed.

"We could go back, you know," Nafer suggested. "We could ask King Skella to protect us and live the rest of our lives in dwarvish lands."

"As much as I like the sound of that right now," Turk said, "I couldn't with a clear conscience."

"How do you mean?" Nafer asked.

"I couldn't leave Erik," Turk said. "He has become a good friend, and he needs us."

"I agree," Nafer said and then, after a pause, added, "I think we need him."

They had passed all of the suburbs of Fen-Stévock, and then the vast farmlands, worked by serfs and peasants destined to a life of servitude, when the sun started to set. The Messenger stopped his company of men and they stood at attention, waiting for his next command. Erik, Wrothgard, Turk, and Nafer stopped as well, waiting.

"Gods be with you," the Messenger said.

"An be with you," Turk replied, his face flat and emotionless.

"I will wait eagerly for your return," the Messenger said.

"As unlikely as that might be," Wrothgard muttered.

"You have as good a chance as any," the Messenger said. "Truth be told, other than sending my five or ten finest soldiers, I believe you four are best suited to the task. I do believe you can be successful."

"Well, thank you for that, my lord," Wrothgard said with a bow.

"These lands are well patrolled," the Messenger said, "so if you choose to camp for the night, you should be relatively safe. If you choose to keep moving, the next village with any sort of semblance of an inn is only a day away."

"Thank you, my lord," Wrothgard replied.

"Erik, a word," the Messenger said as the companions began turning their horses to ride away.

"My lord," Erik said as the Messenger rode his large, black destrier up to Erik's horse.

"I wanted to speak with you a bit more," the Messenger said. "I wanted to speak with you when you first entered Fen-Stévock, but there are times when one must watch who is around him when he speaks."

Erik scrunched his eyebrows and tilted his head.

"For so many years, Erik," Andragos explained, "I have been known as the Messenger, the Herald, the Black Mage, the Steward of Golgolithul, that I sometimes forget that my name was ... is Andragos. Did you know that before standing in front of the Lord of the East?"

Erik nodded. "King Skella told me ... us."

"King Skella," Andragos replied, "he is a good ruler."

"I agree," Erik said.

"This is a dangerous task before you," Andragos said. He shook his head, almost a look of disbelief on his face.

"I know," Erik replied.

"I don't think you do," Andragos said.

"I have faced slavers, dwarves, trolls, wolves, a dragon, and the dead," Erik said, caring little if Andragos understood what he was talking about. "How can this be any more challenging?"

"Be careful, Erik," Andragos said. "Dragons and trolls are not always the worst enemies man will ever face. In fact, at times, our worst enemies are inside of us. I think you already know, everything here is not as it seems."

"Why are you telling me this?" Erik asked.

"I am remembering that my name is Andragos," Andragos said with a smile.

"Andragos," Erik whispered.

"Yes," Andragos replied, "and, in remembering who I am, I am starting to see that the winds of the world are changing. Everything we know is changing."

"What does that mean for me ... us?" Erik asked.

"I'm not sure," Andragos replied. "I'm not sure what that means for me. Just, be careful. Be watchful. And, always, listen to your heart. It has done you well thus far. Follow your heart, and I will see you again."

"You said that to me once before," Erik said.

Andragos smiled.

"Thank you," Erik added. "You once told me my honesty was refreshing. So is yours."

Erik pulled at his reins and turned his horse around.

When Erik looked over his shoulder at Andragos, the man just watched as a father might watch his son leave for a long while, a large smile on his face.

"What did he want?" Wrothgard asked.

Erik waited for a long while before answering.

"I'm not sure," he finally replied.

"The Messenger of the East just wanted to talk?" Wrothgard asked.

"Andragos," Erik whispered so that no one could hear. Then he nodded. "Yeah. Oddly enough, he just wanted to talk."

50

"Have you heard?" Mardirru asked.

Bo nodded his head, slowly, thinking still about the news that had come from the east. It seemed almost unreal. It must have been a myth. He practically shook the eyeballs out of the poor peasant boy he had overheard talking about it. He accused the boy of lying, threatening even to beat him. But even if the news was false, there was truth in that boy's eyes.

A dragon. It couldn't be. They were pure fantasy. Something grandmothers told their grandchildren to scare them into obedience. And this dragon had attacked Fen-Stévock, burned the southern suburb of South Gate to the ground, and killed thousands before being turned away.

And who was able to fend off this mythical beast? Most would say the elite Eastern Guard. Some might even say the Soldiers of the Eye or the Black Mage himself. Perhaps the Lord of the East even. But if there was truth in the rumors that were now spreading to the westernmost reaches of Háthgolthane, it was a boy from Western Háthgolthane who saved Golgolithul from fiery ruin ... a boy named Erik.

"Could it be?" Bo muttered.

"My father knew there was something special about him," Mardirru said with a smile.

Erik Eleodum, the farm boy following his brother and cousin east. The farm boy who really had no desire for adventure. The homesick farm boy.

Bo couldn't help smiling either.

"A dragon, Mardirru," Bo said. "How?"

"I heard that he possessed a mighty weapon," Mardirru replied. "A spell and a magical sword."

"What have you been up to, Erik?" Bo said, staring to the southeast.

The Gray Mountains obscured most of the horizon as they traveled north through the Pass of Dundolyothum. Most refused to travel into the western lands of Nothgolthane this way, but they were gypsies, and Bo had made the journey a dozen times. They would trade with the Northern Dwarves and the Ogres, and the northern men of Hargoleth. Then they would travel along the edges of Ul'Erel into the lands of Gongoreth. And eventually they would find themselves in Wüsten Sahil, in its northernmost city-state of Saman. That would take a year, but it would be a lucrative year and, much to Bo's relief, take them far away from the current chaos that seemed to consume Háthgolthane these days.

Despite the tall peaks of the Gray Mountains consuming most of

Bo's vision, he knew the east was out there, the country of Golgolithul, and Erik. He smiled.

"You are truly an extraordinary man," Bo said. Then he turned to Mardirru. "How do you think he got his hands on some sword powerful enough to fight a dragon?"

"It is said he has a magical elvish sword, but I heard one rumor muttered that he possesses a dagger," Mardirru said with a smile, "a jeweled dagger, that grew into this powerful sword."

"Your father's dagger?" Bo asked with wide eyes. "Could that be true?"

"I don't know," Mardirru said with a shrug. "It was always a mysterious thing. My father never once used it, that I know of, and yet, always had it tucked into his belt. Truth be told, I don't even know when and where he got it. For a long time after he died, I didn't realize it was missing."

"Do you think we will ever see him again?" Dika asked as she sat in their cart, looking east with Bo.

"I don't know, my heart," Bo replied. "I would like to think we would one day."

"We could have stayed in the lands of his people for a while longer," Dika said.

"I know, my love, but it isn't our way," Bo said.

"And I feel we were overstaying our welcome," Mardirru added. "They are a good people, but simple and noble. Their life is hard work, and I feel we might have been a distraction."

"I do hope I see Erik Eleodum again, someday," Bo said, "although, I don't know if I would recognize him."

He looked to his wife, then to Mardirru, and then back towards the east. He laughed, quietly.

"A dragon," he said with a smile and a playful shake of his head. "Erik Eleodum the Dragon Slayer."

Bu sat in the small inn, staring at his cup of spiced wine. His brows furled and cast brooding shadows over his eyes. His men sat around him, but none dared say anything. All the other patrons had left, and the barkeep watched the retinue with worried eyes, constantly wiping the same spot on the bar. South Gate, where he grew up was gone, but that wasn't why Bu ruminated so. A dragon, the Black Mage, and a boy named Erik. Could it be the same one that had killed Patûk had also defeated a dragon? Bu still couldn't believe it as he repeatedly muttered the word 'dragon'.

As soon as the dragon had been defeated, the Black Mage and his Soldiers of the Eye had escorted this Erik, accompanied by a single dwarf, into Fen-Stévock, to the black keep, to the Lord of the East. It was the scroll. It had to be. Luck had smiled on this boy ... the man who had killed Patûk. But a dragon? It had leveled a whole suburb of Fen-Stévock and killed thousands of people. The only way he could have defeated such a creature was the scroll.

"My lord," Bao Zi said, his voice a raspy grumble.

Bu's personal guard held a local villager down, hand around the back of his neck, face pressed into the table. He was the one Bu overheard speaking about the dragon, about the destruction, and about this Erik. He didn't believe him at first. He wanted to kill him.

The man stared at Bu with worried eyes. He was thin and drunk, and dirt smeared his face, his hair hung in matted clumps. He was the kind of man that spent all his coin on drink and whores, and this place had no whores. He was the kind of man Bu presumed was like his own father.

If Erik understood the scroll ... but by the gods, how could he? Maybe the Black Mage translated it, using his black magic. Maybe the Lord of the East translated it. But no. Erik had used it. He had to have used it. Even Li had trouble translating the document, albeit copied from the original. The Lord of the East and the Messenger would know what was in that scroll, and they would be after the Dragon Sword as well, and soon. Who would they send? This Erik?

Bu growled.

"Let him up," he said, his voice even. "Do you know of the free farming families in these lands?"

"Aye, m'lord," the man stammered, sobering a little.

"Do you know the Eleodums?" Bu asked.

"Aye, m'lord," the drunkard repeated.

"Are we close to their lands?" Bu asked.

"Not really, m'lord," the man replied. "They have a large farmstead, a week west of here."

He couldn't afford to let the Lord of the East reach the sword first.

"Release him."

Bao Zi obeyed and pushed the drunkard out the inn's door.

"We cannot afford the time travel to these farmsteads," Bu said.

"My lord?" Bao Zi asked.

"What then?" Sergeant Andu asked.

"We head north now," Bu said, standing, "into the Gray Mountains."

"How early?" Andu asked.

"Now," Bu replied.

"You mean to travel through the night?" Sir Garrett, Count Alger's knight, asked.

"Yes," Bu replied. "We are behind. The usurper will already have men seeking the same thing we seek. We cannot waste any more time."

"This is absurd," Garrett said. "I am quite tired."

"I don't give a pig's fart," Bu hissed, drawing his sword and leveling the tip at Garrett's throat, who had been, up to this point, leaning nonchalantly back in his chair. "You will get on your horse, or I will open you from your eyebrows to your balls."

"You heard the king," Bao Zi yelled, "mount up!"

No one needed any more encouragement.

"When we find this Dragon Sword," Bu said as his followers filed out the inn's door, "I am going to put this Erik in shackles and force him to watch me kill everyone he loves. And then I am going to

Golgolithul, and I am going to command that dragon to finish what it started. I am going to watch it burn Fen-Stévock to the ground, Bao Zi. I'm going to watch every last soul in that city burn."

Bu stared east as if he could see Golgolithul through the inn's wall, the shadows of distant flames spreading across his face.

51

Del Alzon dipped his wooden cup into the bucket of water. After sitting in the sun all day, it wasn't that refreshing, but still welcomed. He wiped the sweat away from his brow and tugged at his pants. All the hard work on the new wall around Waterton, and Del had lost even more weight. All his pants were far too big now and he had poked so many holes in his belt, it had lost its integrity. He drank the contents of his cup in one gulp and refilled it, repeating the process three times.

The wall looked solid, two rows of thick timber sharpened to a point, two stories high and a gatehouse made of mortared river rock.

The men working on the gatehouse were finishing the portcullis, gingerly hanging the iron gate—a gift from Gongoreth—from its chains. It would have taken a year for the blacksmiths of Waterton, led by the dwarf Tank, to finish such a thing, so Lady Elaine donated it. There was space for soldiers to walk along the wall, and at regular intervals, Del had commanded that the workers build guard houses and storage rooms.

Del Alzon smiled at the feat, but a part of him felt saddened by it. Without a wall, someone could always look out at the Blue Forest, which practically surrounded the whole of Waterton and had supplied the wood for the wall. It was beautiful and, until now, Del had never taken the time to appreciate it. Now, it was too late. And for what? Because men wanted more power. Truth be told, if whichever rat turd ruled Hámon, or Golgolithul, or Gongoreth for that matter, decided to march an army through Waterton, their new wall would prove little more than a nuisance, a thorn in the foot. A true army's battering ram would make short work of the gate and portcullis, and a bolt from a catapult or trebuchet would demolish the wall in a single strike. It would have to be replaced with stone eventually.

"Why the sour face?" Maktus asked.

"No reason," Del replied.

"Well, you're looking at the wall with that look," Maktus said, "and it makes me think that there's something you're not pleased with."

"No," Del Alzon said. "It is good. Our men have worked hard. It's just ..."

Del paused.

"Just what?"

"You know its little more than a deterrent," Del said. "If an army really wanted to march through here ..."

"Sometimes that's all you need, Del," Maktus said. "Just make it enough of a hassle to dissuade someone from marching that army through here."

"I am surprised," Del added.

"By what?" Maktus asked.

"At how quickly the wall went up," Del replied, "and how hard the men worked."

"It happens when they have a cause they believe in," Maktus said, and then looked at Del Alzon with a smile, "and when they have a leader they believe in."

"Agh," Del Alzon said with a waving swat of his hand. "Hog's piss."

"Truly Del," Maktus said, "these people trust you and believe in you. I think we have lived in Waterton about the same amount of time, and you cannot tell me you have ever seen its citizens more together. The thieving and fighting have lessened. We have had less issues with traveling adventurers and yet, it seems more men wishing to travel west stay a little longer than they used to. Even the whoring and drinking has lessened a little, although I don't know if that's necessarily a good thing."

"It's not me," Del said. "It's us."

"And who leads us?" Maktus asked.

Del shook his head and grumbled but couldn't help smiling a little.

"Have you heard?"

Yager's bucolic voice stifled whatever comment Maktus was about to make next, and Del was glad for it.

"Heard?" Maktus asked.

"Aye," Yager said, walking up next to Del and Maktus, his elvish wife right behind him.

She didn't bother to cover her ears anymore. Everyone in Waterton either accepted her for her contribution to the victory of what was being termed *The Battle at Blue Water* or they were simply too afraid to say anything, or they just didn't care.

"What's happened?" Del Alzon asked.

"Fen-Stévock is in flames," Yager replied.

"What?" Del asked, turning hard on the blond Northman.

"Well, at least one of its suburbs along its southern walls," Yager added.

"South Gate?" Del Alzon muttered, more to himself than anyone else.

"Yeah, that's it," Yager confirmed.

"How?" Maktus asked.

"A dragon," Yager said, a simple answer for a simple man.

"Do you take me for a fool?" Del asked, furling his brows. "We are busy here, Yager, and you come around telling jokes that aren't funny."

"It's true," Arlayna, Yager's elvish wife, said.

Her voice was soft and mesmerizing. She wrapped her strong arms around Yager's, pulling herself close to him as if the news scared her.

"A dragon?" Maktus gasped. "They're a myth."

"No," Arlayna said with a slight shake of her head, "but they've been gone for many centuries. One hasn't flown the world's skies since I have been born."

"And how old are you?" Maktus asked.

"Don't you know that's no question to ask a lady?" Yager said, and Del Alzon couldn't tell if he was serious or joking.

"Just know I have been on this world far longer than any of you," Arlayna said, squeezing her husband's arm with a small smile on her face. "My people know well the terrors that a dragon can bring, but they were thought extinct a thousand years ago. What's more, a dragon is almost impossible to kill or stop without powerful magic. It is a miracle that the whole of Fen-Stévock is not burnt to the ground."

Where Yager's speech was simple and bucolic, Arlayna's was sophisticated and complex.

"And why isn't it?" Del Alzon asked.

"One man," Yager replied, holding up a single finger.

"Supposedly a single man, accompanied by a single dwarf, drove the dragon away. He purportedly wielded a golden sword, and rumors are spreading that he cast powerful magic," Arlayna said.

"People are calling him a mighty warrior, tall and broad and strong, and he was but a boy from the west."

"A boy?" Del asked.

"Yes," Arlayna said, "a young man named Erik."

"Erik," Del Alzon said, his eyes growing wide. "It couldn't be."

Del reached out and grabbed Yager by the shoulder, pulling him closer.

"What're you ..."

"Erik Eleodum?" Del Alzon asked.

"I don't know," Yager replied with a shrug. "He's being called Erik Dragon Slayer."

"It must be him," Del said, looking down at his feet and speaking to himself.

"He has a strong name," Arlayna said, "that I know. And his sword ... it makes me wonder and remember a fairytale much older than me."

"I know this man," Del said, looking at the she-elf.

"Del, there could be thousands of Eriks out there," Maktus said. "You think it's one all the way from Waterton?"

"Not from Waterton," Del said with a smile growing on his face. "No, from up north. He's a farmer. Dwarves? Mighty swords? Magic? You son of a goat."

Del Alzon started laughing.

"Are you all right?" Yager asked.

"I knew you would be something," Del said, turning and looking east.

"Del, it could be anyone," Yager said.

Del Alzon turned and looked the woodsman in the eyes.

"No, it's Erik Eleodum," Del Alzon said. He could feel a single tear collecting at the corner of his eye. "That idealistic bastard. I knew he would be something."

"Eleodum is an old name," Arlayna said. "He has noble blood flowing through his veins. We will pray to El that he is safe."

Del turned again and faced east. His smile was so wide ... he hadn't smiled that wide in a long time.

"Erik," Del muttered. "You've defied all odds. Keep following your heart, my friend. Keep following your heart."

52

The village to which Andragos had directed Turk and his companions was more of a central meeting place for a small group of famers and their families. It didn't have an inn, but more of a home that opened as the sun set, the wife cooking, the husband serving sour ale, and their children rushing about bussing two long tables and serving. They had built three small rooms on the back of their little home, but anyone purchasing those spaces for a night would have to share them with a cow, some chickens, two goats, and a small pony.

Erik didn't much feel like staying in a place with other people, especially as rumors of a dragon slayer would soon become commonplace in these meeting halls and taverns and inns. When he asked Turk if he was okay with camping just outside the village, the dwarf yielded to whatever the young man wanted to do. It just seemed a shame they had found a space that was covered by a sturdy, wooden roof held up by four thick pieces of timber. The hay on the ground said that a farmer once used it as a storage area for his animals' food, and when they asked the owner of the closest farmhouse if they might use the shelter as a campsite for the night, the old man could have cared less. Wrothgard gave him a gold coin for his troubles, and as they got their fire going, the farmer came to them with several pitchers of spiced wine and a bag full of cheese and fresh bread.

They made quick work of the bread and cheese and took their time on the spiced wine, reveling in the quietness of the night. Where the land south of Fen-Stévock was covered in short, brownish grass, green, tall grass and cedars filled the lands north of Fen-Stévock. A chorus of crickets and night birds filled the air and, as the sun finally disappeared, a welcomed crispness replaced the warmth of summertime.

"This reminds me of home," Erik said.

"I would like to see your home," Turk said.

"Truly?" Erik asked.

"Yes, truly," Turk confirmed.

Turk heard the call of a jaybird and, knowing what it meant, stood and called back. Beldar and Bofim came into view, their forms, at first, ghostly in the shadows of the fire.

"You found us," Turk said.

"You doubted us?" Beldar asked.

"Of course not," Erik replied. "Have you been following us this whole time?"

"Aye," Bofim replied.

"We hung back for a little while," Beldar added. "I think the Messenger of the East saw us. I don't know if he would have cared, but we thought it prudent to be cautious."

The wine lasted only a few more moments once Beldar and

Bofim arrived. Turk took the empty pitchers and bag back to the farmhouse and made small talk with the old farmer. The dwarf's Shengu was rough, but it was enough, and the old man seemed glad for it. His wife had passed two winters past, and his sons had left and created their own families years before. The man gave Turk an extra wheel of cheese and a skin of wine.

"Skull Crusher."

The voice, speaking in Dwarvish, was a whisper, but in the darkness as Turk walked back to the campsite, it still startled him. He turned, dropping the wheel of cheese and reaching for a hand axe stuck in his belt. He peered into the night, barely making out the silhouette of a dwarf walking towards him.

"Long Spear?" Turk asked, keeping his voice low.

"Aye," the voice replied.

Belvengar Long Spear came into view, even though his face was still shadowed by the night.

"What are you doing here?" Turk asked.

"I've been following you," Belvengar replied.

"I know," Turk said. "I saw you ... in Fen-Stévock. Why?"

"I need your help," Belvengar said.

"What is it?" Turk asked. "I didn't know if I would ever see you again ... after you left in Finlo."

"I was upset, for sure," Belvengar said, "but we have been through so much together. We are like brothers."

Turk and Belvengar hugged.

"I missed you," Turk said. "We could have used your skill as a warrior."

"We, as in you and the men you travel with?" Belvengar asked.

"Yes," Turk said. "If you had been with us, Demik might still be alive. He was killed, just a few days ago."

"I know," Belvengar said, "by the hands of men, nonetheless."

"It was a froksman," Turk said, shaking his head.

"Because of men, though," Belvengar said. "These men you travel with, it is their fault Demik Iron Thorn is dead. How many more dwarves must die?"

"They've lost friends as well," Turk said. "Drake and Samus. Erik lost his brother, Befel."

"Necessary sacrifices in searching for the lost city," Belvengar said. "They all would have died if it wasn't for you, yes?"

"We all would have died if it wasn't for them," Turk said, taking a step back. "One of our companions, Vander Bim, died in Thorakest, stabbed in the belly and left in an alley. He was killed by dwarves, Belvengar."

"And did you think to ask why?" Belvengar replied. "Did you ever ask what he might have done to deserve it?"

"Who deserves a death such as that?" Turk asked, but he knew the answer Belvengar would give. Vander Bim deserved such a death because he was a man. "Even Balzarak Stone Axe and King Skella trusted these men."

"That's the problem," Belvengar said softly, and Turk wondered if he was meant to hear what he had said. "How many dwarves died because they trusted men?"

"What are you saying?" Turk asked. "You've been listening to Fréden Fréwin too much."

"You found the lost city, yes?" Belvengar asked, ignoring Turk's last point. "What was it like?"

"It was dead," Turk said flatly.

"Dead?"

"It was a giant tomb," Turk added. "It's where we found the dragon."

"Because of men, no doubt," Belvengar said.

"Because of ... it was because of us," Turk said. "It was because of our greed."

"Do you hear yourself?" Belvengar asked.

"Do you hear yourself?" Turk retorted. "How could men have anything to do with the fall of a hidden dwarvish city a thousand years ago?"

Belvengar Long Spear didn't say anything.

"What are you doing here, Long Spear?" Turk asked.

"We need your help," Belvengar said.

"Who needs my help?" Turk asked.

"The dwarvish people," Belvengar replied. "It is time to take back what is ours."

"Really?" Turk asked, taking another step back.

"We have found refuge in an old dwarvish settlement in the El'Beth-Tordûn. We are preparing to take our cities back. Men will no longer subjugate us and use us and steal from us."

"And who leads you?"

"Fréden," Belvengar said.

Turk knew that answer was coming and gave a scoffing laugh.

"Fréden doesn't want my help, that I can assure you. If you had only come with us, you would see how wrong you are about men."

"They have clouded your vision," Belvengar said.

"I follow a man that is as righteous a person as I have ever met," Turk said. "I would follow him to the Shadow and back if he asked me to."

"You follow a man?" Belvengar sounded appalled by the notion. "Truly, you are joking?"

"No," Turk said, and then repeated, "proudly, no. What has happened to you? Come with me to meet Erik. You will see."

Turk tried to reach for Belvengar, but the dwarf pulled away from him, stepping back into the shadows of the night.

"I hope you come to your senses," Belvengar said, "before you end up like Demik Iron Thorn. War is coming, and those on the wrong side will all end up like Demik Iron Thorn, thrown to the ground and trampled like rubbish."

Turk saw Belvengar turn his back and walk away, but then he stopped and faced him once again. Turk barely caught the silhouette of something flying through the air and, just in time, caught a sheathed broadsword. Looking at the scabbard, it was covered in an intricate scrollwork of iron, a thorny vine ... Demik's sword.

"I buried his body, Turk," Belvengar said, his voice farther away, "before they could throw him away like he was nothing. I said rites over him. This is how men treat our kind. Like trash."

"I hope you come to your senses," Turk whispered, tears in his eyes as he turned and headed back to the campsite.

"Where did you get that?" Nafer asked as Turk came into view.

Nafer grabbed Demik's sword out of Turk's hands and held it close to his chest as if he was holding his dear friend.

"Belvengar," Turk said in Westernese.

"Really? Where is he?" Nafer asked.

"Gone," Turk replied.

"Why?"

"He has changed," Turk said. "As we had heard, he has joined with Fréden Fréwin. They are gathering like-minded dwarves at the El'Beth-Tordûn and preparing for war."

"El'Beth-Tordûn?" Wrothgard asked.

"You probably know it as the Wicked Spire," Turk replied, "the three peaked mountain that rises from the Plains of Güdal."

Wrothgard nodded.

"It was once a dwarvish stronghold," Turk explained, "and many have suggested that tunnels ran from El'Beth-Tordûn to both Thrak Baldüukr and Drüum Balmdüukr. But they were abandoned years ago, around the same time Orvencrest fell."

"And with whom does Fréden plan to war?" Beldar asked. "Men?"

"No." Turk shook his head. "Other dwarves. They are radicals."

"Like the dwomanni," Erik said.

Nafer hissed as Erik said the name, but Turk nodded.

"Yes, like the dwomanni. We have to warn Skella."

Turk watched the fire for a moment, fully aware that his companions, in turn, watched him.

"I have to go back to Thorakest," Turk said. "I am sorry, Erik. I had intended on going to your home with you, but I must warn King Skella of what is happening."

"You don't need to apologize to me," Erik said.

"Yes, I do," Turk replied. "You see, you are the reason I am here."

"I don't understand," Erik said.

"My father believed that dwarves were not meant to live in isolation, hidden away in their mountain strongholds. I believe that too. It is why I left my home because I thought a part of me could help repair ages old rifts between men and dwarves. And as foolish as that sounds, I believed that men like you and dwarves like me can live and work together. But then I chose to go on this quest because I also realized I cannot do such a thing and turn my back on my people."

Turk looked at the water skin full of spiced wine the farmer had given him. He threw it to Wrothgard.

"I accepted the Messenger's task because a part of me felt like I had forgotten who I was, Erik," Turk explained. "I wasn't by my father's side when he died. I watched as dwarves were beaten and robbed and mistreated by men and did nothing. I suppose in some way, I thought that finding a lost city of my people, or at least dying while trying, would ease my guilt. But it hasn't. I feel empty, and I don't quite know why."

Turk looked to Nafer and Beldar and Bofim. Then he looked to Wrothgard and, lastly, Erik.

"I will follow you wherever you go, Erik," Turk finally said. "I trust you with my life. But I must go tell King Skella about what is happening at El'Beth-Tordûn. I have to warn him."

"I understand," Erik said, although his face looked a mixture of sadness and fear. "Will you come back?"

"On my life and my honor," Turk replied. "I will meet you at your farmstead in four weeks. Not even the Shadow could stop me."

"Will you bring Bryon with you then?" Erik asked. "I hope the king's surgeons could heal him."

"I am sure they did," Turk said. "Yes, I will bring him with me."

"And you?" Erik asked, looking at Nafer. "Will you be going with Turk?"

Nafer looked at Turk for a moment and then nodded.

"Yes," he said. "I have to meet with Demik's father. I have to tell him what happened."

"We will all come back," Beldar said, and Bofim nodded and bowed to Erik.

Erik extended his hand to Turk, and the dwarf took it.

"I will wait for you at my father's farmstead," Erik said.

"In a month," Turk said.

"In a month," Erik repeated.

By the time Wrothgard and Erik had their horses packed and ready, the dwarves had disappeared over the horizon.

"Are you going to go home as well?" Erik asked.

"I don't know where home is," Wrothgard replied. "I think I might go to Kamdum, in Gol-Durathna. Maybe I'll travel to Finlo again."

"One month, yes?" Erik asked.

Wrothgard nodded.

"I'll see you in a month then," Erik added.

Wrothgard waited for a long time, staring east. Then he turned in his saddle to face Erik.

"Erik, I have to be honest," Wrothgard said. "I don't think I will make it to your farmstead."

"I don't understand," Erik replied.

"My life has been consumed by fighting and violence," Wrothgard explained, "and I am tired."

"What will you do?" Erik asked. "Where will you go?"

"I don't know," Wrothgard replied with a shrug. "I am wealthier than I have ever been, and I finally have a chance at peace."

"What about the Lord of the East?" Erik asked.

"Maybe I'll go somewhere far away," Wrothgard said. "Maybe I'll go to Wüsten Sahil or to the Isuta Isles. Or maybe I'll go west, to Gongoreth. I'll go somewhere the Lord of the East has no influence.

But if his assassins do find me, then I will die knowing I was a free man, beholden to no one."

"This is goodbye then," Erik said.

"This is goodbye," Wrothgard said.

"I wish I could train with you a little more," Erik said.

"You are the best student I have ever had," Wrothgard replied. "In the short time I have known you and have had the pleasure of helping you, you have become a truly competent swordsman, and you will only get better. Not only that, you have become a trustworthy leader of men—and dwarves—who will willingly follow. Practice your movements, and when you reconvene with Turk, make sure he continues your training."

"Thank you," Erik said. "You have been both a mentor and a friend."

"Thank you," Wrothgard said. "You are an amazing young man. I wish I could watch as you become the warrior and leader I know fate means for you to be."

Erik watched as Wrothgard rode away. Then, he turned his horse to the west. He patted the handle of Ilken's Blade and then rubbed the gold scabbard of his dagger.

"What will I find, my friend?" Erik asked.

He knew his dagger was listening when he felt a tickle at his hip.

"Will I find my family," he asked, "or will I find my farm in ruins and my family dead?"

Sometimes we forget that it is the things outside of battle that require the most bravery. Whatever you find, I will be with you.

He looked down at his dagger and smiled.

"All right, then," he said to the space in front of him, "it's time to go home."

53

Turk breathed deep. It felt like he had been away from Thorakest for so long he had forgotten what it smelled like. Now, having come back only a short while before, he coveted that smell, and his stomach knotted when he thought of the reality that he would have to leave once again, and so soon. The city looked the same, but he could feel the difference—something was off. He and Nafer and Beldar and Bofim approached the castle, and the guards stepped aside and bowed as they passed them.

"Turk!" cried a voice, as they walked through the king's rose garden. "It's good to see you!"

The voice was clearly a man's voice, and one he recognized, but the words were spoken in Dwarvish. Turk looked up to see Bryon running from the castle keep to greet them. The man looked well, his skin back to its original color, and the way he ran spoke to his strength returning.

Bryon practically scooped Turk off his feet, hugging the dwarf tightly and then doing the same to Nafer and Beldar and Bofim.

"Where is Erik?" Bryon asked. "Or should I say, where is the dragon slayer? Word of the dragon attacking Fen-Stévock has reached Thorakest, and I know it was Erik. I just know it."

"He is hopefully home by now," Turk replied. "We are to meet up with him at your farmstead in two weeks. We will take you with us if you would go with us."

"Of course," Bryon said with a wide smile on his face. "Fantastic. Where is Demik? Did he stay with Erik so my little cousin wouldn't be all alone?"

"He's dead," Turk said.

Bryon's smile disappeared.

"I'm so sorry," he said.

"It is one of the reasons we returned," Turk said. "Your Dwarvish has improved quite a bit."

"Yes," Bryon said, a small smile cracking his lips. "It had to get better if I were to make something of my stay in Thorakest."

"Does King Skella know we are here?" Turk asked.

"Of course," Bryon said. "Let me take you to him."

Turk was impressed as Bryon led them to King Skella's quarters. He greeted all the guards by their first names, and the dwarvish soldiers returned the man's greetings with bows and smiles and greetings of their own. And then he remembered why he had ventured into the lands of men and his reason for leaving. This was it. A man and a dwarf acting as brothers. A man living freely in the lands of dwarves, sharing cultures and languages.

"Turk," Nafer said as they stood in front of the door that led to the king's private quarters, "I must go speak with Demik's father, and we won't have much time if we are to meet up with Erik in only two weeks."

"Of course," Turk said.

"Bofim and I are going to see our families," Beldar said. "Who knows when, or if, we will ever come home?"

Turk bowed to each one of them.

"Just you and me, then," Bryon said.

"It looks that way," Turk replied.

Bryon knocked on the door and opened it. King Skella sat at the large round table in a room that had a bookshelf that rose to the ceiling on one wall and a giant hearth and fireplace in the other. Another dwarf stood in the corner of the room, a silver platter holding several cups and a pitcher in one hand and the other hand tucked behind his back.

"Turk Skull Crusher," King Skella said, standing. Bryon and the dwarves bowed. "How good to see you. I've been waiting for you."

"I wish I was here for better reasons, Your Majesty," Turk said.

"Please, sit," the king said. "I assume you are here because of what happened in Golgolithul."

"Partially, Your Majesty," Turk said.

"There is no doubt what you found in Orvencrest is related to a dragon attacking Fen-Stévock?" King Skella asked.

"It is true, Your Majesty," Turk said. "We found something terrible in Orvencrest. I am sure Bryon has told you."

"Yes," King Skella said. He looked to the table in front of him, almost staring off in thought. "All those people, gone in a single dragon's breath."

"The city would still be burning if it wasn't for Erik," Turk said.

"Truly?" Bryon asked, a smile widening on his face.

"Truly," Turk replied.

"That young man is more of a mystery than I think I have ever seen," King Skella said. "To consider the dragons have returned. The terror they brought to this world is beyond imagination. And the one that was awakened—Black Wing—she will return more powerful than before, and possibly with her mate."

"Her mate?" Turk asked.

"Yes," King Skella said. "Our histories tell of her and her mate and the devastation they brought upon the world."

"An be merciful," Turk muttered.

"Indeed," King Skella said. "But you said Fen-Stévock is only partially why you are here?"

"I ran into Belvengar Long Spear," Turk said. "Rather, he had been following us and came to me in the dead of night just weeks past."

King Skella seemed to think for a moment and then nodded.

"Ah, yes, Long Spear," the king said. "A good family. You were friends, were you not? Is a meeting with an old friend such a thing that you would come back home and meet with me?"

"It was the nature of our conversation, Your Majesty," Turk said.

"Oh," the king said.

"He bade me go with him to the Wicked Spire," Turk said. "He is serving Fréden Fréwin, and they are amassing an army there, a dwarvish army. One that they plan on using to overthrow you."

"Really?" the king said, sitting back in his chair. He shook his head with a mirthless smile on his face. "Fools."

"Your Majesty?" Turk asked.

"The mayor is so concerned about the lives of dwarves," the king said, "but he would needlessly waste dwarvish lives over foolishness. You see, Bryon, we are no different than men. Greed. Hunger for power. Prejudice. This is the way of the world, and will always be, I am sad to say. Some out there have notions of peace. There will never be peace, not until An brings it."

"I have come to warn you," Turk said.

"And your warning is well received," the king replied. "And, so, now what?"

"The Lord of the East has tasked me ... us to another mission," Turk said. "It involves the dragon."

"And the Dragon Scroll no doubt," the king said, and Turk's eyes widened.

"You knew?" Turk asked.

"Yes," the king replied. "The Dragon Scroll. The Dragon Sword. Yes, I know all of it. Is he forcing you to do this task?"

"Yes," Turk replied. "We, rather, Erik looked at the scroll and, therefore, this is our punishment."

"You can stay here, Skull Crusher," King Skella said. "You can too, Bryon Eleodum. You can stay in the protection of Thorakest for the rest of your lives."

"I have to get home," Bryon said.

"I cannot, Your Majesty," Turk said with a bow. "Erik is my friend. Truly, now he is my leader. I have made him a promise that I intend to keep."

"As I suspected," King Skella said with a smile. "Be watchful. There are those that will worm their way into the confidence of Fréwin. He is so zealous, he will not realize who they are, and they will use his zealotry against him, us, and the rest of the world."

"Of course, Your Majesty," Turk said, standing and bowing.

As Turk left the king's quarters and walked into the castle's courtyard, Bryon following him, he found Lord Balzarak waiting for him.

"Skull Crusher," Balzarak said, grasping the dwarf's arm.

"My lord," Turk said.

"This man has impressed, nay, impresses me on a daily basis," Balzarak said.

"I would expect nothing less," Turk said. "He comes from impressive blood."

"How are Wrothgard and Erik? I heard about Demik. I am truly sorry," Balzarak said.

"They were well when I left them," Turk said. "I must get back to them now. I am taking Bryon back to his farmstead where I will meet up with Erik and Wrothgard. Then ..."

"You must once again work for the Lord of the East," Balzarak said.

"Yes, my lord," Turk replied.

"I stopped trying to understand the way An works many years ago," Balzarak said, "but I am sure he is using you in this task. Remember that, Turk."

"I'll try," Turk replied.

"I have heard of the nature of your journey to come," Balzarak said.

"As I would expect you have," Turk said with a smile. "Castles have many ears."

"Yes," Balzarak replied, returning the smile. "As you journey on this perilous mission, please tell Erik that he is to remember the gift I gave him."

"The gift, my lord?" Turk asked.

"The circlet I gave him," Balzarak said. "Remind him about the circlet. It is more than a circlet and more than just a simple gift. Remind him, please."

"I will, my lord," Turk said with a bow.

"An be with you," Balzarak, "and with you Bryon."

"You as well, my lord," Turk said with a bow, and with that, they met Nafer, Beldar, and Bofim and made for the northwestern farmsteads of Háthgolthane.

54

His mother's rose garden looked the same, as did his house, his farm, his father's barn, everything. It was as if Erik had left just yesterday. He heard the low moaning of one of their cows and the oinking of their pigs. He smiled at the baaing of their sheep, and when one of the barn cats rubbed up against his leg and purred, it startled him. Then he heard them, inside the house. Their giggles were unmistakable, as was the scolding coming from Beth directly afterwards, only she sounded older. How old would she be now? Fourteen?

His stomach knotted. He wanted to run to the front door and burst into the living room when he first saw his home still standing.

He hadn't even bothered to tether his horse. But as he passed the wooden fence that surrounded the home, as he stepped foot onto the walkway of stone slab his father had lain even before he was born, he stopped. He couldn't go any further. What would they do? What would they think? A thousand scenarios played through his head, from his mother slapping him and running away to his father banishing him.

The door opened, and his heart stopped. Tia. She was taller, looking more like a young woman, but that blonde hair and those blue eyes, that button nose, that mischievous smile ... it was her. She stepped onto their porch, still giggling, stepped forward, saw Erik, stepped back, and screamed.

He didn't know at what at first, but of course ... it was him. As recognizable as she was, he wasn't. His hair was long. His beard had grown full. His shoulders and arms and chest and legs were a sight bigger. He was probably even taller. She screamed at him.

His father came running outside, swooping Tia behind him with one arm and holding a boar spear in the other hand.

"What do you want?" his father called.

Even though his voice was hard and angry, the sound of it caused gooseflesh to rise on Erik's arms. He tried to speak, but something caught in his throat. He found it hard to swallow, breathe even.

"I said ..." his father began, stepping forward and gripping the spear in both hands, but then he leaned forward, squinting.

Rickard Eleodum took several more steps forward, cautious and intentional. Then his eyes went wide, and he dropped the spear. His hands went to his mouth. He ran his fingers through his hair, and Erik could see them trembling.

"Erik?" he said, his voice a whisper.

And then he ran to Erik and wrapped his arms around him. He was shorter than Erik now, but in the moment, he was a giant and lifted his son off the ground. It didn't matter how differently Erik looked. A father would always recognize his son.

"Erik!"

His father cried as he twirled his son about, caring little for how big or heavy Erik had gotten. And, in that moment, Erik cried too. He freed his arms from his father's grasp, and he wrapped them around Rikard and, planting his feet firmly, lifted his father.

"Erik!" Tia cried as she ran to him as well, almost knocking him to the ground as she hugged him.

Beth came, a slow trot in her lady-like way, but nonetheless intentional and, where Tia laughed and giggled, Beth cried. They all stood on that walkway and hugged, and then Erik saw her—his mother.

"Erik," she gasped.

He let go of the rest of his family and stared at her for what seemed like an eternity. The woman who birthed him, cared for him, comforted him when he was scared and bandaged his scraped knees.

They stood, eyes locked on one another. Then, he took a step forward, and before he knew it, he was running to her, sweeping her off her feet and holding her as tightly as he dared. His mother. And even though he was a giant next to her, she cradled his head and pressed it to her chest, kissed his forehead as he melted into her arms.

Erik finally put his mother down, and the rest of his family joined them on their porch. They laughed and cried, and then his mother asked the question he had dreaded.

"Where is Befel?"

Erik had told them some of the details of his adventures, but certainly not all. Befel's death due to a dragon was hard for them to accept, and Erik heard his father—at least once—mention the fact that his firstborn was gone, but they also took comfort in believing that Befel was in the Creator's presence. Erik knew he was. The first thing his parents did was ease his worry that he was to blame for his brother's death. He was a man in his own right and, in reality, the reason Erik left. Rikard Eleodum had felt Befel's desire to leave. They would have to live with the consequences. Besides, they had assumed both of their boys were gone forever, so to even have one of them back was a blessing.

Three days later, Erik sat at his mother's kitchen table, a cup of orange juice and a plate of fresh cheese in front of him. The name his father had mentioned—Bu Al'Banan—sounded so familiar. He knew Al'Banan. He killed General Patûk Al'Banan, but Bu? Apparently, he had led thirty thousand men through Finlo and onto to Venton, the capital city of Hámon. Hámon had fallen in days, Bu Al'Banan its new king.

"Flaming sons of goats," Rikard Eleodum said.

"Rikard," Karita Eleodum said with a hiss in her tone, "must you curse so?"

Erik smiled. Before he had left home, such words would have sent goose pimples along his arms and wonder if the Creator was about to strike his father down with a bolt of lightning. Since then, he had heard—and said—far worse.

"That they are, Father," Erik said, "and worse. Who is this Bu?"

"They say he leads some army of traitors," his father replied, "from the east."

"Patûk's men," Erik muttered.

"Who is that?" his father said.

"A former general from Golgolithul," Erik explained, "who refused to serve the current Lord of the East. He was a dangerous man."

"Was?" his father asked.

"He's dead," Erik replied flatly.

"Oh my," his mother said, putting a hand to her mouth. "How do you know?"

"I killed him," Erik said. When his eyes met his mother's, he couldn't help seeing a mixture of sadness, regret, disappointment, and fear in them. But she was past being shocked anymore.

"And this Bu is his son?" his father asked, trying to ignore Erik's admission.

"No," Erik replied. "I think I know him, but he is not Patûk's son. He probably doesn't know who his father is."

"Erik," his mother scolded.

"But he ... they are dangerous," Erik said. "If we think the feudal lords of Hámon were bad before, now we should be worried."

"What do you mean?" his father asked.

"The east is evil, father," Erik said. "If we have men who wish to make the west like the east, that is a scary thought."

"We don't need to talk about this now," his mother said.

"No, we don't," Erik agreed with a mirthless smile.

"There were gypsies here, not too long ago," his mother said. "They said they knew you. They gave us hope."

"Never thought I'd warm up to gypsies," his father said, "but they were good people, followers of the Creator."

"Bo and Dika," Erik said with a genuine smile, rubbing the handle of his dagger, "and Mardirru. They are very good people. They saved my life. They saved Befel's life."

He knew the mention of his brother would bring more tears to his mother's eyes, but his father had encouraged him not to hide his brother in the past. Just talking of him brought him back in a small way.

"I am glad they are well," Erik said, patting his mother's hand. "I was worried about them. Where did they go from here?"

"North," his father said. "They said they were passing through the Pass of Dundolyothum. I couldn't believe my ears."

"If anyone would, it would be them," Erik said and then finally asked the question he had been avoiding. "Does Simone still live at her father's farmstead?"

It was Erik's way of asking whether or not Simone had married since he left. His stomach knotted as he waited for his father to answer.

"Yes, of course," his father said.

"I would like to go see her if that's okay," Erik said.

"You do not need to ask us," his father said. "Your time away has turned you into a man, and you are able to make your own decisions."

"I will be back by dinner," Erik said, standing, hugging his father, and kissing his mother on the forehead.

Erik greeted Brok Emunaha—Simone's father—as he walked up to the Emunaha house, the home of Simone and her family. Attending to a cart filled with supplies, the man, only a few years older than Rickard Eleodum, had a head of white hair and a short beard. He was taller than Erik when he had first left, but now they stood eye to eye. When Erik extended his hand to shake Brok's, he grabbed his hand and pulled him in for a hug.

As Brok led Erik up to their house, a large home surrounded by fig, apple, and pear trees, they ran into Sindra, Simone's mother. She ran to Erik and hugged him as well, holding him so long he started to feel uncomfortable.

"We have missed you," Sindra said, tears streaming down her cheeks.

"Truly, we have," Brok agreed, "and so has Simone."

"Is she here?" Erik asked, his voice shaky and soft.

"She is," her father replied. "She should be in the kitchen cleaning dishes from lunch."

"May I speak with her?" Erik asked. He felt a lump rise in his throat and his stomach knot again.

"Yes, of course," her father replied.

"I won't be dishonoring anyone, will I?" Erik asked. "She isn't spoken for, is she?"

Brok just smiled.

"Go see her, Erik," he said.

Erik opened the front door. Where his mother's house smelled like roses, Simone's house always smelled like mint and lavender. He pushed the door closed as he stepped forward, but he was so nervous, he didn't push hard enough, and it swung open again. He heard a splash and a deep sigh.

"Close the door," the voice said. It was a voice he hadn't heard in more than two years, but it was a voice he could never forget. "Were you born in the barn?"

She must have thought he was one of her three brothers. He stepped into the kitchen. Simone stood in front of a large basin full of water, her back facing him. Another one next to it was filled with clean dishes. She wore a long, light purple dress that was simple but clung to her curves. She was a broad-shouldered woman from working the farm alongside her father and brothers, and Erik could see the muscles in her arms and back. Her hair was a little shorter than he remembered, the color of the early morning sun—yellow with the slightest hints of roses and lighter shades of blonde.

Erik stepped up behind her and moved his hands so that they hovered just over her shoulders, but he couldn't touch her. It was as if there was some hidden barrier that pushed his hands away.

"I know you're behind me," she said.

She still thought he was one of her brothers. Finally, he let his hands fall, and he gently grabbed her shoulders.

"Timmy, what are you doing?" Simone asked.

She turned, an eyebrow cocked and a weird smirk on her face. The moment she saw Erik, her skin paled, and her smirk disappeared, her mouth opening just slightly. Her eyes wide in shock, Simone reached up and touched Erik's beard and then rubbed a hand along his brow and his cheek. Her skin was soft, and her hands smelled like mint. He had missed that touch. Then, she slapped his face ... hard.

"How could you? How could you leave like that and then come back in here like ... like ..."

That was as far as she got before her face crumpled, and she threw her arms around his neck, her flood of tears soaking his shirt.

"I ... I ..." Erik couldn't find the right words.

"I missed you," Simone sobbed.

"I was afraid you would be married when I returned," Erik said.

Simone pushed back and rubbed angrily at her tears while she studied his face.

"I'm … I'm sorry Simone. I wasn't sure you would wait for me," Erik said, taking his eyes off Simone and looking at his feet.

Simone grabbed his face with both her hands and lifted it up so that he had to look at her. Her touch was soft again, but her hands were strong, and he couldn't have pulled away if he wanted to.

"If it meant waiting to the very last day of my life," Simone said, "I would have waited for you. My heart is yours. My future is yours. There is no one else."

Before he could say anything else, her lips met his, and they kissed. He breathed her in, long and deep, and as he wrapped his arms around her waist, she wrapped hers around his neck again. They fell into one another, pressing their bodies hard against each other as they made up for two years of lost kisses and touches and caresses.

When their lips finally parted, both Erik and Simone now had tears on their cheeks.

"You are back, and that is all that matters," Simone said.

"I have to leave again," Erik said.

Simone looked down, her mouth dropping as she swallowed hard.

"But I will come back," Erik said. "I promise."

Simone looked crestfallen, staring at Erik's chest. Erik lifted her head with a single finger under her chin.

"Marry me," he said, "before I leave. Please. Let me leave knowing that I was at least able to live a few weeks of my life as your husband."

Simone smiled amidst her tears.

"Yes," she said, "of course."

55

Darius, the General Lord Marshal of Gol-Durathna and commander of all its armies, opened the thick, wooden door to a dimly lit, windowless room. As he entered, he heard the scraping of wood against stone, men scooting their chairs back so they could stand and salute him. Darius returned the favor, touching a loosely clenched fist to his left breast. News of death and flames and black magic had reached his ears and, with that, news that his men—Ranus and Cliens—were also dead. He had just delivered the news of her husband's death to Cliens' widow. He didn't have to, but it was the least she deserved.

She cried and wailed, as did his children. His oldest, also Cliens, vowed to avenge his father.

"I will kill every easterner," the boy, almost a young man, had said.

When Cliens' widow finally looked up at Darius, he could see hate in her eyes, hate for him, for Golgolithul, and for the world.

Ranus' family was harder to read. They had sought refuge in Gol-Durathna when both goblins and Golgolithul displaced the frog people from the Shadow Marshes. Darius didn't understand their language, and when he told Ranus' widow, she simply looked away and closed the door. He had waited a moment, listening for crying or yelling, but they never came.

"Please, sit," Darius said, his voice low.

"This must be a lie," Fabian said, scratching nervously at the patchy brown beard that tried to cover his chubby chin. "A dragon? They don't exist."

"So, a thousand people are lying?" Amado asked.

"You are young," Fabian said. "Young men have a tendency to believe in fantasies."

Amado stood quickly, pointing a finger at Fabian.

"Sit," Darius said, his voice calm. "It is no fantasy, Fabian. A dragon destroyed South Gate."

"Is it true?" Callis asked. He rubbed his thin, crane's neck. "Are they ... are they dead?"

Darius nodded but doubted the men could see him doing so in the dim light.

"Yes," he finally said. "Cliens and Ranus are dead."

"Their bodies, Lord Marshal?" Callis asked.

"No bodies," Darius replied. "The dragon fire ... it ..."

The General Lord Marshal stopped. His stomach knotted, and something caught in his throat. It was all too surreal.

"I hear it was a man barely twenty years old who stopped the dragon," Amado said. "That is what my spies say."

"What else do your spies say?" Darius asked, but he had already heard the answer from others in the Keep of Amentus.

"They say that the reason the Lord of the East sent mercenaries to a lost dwarvish city was for a spell," Amado replied. "It is a spell to control a dragon, but the spell alone is not enough. There is a sword ..."

"A sword?" Darius asked. That part he hadn't heard.

"Yes, Lord Marshal," Amado replied, "a sword that can kill a dragon. And this man who defeated the dragon has been tasked with finding the sword for the Lord of the East."

"Who is this man?" Darius asked, more to himself than to anyone else.

"All we know right now is that his name is Erik Eleodum, that he is from the northwestern farmlands of Háthgolthane," Amado replied, "and that he was traveling with dwarves."

"Dwarves?" Darius questioned.

"Shall I prepare the Dragon's Teeth, General?" Marcel asked, the thick, well-muscled man clenching his jaw as he rolled his head, popping his bull's neck.

"To what end?" Darius asked.

"We will intercept this man," Marcel replied.

"No," Darius replied. "We are on the brink of war as it is. If we were to openly attack an agent of Golgolithul ..."

Darius trailed off and stared at the dark ceiling.

What is happening? What is this world coming to?

"The Atrimus?" Amado asked, referring to the Golden City's secret guild of assassins.

"Yes," Darius replied. "Send them, right away."

"And your orders?" Amado asked.

"Whatever means necessary," Darius replied.

"And what about Hámon," Fabian asked, "and this new king who claims to be the son of Patûk Al'Banan?"

"For this, Marcel, we can prepare the Dragon's Teeth," Darius said. "He has overthrown a king who openly traded with Gol-

Durathna. King Agempi, nor the council, will declare war, but we must be ready."

"Very well," Marcel replied with a quick bow.

Darius stood, the other four men standing with him. He bowed, and they returned the favor.

"Find this Erik Eleodum," Darius said before exiting the room, "and stop him."

56

Erik watched the horses and cart approach with a smile on his face. They were a few days late, but they had returned, as promised, and with Bryon in tow. He hadn't expected to see Beldar and Bofim, but it was a pleasant surprise as the two dwarves came into view. He lifted a hand and waved, and Turk returned the gesture, followed by Nafer.

"Who are they, son?" Rickard Eleodum asked.

"My friends," Erik replied.

"Are those dwarves?" his father asked.

"Aye," Erik replied, looking at his father with a smile.

"Bless me," his father said, "I haven't seen a dwarf in years. Gypsies and dwarves in a matter of months. Bless me."

"It's good to see you!" Erik yelled in Dwarvish. "And only a few days late!"

"You're speaking their language?" his father asked, eyes wide and hand rubbing his cheek.

"Well, when you live among them for so long," Erik said, smiling even wider, "you have to make sure they're not talking about you."

"Uncle Rickard!" Bryon called as they reached the Eleodum house.

Erik's father simply waved, a dumbfounded smile on his face.

"Erik, it is good to see you," Turk said, dismounting and hugging Erik.

"Father, this is Turk Skull Crusher," Erik said, and the dwarf grasped Rickard's hand.

"Skull Crusher?" Rikard said with some apprehension.

"Family name, sir," Turk said, laughing a bit.

"Nafer Round Shield, Beldar White Tree, and Bofim Black Stone," Erik continued, and each dwarf followed Turk in shaking Rickard's hand.

Bryon met his uncle with a firm hug, and it had been a long time since Erik had seen tears of happiness in his cousin's eyes.

"You should go see your father, Bryon," Rikard said.

"I'm worried," Bryon confessed.

"Son, go see your father," Rickard repeated. "He and your mother have missed you. The rest of you, you are friends of my son and, from what he has said, are to thank for his return home, so you are welcomed guests of the Eleodums. Please, come inside."

Bryon hugged each one of his sisters for longer than they had expected. He didn't realize how much he missed them, having been a constant annoyance in the past. His mother was next, and she greeted him with more kisses and more tears than he could bear, and he thought she might smother him to death. But his heart stopped when his father entered the room. He wasn't as big as Bryon had remembered him, and he didn't have that lazy-eyed, red-nosed look he typically had at this time of the day. He was sober.

"Father," Bryon said, straightening his back.

"Bryon," his father replied, a slight shake in his voice.

"I'm sorry I left," Bryon said. He didn't know what else to say. "I know it's probably been a strain on you and mother."

"Yes, it has," his father replied, face straight and stoic, with the slightest hint of a tremble in his voice.

"I'm a rich man now," Bryon said. He kneeled, opening his haversack to show his father the coin and gems and jewels he had. "I don't know if it will make up for it, but you can have it all. It will pay off your debts. You can hire more men. Buy more land. I ..."

His father pulled him up to his feet, and as Bryon expected his father to hit him, he wrapped his arms around Bryon and squeezed and cried.

"My son has come home," he said. "Oh son, how I have missed you. I thought I'd never see you again. You are worth more than all the jewels in the world."

Bryon didn't know what to do or say and, for a moment, just stood there, but slowly, he wrapped his arms around his father and completed the embrace.

Later, Bryon met Erik among his father's orange groves, away from their families and away from the buzz of the farmsteads. So many rumors had begun to spread about dwarves and warriors and dragon slayers being in their midst, both Bryon and Erik barely found time to be alone.

"My father stopped drinking," Bryon said. "Hasn't touched a drop almost since we left."

"That makes my heart happy," Erik said.

"I hear you are finally going to marry Simone," Bryon added.

"Yes," Erik said with a smile.

"That makes my heart happy," Bryon said.

"Now we have to find you someone," Erik said.

"Oh, I don't know about that," Bryon said with a laugh. "Perhaps, someday. But for now, I still need to heal."

"The dragon wound?" Erik asked.

"I still feel it from time to time," Bryon explained. "King Skella said it will never truly heal. I have vivid dreams of the dragon and of wolves and darkness. The king said that was because of my wound. But not all wounds are physical, Erik. Not all healing is physical."

"You don't need to go with us," Erik said. "You weren't there. The Lord of the East didn't command you to do anything. He spoke my name, not yours. You can stay here and mend your wounds, physical and otherwise. I don't mind."

Bryon looked at Erik and shook his head.

"We are in this together, cousin," Bryon said. "That is one of the biggest mistakes I have been making ... that this life is just about me. No, I will go. Where you go, I go."

News of Erik Eleodum returning home, now a warrior, had spread through the farmlands quickly. Most couldn't believe their ears, that the younger Eleodum, known for his gentle nature, could be a mighty soldier, but when they came to see for themselves and saw him not only training with his cousin—a much humbler version of his cousin—and dwarves, not only did the farming settlements buzz with the talk of mighty fighters living in their midst, but also the talk of dwarves, who hadn't been seen in the farmlands for years.

Now, as another day ended bringing him nearer still to his departure again, Erik stood in front of the fence surrounding his home. He stared north, towards the Gray Mountains. He grew up in their shadow, always wondering what could possibly live and dwell in such a place. Now that he knew, part of him wished he could go back to his ignorance.

As he stared at the Gray Mountains, large and looming, much of them covered with snow, they seemed to change shape. They turned black, and black clouds hung over them. Thunder rumbled and purple lightning erupted from the ominous clouds. He remembered those clouds from a dream, but now he wasn't in his dream.

He blinked, and the clouds and lightning went away, and the Gray Mountains were as they were before. Erik felt an overwhelming sense of peace, and he smiled. He knew Simone stood behind him, and he smelled her usual scent of lavender and mint. Her smell mixed with his mother's roses brought a bigger smile to his face, and he imagined living here in peace for the rest of his life. But, among that sweet aroma, he caught a whiff of something familiar and sour, something he only experienced in the deepest, darkest places, whether it be in his mind or in this world ... death. He could hear them, in the distance, far away in the tallest peaks of the Gray Mountains. But he could hear them, the minions of the Shadow. They were there, waiting, bound by the flames of the shadow, and he would have to break them.

Simone wrapped her arms around Erik, and after he turned to face her, she held him tight. She was a tall woman, but he was bigger and looked down at her, her blue eyes staring back up at him. She would be his wife on the morrow and for a moment, their life would be perfect. But then he would have to leave again. For now, though, everything was perfect.

Erik looked once more to the Gray Mountains. He smiled, breathed, and closed his eyes. They were already calling him Erik Friend of Dwarves, Erik Wolf's Bane, Erik Troll Hammer, and Erik Dragon Slayer, but for now, he was simply Erik Eleodum, son of a simple farmer.

DRAGON SWORD: CHAPTER 1

DEMON'S FIRE BOOK 1

Darius, the General Lord Marshall, marched down the hallway leading to the throne room. Reflecting his urgency, his thudding boots echoed off the cavernous walls of the capitol building of Amentus, a building hundreds of years old, built from white marble. The arched ceilings, painted to look like a crystal blue sky with puffy, white clouds, aided the acoustics of the corridor, and the ancient builders had a purpose behind such construction. One man could stand at one end of a hallway and shout anything—a command, a proclamation, or a call for help—and someone standing at the other end, some fifty paces distant, could hear him as if they stood next to each other.

As the Lord Marshall stomped by, guards placed at regular intervals slammed their right, gauntleted fists into their breastplates as they saluted. Positioned next to the pillars which formed part of a fake colonnade—they didn't hold up any weight but were simply an architect's embellishments—these men and women who guarded the capitol building were the best trained, most fearless, and most devout soldiers. As they saluted Darius, it meant more than any other salute—it was true respect.

He came to the tall, solid double doors made of a light oak leading to the throne room, each etched with the carving of a gigantic sun. The two men who guarded the doors saluted. As with all of the guards, they wore plate mail that covered every part of their bodies and made from the best steel, save for Dwarf's Iron. A sun with seven points—the symbol of Amentus—was emblazoned on their breastplates. They lifted their visors.

"Open," the General Lord Marshall said.

"Sir ..." one of the guards began.

"I don't have time," the General Lord Marshall snapped. He knew King Agempi was in a meeting with his advisors and politicians. It was an important meeting, something to do with the economic situation of their country and the steps they needed to take to rectify whatever issues they were having. It was all over Darius' head and the reason why he loved being a soldier and never accepted the King's offer to make him a senator or advisor of state. "Open the damn door."

Both men lowered their visors and stepped to the side, drawing their tower shields—painted blue with a yellow sun at the center—close to their bodies in attention. One of them knocked on the double door. They opened.

A colonnade—this one real and made of the same white marble as the rest of the building and inlaid with suns and moons and stars—led to the wide dais on which the thrones of the King and Queen of Amentus had been placed with perfect precision. Guards stood next to each column, but unlike the ones who stood at attention in the building's main hallway, these didn't salute as the Lord Marshall walked by. It wasn't for lack of respect. Darius had trained each one of these men, personally ensuring they were the most loyal and most fierce—the last line of defense if the capitol building fell in battle. They saluted no one, not even the King. It was their command. They were the Warriors of the Sun, the most elite of knights in Gol-Durathna's military, and their loyalties were to the state ... and the state only.

The king was in a meeting with several advisors and senators, but he looked up as the General Lord Marshall stepped onto the blue carpet that led to the dais, caring little for the dirt on his boots. A broad-shouldered man, the king had dark ringlets in his hair that spilled over his shoulders, and his thick beard had gray streaked through it. Despite the thickness of his beard, Darius could see his red lips and still white teeth when the king smiled. He stood and lifted his hands to silence one of his advisors before he opened his arms as if he might even hug his general.

"Darius!" the king called, "I thought you were away."

The General Lord Marshall didn't answer. He simply approached the dais and, reaching the bottom step, knelt, right fist to his left breast, and head bowed low.

"Stand, Darius," the king said, pushing past one of his advisors, "and dispense with these formalities. It is good to see you."

The General Lord Marshall stood. His eyes met the king's. Those eyes—a brilliant emerald green—were the kindest eyes Darius had ever known. He had seen rulers from other countries on the brink of war with Gol-Durathna, red-faced and angry, stand in front of King Amentus and soften simply because of those eyes.

"To what do I owe this pleasure?" King Agempi asked.

"Sire, we weren't done," one of his advisors said.

"Silence! I can interrupt a meeting with my advisors and greet one of my oldest friends if I want."

"Of course, Your Majesty," the advisor said, head hung low and backing away a few steps.

King Agempi X was a powerful man and a good ruler. He surrounded himself with well-educated advisors and politicians of character and integrity but hated the mundane nature of most meetings concerning the state. He was a man who believed his real place was on a battlefield, and his shoulders, chest, arms, and legs evidenced as much.

"As much as I take great joy from discussing taxes, the level of our wheat stores, and our economic concerns east of the Giant's Vein,"

King Agempi said, "I think I can manage a small break for you, Darius."

"I wish my presence was for pleasure, Your Majesty," the General Lord Marshall said.

"That concerns me," King Agempi replied, some of the sparkle leaving his eyes.

"It should," the General Lord Marshall replied.

"Well, then, speak, General Lord Marshall," the king said.

The General Lord Marshall shot a quick look to the advisors and senator who had been conferring with the king.

"Belisarius, you may stay, but the rest of you, leave us," the king said.

As the advisors filed out, some showing their dislike of being dismissed, the senator, an older man with curly, gray hair and a short, white beard, bowed and stepped aside, next to the king's throne. His slight frame belied the fact that he was once a soldier too ... a very good soldier. Unlike Darius, he had accepted the king's offer to throw off his armor and put away his sword for a life of politics; it had not treated him well. He was barely older than the Lord Marshall, but he looked as if he could have been Darius' father.

"We have dispatched the Atrimus," the General Lord Marshall said.

"The Shadow Men?" Belisarius gasped.

"I trust there is a good reason for this," the king said.

"There is, Your Majesty," Darius replied. "This ... this dragon attack on Fen-Stévock. We have gathered information that leads us to believe there is more to this. The Lord of the East seeks a powerful weapon; he has part of it, a scroll with a spell, but now seeks a special sword. With that he can control dragons ... even kill a dragon."

The king sat down again, resting an elbow on an armrest of his throne and his chin on his fist.

"Dragons?" the king said, as much to himself as to Darius and Belisarius. "A year ago, the mention of such a thing would have made me laugh. They were a fable, a myth, Darius. A child's tale."

The king leaned forward, resting his arms on his knees, his thick brows furling into a concerned look.

"To be able to kill a dragon, let alone control one," the king muttered under his breath.

"It is the stuff of legends," Belisarius offered.

"This would turn the tide, Darius," the king said. "The Lord of the East would no longer need to hide behind diplomacy. War would be imminent. And we would be on the losing side."

"All of Háthgolthane would be on the losing side, Your Majesty," Belisarius added. Darius felt the old soldier adding nothing of value with his comments; politics had turned him into a 'yes man'.

"The man who saved Fen-Stévock is the one who the Lord of the East has tasked with finding this sword," Darius explained, "the Dragon Sword."

"He is a man of Western Háthgolthane, yes?" the king asked.

"A pity he didn't let Fen-Stévock just burn," the senator said, and the king rebuked him before Darius could.

"He saved thousands of lives, Belisarius," the king said. "Remember that. Those people haven't a clue who their ruler is. Most of them don't care. All they care about is putting food in their children's mouths."

"How is a man from Western Háthgolthane so willing to serve Golgolithul?" Belisarius asked, his first sensible input to the conversation.

"Truly," the king added. "The men of Western Háthgolthane ... descendants of Gongoreth and Hargoleth, who stayed after the Great War and the Treaty of Bethuliam rather than returning west. They oppose the east more than we do. By the Creator and the old gods, they oppose the east more than the men of Mek-Ba'Dune."

"His service is not given willingly, Your Majesty," Darius said. "Our informant tells us that he must do as the Lord of the East bids. The Lord of the East has threatened him ... threatened his entire family."

"That is a pity. The men of Western Háthgolthane used to be

allies to Gol-Durathna." The look on the king's face was distant, staring past Darius and Belisarius as if he was remembering a sad memory. "They are the reason we won the Great War. Without them, all would have been lost, and they sacrificed much. Such a man would have been a valuable ally. Is there hope for this man, Darius? Can we sway him to our side?"

"We know where he lives, where his family lives," Darius replied. "However, at the same time, this Bu Al'Banan, self-proclaimed King of Hámon, is also after the sword. Our informants also tell us he thinks it will legitimize his claim to Hámon's throne and give him the needed power and support to conquer Golgolithul."

The king sighed, rubbing a hand along his brow as he looked down at his feet. He removed the gold crown—a simple circlet of gold studded with diamonds at regular intervals—and once more rested on an armrest of his throne.

"Does this mean we must kill an innocent man, one who saved thousands ... tens of thousands of lives to prevent the sword from falling into the hands of the Lord of the East or this King Bu Al'Banan?" King Agempi asked.

Darius felt his stomach knot.

"Can we sway him, as you mentioned?" Belisarius asked.

"To what end?" Darius asked. "The Lord of the East will surely kill his family for the man's betrayal. And this new King of Hámon will probably kill his family anyways."

"Then he must not find the sword," Belisarius said.

"But ..." the king began, but his senator interrupted him as all good politicians should.

"The greater good," Belisarius said. "A small evil for the greater good."

Spoken like a true politician. Darius glared at the former soldier, hard and cold, a moment of hatred in his eyes. But he knew his words were the truth. There was no other way.

"He must be stopped," King Agempi said. "This man from

Western Háthgolthane. And Golgolithul. And this King Bu. You know what must be done, Darius."

"The Atrimus are on their way to Hámon and the farmlands of Western Háthgolthane," the General Lord Marshall said with a bow and began to turn to leave.

"Let me know if you hear anything else from our informant in Fen-Stévock," King Agempi said.

Darius stopped and gave a half-turn to face the king again.

"I don't think I will, Your Majesty," Darius replied. "We haven't heard from him in a while. I believe he has been discovered."

"The gods be merciful to him," King Agempi said. "His death will not be quick."

"And to his family," Darius added. "His last message to us told us Golgolithul is mobilizing troops to their northern borders."

"When did things get so complicated?" King Agempi asked. "I mean, a dragon? Mobilization of troops? We have had relative peace for more than two hundred years. And now what?"

"I don't know, Your Majesty," Darius said. "Shall I garrison our southern borders as well?"

King Agempi waited for a while before looking at Darius with hard eyes, giving the General Lord Marshall a quick nod.

"Make it so."

Andragos—the Messenger of the East, the Black Mage, the Steward of Golgolithul, the Harbinger of Death—stood next to the Lord of the East, shadowed by the darkness of the dungeons under the main keep of Fen-Stévock, barely illuminated by floating red balls of magical light. The thick smell of stale blood, sweat, piss, and feces hung in the air, and a film of vaporous fungus covered much of the dungeon's stone, its spores the descendants of poisonous mold hundreds of years old. There were twenty cells in this dungeon, and the only way to get in and out was a magical portal. There were two such portals, one in the Lord of the East's quarters and the other in a hidden room in the keep of Fen-Aztûk, the sister city to Golgolithul's capitol. Magical rods of an ancient metal barred each of the cells without a door. One simply needed to know the magical word to get in and out of a cell, the bars simply disappearing and then reappearing again. Only the worst criminals—traitors, politicians inciting unrest against the Lord of the East, and people who needed to stay quiet—called this place home.

One such man hung naked from the ceiling of a cell by his hands, his feet just off the ground. Melanius, the Lord of the East's new mage and advisor, stood just inside the cell, playing the role of inquisitor. Kimber and Krista, the Lord of the East's two witches, stood just behind Melanius. Blood dripped from the prisoner's mouth as his chin dipped to his chest. This man was strong, with knotted, lean muscle ... once. Now, he was beaten and bruised, little more than an animal, his skin torn and scarred and burned. Before his physical torture, the Lord of the East would have put him through magical torture. He would have crushed organs, only to heal them just to crush them again. Magical heat would have seared the man's brain, skin, blood even. The Lord of the East, or Melanius, or the witches would have put images in the man's head, images of his wife dying, being raped, cheating on him, slitting her own throat, murdering their children, anything that would drive someone insane. Andragos knew this was what the man had endured before coming here ... because he used to be the one doing it.

The Lord of the East nodded to Melanius, who, in turn, nodded to the torturer. A large man, his upper torso as bare as his shaved head, took a curved knife to the prisoner's chest. The naked man lifted his head and screamed, jerking sideways violently as the torturer removed another piece of skin from his body. When the torturer threw the skin to the ground, the prisoner dropped his head again and wept, a low, moaning cry.

"Speak," Melanius said, his voice a croaking hiss, "or your wife and children will meet the same fate."

Andragos looked over at the smiling Lord of the East. He then looked down at the cell floor and saw a dozen squares of flayed skin; one of them bore ten scarred lines. It was the first piece of skin removed from the man's body, a symbol of his service to Golgolithul's army. The second piece of skin to be removed was a tattoo on his chest, one of a black gauntlet gripping a red fletched arrow, a symbol of his service as the Lord of the East's personal guard. Andragos frowned.

"You don't approve," the Lord of the East said.

Andragos steeled his resolve and met the Lord of the East gaze for gaze.

"He is a traitor," Andragos replied. "He deserves this and more."

Andragos tried to believe his own words, but something in his chest tightened. He had seen such punishment hundreds of times over hundreds of years. He had directed such punishments. And he had no room for traitors and liars, but something about this time, this torture, this man made him frown. It felt wrong.

Am I growing soft?

"Very well," the Lord of the East said with a smile. "But you do understand I must use him as an example. His family. His friends. His acquaintances. Anyone he did business with. They will all meet a similar fate. And then we will see who dares to challenge me. Who dares to spy for lesser men? This man must pay in full for his sins."

"Please ... no more," the man whispered through sobs of pain.

"Perhaps you should have thought of that before making a pact with that incestuous cockroach in the north," Melanius hissed, a hint of glee in his voice.

The man cried and screamed as the torturer removed another piece of skin.

Andragos closed his eyes for a moment. It would take much of his energy, but he wanted to make sure the other four wizards in the room—Melanius, those two bitch witches, and the Lord of the East—couldn't read his thoughts as he passed a message to the unfortunate prisoner.

Your family will be safe. I cannot do anything about you or most of your friends, but your family will live.

The man looked up. His eyes met Andragos'. They were swollen and bruised, barely visible through the tears and blood that covered his face. But at that moment, he smiled. As the executioner removed another piece of skin, he groaned and gritted his teeth, but he did not scream out again. He steeled his resolve and just stared on as the Lord of the East had him executed, piece by piece.

"I have things to do," Andragos said.

"You don't want to stay and watch this man break?" the Lord of the East asked.

"He won't break," Andragos replied, "and you have tasked me with the rebuilding of South Gate. It has proven an arduous task. Besides, I have seen such things more times than I can count. They all end the same."

"Very well, then," the Lord of the East said.

Andragos snapped his finger and appeared in the main hall of the Fen-Stévock's keep. Raktas and Terradyn, his two personal guards for the last hundred years, were there to meet him, and they followed him as he left the keep and met his own elite soldiers—the Soldiers of the Eye—in the courtyard. After a few words, Andragos and his guards stepped into a dark carriage that was quiet as it rolled away.

"Find Ja Sin's family," Andragos commanded, "and escort them to safety. The Lord of the East means to flay his wife and his little daughters and sons for his iniquities. I shouldn't care, but I cannot let that happen."

"Where should we take them?" Terradyn asked. "Surely, the Lord of the East will be coming for them soon."

"Take them to my cottage," Andragos said, his voice hard and his face dark. "They will stay there for a while, and then I will find a suitable place for them to live. Did Ja Sin have close friends?"

For the last two years, Ja Sin had been a high-ranking officer in the Lord of the East's personal guard. He was a powerful warrior, a dynamic leader, and a spy for Gol-Durathna. The Lord of the East couldn't prove it, but they knew he was. And he was willing to face his punishment with head held high. But to punish his family ... Andragos shook his head. A hundred years ago, he wouldn't have cared, but the increasing cruelty of the Lord of the East began to weigh on him. He grew tired as much as the Lord's actions became pointless.

"Yes, my lord," Raktas replied.

"We cannot save them all," Andragos said, "but we can save some."

"What is happening, my lord?" Terradyn asked.

Andragos didn't answer. Then he looked at his two guards, confidants, friends ... if they could be called that.

"Are you with me?" Andragos asked.

"To the death," they replied in unison.

"Just be ready," Andragos said.

"My lord," Raktas said.

"Yes."

"We have found our own spy," Raktas continued. "A man who has infiltrated the Soldiers of the Eye."

"Truly?" Andragos asked.

"Yes, my lord," Raktas replied.

"Another spy for Gol-Durathna?" Andragos asked.

"No, my lord," Raktas replied. "For the late Patûk Al'Banan."

"Does he now spy for this Bu Al'Banan?" Andragos asked.

"I don't know, my lord," Raktas replied.

"Bring him to me," Andragos said, "unscathed. And hurry with Ja Sin's family."

Both men bowed.

DRAGON SWORD: CHAPTER 2

DEMON'S FIRE BOOK 1

Towards the end of the summer, early mornings on the Eleodum farm were cool. The new sunlight glistened off the dew that collected nightly on the grass and wheat and corn stalks of the farm. A rooster's crow signified the beginning of the day and, as if in response to the rooster's morning call, the low moaning of cows echoed through the farm.

Erik Eleodum smiled as he put his left hand on his hip, breathing heavily. The rising sun, so slow at first, barely a sliver of light peeking over the eastern horizon, dared to rise more and more, its light causing the wheat of his farm to glow as if he had planted golden thread. Life ... this was what life looked like. The world around him celebrated the bounty of the land, the perfection of the Creator's work in nature stood better than all the treasures of the lost dwarvish city of Orven-crest, greater than the work of the most skilled artisans.

As he twisted it in his hand, the rising sun glimmered off Ilken's Blade, his sword, a gift from a dwarf named Ilken Copper Head, one of the most renowned blacksmiths from the dwarvish city and capitol of Drüum Balmdüukr, Thorakest. He smiled again. He trained every morning and, occasionally, in the evening. As he did so—sometimes alone and sometimes with his cousin, Bryon, or his dwarvish friend, Turk—his movements felt fluid and precise. They were a part of him, second nature now buried deep in his subconscious. As he walked or used his arms without real conscious thought, his blade was simply an extension of the movements, his body a weapon in itself.

"Thank you, Wrothgard," Erik said, pretending his friend was still right next to him. Once a soldier of Golgolithul, an Eastern Guardsman, who had become a mercenary, Wrothgard had trained Erik, but he was gone, having run away from further duty to the east and Golgolithul's ruler, the Lord of the East. Erik hoped he was safe, wherever he was.

Erik walked over to a towel that hung on a wooden fence and used it to wipe the sweat from his face and the ever-growing muscles of his chest and arms. Each day he trained, he grew stronger and his muscles bigger. Growing up on a farm, he was always stronger than most, but now, when he did work on his farm, he could do the work of two men. He didn't grow up to be a soldier, or a warrior, or a wielder of any weapon for that matter; he thought he was going to be a farmer. He grew up wanting to be a farmer ... and part of him still did. He never wanted fame, notoriety, fortune, or anything like that. But now, they were all his. People called him Erik Friend of Dwarves, Erik Troll Hammer, Erik Wolf's Bane, Erik Champion of the East ... but mostly, they called him Erik Dragon Slayer.

He didn't really slay a dragon; she was still out there, licking her wounds and biding her time. He simply fended her off as she laid waste to the southern portion of Fen-Stévock—simply called South Gate. He dispelled her with an ancient scroll containing an even more ancient spell he had found in the lost city of Orvencrest. He saw her—the dragon—often, in his dreams. She was there, as were the dead ... always the dead. They could hurt him in his dreams, but he could hurt them as well—destroy them. He could hear her at times, too. She cursed him in his mind. He sensed her, somewhere, out there. Gooseflesh rose on his arms as he thought of a question that plagued his mind every day: If he could feel and sense her, could she sense him? Most likely. She was as powerful as the greatest wizard and wielded magic more potent than Andragos could conjure up.

Putting his towel back on the fence post and pulling his shirt over his head, Erik watched the sun rise, knowing she was out there in the east, beyond the Giant's Vein that separated the continents of Háthgolthane and Antolika. She was even further, beyond the Jagged Coast and past the Sea of Knives. Even past the Isutan Isles.

He slowly turned his head and looked south. They had waited an extra month—he and his cousin and the dwarves. The Lord of the East, ruler of the Eastern Empire—Golgolithul—had commanded them to retrieve the fabled Dragon Sword—described on the same scroll that contained the spell that helped him defeat the dragon—and he gave them a year to do it. That command came two months and some weeks ago. They had agreed to meet at the Eleodum farmstead after a month of rest. When Wrothgard didn't show after a month, they agreed to wait another month. He still hadn't shown. Erik knew he wouldn't, and his heart sank a little even though he smiled at the thought of the eastern soldier. He was a good man, a good warrior, and an even better friend. But he was tired of fighting. He told Erik as much. He needed more than a month to rest. He needed a lifetime.

Wrothgard had told Erik he probably wouldn't meet them. It would mean his death because failure in service to the Lord of the East meant death. But Wrothgard didn't care. He was going to take his chances. In the coastal city of Finlo, the desert continent of Wüsten Sahil maybe, or maybe even further. If the Lord of the East sent assassins after him, and they did find him, at least he would die a free man.

With the thought of the Dragon Sword, Erik looked to the north and the looming Gray Mountains, gigantic along the northern horizon even though they were a long way away. He had grown up in the shadow of those mountains, always wondering what they truly looked like, never thinking he would get to find out. On bright, sunny days such as this, they didn't look so formidable, serene almost, painting a pleasant backdrop to the northern horizon. But on cloudy or stormy days, when the mist hung low, those mountains were the stuff of shadows ... of *the* Shadow.

In his youth's mind's eye, the worst kind of monsters lived in those mountains, which seemed to be huge, evil creatures in themselves, especially the two tall peaks simply referred to since his childhood as The Fangs. Erik gave a mirthless smile. The honesty ... the truth of youth. Now it was time. He would leave his parents again, his home, his wife—Simone—for some fool's journey he didn't care about. Erik sighed. It would be a long day. He had a lot of work to do.

Erik pushed on through the darkness, feeling the crunch of twigs and pine needles beneath his feet. The sound broke the silence of the night as the cold numbed his face, but he kept moving, pushed branches out of his way that sought to peck at his face like hungry birds. He could barely see in front of him, the moon hidden by black clouds, and what he could see appeared as ghostly silhouettes. He shivered. He rubbed his palm on the pommel of Ilken's Blade. Knowing his sword was there gave him a little comfort ... but not much. Not in this place.

Erik finally pushed past the last tree and edged slowly into a small clearing. He remembered this place; it was a long time ago. This place was from a dream he once had—now he was dreaming again. His dreams were always so vivid, so real it was hard to differentiate this Dream World from reality, but he spent so much time here—every night for long periods—and he could tell the difference now. Normally, the undead were there, waiting. They hadn't been, in a while, though, not since he had destroyed Fox. Fox was a fiery haired slaver he had killed. The man's master, a slaver named Kehl and hailing from Saman—northern most city in Wüsten Sahil—had tried to enslave Erik, his brother, and his cousin, but they failed and many of them died, along with Fox.

For some reason, the dead had elected Fox as their leader. He was anything but in life. And no matter how many times Erik killed the man in his dreams, he would always come back ... except for the last time. Now he was gone forever, his deathly form dispatched into oblivion when Erik struck him with Ilken's Blade. Since then, his dreams had been of a vast grassland and a single hill topped by a large, weeping willow. A man sat under that tree, a man Erik knew but could never remember from where or what his name was. And in his dreams, he would sit and talk with the man and wake refreshed, next to his wife, Simone.

That had been his dreams since he came home, but now, on the eve of his departure once again, things had changed. He was in a dark place he had only been to once before. Before, in stark contrast to the darkness of the surrounding forest, there had been a fire blazing in the center of the clearing, and a cloaked man had stood warming his hands. He was a mysterious and powerful man, and just the one time, Erik had peered into the man's hood and he had seen every face he had come across in his life, one after the other like the flicked pages of a book. Erik knew he was more than a man, something otherworldly.

In dreams past, the hooded man had led the dead to a golden carriage that would carry them away to heaven, or so Erik presumed. The man had also denied men access to the carriage, those such as Fox and the other slavers. The man had made Erik feel powerful, like he had control in this dream world. It was because of that man that he was able to walk in his dreams unafraid.

But now, the fire was gone, as was the man. In the darkness, Erik could just make out cold ash and charcoal sitting within a stone circle. He knelt down, sifting through the extinguished campfire, stirring the remains with a short stick and not a single ember glowed. Wind howled through the forest trees and swirled through the clearing. It picked up ash and dirt and created tiny tornadoes.

There was another clearing, just through another copse of trees. He passed through there and the open space was empty like the first. The last time he was here, this was where he found the caravan of golden carriages, waiting to carry the dead away. Now there was only darkness and cold silence as the wind dropped once more.

Erik shivered as he saw a single pinpoint of light at the far end of the clearing. It was tiny at first, a pinprick of silver, but then it quickly grew into a tall oval of blinding brilliance. It was a doorway, and a man stepped through it, cloaked and hooded, but not the hooded man from before. Erik couldn't see a face, but frail hands emerged from the wide sleeves of the cloak. They formed the shape of a cup, and another pinpoint of light floated above them. The ball of light flashed, causing Erik to close his eyes, balls of light dancing behind his eyelids like fireflies. When he reopened them, the cloaked figure held a sword, long and broad, its steel a golden color. It reminded Erik of the shape his golden-handled dagger took when he defeated her ... the dragon.

The man placed the sword on the ground, and after another ball of light flashed, he held a golden crown. It had a total of five points, and the one taller than the rest was studded with a large diamond, a brilliant gem that emanated its own light. He placed the crown next to the sword, and from one more ball of light, he produced a green stone, an emerald perhaps, that was round, almost in the shape of an egg. He placed it on the ground, next to the sword and the crown. The emerald egg flashed and the sword and crown were gone, leaving it alone in front of the cloaked figure.

When Erik stepped forward into the center of the clearing, the cloaked man lifted a finger and pointed. Erik looked over his shoulder and saw another cloaked man standing behind him. He looked almost exactly like the first figure, although Erik could see silver runes outlining the man's hood and sleeves. There was a shadow behind the man, if that was possible in the darkness. The shadow was large and looked like it had horns and wings—the dragon perhaps. But the shadow had two arms and two legs and as it moved, the second robed man moved, the shadow's puppet. A cackling laugh emitted from underneath the puppet's hood.

The first man clapped, and the forest faded away, and Erik was on his farm in the middle of the night. He heard screams as he smelled smoke and the heat of fire caused him to step back.

Erik stood in the middle of his farmstead and spiders the size of horses ran about him, spraying everything with silver silk and sinking their fangs into faceless victims they had entwined in their webbing. Giant men followed them, killing those who had not fallen victim to the spiders with clubs the size of tree trunks. Soldiers rushed in behind the giants, their skin green, their eyes blank and black, spears spilling guts and swords removing heads. Buildings burned, people screamed, and livestock lay slaughtered as, for the first time in a long while, Erik felt scared in his dreams. That was when the dead came, rising up from the ground, consuming anything still alive and pulling them down into earthen graves. That was when Erik heard distant scream. The earth shook and the fire intensified around him. The dragon.

But when he turned, there was no dragon. All he saw was a massive shadow, the same shadow that had controlled the cloaked man, only larger. It moved about without any true form, twisting, contorting, and directing the ensuing death. The shadow was over him, above him, all around him, its wings spreading and flapping up hurricane-like winds, threatening to blow him away. The shadow roared, the sound a mix of rage and anger-filled laughter. It reached out with a black, clawed hand and ripped up a whole grove of apple trees by the roots, then a grove of orange trees. The hands crushed buildings that still stood, smashed barns, and carved deep gashes into the soil.

He saw everyone he loved standing in front of his home—his parents, cousins, sisters, the dwarves ... Simone. The shadow breathed a single, fiery breath, fire consuming them, and the moment they were gone, silence descended. The air around him became stale, and he knew what that silence meant. The giant shadow hovered above him, sucking in all the air. It was the same when the dragon showered his brother in fire. He heard laughter, saw fire, felt pain like he had never felt before, and then came the darkness.

Erik awoke with a start, sitting up quickly in his bed. Sweat poured down his face and chest and back. The bedroom of his and Simone's new home was dark. Beside him, his wife groaned softly as she turned slightly in her sleep. Erik took in a deep breath and let it out slowly, feeling the beat of his heart slowing in his chest. He shook his head both in disbelief of what he had experienced, and as if to rid himself of the memories.

He knew he had been dreaming, but as of late, his dreams were just his grassland, his hill, his tree, and the man. He had come to learn that powerful men and women—and powerful creatures—used the Dream Land for communication, to send messages, to intimidate. He saw them, every night.

Something strong had controlled his dream. Was it the dragon? Was that the shadow? He could still feel it. Even now, awake, he heard anger-filled howling, malicious laughing, and it wasn't just the memory of his dream. He knew the dragon was somewhere, biding her time. It had to have been her. She desired many things, Erik had learned, but he knew one thing she truly desired was his death, and the death of everything he loved. Was his dream a vision of what was to come? Was she infiltrating his dreams and showing him what she meant to do?

He nodded slowly. Surely, that's what it was. But something felt wrong. The giant shadow—could that have been *The Shadow*? What of the two men? The sword—the Dragon Sword Erik suspected. The crown—maybe a symbol of leadership, for the dwarves or the Lord of the East or someone ancient. But what of the stone? It seemed to have no significance, and, yet, it consumed the other two.

Whatever the message, he knew it was time to leave, time for him to go in search of this Dragon Sword. Presuming he discovered its whereabouts, he did not know if he would give it to the Lord of the East as he had promised or if it had some other fate. But he could not make any such decision until he found it.

He rubbed his temples with his index fingers and then pressed the heels of his palms into his eyes, hard, trying to get the images of his dream out of his head. He pressed his hands into his face so hard he saw stars and had to stop. He sucked in a deep breath again and ran a hand through his wet, sweaty hair, pulling the last bit just to make sure he was surely awake.

"Are you alright?" Simone asked, her voice groggy with sleep.

"Yes, my love," Erik replied sweetly.

"Another dream?" Simone asked.

"Yes," Erik replied, "another dream."

Simone sat up, her night shift hanging off one shoulder. She looked at Erik with half-closed eyes and wiped a clump of matted, blonde hair away from her face. She touched his bearded cheek. Her hands were so soft and always smelled like lavender and mint.

"I am so sorry, my sweet," Simone said. "Is there something we can do?"

"I don't think so," Erik replied. "I could drink sweet wine or dream milk, but a wise man—a dwarf—once warned me about doing so."

Erik stared at his wife, making out the outlines of her facial features in the darkness of the room, the only bit of light coming in through a small crack near the window. She was beautiful, even in her sleep. His heart raced again but for a different reason, and, for that brief moment, he forgot about his dream and the mysterious shadow. But when he looked away, they were there again.

"But if it helps you sleep ..." Simone began to say.

"No," Erik said, gently, grabbing one of her hands, pressing her fingers to his lips, and kissing them. "This is my burden. My dreams have a purpose, even if I don't know what they are sometimes. Go back to sleep now; I will be alright."

"Are you sure?" Simone asked.

"I am," Erik said with a smile, touching his wife's cheek with the back of his calloused fingers.

As Simone lay back down, Erik pulled on his trousers and walked out onto his front porch. He looked out over his lands, farmland his father had given him, and to which lands Simone's father, Brok, had added. Erik could have bought three times the land again; he was a wealthy man and had more coin than any other farmer in their farmstead But that meant nothing to Erik; he had fertile lands, and he had a beautiful wife, but he was about to leave it all behind.

He stood and opened the bedroom window and stared at the Gray Mountains again, looming like shadowy giants in the dim moonlight. He knew what he had to do. There was no way around it. But what fate awaited him in those mountains? What horrors, in this world and the dream world, had yet to come?

ABOUT THE AUTHOR

Christopher Patterson lives in Tucson, Arizona with his wife and three children. Christopher has a Masters in Education and is a teacher of many subjects, including English, History, Government, Economics, and Health. He is also a football and wrestling coach. Christopher fostered a love of the arts at a very young age, picking up the guitar at 7, the bass at 10, and dabbling in drawing and writing around the same time. His first major at the University of Arizona was, in fact, a BFA in Classical Guitar Performance, although he would eventually earn a BA in Literature and a BFA in Creative Writing.

Christopher Patterson grew up watching Star Wars, Dragon Slayer, and a cartoon version of The Hobbit. He started reading fantasy novels from a young age, took an early interest in early, Medieval Europe, and played Dungeons and Dragons. He has read The Hobbit, The Lord of the Rings, and the Wizard of Earthsea many times and heralds Tolkien, Jordan, and Martin, among others, as major influences in his own writing.

Christopher is also very involved in church, especially music and youth ministries, and is very active, having been a competitive power lifter since high school.

He thanks his grandmother for letting him waste paper on her typewriter while trying to write the "Next Great American Novel" and his parents for always supporting his dreams.

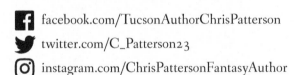

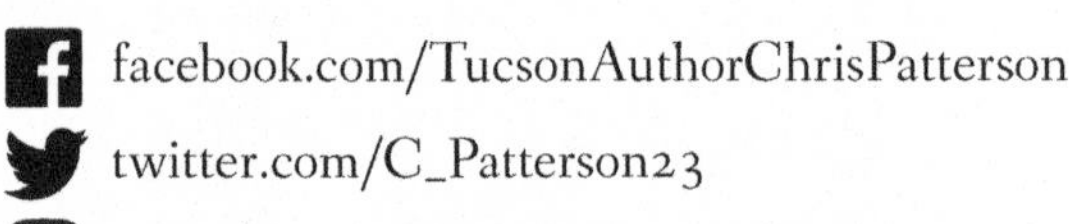

facebook.com/TucsonAuthorChrisPatterson
twitter.com/C_Patterson23
instagram.com/ChrisPattersonFantasyAuthor

ALSO BY CHRISTOPHER PATTERSON

The Shadow's Fire Series

A Chance Beginning

Dark Winds

Breaking the Flame

The Demon's Fire Series

Dragon Sword

Stone of Chaos

Demon Rising

Holy Warriors

To Kill A Witch

Made in the USA
Las Vegas, NV
20 July 2021

26744805R00281